Dax groaned when he took his first bite of chicken and waffles, and that deep sound pinged something low in her belly.

She wanted him groaning like that with *her*. "Good?"

"You're right." He closed his eyes in pure bliss, so manly, she wanted to leap across the table between them and launch herself at him. "I'm ruined for them elsewhere."

Or he could come back here with her...

Was it crazy to start hoping he might actually want to relocate here? Yeah, but crazy ran in the family. "Another thing to love about Charleston."

Seed thrown down.

"Honey, you're the best thing about Charleston. Chicken and waffles are like here." He set a reasonably high bar in the air before he raised his hand over his head. "You're here."

Her heart fluttered. "That's mighty high praise. I'd say the same about you, and I really love me some chicken and waffles."

The way his mouth curved as he forked another bite had her clenching her thighs. Goodness, this man was hot and she wanted him like a plate of chicken and waffles. With butter and syrup on top.

"You're not eating."

The implication was in the rough edge of his voice. *You're watching*.

Her inner reply was immediate. *Yes, Captain Hotpants, I am*.

PRAISE FOR AVA MILES' NOVELS
SEE WHAT ALL THE BUZZ IS ABOUT...

"Ava's story is witty and charming."

BARBARA FREETHY #1 *NYT* BESTSELLING AUTHOR

"If you like Nora Roberts type books, this is a must-read."

READERS' FAVORITE

"If ever there was a contemporary romance that rated a 10 on a scale of 1 to 5 for me, this one is it!"

THE ROMANCE REVIEWS

"I could not stop flipping the pages. I can't wait to read the next book in this series."

FRESH FICTION

"I've read Susan Mallery and Debbie Macomber... but never have I been so moved as by the books Ava Miles writes."

BOOKTALK WITH EILEEN

"Ava Miles is fast becoming one of my favorite light contemporary romance writers."

TOME TENDER

"One word for Ava Miles is WOW."

MY BOOK CRAVINGS

"Her engaging story and characters kept me turning the pages."

BOOKFAN

"On par with Nicholas Sparks' love stories."

JENNIFER'S CORNER BLOG

"The constant love, and the tasteful sexual interludes, bring a sensual, dynamic tension to this appealing story."

PUBLISHER'S WEEKLY

"Miles' story savvy, sense of humor, respect for her readers and empathy for her characters shine through…"

USA TODAY

OTHER AVA TITLES TO BINGE

The Paris Roommates

Your dreams are around the corner...

The Paris Roommates: Thea

The Paris Roommates: Dean

The Paris Roommates: Brooke

The Paris Roommates: Sawyer

———

The Unexpected Prince Charming Series

Love with a kiss of the Irish...

Beside Golden Irish Fields

Beneath Pearly Irish Skies

Through Crimson Irish Light

After Indigo Irish Nights

Beyond Rosy Irish Twilight

Over Verdant Irish Hills

Against Ebony Irish Seas

———

The Merriams Series

Chock full of family and happily ever afters...

Wild Irish Rose

Love Among Lavender

Valley of Stars

Sunflower Alley

A Forever of Orange Blossoms

A Breath of Jasmine

The Love Letter Series

The Merriams grandparents' epic love affair...

Letters Across An Open Sea

Along Waters of Sunshine and Shadow

The Friends & Neighbors Novels

A feast for all the senses...

The House of Hope & Chocolate

The Dreamer's Flower Shoppe

The Dare River Series

Filled with down-home charm...

Country Heaven

The Chocolate Garden

Fireflies and Magnolias

The Promise of Rainbows

The Fountain Of Infinite Wishes

The Patchwork Quilt Of Happiness

Country Heaven Cookbook

The Chocolate Garden: A Magical Tale (Children's Book)

The Dare Valley Series

Awash in small town fabulousness...

Nora Roberts Land

French Roast

The Grand Opening

The Holiday Serenade

The Town Square

The Park of Sunset Dreams

The Perfect Ingredient

The Bridge to a Better Life

The Calendar of New Beginnings

Home Sweet Love

The Moonlight Serenade

The Sky of Endless Blue

Daring Brides

Daring Declarations

Dare Valley Meets Paris Billionaire Mini-Series

Small town charm meets big city romance...

The Billionaire's Gamble

The Billionaire's Secret

The Billionaire's Courtship

The Billionaire's Return

Dare Valley Meets Paris Compilation

———

The Once Upon a Dare Series

Falling in love is a contact sport...

The Gate to Everything

———

The Standalones

A Very UN-Shakespeare Romance

The Hockey Experiment

Love and Other Trials

———

Non-Fiction

The Happiness Corner: Reflections So Far

The Post-Covid Wellness Playbook

———

Cookbooks

Home Baked Happiness Cookbook

Country Heaven Cookbook

———

The Lost Guides to Living Your Best Life Series

Reclaim Your Superpowers

Courage Is Your Superpower

Expression Is Your Superpower

Peace Is Your Superpower

Confidence Is Your Superpower

Happiness Is Your Superpower

———

Children's Books

The Chocolate Garden: A Magical Tale

———

To see all of Ava's titles, check out her handy printable booklist.

LOVE AND OTHER TRIALS

AVA MILES

Copyright April 2025, Ava Miles.
ISBN: 978-1-949092-90-5

All rights reserved. No part of this book may be reproduced or transmitted in any form by any means—graphic, electronic or mechanical—without permission in writing from the author, except by a reviewer who may quote brief passages in a review.

This is a work of fiction. All of the characters, organizations, and events portrayed in this novel are either the products of the author's imagination or are used fictionally.

www.avamiles.com
Ava Miles

A NOTE FROM AVA

Glen Powell inspired the hero in this book, Naval Pilot Dax Cross.

What I haven't shared was what came next...

I'd only seen a couple movies of Mr. Powell's when Dax came to light, but I was on a plane to the U.S. and ended up watching one of the in-flight movies, *Twister*—something I normally might not have watched. The reason is that I have been in two tornadoes, one as a child and one as a woman.

If you haven't seen the remake of the original movie, which I have not seen, you might think it's only an action flick, but somehow the loss of the heroine's friends in her pursuit of storm chasing makes it deeper in a way that completely surprised me.

And that's where the line that changed my life came in.

I had no warning, and in that respect it struck as quickly as a tornado. The hero was speaking to the heroine about her friends dying in a tornado, and honestly, I don't even fully remember the details. But suddenly he looked at her and said with great empathy something like, *How much longer are you going to let this take from you?*

A NOTE FROM AVA

Delivered with empathy—love even—I received this question. Obviously I was ready. I sat back as tears filled my eyes. My heart was like, yes, how much longer am I going to let that first horrible event in childhood take from me? Keep me from being fully happy and all that I can be. Some moments happen like that. Awareness. Insight. The surge of grief and loss. Determination. Healing. Peace.

I cannot express how deeply grateful I am for that line and how it changed me. I even thought how funny and wonderful it was to happen in something supposedly billed as an action flick. Entertainment is wonderful like that as are books.

That's why it's an art.

A couple of days later, I was sitting in the lobby of a major office building waiting for my soul sister, international bestselling author Kate Perry, to finish with an appointment. It was taking a while, and the women at the security desk, who had been especially welcoming and kind, told me they were a little worried about her, that the appointment shouldn't be taking that long. Anyway, the extra time allowed for another miracle.

One of the women, who was in her late twenties came my way and said her guidance had told her to come talk to me. She knew I was an author of both fiction and self-help, because we'd gotten to talking beforehand. She said she'd been feeling very stuck and having trouble with the man in her life, and honestly, the rest is a blur, because my guidance suddenly was telling me to mention the line from the movie to her and how it had helped me. I knew she also needed to hear it.

I put my hand on her shoulder and told her that I was supposed to say this next thing but that it was going to be hard to hear. Our eyes met and I said the line. She instantly started crying, the healing kind, and she whispered, "I needed to hear that so bad. I lost my child."

I was stunned, and truthfully, I'm not sure I would have told her that line had I known she'd experienced such an unimaginable loss. Clearly I wasn't meant to have known, because she hadn't told me that part of her story. The rest of her journey poured out with cleansing tears, and since I saw her the next day, I learned she had made some major changes to move forward, the kind that change your life. And all because of the reason we both had in common: she wanted to be happy.

The title of this book is LOVE AND OTHER TRIALS, and it wasn't until I started writing the dedication that it all came together. What happened when I was a kid was a trial. That woman losing her child was a trial. The hurt that comes, and sometimes even the people that keep the hurt alive or prevent us from healing, sometimes for reasons they believe are well intentioned, are sometimes family and the men in our lives. I speak as a woman here. I'm sure there are men who can say it was a woman in their life that prevented them from moving on until that moment when you hear the right thing. When you finally say, no, this is not going to take from me anymore. I'm healing. All the way.

These trials, dear friends, are the ones that keep us from experiencing and being open to the love that's out there. So if you are reading this rom-com, you'll be entertained for sure. The heroine realizes love doesn't have to be a trial because the hero shows her a different way.

And who knows, you might also be open to a line in this book being the one you needed that will help you change your life. Because trials are hard, they're heavy, and they can take us down. Whether with family, men, or something else.

So if that's you, let me be the one to ask: how much more are you going to let it take from you?

Let's be done with it together, and let the love in. Happily ever after is waiting.

Ava

To Glen Powell—and other actors like him who uplift and change our lives through their talent and art.

UNKNOWN

Hey Ariel! This is Dax Cross, best man, telling you he's locked and loaded for the wedding. 👍

> Hey Captain Hotpants! Good to hear. 😅 Because we're in for the trial of our life... 🫡

CAPTAIN HOTPANTS

Trial? 😁 Aren't weddings happy occasions where people dance, drink, and get laid? 💃

> Not in my family. 🚫 Think tornadoes and hurricanes. 🌪️🌀

CAPTAIN HOTPANTS

Yeah, I heard your half sisters are called the Three Tornadoes. 🌪️ I wondered what that was about. 👀

> You're about to find out. 💀

CAPTAIN HOTPANTS

Good thing they're your specialty. 😉

> I'm not sure it's gonna help. Bring a strand of garlic. 🧄

CAPTAIN HOTPANTS

😱

ONE

The trials had begun—her family had forgotten her at the airport.

At least Ariel Holmes' battered black luggage didn't make for an uncomfortable seat. Other than a handyman fixing a broken baggage turnstile, she and her bloodhound were alone in the abandoned Charleston airport. Not a surprise, given it was one thirty in the morning. Hers had been the last flight in, arriving over an hour late.

Enjoy the peace and quiet, Ariel, because it's about to get freaky. And not in a hip-hop music kind of way.

Then she remembered the trials had already started five months ago, when her oldest half sister had blackmailed her into being her wedding planner. She laughed harshly under her breath in the quiet airport. Right. How could she have forgotten that little *two-by-four in the face* display of family love?

Ariel gave her bloodhound a good rubdown when he leaned his tired caramel head against her side and straightened his service vest. "Well, Sherlock, we've missed the last of the cabs. And with that storm kicking up, I'm not sure they'll be coming back anytime soon. I wouldn't say we're screwed, but it's no luck of the Irish either."

She unzipped her suitcase enough to pull out the silver flask she'd brought, filled to the brim with her favorite plus-one for family weddings: Jack Daniel's. But her phone pinged before she could take a healthy sip. She rummaged through her purse for it, relieved to see an incoming text from the one person in her family who would be outraged on her behalf—Jeffrey, her half brother.

> BEST BROTHER EVER
>
> The Three Tornadoes FORGOT you? 👤 $*#&# You'd think with Tiffany threatening you to make her wedding the best Charleston has ever seen—on a piddly budget no less—she'd have arrived in a magical winged horse carriage to pick you up. 🦄

> Are you drunk? 🥴 This is Tif-fa-ny we're talking about, and don't get me started on the gang up from Terry and Tricia. Aren't you lucky you don't share any blood with them? 🌿

> BEST BROTHER EVER
>
> I say a little prayer of gratitude every morning. 🙏 You though… 🗡 Their brilliant idea to spend a week at the beach before the wedding is going to kill you if you're not careful. 💀 It's Saturday. Barely. The wedding is next Saturday. You do the math. Girl, you'd better have brought your flask. 🥃

> I brought two. 😏 Regular and garter. Sending you the Three Tornadoes' texts now so you can stomp around for me in indignation. 😤

BEST BROTHER EVER

😈 The only thing that looks better on me is my honey. Have I told you how much I love Antonio? I think he might be my one and only. Which is why he's NOT coming to this wedding.

Good plan. 😉 He might run for the hills. Keep sending up good thoughts for me.

BEST BROTHER EVER

Always. 🩶 I wish I could say I'd love to come earlier, but Friday is plenty early. My hair is already standing on end. Also, you should have rented a car besides the golf cart.

I was assured Captain Hotpants could haul anything I need. 🌶

BEST BROTHER EVER

Snicker. With those prime muscles, I'll bet. 🌶 Ariel, I say this with love. You'd better check him out because I have a feeling about him for you... 💘

And we always trust your feelings. LOL. 🖤 All right, texts incoming.

BEST BROTHER EVER

I'm starting my Zen breathing. 🧘 Also—DO NOT APOLOGIZE FOR CUTTING YOUR HAIR.

Her hand went to her newly shorn hair before she sighed heavily. "Right. No apologizing. It's not like I had a choice."

Not that her sisters would care. Exhibit A. Their texts. She opened them and forwarded them to Jeffrey. Moral support rocked. In her phone, their numbers were saved under their nicknames, the Three Tornadoes, and their birth order number, with Tiffany being the oldest, and Terry being older than Tricia by two minutes. But Jeffrey knew all about that.

> **TORNADO #1**
>
> Are you finally here??? 🛬 I needed you like yesterday. There's oodles of things to do. You remember our deal, right? You'd better make my wedding the best one Charleston has ever seen. 🏠 Grandma's house won't be yours if it's just average.
>
> **TORNADO #2**
>
> Wasn't Jeffrey picking you up? 😂
>
> **TORNADO #3**
>
> They let you land in this weather? 🌧 I thought your flight would be canceled. It's ghastly outside.
>
> **TORNADO #1**
>
> Good thing you didn't crash in the storm. ✈ I need you so bad this week. 🥺
>
> **TORNADO #3**
>
> God, we've been drinking. 🍺 We'll have to figure out who can come get you.

She tossed her phone back in her purse and imagined Jeffrey swearing a blue streak. Made her feel a little happier on the inside. Because she wasn't relieved by her sister's assurance that someone would come. God, she should probably call an Uber, but she had no guarantee she'd find one at this hour, especially since there was a storm on the way and not all car services accepted dogs. Might as well enjoy the quiet and a little more Jack.

She stroked behind Sherlock's floppy ears as he gave a

sympathetic ruff. "Maybe if they forget us, we can hop on the first flight out of here in a few hours."

His rueful gaze had her laughing. God, he was such a trooper at family events.

"Yeah. I'm delusional. Don't mind me."

If it weren't for her desire to have her grandma's house, Ariel would have arrived at Tiffany's wedding right before the rehearsal this coming Friday. But no...

Her mother had teamed up with her sister to blackmail her. Blackmail her! Ariel's organizational skills were legendary, sure, as were her contacts in Charleston. They thought she could hit this wedding out of the park and stop the Deverell wedding curse. While she was known as a miracle worker of sorts, working in disaster recovery as she did, this was totally different.

Sure, she and Sherlock had pulled off some amazing search and rescue operations, but she wasn't confident even they could do anything to combat the wedding curse—if it were real.

Ariel's grandmother had married her (former) friend's ex-husband, and the woman had cursed her and her offspring on the steps of St. Michael's Church the day of the wedding.

More startling, there was plenty of evidence it had worked.

Case One: Her grandmother, who'd been married three times. Her first wedding had been the *talk* of Charleston, but her former friend's curse had immediately set in—the lights had flickered in the church and the seven-tiered cake had broken in half and crumbled to the ground as she and her friend's ex were about to cut it.

And then there was Grandma's third wedding...

Well, a tropical storm blew in and canceled the darn

thing on the day of, only to be held days later in city hall under muted circumstances to say the least.

Case Two: Her mother's three weddings had only added more proof to the pudding, and don't get her started on her aunts'. The carriage horse carrying her mom and the Three Tornadoes' dad off into the sunset reared and took off at a gallop before the driver got him under control. And when she'd married Ariel's dad, a nest of mice had run through the reception hall, causing a massive exodus, and her father still shuddered when he saw one. But that was not to be upstaged by what happened during the reception for wedding number three—the porch steps to the mansion had given way from wood rot when the women were gathered to catch the bouquet, causing a few turned ankles and bumps and bruises.

And then there were her sisters' previous weddings. Oh Lord. The chandelier taking the tent down during Tricia's wedding dance was still talked about at family reunions over mint juleps. Six people had been rushed to the ER.

The oyster bar at Terry's rehearsal dinner had made everyone hang over the porcelain throne all night.

And Tiffany's first wedding...

Well, not only had she set a new record for bad taste with nude Adam and Eve ice sculptures, courtesy of her artist ex-hubby, but one of the Sterno cans under a nearby chafing pan had somehow melted their genitals, causing Adam's giant junk to drip and shrivel in size, making every guest there totally uncomfortable or wheeze with laughter until they were wiping tears.

She and Jeffrey had laughed themselves silly. They'd bandied back *who knew Adam had been so hung?* remarks with them concluding he had to be, to father all humans according to the biblical account.

And that wasn't counting the others' woes at that wedding... There'd been a poison ivy outbreak after the wedding rehearsal, held at an idyllic farm, and the next day the top of the holy water had popped off violently during the blessing, knocking out one of the bridesmaids. Cold. For two minutes. Tiffany had wisely not asked her to be in the wedding party this round.

Who had rushed in to help with every disaster at her sisters' weddings? Ariel. She'd bought and distributed the calamine lotion and Pepto. She'd found event staff to shore up the tent and remove the broken chandelier. Heck, she'd even called the paramedics when necessary.

Despite her being dubbed the family fixer, Ariel didn't know if she could stop a curse. The research on that was fairly hair-raising, involving crazy incantations under a full moon and one-eight-hundred numbers to voodoo priestesses named Madame Renfro on Bourbon Street. So not going there.

But she would do everything in her power to make this wedding into the fairy tale her sister had in mind—somebody in the family needed a wedding win—and she had readily agreed to help from afar. With a skilled wedding planner at the helm.

Of course, that hadn't been enough...

She did love her sisters. And her mother. But God, they were hard to please and even harder to feel connected to. They were the exciting and fun ones, and she was the wallflower. Some might say she had an exciting job, but she considered herself a no-nonsense professional who trucked through mud and debris to find people. She was a mere daisy. Not a bold dahlia or bird of paradise like her sisters. Maybe it was because they all had the same father, while she'd gotten her father's practical, grounded side, like

Jeffrey, who'd been a toddler when their father had married her mother.

It sucked not fitting in.

A part of her—which clearly needed therapy—was still chasing family approval. Love even. Like that silly mouse with the wheel that never stopped. She'd tell herself to not let them push her around, but then she'd see them all huddled together or smell her mother's familiar perfume and want to be wrapped up in them. To have them praise her and tell her she'd done a good job, accepting her, for a brief moment, as one of them.

This wedding was her chance. Tiffany had even made her the maid of honor to give her the proper authority. For a moment, it was like they'd handed her all her dreams, wrapped in poofy pale pink tulle, the fabric for her bridesmaid's dress.

Or so she'd thought. Then the threats had kicked in.

Tiffany had wanted her to lead the whole shindig. Even knowing she had a demanding full-time job. It hadn't taken her long to realize why they'd been so inviting: she wasn't one of the Deverell women. Her mother had reverted to her maiden name after her first divorce—and she'd changed her three daughters' names too, out of spite. Ariel had balked at giving up her father and Jeffrey's last name of Holmes after the divorce. Her mother hadn't cared enough to fight her, saying it was probably less confusing anyway since she didn't embody the Deverell women characteristics.

Which her sisters had taken to mean the curse didn't apply to her. Surely if she planned everything, the bad luck would stay away. Logic had never been their strong suit, God love them. She'd pretty much told them Madame Renfro, the voodoo priestess, would have said there was no way the spirit world worked like that. Or so she figured...

They hadn't liked her response or her insistence they needed a dedicated wedding planner. That's when her sister and mother had brought out the familiar big guns of family manipulation. Because a Deverell woman would do anything to get what she wanted...

Which was why Ariel really wasn't one of them. She couldn't go that low.

God. Families. You can't live with them and you can't live without them.

She took a sip from her flask to stave off the bitter taste in her mouth. The blackmail was like tea left too long in her grandmother's Royal Doulton rose teapot. What would her grandmother think of their deviousness? Maybe she would have understood. She'd wanted the wedding curse broken long ago. She'd consulted multiple psychics on the subject to no good end, obviously.

Ariel had been close to her. Her grandma hadn't been able to do much with the Three Tornadoes. They were a unit and tight as a sailing knot, and oddly, Grandma had said maybe they were too much like her for the four to get along. Ariel hadn't had anyone to really play with, and since she'd always been wise beyond her years, she and her grandma had bonded. She'd also loved Ariel taking good care of her.

Her cute little white house on Folly Beach with the green shutters was supposed to go to Ariel because she'd been the one to call her grandma at least three times a week and look out for her in her later years. Grandma had known how much Ariel loved that house—and also that her own daughter wouldn't hesitate to sell it to a developer. But being old-fashioned and trusting in family to abide by her wishes, Grandma hadn't imagined hiring a lawyer to create a will. She was old-school Charleston that way and frugal with her money.

But after she'd passed five months ago, her mother had given the deed to Tiffany with the understanding she could give it to Ariel after she made her wedding come off. Was she a little bitter at the blackmail?

Yes. But she was focused.

Grandma's house was going to be hers, and she was going to do everything her sister wanted to make this wedding the event of Charleston.

If they ever picked her up…

She turned to her faithful hound. "You've got my back, right, boy?"

Sherlock gave a muted ruff and looked up at her with his sad, expressive brown eyes, the wrinkles on his angular face lending him the kind of wise visage people trusted, her most of all. Whenever they visited her family, he stayed glued to her side. He knew what they were up against.

"Well, buddy, we knew how it was going to be. Back in Tornado Alley, family style. No pity parties." She took another drink from her flask. The whiskey was a welcome streak of fire down her throat as she stared at the empty baggage carousel making lazy circles around the airport.

Sherlock suddenly gave a low ruff, his droopy head lifting as a light blue vintage Bronco pulled up along the curb outside baggage claim—noticeable because up until now it had been as empty as the rest of the airport. A tall man with broad shoulders wearing a gray sweatshirt and jeans headed around the hood after letting himself out and jogged toward the entrance. The sliding doors slicked open. He paused, putting his hands on his trim hips as he scanned the area before sighting her. The frown on his handsome face changed into a killer smile. Her heart gave a lurch, like she'd just hit her bicycle's brakes because she'd seen something amazing and wanted to stop.

Wowza.

She'd seen photos of Naval Captain Dax Cross on social media after he'd first texted to introduce himself as best man. She'd already been told his nickname was Captain Hotpants, and wasn't that cute as hell? That he was H-O-T hot wasn't in question. He was absolutely gorgeous, whether in his dress whites or in faded jeans and a ripped T-shirt on the beach.

The beach pics were especially yummy, and she might have looked at them a few times. Not in a stalker like way. But in a *I want to make sure I'll recognize him when I meet him* way. Okay, and maybe she'd drooled a little.

Like she was now. His sandy hair was windblown from the storm. His square jaw carried a day's stubble from not shaving. But it was his piercing moss green eyes that had her breath freezing in her chest.

She'd been attracted by his good-humored texts as much as his photos and posts online, but he was even better-looking in person. Attraction confirmed. Body temperature rising. Jeffrey would be thrilled. She certainly wanted to give a little cheer. If he was her consolation prize this week, she could get through anything.

Suddenly being the maid of honor to his best man didn't seem like a chore. No, this task was going to go down like red velvet cake and extra dry champagne.

She lifted her hand and waved. *"Captain Hotpants!"*

"Ariel Holmes!" He walked over in determined strides, a mouthwatering picture of pure, all-American male in action. "I heard your family forgot to get you, so I headed out while they were arguing about who would brave the storm. You'd think with your mother being named Stormy and your sisters being called the Three Tornadoes they wouldn't make such a fuss over a little rain."

There was an edge to his voice already, one that had Sherlock's head lifting as he gazed up at the captain. "You brought the garlic, right?"

His mouth flattened and a forced exhale was audible beyond the baggage claim turnstile noise. "I thought you were joking when you texted that. Now I know better..."

The ominous tone was clear. Something had happened. Poor guy. He was only a good-natured best man trying to do his best by his fellow pilot and former college roommate from the Naval Academy. Rob Abrams was clearly the fiery one in their brotherhood. When she'd met him at Thanksgiving, she'd found him to be exactly the sort of magnetic, rugged male Tiffany usually went for. They'd gotten along fine, sticking to work talk, but Ariel could tell Rob had some baggage from childhood. Tiffany had plenty of her own baggage, so Ariel was hoping the discipline Rob had learned in the military would help them create a more stable foundation for their lives. Because Tiffany needed it—and so did her son, Marshall, from her first marriage.

Suddenly she wondered if Dax was upset because he'd seen a few other sides of her sister and was worried about his friend. That was only natural. Except it seemed like something bigger had happened, she decided.

A flash of lightning had him looking off toward the windows as the first plops of rain sounded on the roof. "But how are you? You must be pissed they forgot you."

She stood up, feeling like a shrimp compared to his tall frame as a crack of thunder boomed outside. "I'm used to it. Two weddings ago, I started bringing my own flask."

When she waggled it, he rolled those gorgeous green eyes dramatically. "That's both sad and ingenious. I've been here a day, and I'm already feeling like I'm in a parallel universe. I'm only saying that since you suggested the garlic. Here, let me get your bag. Also, what are my rules of engagement with Sherlock? I know search and rescue dogs don't like people getting up in their business."

Impressed, she straightened Sherlock's drool bib hanging over his vest. "That's correct. Put your hand out and let him get your scent. After that, it's up to him. Oh, and I can get my own bag."

"Please. I have to keep up my reputation as Captain Hotpants." His flirtatious wink had her wanting to do a cartwheel as he held out his hand to her dog. "Besides, I need to lift things. You're doing me a favor."

Okay, that had her mouth twitching. Especially since her luggage had wheels. "My sisters tell me you're known for having the best buns this side of Biloxi." That had not been on his social media account.

The winning smile he shot her as he cocked his very taut butt playfully to the side was as welcome to her eyes as summer sun on a windy beach. "The other side of Biloxi was already taken."

Goodness, he was too good-looking for words. And that cute little tush...

Seeing that every day would be no hardship. Captain Hotpants was going to be her one pleasure this week, helping her make this wedding come off.

"I find that hard to believe, seeing it in real life," she flirted back.

He flashed another *take your breath away* smile. "No, really, it's a longstanding joke between me and Rob. You can't take us too seriously sometimes. Working as a pilot, you get a sick sense of humor because of the risks you navigate. But you know what I mean, going into disaster sites, looking for people."

"I do."

She knew Rob had grown up as a single child, not really knowing his father, and he'd chosen the Navy as much for its adventure as to make something of his life. He must be an adrenaline junkie, the kind of person who chased storms. Her job had its share of adrenaline, but she didn't feed on it. Not like Rob seemed to as a fighter pilot. He'd loved telling her how fast he'd gone and some of the dangerous maneuvers he'd pulled. Now his personal life was going to be filled with the same kind of turbulence. That was Tiffany—and her other two sisters.

Mesmerizing. Chaotic. Destructive.

Most of the men who'd hooked up with her mother's side were like that, but none of the marriages had lasted.

"Whatever the reason for the joke, Captain Hotpants, it sounds like a good story."

He gave a heartfelt wince. "You could say that. We came down this way for spring break back in college, and I got to talking up a girl, which led to her coining the phrase one night over Jack and Coke. My call sign—Hercules—didn't stick in the Navy because Rob is an asshole."

Ariel laughed, knowing he said it like guys do. She hung out with guys so much for her job she was used to being treated like one of them. "Let's hope he's an endearing asshole, if he's marrying my sister."

Something hard flashed in his eyes. She noted it as Sherlock nudged her hand. Yeah, her dog had sensed there was a problem too.

"Something like that." He inclined his head to the exit. "We should head out before it really starts to pour. I'm glad I left the hard top on coming down here."

The rain was falling in giant plops, but so far it wasn't a raging thunderstorm despite the ominous lightning and thunder. She followed Dax out to the curb, feeling the large drops hit her hair. She was touched when he opened her door first and then the back passenger side for Sherlock. After seeing them to safety, he ran around the front of the car and climbed inside himself as a white flash lit the sky. Raindrops had wet his face, highlighting his strong brows and rock-hard jaw. My, oh my, was he one tall drink of water, as Grandma had liked to say.

"Everybody good?" he asked as he buckled up.

A boomer shook the car, making Sherlock bark in response. "You're all right, buddy," she reassured him. "We're good, Dax. But I'm starving. Do you mind if we hit the Waffle House nearby for burgers or something?"

He turned the engine on. "You bet. I can always eat. Just show me the way. I'd heard you love it here. But I didn't know you were moving here from Charlotte until Rob mentioned it."

She'd made those plans on the contingency of getting Grandma's house, but she wasn't going to say anything about the blackmail. She grabbed her phone and brought up the directions for the Waffle House she had in mind, planting it on the console where he could see it.

"Charlotte isn't a place I've ever felt I could plant roots. My grandma lived here, so we used to come as kids for the summer. Later I came when I wasn't working. She recently passed."

"I heard," he said gravely, "and I'm sorry."

Ariel felt her throat tighten. "Thank you. It's still weird, having her gone. But she has a beautiful house on Folly Beach I'm hoping to move into. I know it might sound like a funny place to move, coming from someone who's done disaster recovery after a hurricane, but every place has its dangers, I personally think. And this place is special. The kind where you can put all your troubles aside, dig your toes into the sand, and just be."

Her job was so stressful Ariel had few places where she could let go. Her grandmother's place had always been a refuge. First, from a broken, chaotic home when her mother had divorced her father, and then later, when she'd needed a place to heal after all the disasters she'd seen.

Searching for people in wreckages with Sherlock and pulling them out alive was powerfully fulfilling. But not finding them in time—break-you-in-two heartbreaking.

"Sounds like a nice place," Dax commented, cranking the windshield wipers up to high as the rain fell harder as they left the airport.

"It's the best. If I can swing it, I plan to take Sherlock out that way for some exercise. He doesn't like being caged up. You're welcome to come along."

He glanced her way, a sexy smile touching the corners of his tantalizing mouth. Pure temptation, like the rest of him. "I'd like that. You seem like good company. I thought you would be. Ariel Holmes, I'm really glad you're here."

So was she—and that was a downright miracle. "I'm happy you're here too, Dax. I won't need to bring my garlic necklace out when I'm around you."

He laughed before falling silent.

The quiet in the car was the easy kind after that, and she savored it. She'd liked Dax from his first text, and everything she'd seen on social media and heard from her family had backed that up. He seemed to be a decent kind of guy. A loyal friend. A dedicated military officer. She sometimes worked with active and retired military personnel in her job, and she enjoyed their company a lot. She knew Rob had conscripted Dax as much as Tiffany had enlisted Ariel for the wedding, though blackmail had likely not been involved in Dax's case. Lucky guy.

The sound of Dax drumming his fingers on the steering wheel as he drove made her look over. His mouth was tense again, and he seemed troubled. They were on the same team. She might as well get it out of him.

"I know we've only just met, but I have a good sense of people from my work. I also know my family. You seem upset. Did something happen already?"

He exhaled sharply. "Yeah, and because I like and respect you, I'm going to be completely honest with you."

She turned in her seat to give him her complete attention. "Great. Honesty is my jam. Lay it on me."

He swung his head her way, his cool green gaze locking on to her. "Tiffany hit on me."

"*Oh no!*" She wanted to sink into her seat and howl like Sherlock chose to just then.

"Yeah." He drummed the steering wheel louder this time. "Ariel... I'm going to have to stop the wedding."

Shit. Stopping the wedding meant she couldn't earn her grandma's house.

The Deverell wedding curse had just sent her a curveball.

TWO

He should have packed a strand of garlic and hung it around his neck like a vampire lei.

Because maybe him reeking a bad odor would have kept Tiffany from making a pass at him and patting his butt when Rob was off in the men's room.

The *Abrams-Deverell Mission Briefing Book* he'd put together had not even hinted at this possibility. Then again, Dax's book had only listed top-level information about the wedding and Tiffany's wedding party, with the understanding of more to be gathered on-site as needed.

Wedding Location: Charleston Estate Resort; lodge on-site for socializing, welcome party, and rehearsal. Cottages used for main guests. Outdoor site by beach for wedding.

Bride: Tiffany Deverell; thirty-four; married once to an artist for seven years; thirteen-year-old son, Marshall. Oldest of the Three Tornadoes. Met Rob at a bar on a girls' night in Pensacola. Dated eight months before Rob popped the question in November.

Maid of Honor/Wedding Planner: Ariel Holmes; thirty-one; half sister; unmarried; dog Sherlock. Lives in

Charlotte; relocating to Charleston. Works for disaster recovery organization like Red Cross. Dax's main point of contact.

Bridesmaid: Terry Deverell; thirty-three (twins); on second marriage to Morris; two kids named Billy and Brooks. Lives in Dallas; second of the Tornadoes.

Bridesmaid: Tricia Deverell; thirty-three (twins); on second marriage to Bartlett; two kids named Ripp and Ryland. Lives in Atlanta; third of the Tornadoes.

Mother of bride: Stormy Deverell; sixty-two; on third marriage to Trey. Lives in Savannah.

Incomplete information was part of every mission. Dax knew that. Even with complete intel, he didn't think he could have seen this one coming. He'd been so shocked—and he was a naval pilot trained to handle enemy pilots shooting at him!—that he'd just stood there afterward, frozen solid, as Tiffany sauntered over to join her sisters.

Rob joined him a minute later. His closest and dearest friend had nudged him in the ribs and tipped his head over to his soon-to-be bride and said, "Isn't she the most beautiful woman in the world? I used to think there was no other place I felt as alive as in the cockpit, but with her, I feel that way. Like every sense is heightened. God, I'm so lucky to be marrying her, and I get a son in the bargain. Who has it better than me?"

Dax had glanced over to the platinum blonde in question before he found Marshall running around with his cousins, all up way past their bedtime. He'd only grunted—unable to think of a good way to tell Rob that his fiancée had just come on to him. How the hell was he supposed to tell him something like that? *Hey, man, I hate to break it to you, but your fiancée likes ALL men to feel alive. She just made me feel like I was going to stroke out. From shock, sure, but there's no denying every sense was heightened. Are you sure getting hitched is a good idea?*

Drama from the Three Tornadoes had interrupted further musing. He and Rob had overheard them talking about Ariel being at the airport, and they'd wandered over. Arguments had erupted about who was to blame. No one seemed inclined to do anything about it, so he'd offered to pick her up. Everyone had been drinking heavily but him. Being on call as a pilot, he didn't drink more than a social beer on occasion.

The blustery drive to the airport had done him good. He'd gone through the incident and concluded he could do only one thing.

Talk to Rob.

Stop the wedding.

Which really sucked, since his friend thought he was happy. But what choice did he have? Rob was his pal. His buddy. He had a duty to him. Even if he suspected his friend wouldn't handle the news well based on how he'd reacted to his college girlfriend cheating.

Ariel reached across the gearshift and laid her hand on his tense arm. Heat rocked through him as he quickly glanced her way—that quick glance enough to make him aware of every little raindrop that wet her skin. Jesus, his electrical system was going haywire. Usually that meant bad things for a pilot, but with her, he didn't feel any danger. Only a surprisingly deep connection.

But this attraction could be yet another problem since he wanted to stop her sister's wedding. Shit. He'd known from the beginning she was coming alone to the wedding— like him. He wasn't seeing anyone, and while he could have found someone to be his plus-one, he hadn't thought it wise.

He was the best man, and Rob had asked him to bring his A game. She'd clearly felt the same.

"I'm so sorry, Dax. Tell me exactly what happened."

That she believed him was a relief. She was sitting up straighter in her seat, one hand fisted on her jean-clad thighs. Calm outwardly, like he imagined she would be as she was searching through rubble trying to find victims who were still alive.

"*I'm* the one who's sorry to put this on you. It can't be easy hearing something like that about your sister. And they're getting married in less than a week. Jesus, what a mess!"

He'd hated to tell her, but he liked her and respected her. He didn't want her—or anyone for that matter—to think he was the kind of guy who'd encourage or welcome his best friend's fiancée hitting on him. He'd even hoped he and Ariel might flirt a little and see where things went this week, but that seemed up in the air now, given his impending talk with Rob.

And Jesus fucking Christ, what would his buddy say when he told him? His best friend would never believe he'd done anything to invite it, thank God. They had a code. But how was Dax supposed to live with knowing he'd fucked up his best friend's happiness?

Shit. Shit. Shit. Shit.

"Start from the beginning, Dax," she calmly repeated.

His hands gripped the steering wheel. He'd wanted to pretend he'd read it wrong, but the invitation and flirtatious comments had seemed clear. The hand on his butt had certainly been filled with intent.

Something touched his arm again, but it didn't feel like Ariel. When he looked over, he saw Sherlock was resting his head against his shoulder. God, it made him long for a dog.

He hadn't had one since leaving home for college. Being away so much, he couldn't keep a dog. But his heart squeezed a little at the gesture. Dogs always knew what to do. His Lab growing up had slept with him after he'd lost a baseball game. Damn, Jasper had been a good dog, and so had Rover after him. "You're lucky to have this guy."

"I know." She gave Sherlock a good rub under his ears. "Dax, let's still go the Waffle House, if you don't mind. You can tell me what happened when you're not driving."

Again, she showed the kind of poise he was used to in military officers and emergency personnel. She must be shocked, too, but she wasn't showing it. "Sounds like a good plan. So how about we talk about you on the way there? Before coming here, I heard you were helping in Omaha after that horrible tornado touched down."

"Yeah, I was." She settled more comfortably into a slouch in her seat. "Seven dead, which was horrible. But we managed to save six, and for that I'm deeply grateful. You might have the best buns this side of Biloxi, but Sherlock here has the best nose this side of... Sherlock, what should we say here? The Himalayas? Sherlock has done some of his biggest rescue efforts in Turkey and Bali, so that won't work. Maybe Perth?"

What did her passport look like?

"I've only gotten to Mexico and Dubai and some parts of Europe for fun. Naval aircraft carriers in the Gulf don't count."

"I heard you're leaving the Navy."

"Yeah, I'd always planned on becoming a corporate pilot at some point. Your shelf life as a naval aviator is only so long, and my new job landed in my lap, so to speak. Got such a nice signing bonus, I could buy this baby. Fully refurbished '72 Bronco. It's a honey."

"Congratulations. Where will you be based out of?"

"Somewhere in the South, although I haven't decided yet." He let his gaze track to the online navigation to check the upcoming turn. "I can choose where I want to be based out of. I drove this way after seeing my family in Austin so I could take in my choices. There are a lot of great cities out there."

"Charleston is a nice town," she commented softly.

He looked over as the hair on the back of his neck stood up. The way she'd said it was nostalgic and full of yearning. "So you love Charleston that much, huh? It's my first time here."

The slow shake of her head, along with the way her blue eyes warmed, had a powerful effect on his heart. He wanted to see why she loved this place so much.

"Well... That makes this city a little more interesting to me. I'll keep an open mind while I'm in town. It would be great to know someone here. Most of my buddies are on carriers like I just was, and of course Rob has new orders in San Diego as you know."

Maybe not living in family housing like he'd thought. Jesus, how was he supposed to break the news?

She twisted her hands in her lap as the unspoken reminder hung in the air. "I'm hoping to take over my grandmother's house shortly, but it's a little complicated."

With her family, he could believe it. She should plant garlic in front of her house.

"I have an offer from the hurricane relief center in this area, so Sherlock and I wouldn't have to travel as much. He's seven years old now, and we've had a really good run. Haven't we, boy?"

She gave the dog a good rubdown as Dax took the exit and headed down the curve and turned right. The yellow sign for the Waffle House was visible through the rain a short distance ahead. He pulled into the closest parking spot and was out the door to open Ariel's before she could do it herself. He still liked to treat a woman like a woman.

Her smile was bright as he opened it, first for her and then for Sherlock. Running inside, he fought the urge to put his hand to her back. Being early May, she didn't have a coat, so she had to be getting wet from the rain. He beat her to the door, and opening that too, he let her and Sherlock precede him.

A tired waitress greeted them and told them to sit wherever they wanted. They picked a spot in the middle, since the place was empty save them, and when he sat across from her, he took a moment to take her in.

Her hair was a messy brown tangle of curls, slightly wet now, cut close to her face. Pixie chic, he might say. Not the shoulder-length hair he'd seen in her photos online and at her sister's place when he'd visited Pensacola to meet Tiffany after Rob had proposed.

Unlike her sisters, she didn't seem to wear much makeup or fake eyelashes. Her natural beauty was pure girl next door—just the way he liked it. Fresh-faced. Peachy skin. A little spattering of freckles from where the sun had kissed her. She wouldn't be the kind of woman he'd wake up with and wonder at the difference in her appearance.

He pulled his thoughts back from that tantalizing door and let his gaze wander to her awesome dog. Sherlock stood calmly beside the table. When she was sitting down, Ariel wasn't too much taller than the bloodhound, who probably topped out at twenty-seven inches if he were to guess.

His gaze couldn't stay on the dog long. Not when there was such a beautiful, compelling woman sitting across from him, smelling like spice and fresh rain. He knew Ariel was called "The Runt" by her family because she was tiny, and she *was* petite, with a hot little body he could easily imagine picking up and wrapping around him. Her skin was wet from the rain and looked luminous, but it was her baby blues that held him in thrall until the waitress slapped a menu in front of him.

"What can I get y'all?"

Ariel didn't even pick up the menu. "Iced tea, sweet, of course. Angus burger with bacon and hashbrowns."

He gazed at the menu quickly and noted the options. "First thing. Is there any way we can get some water for her dog? He's just gotten off a plane. Like my friend here."

Ariel reached into her purse. "Don't worry. I was going to give him some of mine. I have a collapsible water bowl."

"Isn't that clever?" The waitress touched the blue-ribbed rim when Ariel held it up. "What else strikes your fancy?"

He patted Sherlock's head when the dog wandered over as if to thank him. "I need some help deciding. If it were you, what would you go for? Pecan waffle? Pork chops and eggs breakfast? Or Texas Cheesesteak Melt?"

The waitress tapped him on the back with gusto. "Why not get all three, honey? You look like a man who could handle all that food and then some."

He was used to women flirting with him. Erika in second grade had been the first. She'd asked him on a hot day in Austin if he wanted a lick from her fudge brownie ice cream cone. Of course he'd said yes, and that had been the beginning of his longstanding enjoyment of women. He had no trouble flirting back.

Just not with his best friend's fiancée.

Again, he wondered if he'd done something to inadvertently invite Tiffany to go there. He didn't think so. He didn't cross uncrossable lines. Ever. "Ariel, any thoughts?"

The right side of her mouth was curled up in a sexy grin, as if she were enjoying a little secret. "Sweet or savory?"

If it were her sweet little body, he'd say sweet in a heartbeat. "How about a little of both?" he asked with a touch of naughty in his voice.

Her blue eyes flashed with heat as their waitress gave an *Mmm-hmm*. "How about pecan waffles with a double side of sausage?"

He didn't take his eyes off hers, watching the way her chest rose with her breath, as if her heart was beating fast, like his was. "Perfect."

"Sweet tea, for you too, sugar?" the waitress asked with a touch of sauce in her syrupy voice.

"Is there any other kind?"

She picked up the menus. "No, baby, there ain't."

When she left, he kept staring back at Ariel, whose blue eyes seemed almost navy now. The attraction between them was growing in power. Like the storm had. He'd watched the clouds swirl and gather before coalescing. He imagined the connection between them would be the same if they were somehow able to continue down this road.

He'd hopefully make her laugh away the worry he sometimes caught winking in the corners of her eyes. And he'd sure as hell make her moan, because this was the kind of woman you gave everything to, a woman who was confident enough to enjoy herself and let go.

"Ariel, I'm glad we stopped here. I've heard a lot of great things about you, and honestly, I read a few things online about you and Sherlock. Plus, Rob can't talk about you enough. He thinks you're a cross between Mother Teresa and Joan of Arc."

She turned her mouth up at that. "That's ridiculous, but Rob is strategic, which makes him a good aviator, I imagine. He thought it was important to get to know me when he came for Thanksgiving to meet the family for the first time after he proposed."

His diaphragm seized up, prompting him to sit up straighter to ease the tension.

Ariel immediately reached across the yellow table and gently touched his hand. "Ready to tell me?"

He nodded crisply. "Best get it over with. Here goes. I was talking with Rob. About you, actually, and how I was looking forward to meeting you."

Her face registered shock before she glanced over and rubbed Sherlock under the ears, almost as if she couldn't maintain eye contact after that admission.

"We'd read about you and Sherlock saving those people in Nebraska. Maybe it's being in the military, but me, Rob, and our other military buddies have a lot of respect for you. Sherlock too, of course. It takes guts to do what you do. Maybe even more than what we do."

"Let's not start comparing."

They paused to thank their waitress as she set down their iced teas and three glasses of water, with a wink at Sherlock.

"We all do what we do," Ariel continued. "But you're digressing..."

He was, and he knew it. "Anyway, your sister came over. She'd been drinking with your other sisters, if you don't mind me saying. Another reason I didn't want them driving." Rob hadn't been a candidate either, but that wasn't unusual. Dax had been the designated driver since college.

"Tequila, likely." Ariel frowned as she filled the dog's water bowl. "My sisters and tequila have a longstanding relationship. Keep going."

He could still see the way Tiffany had cozied up to Rob and wrapped her arms around him before leaning in and giving him a long, deep kiss. Dax had almost excused himself to give them a moment, but before he could, Rob had pulled away and said he had to hit the men's room, leaving Dax with Tiffany.

"Rob went to the head after they'd had an affectionate moment. She looked at him like a bride should, I thought. But then she turned to me and smiled. The vibe felt a little off when she kept staring at me. Then she said she could see why people thought I had the best buns this side of Biloxi. How she'd been watching me... Jesus, this is mortifying."

He never blushed, but heat was crawling up his neck.

"Keep going. It can't be more embarrassing telling it than having it happen."

That was a perspective. "After that, she did some itsy-bitsy spider thing with her fingers up my chest before sliding her hand around and patting my butt, saying I looked good enough to eat."

"Grabbing it or patting it?" she asked seriously.

"Patting." He gave her a strained smile. "Like I was her pet." Or her love slave, but he would never say those words out loud.

Ariel heaved out a breath. "And then what?"

"She leaned in closer." He could still smell how strong Tiffany's perfume was, but oddly he hadn't smelled any alcohol on her breath. "Then your sister, Tricia, shouted out something about you being at the airport, and all hell broke loose. Tiffany headed over. Rob returned. Phones came out.

Arguments ensued. I was upset no one had remembered to pick you up."

Her lopsided smile grabbed him by the throat. "That's really sweet."

God, she was easy to impress, but then again, her family had forgotten her. Who did that? Whenever he flew into Austin, his family met him with signs saying, *Welcome Home, Dax* or *We Missed You, Captain*.

"If I'd known, I would have been there when you landed, but I thought it was handled. And that's when I volunteered to get you." He fiddled with his straw. "I left in shock, trying to make sense of things and then figure out a way to tell my buddy."

That lovely hand of hers found his again, and this time, he took it and held it firmly. Her hand was slender and fit his perfectly, her touch carrying warmth all the way to his rapidly thudding heart.

"I'm so sorry that happened, Dax. You can't know how much. I've been on the front lines of a lot of the so-called Three Tornadoes' damage, and this is top of the charts. But while it doesn't make any of it better, I can tell you that my sisters are all abominable flirts—even while involved or married. It's mostly harmless, although that doesn't justify it. They have this compulsion I've never understood to make sure every living and breathing male between the ages of twenty and seventy wants them."

Call him old-fashioned, but he still didn't think it was right. Even flirting had intent, and it wasn't how someone should act when they were in a committed relationship. Also, it would surely make Rob crazy given his past with Erin. "I've known women like that, Ariel. I just don't want my best friend to marry one of them."

"I get that." She gave Sherlock another pat when he

leaned his head against her side. "But it's possible Tiffany got jealous of you talking about me and wanted to assert her..."

"Dominance?" He scoffed. "Doesn't pretty it up."

"No, it doesn't." She bit her lip, her inner turmoil obvious now. "You said you plan to stop the wedding. You're going to talk to Rob?"

"I have to, Ariel." He squeezed her hand since she looked pale now, his own mouth flattening at the coming conversation. "He has to know. I wouldn't be his best friend if I didn't tell him. Do you disagree?"

"No, of course not." Her hand tensed in his grasp. "*I'd* want to know. But you should know... Oh, never mind."

She pulled her hand free and rubbed her face, as if the lateness of the hour had finally hit her.

"Know what?"

"Nothing." She picked up her glass and drank deeply before setting it down with a clack. "So you'll talk to Rob? When? Tomorrow? Because it's Friday—"

"Saturday actually," he countered, holding up his watch showing 2:11 a.m. "Early hours."

"Right." She rubbed her face again. "Oh God! What a mess. If he wants to cancel the wedding, maybe I can get back deposits. You'll tell me right away, right?"

"Of course." Dax reached for her hand and leaned forward, searching her tired eyes. "Hey! I'm sorry I'm stressing you out. I know there's a lot on the line here. But we'll figure things out. Together. Think of me as your wingman. Your sister said Lisa wasn't working—"

"*Wasn't working?*" Her mouth gaped as their waitress put their plates down and left quietly, her sensible shoes squeaking. "But Lisa— I'm sorry. I think I just left my body.

She got rid of Lisa? How could she? Lisa is my wedding assistant. Oh God! This is awful."

"Maybe the wedding being called off wouldn't be such a bad thing for you?" he joked before wincing. "God, that was an awful thing to say. Chalk it up to me trying to see a silver lining where there probably isn't one."

She tipped her head back to the ceiling. "My sisters aren't called the Three Tornadoes for nothing. I've always thought my family should come with tornado warnings. Seems like the sirens are screaming already."

He studied her, his thumb finally giving in to the urge to caress the back of her hand. "I just got it. You went into disaster recovery because of your family. Jeez, I'm slow."

"You're far from slow, Dax." She gave him a smile that caught him right in the center of his chest. "And you're right. I'm compelled to bring order to chaos. Since I was a child, I've come in after my sisters wrecked things and put them back together. My mother too, although she's tempered some. I should thank them really. I found my life's purpose because of them, and I'm damn good at it. We'll get through this."

She sounded convincing, and for a moment, the Joan of Arc comparison seemed more than apt. He stroked her hand, trying to assure her he was with her. All the way. "Then we have nothing to worry about."

She didn't say anything, and who could blame her?

Ejecting from a burning aircraft would be easier than stopping this train wreck.

THREE

Ariel couldn't believe it.

Her grandma's house might as well have slid into the ocean. All hope of fulfilling her part of her bargain with her sister had blown away, like dandelion seeds in the wind.

How could Tiffany have done this?

Her sisters liked to be the center of attention, sure, but flirting was one thing, and grabbing the best man's butt was another.

"How come you're so normal?" Dax asked as they drove back to the wedding venue—Charleston Estates Resort. "If that's not a rude question? Is it because they're your half sisters?"

Sherlock gave a low howl, as if he understood the kind of agony this line of questioning gave her.

"Maybe. My mom will tell you she and their father ran pretty wild when they first met, and they were still going when she had Tricia and Terry, who are fraternal twins, after Tiffany. Then their relationship crashed and burned. Grandma had two other daughters besides my mother, you should know, and she named them the Hurricanes when they were little because of how crazy they could get. Said she got what she deserved for calling her first child, my mother, Stormy, and her second daughter Gail—although the term gale is spelled differently—and then giving Brianne the nickname Breezy. So you see, wild blood runs in the family. Although I've found a way to channel mine into my job and overcome the rest. I like to say I have a louder good angel on my shoulder than a bad one."

"Interesting."

The word was loaded with meaning, but she wasn't going to analyze it. "Mom didn't like being without a man, and with three girls, she wanted stability. Dad's a financial planner—very logical, patient, and steady. She made him a little wild, and he made her a little calmer. They balanced each other out until my mother wanted more. I was thirteen when they divorced."

The worst year of her life. Suddenly she was the only person who didn't fit in, except when she spent time with her dad and Jeffrey two nights a week.

With one hand resting on the steering wheel, Dax used the other to give Sherlock a good rubdown, making the dog's soulful eyes nearly roll back in his head, which made her smile. She could always tell something about people by how they treated Sherlock and how he reacted. Dax clearly loved dogs. More, he longed for one himself.

"So you're more like your dad."

"Yes. He's good with his clients and manages risk for a living, which I inherited from him. Except I was an accident. On some wild night my parents had in Vegas. Feel free to laugh. It's cliché."

He bit his lip, clearly trying to keep a straight face. "I won't. But you have a half brother, right?"

"Yes, Dad already had Jeffrey from another marriage.

He was three when I came on the scene, and instead of being jealous of me—like Terry and Tricia were at the same age—he considered me his baby princess. We adore each other with a capital A. The Three Tornadoes—as Mom called them when they were toddlers—were always their own unit. Jeffrey and I never fit in. But that's a simple answer about why I'm different..."

The rain had lessened, but lightning flashes still lit the distance. "What's the complicated answer?"

Maybe it was fatigue or the easy way he listened—like he was becoming a good friend beyond the sizzle between them—but she decided to tell him. "Since the first Deverell woman in the family—Augusta Deverell who came to Charleston from England with her husband in 1801— Deverell women have been raised to do two things: to please their mothers and entice men. I've failed at both. That makes me different straightaway."

That green liquid gaze of his slowly slid her way. Making her shiver. Making her aware of the rain still wetting her skin.

"As someone who finds you very attractive in addition to funny, kind, and interesting, I would take issue with that last statement."

Her insides tightened. Did he mean she enticed *him*? She felt another little shiver, this one hot.

"Perhaps you're different too." She shot him a rueful smile. "Look, I'm a gentle wind in comparison to my sisters. By the time I came around, my mother had little energy left for me after my sisters. Dax, the truth is, my mother didn't even name me. She was in shock at having another child. Three girls had tested her trim waistline plenty. She didn't know what to do with Jeffrey. My sisters named me. Guess who they chose?"

She caught his wince. "I don't want to assume it was a Disney princess."

"That's me. With the last name Holmes, I'm a hodgepodge of crazy characters. I named Sherlock something else, but my first search and rescue crew kept calling him Sherlock. It stuck."

"Kinda like Captain Hotpants." He hung his wrist on the steering wheel, looking manly and as delectable as the apple pie she'd passed up at the Waffle House. "We're a pair. I mean, my last name is Cross. When someone calls me Mr. Cross, I wonder if they're thinking I frown all the time. And what woman would want to be Mrs. Cross, assuming she'd take my name? Then there's the teasing I got as a kid. Dax the Axe."

Her lips twitched. "Maybe we should both change our names and pick new ones."

"Fresh start." His sexy wink sent tiny shivers licking across her skin. "I like that. What would you choose?"

She rubbed Sherlock behind the ears as she considered. "Something classic. Like Elizabeth Harvey. You?"

"Albert...no...Stephan St. James. That sounds more fun. Especially with my Southern accent. People's brows would slam together when I said, 'How y'all doing? I'm Stephan.'"

God, he really was a hoot. "I'll call you Stephan if you'd like, but I'm warning you, I might have to bring out Captain Hotpants on occasion."

"And you haven't even seen this butt in dress whites yet." Another sexy flash of a smile. "All right, *Elizabeth*. I hate to tell you, but I really like Ariel. I've never met one before, and it makes you seem even more unique."

Could he just kiss her now? Because she wanted his hands all over her after that comment. "Well, I like Dax too. Do you know what it means?"

His indelicate snort came before a cutoff laugh. "My mother didn't look it up until after she chose it. The name can mean water, leader, or badger. A hot mess, if you ask me. What about yours?"

Oh God, was she going to tell him? Yeah, because they were getting to know each other. Embarrassing things and all. Still, she peeked between her fingers at him. "Don't laugh, but it means lion of God."

He angled back further in his seat, making her even more aware of his powerful chest and shoulders. "I told you Rob thinks you're a cross between Mother Teresa and Joan of Arc, so he got it sorta right."

"Never say so." She wiped Sherlock's mouth with his white drool bib before he rested his head against her arm. "I'm more of a mermaid than a saint."

"After meeting some of your family, I think you're saint quality." He pulled into the front parking lot for Charleston Estates and swung into an empty spot near the double door entrance. "Now—we're finally here. We should get some rest and huddle in the morning. You have my number, but I'm in Cottage 4. Let me help you inside with your luggage."

He was out of the car before she could answer, running around to her side and opening the door for her as the rain continued to fall. "From the way the lodge is lit up, I have a feeling the party is still going."

"We'll get you to your room so you can get some shuteye." He popped open the back passenger door so Sherlock could leap out. "You've been traveling after saving people's lives. Take a break. We'll start fresh in the morning. Together. Wanna have breakfast?"

Her pulse picked up. His face was slightly wet and shadowed despite the soft glow of the exterior lights, but she could see the interest in his eyes. She felt the same interest coursing through her. "I'd love that."

When they entered the resort's lobby, Dax toting her luggage, she gave a tired smile to the young man behind the desk. "Hi there. I'm Ariel Holmes."

The attendant returned her tired smile. "Welcome to Charleston Estates, Ms. Holmes. Mari said to give you a special welcome. We're looking forward to making your sister's wedding the special occasion y'all hope for."

If only you knew...

She and Dax shared a look before she pasted a polite smile on her face. "Thank you." After Dax talked to Rob tomorrow morning, she might be canceling everything by noon.

He typed into his computer, a frown emerging. "I'm having a little trouble finding your reservation. Would it be under a different name?"

Impending doom filled her stomach. "No. I talked to Mari specifically about my cottage because I wanted my bloodhound to be comfortable. He likes his space."

Dax put a comforting hand to her back as raucous laughter reached her ears from the lodge area tucked around the back. She knew that sound. Her sisters were still up. Probably on their second bottle of tequila.

"It seems your sister, Tiffany, moved into your cottage when it was ready." He glanced up, a frozen smile on his face. "I wasn't on duty yet, so I'm not sure—"

"That's all right." She could feel acid already boiling in her stomach. "I'll talk to her."

She took off for the lodge's entrance, holding Sherlock's leash. Part of her wished Jeffrey were here because he'd rage at the Three Tornadoes for her. She wasn't usually the type to rage. It wasn't her style. Besides, it never worked. "I'm so sorry, buddy. I know you're tired."

The dog gave her a mournful gaze, trotting alongside her.

Dax matched their strides. "Anything I can do here?"

"Find some garlic?" Her joke fell flat as she stopped in her tracks. "I'll figure it out. Go on to bed."

"No, not until you're settled. I've got your luggage."

"Really. I'm fine. You can leave it in the lobby and get to bed."

"*Elizabeth.* I'll see you to your door."

A strained laugh emerged from her throat. "If you insist. *Stephan.*"

"I do."

A part of her wanted to take his hand and sail off into the sunset, because that's what Elizabeth and Stephan would do.

Another round of naughty laughter interrupted her reverie, so she started toward the doorway. She'd chosen the resort for its homey luxury as much as its convenience—the whole place was available for rental for the wedding. Her sister was supposed to take her second plunge into marital bliss here, but now it was all in jeopardy.

They had one hundred and fifty guests coming to the wedding...

Suddenly she felt like she was under the rubble of an earthquake after her exit had caved in, and she didn't know the way out. When she reached the entrance, her gaze landed on her three sisters, clustered together on the buff-colored U-shaped sofas in their usual Lululemon yoga outfits. Two empty bottles of tequila—gold and silver—lay in the center alongside half-drunk cocktail glasses. The silver bottle was new. Everyone else seemed to have gone to bed, and Ariel wondered if Dax was relieved Rob wasn't there.

"Ariel!"

Tiffany's scream lit off two more piercing squeals from Terry and Tricia, who were on their feet immediately, rushing after their older sister. She braced herself as Tiffany plowed into her and wrapped her up in a tight hug, all sweetness amidst the smells of fading perfume and hair spray.

"Oh, thank God! We were *so* worried about you. Where have you been? It's after three in the morning. I texted you and Dax. Why didn't you text us back?" She gave Dax a flinty look even as Terry and Tricia grabbed Ariel and bussed her cheeks. That was normally how Deverell women greeted others. They didn't hug or kiss—they did both.

"What happened to your hair?" Terry cried out, blasting her with waves of tequila.

Tricia gave a bloodcurdling cry as she pressed her hands to her oval face. *"You cut it!"*

Tiffany stopped staring Dax down and swung her head to look at Ariel. "What did you do?"

Three unified sisterly cries pierced her ears and kicked off a soulful howl from Sherlock.

"How could you cut your hair before my wedding?" Tiffany raged, eyes bulging out like a possessed doll's. "You'll spoil my pictures."

Goodness. She'd anticipated the drama, but not after three in the morning. Certainly not after what Dax had told her. Didn't Tiffany realize how much trouble she'd caused?

"It was unavoidable. If I could have done anything else, I would have, so let's make the most of it, shall we?"

"Make the most of it!" From the look of it, Tiffany's

head was about to start spinning around. "But I want everything to be *perfect*. You knew that, Ariel."

"We'll have to get her extensions—or a wig." Terry's face screwed up in horror as she touched Ariel's short curls, making her want to swat at her sister.

"Yes!" Tricia agreed, eyeing her like a new decorating challenge. "A wig. Maybe something Marilyn Monroe-like."

Wig talk had calmed Tiffany, but her sister still had her nose scrunched up in a prime Bridezilla pose. God, this was too much.

"Really, Ariel," she said, shaking her head like Ariel was a naughty girl. "You know how important wedding photos are."

"No, she doesn't," Tricia said, proving she'd taken her daily bitch pill. "She's still single."

"If Ariel said it was unavoidable, I'm sure it was," Dax broke in, stepping protectively behind her, warming her now-numb heart. "She's had a long day. How about we find her cottage?"

Tiffany gave him another hard look, and Ariel wondered if it was because Dax hadn't flirted back or because she knew she was in trouble with her fiancé's best friend. "Dax is right. Sherlock and I are tired and want to go to bed. We can talk more in the morning. I heard you have my key."

"Sleep always helps your mood." Tiffany reached out and rubbed her arm. "About the room... I needed a little more space for the wedding and the gifts, so I moved you in with the boys."

"*What?*" She fell back a step in shock, rocking into Dax's warm, comforting body.

"We put all five of them in their own cottage because Marshall is thirteen and Ripp is twelve, but us girls got to thinking it would be nice to have an adult around. You didn't bring anybody, so we didn't think you needed the extra space, and the boys love to play with Sherlock. There's a nice pull-out couch in the living room for you and a homemade doggie bed on the floor for Sherlock."

This was a new low. "You got rid of Lisa assisting me with the wedding *and* you want me to babysit? Tiffany, I've been working a tornado site this past week, and you know how rowdy the boys are."

"You're always doing something like that." Her sister blew her platinum bangs off her forehead. "It's what you do. Besides, it's not babysitting. It's just minding your nephews, whom you don't spend enough time with. And they only get a little rowdy, being boys."

Five boys between the ages of eight and thirteen would only get a little rowdy? Was she kidding?

"It'll be fun." Tiffany jostled her with that beaming smile of hers, something even three in the morning didn't dim. "Think of all the memories you'll make. And—we don't need Lisa now that you're here."

The change from one shocking subject to the other wasn't unheard of with her sisters, but she was a little slow given the lateness of the hour. "I need her—"

"She wasn't doing things the way I wanted." Tiffany glanced at their other sisters, signaling them to join her side, as always. "Ariel, she was trouble. I would think you'd be thanking me."

"Thanking—"

"Plus, she and Rob get to save some money," Terry put in, smoothing back her strawberry blond hair from over her shoulders. "Do you know how much Lisa's services cost per hour?"

She felt Dax's hands come to rest on her shoulders and

savored the strength they imparted. Because she was about to blow her top. "Yes, I know how much Lisa costs. *I* found her. She's essential to things coming off."

"No, you are." Tiffany crossed her arms, and Terry and Tricia mirrored her stance. "Besides, you have Dax here to help you. Right, Dax?"

He was silent a moment. "Of course. I plan to help Ariel in any way I can."

"See." Tiffany jostled her and cut Dax a saccharine smile. "You have a big, strong man to help you. Better than Lisa."

Unbelievable.

"I really want my own space, Tiffany," she said.

Her sister's dismissive wave had her gritting her teeth. "Don't be like this. It's my wedding. Besides, you love your nephews."

Guilt. The oldest trick in the book. "That's not the point—"

"This way we get to spend some quality time with our honey pies, Ariel," Terry drawled as Tricia nodded. "Do you know how long it's been since we've been away from the boys? We need a break."

"So do I!" Ariel cried out.

"It's different with kids." Tiffany gave her a hard look. "Ariel, you must be tired. Why don't you head along to your cottage? You and the kids are in number 7. Let me get you the key card."

"Make sure to sneak in quiet," Tricia added, putting a finger to her lips. "Ryland is a light sleeper."

She couldn't make her feet move. She was sleeping on a pull-out bed in a three-bedroom cottage filled with five boys. Ones she was supposed to be *minding*. Of all the things she'd imagined coming out of the Three Tornadoes' infamous minds, she'd never imagined this nightmare.

Sherlock nudged her with his head, his sad eyes likely mirroring hers. She shook herself. There was nothing she could do about it tonight. She knew the resort's availability. Every cottage was accounted for by other guests until they fully occupied it starting Thursday. There was her grandmother's place on Folly Beach, but it was much too late for her to go there, not to mention she didn't have her own car.

After Dax talked to Rob, all of the arrangements might very well change anyway. She just had to get through tonight. It wasn't long until morning anyway. God knew, she and Sherlock had stayed in rougher accommodations.

"Ariel will stay with me for the moment so she can get a decent night's sleep." Dax's deep voice held the note of military command. "I have a two-bedroom cottage, and Carson won't be getting in from Norfolk until Thursday. Come on, Ariel. You and Sherlock are dead on your feet. Good night, ladies."

He turned her around with gentle hands and started to walk her toward the exit as her sisters cried out her name.

"Just keep walking," Dax muttered.

Sherlock was trotting quickly, clearly eager to be gone.

"Are you sure about this?" she whispered.

"You betcha." He let go of her arm when they cleared the lodge and glanced her way, making a face as the rain gently fell. "Five boys aged eight to thirteen? Between the farting and some other things boys do that I won't mention, I'd be having nightmares for you. Jesus, I'm still a little stunned at their tactics, and this is after my butt got grabbed."

"The sad thing is that I shouldn't be surprised, but I kinda am." She welcomed the humid air and gentle rain on her face as they left the main building and headed down the meandering walkway to the cottages illuminated by outdoor lighting. "They always make a big deal about me still being single. And not having kids."

"So I heard, and it's bullshit. You deserve as much respect as anyone else."

The Three Tornadoes thought she was a freak for not having gone down the aisle at least once yet. Wasn't she thirty-one? Why hadn't she gotten married yet? The implication: something was wrong with her.

"It's understandable why they'd want alone time with their partners, but it doesn't mean they get to take advantage of you," Dax finally commented as they arrived at his cottage.

He dug out his key card, and she took a moment to breathe in the sea air and listen to the crash of the waves along the property's edge and the rustle of the palm trees as the rain hit their towering leaves. She'd been so looking forward to this little piece of heaven. Most of the cottages sat within a stone's throw from the beach. All had screened-in porches with comfy chairs and couches and dining nooks. Thank goodness for Dax. She and Sherlock would have a quiet sanctuary after the long days she'd put in. It wasn't Grandma's house, but it held the same flavor, which was its own comfort.

Her dream of being given the deed to her grandma's house had fortified her for this trip. But that dream felt pretty far off now, and she was suddenly sad and dispirited. If the wedding got canceled, her sister would hold on to the deed for future leverage. Or, worse, sell the house. Yes, she could find another place to live here in Charleston, but that would break her heart. Especially since her grandma wanted her to have it.

"My family doesn't see it as taking advantage," she commented quietly as she glanced around the porch before entering through the front door he held open. "They think you do everything for family because it's *family*. That's it. Grandma always said life is composed of love and other trials with family in the mix." Of course Grandma had also added men to the list of trials. Ariel had always been extra wise on that score, having seen the fallout of her mother's and sisters' relationships.

Dax turned on a brass lamp beside the front door, illuminating the family room area that rolled into a kitchen and dining nook. A tall ceiling was decked out with a large white plantation-style fan and clerestory windows. Elegant colonial era furniture, seaside paintings, and antique knick-knacks made the space feel welcoming and luxurious, as did the hardwood floors and brick fireplace.

She unclipped Sherlock's leash. He immediately plopped himself down on the blue rug beside the fireplace and laid his head on his paws, clearly ready to sleep. "Poor fella. He's my rock when I come back to see my family."

"I'm glad you have him." Dax set her luggage aside and leaned against the couch. "I've always known I'm from a great family. We have fun with each other. We all love and respect each other. When I think of my family, the concept of trials doesn't even register."

God, that sounded like a dream. "I'm glad for you."

He crossed and laid a hand on her shoulder again, lightly stroking the tension in her muscles there. She wanted to lean in and bury her face against his chest. At five-two, she didn't come up to his shoulder. He was a solid refuge, the way the famous Morris Island Lighthouse on Folly Beach always looked in a storm.

"Thank you for stepping in." Their eyes met and held. "It helped. Knowing you had my back."

"It was my pleasure."

She searched his face. Fatigue was there, but so was heat. Her awareness of him grew, and the only sound was their breathing. God, she wanted him. He'd come and gotten her. He'd made her laugh. He'd been honest with her. Okay, sure, he wanted to stop the wedding, but that wasn't his fault. He'd even protected her. How many more boxes did she need to check?

"You should get some sleep." He caressed her shoulder, his thumb grazing the hard line of knotted muscle there. "You'll feel better."

His warm, compassionate look finally had her doing what she wanted. She closed the distance between them and laid her head against his strong chest. His arms came around her, and for a few minutes, all he did was hold her. There was comfort in the embrace, and there was sweetness in the way he ran his hands up and down her back.

"Come on, you're dead on your feet," he finally said, easing away and taking her hand.

After she said good night to Sherlock, he led her through the doorway to the small hallway and then to another door. She knew he was right. They were both beat, and this awareness between them would keep. He wheeled her luggage inside and gestured to the brass bed. "Good night, Ariel."

His mouth tipped to the side, and then he was gone, shutting the door behind him. She stared at it and felt as if her heart had risen up like a birthday balloon and lodged in her throat.

Everything with her family was rock-bottom bad. But Dax Cross was oddly the bright spot. Yes, he was exactly like the Morris Lighthouse. Not only beautiful to look at but a much-needed light in the middle of turmoil.

They were going to need each other to weather the storm they were facing, because her sister would not back down easily if anyone tried to stop her wedding.

A part of her wanted to dive into *I need to fix this* mode. Disaster recovery was her wiring. But how could she? Even worse to contemplate: should she? Dax was justified in how he felt, but he didn't understand the full scope of the situation. Then again, did Ariel? She and Tiffany lived in different towns and saw each other two to three times a year. Maybe her relationship with Rob wasn't as strong as it had seemed back in November. Certainly, Ariel wasn't ruthless enough to help her sister put a ball and chain around his ankle just so she could get her grandma's house. How could she justify going into fix-it mode without more information?

She fell back on the bed, knowing she was exhausted. But her thoughts just wouldn't settle. Her dream wouldn't die. Because her grandma's house!

Somewhere in hell a Deverell ancestor was laughing at her conundrum. The man who could ruin everything was the man she was attracted to. Really attracted to. Not just a passing fancy, as Grandma liked to say. Because if Rob decided to call off the wedding after talking to Dax, her time with the best man could be over. Even if it wasn't, by some miracle, how in the hell was she supposed to date the man who'd stopped her sister's wedding?

The trials were swirling like killer bees, and Ariel closed her eyes as her mind continued to spin images of the possible wreckage ahead.

FOUR

Today might as well be called *Ruin Your Best Friend's Life* Day.

Dax sat up in bed and grabbed his watch. Six a.m. His internal clock was as consistent as his flying stats, even after hitting the hay as late as he had. Would Rob be up and about too? Maybe they could take a run? Talk on the beach? Surely it would be best to have this out away from the property.

When he picked up the phone, his gut tightened. Rob had texted ten minutes ago.

> ROB
> Hey dipshit! You up? I need to talk to you.

His already tense stomach dropped to the floor. Had Tiffany struck first? He could see her spinning a tale to suit her interests. Her hard looks last night had portended bad things.

He rubbed his morning scruff, wishing for once he was back on an aircraft carrier where trouble like this didn't happen. But that wasn't his reality, so he texted Rob back.

> Up and ready for a run. Meet you in ten on the beach.

ROB

Dax hauled himself out of bed and did a hundred pushups before throwing on an old Navy T-shirt with a pair of gray shorts. After pulling on socks and running shoes, he headed to the bathroom. Normally he wouldn't check his hair for a run, but if Ariel was awake, he didn't want to greet her with bedhead. Or bad breath. After using a comb and a toothbrush, he opened his bedroom door and ducked into the hallway.

Her door was still closed, but as he tiptoed to the front, Sherlock rose and shook off his sleep and headed to the front. Dax wondered about letting the dog out, but he couldn't deny him.

He grabbed the leash from where she'd laid it on the entrance table, clipped it on, and opened the door. "You take care of things and then it's back inside. I don't know you guys well enough to take you with me."

Bloodhounds were good dogs, and Ariel had trained this one well, but they were like every other dog. Presented with the chance to be outside, they'd want to stay there. He waited for Sherlock, stretching. Sunrise was breaking out in reds and oranges, and God, what a sight. As a man used to being on carriers and in planes, he saw more sky than most, but this sunrise was a doozy. The ocean was still black and navy in spots, the undercurrent visible.

Sherlock trotted over to him and nudged him as if to say thank you. He rubbed him behind the ears. "You're a good boy. I'm promising myself right now that pretty darn soon I'll have my own dog. Let's get you inside."

Opening the door, he unclipped Sherlock's leash and stowed it before exiting and heading to the beach. Rob was a dark form only a few meters up, jogging toward him like he had since they'd first met at the Naval Academy as roommates in Bancroft Hall. They'd run together nearly every day afterward. Those rituals of brotherhood had seen him through his homesickness, and their friendship had only deepened.

While Rob had always pulled Dax away from the books when he was hitting them too hard, Dax had returned the favor by helping his buddy buckle down for schoolwork. They'd helped each other meet girls, too. Dax was the one who'd helped Rob make a move on Erin at a local Annapolis hangout, which had led to a two-year relationship. Until she'd cheated on him and broken his heart...

Now he was about to have it broken again. God help him.

"Did I just see you take Ariel's dog out?" Rob asked quietly when he halted in front of him, also sporting morning scruff.

A leading question if he'd ever heard one. He looked his friend in the eye, which was easy since they were the same height at six-two. Whether he'd be a few inches shorter after Rob tried to knock his block off would be another story. "You know dogs."

Rob jerked his dark head toward the ocean. "Come away from the house. We have some things to discuss."

His clipped tone would have made plebes pee their pants back at the Academy. As his friend, Dax usually didn't take it personally. But today it felt personal.

The tide was low, so he followed Rob out closer to the water's edge, crunching seashells in his wake as they started jogging. The seagulls cried out. He caught sight of two black shapes leaping in the distance and usually would have smiled at seeing porpoises. Not today.

He came abreast of his friend and wondered if he should stop so they could have it out. Best to keep moving, he decided. Rob had a fiery personality, and when he got going, he was like a bottle rocket. Better to let him erupt and burn out.

"I didn't want to believe Tiff, but when I saw the dog, I knew. What in the hell were you thinking, inviting Ariel to stay with you?" Rob shot out.

He was getting the riot act for being a good guy? Really? "She was exhausted and needed a bed. She'd wanted space for her and Sherlock, and dammit, she'd just finished working a tornado site. I had a free room. Seemed obvious to offer it."

"I know you like to be the good guy, but you shouldn't have butted in." Rob pumped his arms harder as he picked up his pace, which Dax matched. "Tiffany woke me up right after you left with her sister, upset as all get-out. She and her sisters had everything planned with Ariel staying with the boys, and you screwed that up."

"They didn't ask her—"

"Not. Your. Problem." Rob punched the air, his frustration visible in the smashed brows on his wide forehead. "Dammit, Terry woke her husband up and had him sleep in the boys' cottage. That's on me since you're my friend, and this when I'm trying to put my best foot forward with my new in-laws."

Shit. He hadn't thought about anyone else needing to mind the boys. The in-laws thing might not be an issue much longer. But one thing at a time. "I didn't know that would happen. Tiffany said they thought it would be okay with Marshall being thirteen and Ripp—"

"That's what I said, only to get my head blown off." Rob scowled fiercely. "Let's review. You're the best man. Your duties are to help Ariel in any way, not get in her pants—"

"Hey! I resent that." But they *were* attracted to each other, so he couldn't deny he'd like to go to bed with her. Only it wouldn't be crude like Rob was suggesting.

"Dammit, Dax, I know you're the first guy in a crowd to be the gentleman, but keep out of things between Ariel and her sisters. They have a complicated relationship. You're the sailor in the port, passing through. Remember that."

"Aye, aye." He shot his friend a jaunty salute, to which Rob only grunted in response. "Now, are you done?"

"Yeah. Jesus, I'm revved. I hate it when Tiffany is mad at me. It feels worse than having a missile locked on you."

Another spasm raced through Dax's stomach. That bad? They hadn't even talked about his stuff yet. "Can we stop a minute? I need to talk to you."

Rob halted beside him and put his hands on his hips. "Fuck. You didn't sleep with Ariel, did you?"

"No." He scratched an itch in his brow, likely from the headache starting. "What I want to say isn't about Ariel. It's about Tiffany, and I need you to listen to me. All the way through."

Rob rubbed the back of his neck. "You're already taking sides between Ariel and her sisters? I knew you'd react like this when I heard you'd come in as Knight Valiant and swept her off to your cottage. Dammit, Dax, I can't have this. I like and respect Ariel—you know how much—but I *love* Tiffany. I'm marrying her, and you're my best friend, so you need to—"

"She came on to me last night." He couldn't let Rob go on any longer. "When you were in the head."

Rob's entire face tightened, the bones of his face visible in a scary way now. "What the fuck did you just say?"

He set his weight in the sand and fell back into reporting mode like he would with a superior officer. "When you left for the head last night—right before I went to the airport—Tiffany told me she found me handsome. She ran her fingers up my chest before patting me on the butt. I did not at any point invite this or respond favorably."

"What the fuck, Dax?" Rob shoved him back hard. "This is bullshit! Tiffany loves me. We're getting married Saturday."

"I know." He didn't flinch from Rob's dark glare. "As your best friend, I had to tell you. Especially after Erin!"

"Forget Erin!" Another shove drove Dax back a couple steps. "We're not talking about this. Any of it!"

"Jesus, you know it's the last thing on earth I want to do. But our bond is stronger than blood. Dammit, Rob, how long have we known each other?"

Rob held up a hand like he was stiff-arming him in football. "You misunderstood. Tiffany is crazy about me. Heck, she's even—"

Dax waited while Rob pressed his fingers to the bridge of his nose, his mouth grim. "What?"

"Nothing." Rob's mouth worked before he shook his head slowly. "Look, you misunderstood. Jesus, this has got to be related to all that wedding curse stuff Tiffany keeps harping about."

"What?"

"Forget it. Ask Ariel. Wait, weren't we talking about Ariel when Tiffany came over?"

"We were." Rob was obviously grasping at straws to explain away his fiancée's behavior—because a wedding curse? "Ariel thought she might have been jealous—"

"You told Ariel?" Rob stalked off, the tide coming in and touching his shoes. "Fuck, man, what's gotten into you?"

Dax followed him. "I was upset. She sensed it. I told her because I didn't want her to think badly of me. I also needed her to know what I had planned."

"And what was that?" Rob lashed out, extending his hands wide open. "What, Dax?"

He didn't flinch, although his insides felt like he was pulling 9 Gs. "I said I was going to tell you and try and stop the wedding."

"Fuck!" Rob kicked at the sand. "This wedding isn't going to be anything but brilliant. Like my bride-to-be wants. That's your mission, Captain. Do you hear me?"

He looked at his friend. "Rob. Didn't you listen to a single thing I said?"

"You got it wrong." He sliced his hand through the air. "All the way. Tiffany and I love each other. We're getting married Saturday. I don't want to hear another word about this."

"*Rob.*"

"No!" His dark eyes sparked. "I know you and your damn code and what you think you know about me, but I don't want to hear another word. Or we're done."

He went numb, like he'd been in the ocean too long after ejecting from his aircraft. This was the first time Rob had put someone else over their friendship. "Fine."

Rob came over and gripped his shoulder. "You're my best friend. I'd die for you. God knows I've bled for you. But this is my wife we're talking about. My life. My family."

Suddenly he couldn't swallow.

"You misunderstood last night." Rob's face was turning red. "We're never going to speak of this again. I want your word."

He nodded crisply. What the hell else could he do? "You have it."

"Good." He gripped him again before slapping him on the back like old times. "Okay... Let's finish our run and then get some chow."

He watched Rob take off, his stride angry and almost erratic. Dax started after him, hugging the water. He was quickly out of breath, probably because he wasn't breathing. Hearing Rob tell him he'd end their friendship—one they'd had for almost eighteen years—had shaken him.

They ran in silence the rest of the way, and Dax used the time to work out his remaining angst and let it go. Rob had decided what he wanted. It was his life. Dax had done what he'd thought best.

No point in holding on to the past or nursing a grudge.

Still, he was going to be careful not to be alone with Tiffany ever again. His friendship with Rob meant too much to him, and now he knew who his friend would choose when push came to shove.

Their friendship had radically changed though, and that was a genie he couldn't put back in the bottle.

Rob begged off from eating breakfast when they returned to the cottages, saying he'd grab something with Tiffany. That was fine with Dax. After another healthy slap on the back, his best friend was gone, leaving him alone in the quiet morning. He headed back to the cottage, armed to return to his original mission. Be the best man. Help Ariel out. Make this the wedding his friend wanted—even if he privately thought it was a disaster.

When he let himself inside, Sherlock met him at the door, his sad expressive eyes seeming to stare right through him. He was rubbing him under the ears, taking some comfort in the dog's presence, when Ariel appeared in the doorway. She was wearing a jean skirt and an off-the-shoulder cream shirt tucked to the side with flip-flops. Her hair was wet from the shower, and her natural beauty was more luminous after a night of sleep.

All he wanted to do was cross to her and fold her into his arms.

Instead, he tried to give her a convincing smile. "I talked to Rob. He thinks I misunderstood. The wedding is still on."

She seemed to deflate like the washed-up jellyfish he'd run by before she drew herself back up, relief written all over her face. "You okay?"

"Peachy." He rubbed the scruff on his face. "I need to shower and shave, but then I'm yours. One thing before we get started. I'm almost afraid to ask, but Rob mentioned some wedding curse."

Her grimace made him feel even peachier. "Yeah. About that. Let me walk you through the basics."

By the time she finished reciting a long list of wedding disasters that seemed statistically significant in a way he couldn't make sense of, he was frowning. "Now I *really* understand the garlic comment. I have to admit that list of disasters blows my mind. If it were me, I'd call it bad luck, but I'm a tangible reality kind of guy, so this curse thing stretches my comfort zone."

She nodded. "Understandable. You did ask."

He was already regretting it. "I did. How about we stick to the plan and hope for the best, then?"

"That sounds good to me." She tucked her hair behind her ear as she ducked her head. "You must think we're all crazy."

"Not you. So… What's on our agenda this morning?"

Her pointer finger traced something in the air before she said, "Koi."

"Huh?"

"You heard me." She covered her hands over her eyes playfully before letting them fall to her sides. "Tiffany wants a koi pond at the wedding. She read in some bridal magazine that they symbolize passionate love and a lasting marriage, the latter of which isn't something the Deverell women are known for. Apparently, you can rent the fish and the tank."

He wasn't going to snort. He was going to be a good person. Forget he and Rob had ever talked. *"Okay..."*

"It's a terrible idea, I know, but at least I talked her out of putting goldfish in jars on the wedding tables. PETA and animal lovers—myself included—aren't in favor of using animals for entertainment purposes. I tried to convince her to have a cocktail party at the aquarium, but she wouldn't spring for it. This was the best I could negotiate."

"I'll shower and get changed." He passed her in the hall. "Maybe we have something we need to pick up before we land the fish."

"What's that?"

"Garlic," he called teasingly over his shoulder.

Her hearty laughter rang through the house.

FIVE

Garlic.

Maybe they really should stop and buy some when Dax got out of the shower.

The shower...

Oh, good heavens, the images in her naughty mind. Dax all wet and naked with steam rising around him, muscles rippling as he washed. In her relieved *the wedding was still on* euphoria—okay, she was a little conflicted for Dax—she could all too easily see his hot body and smell the clove-scented resort shower soap as he slicked his skin with it.

But she was getting a little hot herself as she waited for him in the living area, so she picked up her phone and smiled.

Jeffrey had texted. Yeah. She needed to update him. Or maybe not the part about Tiffany. He might rib Tiffany about it, causing unneeded explosions.

BEST BROTHER EVER

> Hey! I heard you'd shacked up with Captain Hotpants already. 🍆 Oooh! Way to trust my feeling about you two. Girl, I am so proud of you. Forget the Three Tornadoes bitching about you not babysitting their babies. Yes, I heard. 😏 Take that tall hunk in hand. 🥒

She snorted, all too easily imagining taking Dax's eggplant in hand. He'd be big and gorgeous and hot.

> We're bonding. It's crazy. 😸 Maybe it's the fact that we both have high-risk professions. Also—he's normal. 🤍

BEST BROTHER EVER

> I knew it! 🏆 He looks like the all-American boy. 🏈 Perfect for you. Have you smooched? 💋

> Not yet. Close. Last night it would have been like kissing a narcoleptic or someone sleepwalking. 💀

BEST BROTHER EVER

> You're not tired now, right? 😏 Girl, you'd better jump that man, or I will tie him to your bed for you. 🛏️😬

> You're the best. 🥰 Best to have him the first time without zip ties...

BEST BROTHER EVER

> Depends on what you're going for. 😉 You know where Home Depot is... 🔧 Talk later. Antonio is finally stirring. 🏃

Ariel was so glad Jeffrey was happy. He'd had a few long-term relationships, but none had worked out so far. But that hadn't stopped him from believing in love, and that was where they differed.

She wasn't sure there was happily ever after for people like her. Although she'd never been married, she had one failed engagement in her past, which seemed to prove that she was a Deverell woman after all. Part of a family tree that looked more like a bush, honestly, because no one in her family had lasted. On either side.

But her brother was determined to find his prince, and if Antonio was his forever plus-one, she'd be cheering them both on with all her might.

She checked on a few more wedding items before heading to the front door to see if her golf cart rental had arrived since Dax still hadn't appeared. Opening the door with Sherlock, she stopped short as her mother halted halfway up the steps. "Mother!"

"*Ariel!*" She sprang up the final stairs in a green linen sundress with youthful pep for a sixty-two-year-old, something fostered by her regular yoga classes and daily wellness juices. "I'm sorry I missed you last night, but I was beat from traveling. If I'd been up, I would have run to the airport for you."

Could she believe that? Historical evidence suggested otherwise. "That's sweet, but I got a ride."

They bussed cheeks, because no one messed up a woman's carefully applied makeup.

"I also would have offered to let you stay in my cottage until your aunt Gail arrived."

Like hell she would. Another intense *mother* look had Ariel wanting to shift on her feet because she *knew* that tone. "It was late, and Dax offered since he had a spare room."

"So I heard."

Doom and gloom organ music started to play in her head. Sherlock plopped down at her feet, knowing they weren't going anywhere.

She felt her mother's slender hand finger the ends of her short hair, her diamonds flashing in the sunlight from the ring she'd kept from Ariel's father. Because a woman could never have too many diamonds… "Your sisters said you'd cut your hair last minute. Between staying with the best man and this change, that's pretty wild for you."

Ariel wished she could laugh that one off, but she knew what was coming…

Their eyes met, her mother's familiar floral perfume wafting over her. The familiar feeling of never measuring up started to rise within her. She never felt good enough when her mother looked at her that way. Like she was assessing all the reasons Ariel didn't pass muster.

Because no one could say Stormy Deverell didn't pass muster. She had exotic green eyes, a full mouth, and cheekbones a swimmer could dive off. She still turned heads, so far without plastic surgery, she liked to joke, and every time Ariel looked at her, she wondered how this woman could be her mother.

They were as alike as South Carolina peanuts and California cabernet—and she was the peanut.

"Mom, I didn't have a choice about the hair." She was going to have to give some excuse or their complaining would never cease. "Something happened on the disaster site."

"Don't tell me any more." Her mother fingered her hair one last time before touching Ariel's waist, measuring it like usual. "You know I don't like to hear about the danger you put yourself in. But at least it keeps your weight in check."

The choking feeling was starting in her throat.

"Your risk-taking must be some Deverell trait that Grandma never knew about." She worried her perfectly painted mouth in an evening nude pink. "Pirates possibly. Charleston was infested with them at one time. You certainly didn't get it from your father's side. But we'll make do. You'll wear a wig. I asked around for recommendations and one name stood out. I already called for you. The wigmaker is expecting you today at two."

She held out a piece of paper with the name handwritten on it in bold print. Ariel suddenly wished lightning would strike her. "Mother, I'm not wearing a wig."

"Ariel—" The clipped tone would make a puppy tremble and pee himself. "Wedding photos are the most important photos a woman ever takes alongside baby photos. They line the walls of your home. They go in your wallet. They grace your first Christmas card. They impress your friends and family. How could you not want to make your sister's wedding photos special? This is her second chance at love. With a good man. A naval pilot! Didn't you ever see *An Officer and a Gentleman*? Well, I did, and if you think of Rob as Richard Gere, you'd understand why I've been behind this relationship since Tiffany first told me about him. As for you, you *will* wear the wig. In fact, you should be thanking me for finding an easier, faster solution. Extensions would take hours."

Hours! "But my hair is fine at it is—"

"No, it's too short. It makes your hair appear even thinner than it already is. Besides, it accentuates the narrow thrust of your chin in an unpleasant way. We need to soften the angles to make you look pretty."

Okay, that one hurt. Ariel knew she wasn't as much of a beauty as her mother and sisters, but she thought she looked pretty good usually. Like a pixie. Or a fairy. Not that her mother or sisters ever thought that. They were always trying to make her prettier. Fake eyelashes at Christmas. Brow tinting for her birthday. Even a bottle of castor oil to make her thin brows fuller.

Stuff she threw away with knots in her stomach.

"All the girls in our family need to have long hair in the photos to work with the family appearance and the bridesmaids' dresses. Your neck is too long without hair covering it up."

She clutched her neck as the urge to defend herself rose up. "No, I'm—"

"Stop this, honey." Her tone was as hard as her eyes, but then she laid a tender hand on her forearm as if she could soften the blow. "I know what's best for you. You're being selfish."

Selfish.

She clenched her hands into fists at her sides. Selfish was the word the women in her family threw around when they wanted to get their way. Make you feel so bad you caved. *They* were never selfish, of course. She could feel herself getting riled up as she tried to figure out what to do. Arguing would only lead to more bullying and shaming, and she would lose. Her mother prided herself on winning every argument.

If she agreed, she would be expected to wear the damn wig. Which she was completely opposed to. First, she didn't want to. Plus, a fake hairpiece would itch and make her look like an idiot.

What to do? Maybe it could disappear. Too bad she loved Sherlock too much to lie about him. She could have told the tall tale that he'd thought it was an animal and dragged it off and buried it. Except wait! Uncle Johnny was bringing his beagle. She hated to do it, but she could blame him. God, she was a terrible person, but desperate times...

She took the paper from her mother's hand, telling herself she had a plan. "Dax and I are heading out to start our errands. We need to get going."

Her mother's slender brows rose, and the hard look in her eyes told Ariel she didn't like that response. Well, too bad. "I see. I'd planned to invite you to breakfast with me and Trey."

God, she'd rather poke her eye out with a fork. Trey was a douchey real estate agent from Palm Beach who excelled in mansplaining and drinking piña coladas. But he liked to party, like her mother, and they'd been together for eighteen months.

One thing was certain: Ariel wouldn't be planning *that* wedding.

"Thanks for thinking of me." She did her best to smile. "But I need to hit the ground running to make sure Tiffany's wedding is all she hopes for."

"And to get your grandma's house," Mother had to add. "You and Captain Cross appear to have gotten rather close rather quickly. As for staying here in his cottage, it looks bad, Ariel. Shacking up with the best man. Also—you've upset your sisters. You were supposed to mind your nephews. Terry had to wake poor Morris out of a dead sleep to take your place last night."

"They didn't run it by me, Mother." Sherlock gave another whine. "I'd been looking forward to having a quiet place with room for Sherlock, especially after staying in temporary housing this past week."

"But why wouldn't you want to spend time with your nephews, Ariel?" Mother's usually smooth forehead was wrinkled. "This is family time. You can be alone when you go home. Don't you ever get tired of being on your own?"

She bit the inside of her cheek. *Don't argue. It will only make things worse.* But she was fed up with this kind of treatment. She was thirty-one years old. She was paying for her own cottage. It wasn't right.

"Mornin', Stormy," Dax drawled with a flash of a smile as he stepped out onto the porch and joined them, hair wet from his shower.

He shot Ariel a quick smile, and she managed a weak one as he stepped close. Yes, focus on him and not her mother's glare.

Turning to him, she punched up her smile. Freshly shaved and smelling delicious of pine and spice, he looked absolutely like Captain Hotpants. He wore a white T-shirt that fit his muscled chest to sheer perfection, along with tan cargo shorts and flip-flops. God, even his feet were perfect.

Ariel caught her mother's appraising glance and watched as she smoothed her cool white blond hair over her shoulder, a glimmer of a femme fatale smile appearing on her now-relaxed mouth. Because Deverell women always wanted to turn men's heads with their charm.

"*Dax,*" she drew out with equal sweetness, looking pointedly between the two of them. "Pleasure seeing you again."

"Thanks for letting Ariel bunk with me." He might be channeling sunbeams given the wattage of his smile. "Turns out it's the best thing ever. We're plowing through wedding stuff and getting on the same page, so Tiffany's day is going to be the best Charleston has seen. I know how important it is to Rob for his bride-to-be to be happy. Well, isn't that lyrical of me?"

He laughed. Neither Ariel nor her mother joined in, the tension as thick as August humidity.

"We've got to go see about some koi and a bunch of other things, but I promise to have Ariel back later so you ladies can catch up more." He extended his arm to her. "Shall we?"

Ariel wondered if her mother was going to let Dax get away with such a ploy. But her mother only smiled that siren smile of hers. "Can't keep a naval officer from his duties, can I? Y'all have fun now."

She gave Ariel a hard look before sending a flirtatious wave that made Ariel queasy. Then she hurried down the steps and was gone.

Dax let his hand drop to his side. "I did my best, but she's a tough customer."

"The poor grass would probably fry under her glare," she told Dax. "But thanks. Let's go before we get derailed by anyone else."

He pointed to the beach. "I found a way to access the parking lot from the beach so we won't have to walk around the lodge. It's a little longer but—"

She grabbed his hand and started off, Sherlock trotting beside her. "Brilliant! I'm not above taking an alternate route if it helps me avoid everyone. My mother made me a wig appointment. For two o'clock."

He was biting the inside of his cheek when she glanced over. "What are you going to do?"

Seeing the beach, all she wanted to do was dive into the water and spend the rest of the day swimming with him. "Would you think I'm a terrible person if I get the wig and then blame our uncle's beagle for snatching it and burying it on the wedding day?"

His chortle scattered a trio of seagulls pecking at

washed-up shells. "Not a bit. That's genius actually. I'll be an eyewitness. How about this?"

He struck a considering expression, shaking his head thoughtfully as they continued to walk. "That beagle had Ariel's wig in its mouth in two shakes of a lamb's tail and was off. I chased it, heaven knows, but the damn dog up and vanished on me like a ghost in New Orleans. Poor Ariel. She's just going to have to make do with the hair God gave her."

She burst out laughing. "That's perfect!"

He held out his fist for a fist bump. "We're a team. I've got your back. As for your wig appointment, we'll get you plenty ready with some margaritas beforehand."

She gestured to her purse. "I was thinking it would be a flask moment, but margaritas work. Chips and salsa too."

"Done," he said as they reached the parking lot. "Elizabeth, I think this is the start of a beautiful friendship."

Her heart fluttered, and who could blame her? The morning sun made his sandy hair nearly golden, and he'd just managed to save her from a trial. "Stephan, I couldn't agree more. Now, let's find my golf cart."

"Your what?"

She took off toward the front of the lot and spotted it parked near the door to the Charleston Estates' lobby. "There it is!"

Her feet picked up their pace as Sherlock took off toward it, his tail going to its excited saber-like position. The glittery pink golf cart had her grinning. When she'd looked for a rental and seen this one, she'd thought it would be fun. A roomy two-seater so she wouldn't be carting wedding guests around, and a rear cargo box that allowed for her to haul wedding items. "Trust me. Charleston is a nightmare to park in. Smart people—like me—use a golf cart.

Grandma drove one for some fifty years. Didn't ever use a car much."

Sherlock climbed in, his tail tapping the floor. Dax scrubbed a hand over his jaw. She wasn't sure yet which she liked better on that rock-hard jaw. Morning scruff or clean shaven. God, she couldn't wait to touch it.

"Did you choose the pink? Or is someone having a little fun with you?"

She punched him lightly in the shoulder and climbed in the driver's seat. "I chose it. I confess I thought my nephews would be less inclined to beg me for rides if it was pink and sparkly."

He folded his tall frame into it and patted Sherlock on the head since he was sitting right behind them. "Your strategic mind continues to awe me. Good thing I'm comfortable in my masculinity and am okay with being pressed up against your dog."

She glanced over and fought a hum of feminine appreciation as she entered the code the rental company had texted to start the cart. His powerful frame made her feel tiny in comparison, in that delicious way a large man made a woman feel. "Hang on to your butt, Captain Hotpants. We're about to take off."

His snort accompanied more laughter, but he secured his grip on the grab handle. "I should warn you. I'm not a great copilot. But I am used to a tight fit."

Oh, how naughty of him... She patted his heavily muscled thigh with a flirtatious wink. "Don't worry, I'll be gentle with you."

Except she couldn't help reversing the golf cart with a little extra oomph as she pulled out, making him grunt and grip the bar overhead. Sherlock was panting excitedly, tail wagging. He'd always loved driving in her grandma's golf cart when they'd visited. Grandma's eyesight had gotten bad, so she'd only driven to the small grocery store on Folly Beach for groceries.

"My first driving lesson was in a golf cart," she told Dax as she headed downtown.

"That explains your driving." He was quiet for a while as she navigated the golf cart before sending her a playful smile as they hit King Street. "People are staring at us."

They were in the hub, where tourists, college students, and local shoppers lined the streets. "They're probably staring at you, Captain Hotpants."

He gave a playful wave to a trio of college girls after one boldly waved at him. "You didn't see that guy in the camo shirt and shorts combo tip his invisible hat to you? Ariel, I swear he was ready to go out hunting and lay a freshly killed deer at your feet."

"That's disgusting," she told him as she navigated the traffic toward Spring Street. "I love me some deer jerky, I won't lie, but I don't want a fresh carcass on my flip-flops."

Sherlock gave a bark as if agreeing.

"Wait!" Dax pointed toward the right. "I know why the camo guy was here. He was visiting the taxidermy place. Did you see it? It had a deer ringed by pink strobe lights in the store window."

"It did not!" She chuckled.

"Did too! You'll see it when we come back. Austin is clearly behind the taxidermy times. And I think the store window was displaying leather handbags. You can get your animal stuffed or make it into a fashion accessory."

"That's so Charleston," she told him as she let her gaze run along the charming shops that lined the street. "Grandma and those of her generation made a little go a long way, and the prettier the better. She swore Charleston was the first city to scent pine cones with cinnamon, which later became a big decorating trend."

"I'm clearly behind the times since I've never been around cinnamon-scented pine cones."

"You poor baby." She gave in to the urge to pat his knee again. "Grandma laughed when some ladies called it Southern potpourri and sold it for nearly twenty dollars in these shops. Said that was the Holy City for you. Making money for one's family using all the wiles God gave you. I don't know that I'd go that far, but that was her thinking. God, I miss her."

This time he laid his hand on her knee, and she almost fumbled with the accelerator pedal at the electricity that shot up her leg to a rather sensitive area. "When did she pass?"

"Six months ago." She wiped her nose as tears filled her eyes. "Before Thanksgiving—a few weeks after Tiffany announced her engagement. Her heart gave out as she was walking back to her house from her daily stretch of her legs on the beach."

"I was close with my grandpa Cross. He used to take me fishing every Saturday morning growing up. When I lost him two years ago, I felt like someone had dug a fishing hook in my heart. One I'd never pull out."

She continued navigating them to Johns Island with emotion balled in her throat. "That's exactly how it feels." She laid her hand on top of his hand on her knee, and it felt like a new bond was forming between them from comforting each other.

She was used to intense moments of connection with people in her job. Trauma and loss opened people up, but with Dax it was more than that. There was attraction and good humor and a certain intimacy—like she could tell him anything. It felt inevitable that they'd end up in bed together, and she was trusting herself on knowing when the time was right.

He took her hand in his, stroking the back before he teasingly set it back on the wheel with a pat. "I haven't told anyone this—not even Rob since he'd drag me out on a boat and say it was for my own good—but I can't bring myself to go fishing without my grandfather. Grabs me by the throat just thinking about it. I was wondering about trying to do it here if there was time since I've got my buddies coming. I need to push past it. Gramps wouldn't want me to give up fishing because of grief over him. He'd likely shove me off the boat for being so silly."

"It's not silly." She pulled into the dirt parking lot for the tropical fish farm, whose logo had dancing starfish, and parked. "Grief is normal."

"It's different for guys," he bantered back. "I know I'm being ridiculous."

"You said you think I'm pretty tough, right? Well, I still dread going to my grandma's house in Folly. I'm worried about that moment when I get to the first step of the porch. She'd usually call out my name from an open window, and the way she'd say it—like I was precious to her—always made me feel like I was walking on the clouds. That won't happen ever again. I want to live there because I'm hoping it'll help me find peace by settling in a place we both found happy. She wanted that."

She was hoping to take the deed her sister had promised to give her after the wedding and start the process of putting it in her name. Because she was going to lock that up legally. Her family could not be counted on to keep promises.

He unfurled from the golf cart and was around to her

side a moment later, extending his hand. "Since we're in the same boat, so to speak, perhaps we can help each other."

Just like that, their new bond went deeper, and she felt her heart pulse harder in her chest as she laid her hand in his. "I'd love that."

The morning sun glinted on his hair, turning it gold. His gaze was thoughtful and filled with heat. They could kiss right now, she knew, but then Sherlock jumped out of the golf cart as the screen door to the store creaked open.

"Nice dog. Y'all here about the wedding?"

She reluctantly looked away and felt the loss of Dax's hand as he released her. Turning, she pasted a polite smile on her face and nearly did a double take. The man who'd asked looked like an old pirate, a common enough occurrence in Charleston, but he sported an old smoking pipe in addition to long, straggly gray hair and a T-shirt with dancing starfish. The starfish on his belly looked like they were stretching, as if for fish yoga. "Yes, I'm Ariel."

"Like the mermaid." He chortled before puffing on his pipe. "Hard to forget that name. I'm Scooter. And the fella? He the groom?"

"No, he's the best man and a Navy pilot to boot."

Dax shot her a look, but she had good instincts about people. She'd peg this guy as a veteran.

"Captain Dax Cross. Pleasure to meet you."

"I was in the Marines way back in the day." Another puff of his pipe reached Ariel's nose, the spicy tobacco reminding her of an old library. "You sea biscuits still have it easy?"

"Yes, sir," Dax drawled. "You know, my grandpa had a joke for his old Marine buddies when they gave him shit for being in the Navy."

So Dax and his grandfather had more in common than fishing. He'd followed in family footsteps.

"Do you know why the Navy carries Marines around the world on its ships?" he asked before answering with a cheeky grin, "sheep are too obvious."

Scooter grinned, showing a gold tooth. "That one is older than dirt, sonny. What about this one—how do you separate the men from the boys in the Navy?"

Dax laughed heartily, a sound as tantalizing as a slice of warm pecan pie. "My grandpa loved that one. With a crowbar."

"I've got me one around back." Scooter jerked his head to the right. "With the koi you want to see. Come along and see my babies."

She was so happy she wanted to lock arms with Dax and mosey on back. God, call her crazy but she loved men like these two. They gave each other shit, but she knew they were also the type to get shit done. No muss, no fuss. Her motto. She was hoping it would carry her through the wedding.

Sherlock was already sniffing at the brush under the palm trees as they followed Scooter. A sea of troughs waited behind the front building, each containing a special kind of fish. The tanks were labeled with black sharpie, and she read signs for angelfish, swordtails, tetras, American cichlids, and goldfish before arriving at the koi. Large orange and white fish swam in the clear water.

Scooter tapped the tank. "These here are mighty popular, even though they're pricey. I had a bride about five years back come out and ask if she could rent them. Saw something about them on one of those fancy wedding shows ladies love to watch. Said she knew a whole bunch of brides here in Charleston who'd go wild for them at their special day. Got me to thinking, and when that happens, my missus says to look out."

Both she and Dax chuckled. What did his missus look like? Ariel wondered if she had a pipe to smoke too.

"Sure enough, she was right. After I started renting them out, I could finally afford the boat I'd been saving up for. Can you believe it? But what men fork out for rings today really blows my mind. Back when I proposed, you were lucky to be able to afford a simple gold band. Now a rock the size of Texas is expected, and more often than not, the marriage barely lasts as long as the payment plan. Crazy, if you ask me, but I'm not complaining. How many do y'all want?"

What a character. But that was Charleston. She told him her budget. "I'll need the special wedding tank I saw online as well. With the installation, of course."

"It won't fit in that Barbie golf cart of yours." His gold tooth winked as Dax smothered a laugh. "I don't include it because I've had some people rent kiddie swimming pools instead. Depends on the bride. The plexiglass one I have is perfect for a wedding with lots of people running around. Weddings can get wild."

She thought of her family. Wild didn't cover it. "Do you have insurance?"

"You betcha. I'll write up your invoice inside if you want to look around. You might enjoy checking out my African cichlids on the back left. They're freshwater and colorful. I specialize in the blue ones. You being a mermaid, they're your kin."

With another flash of his gold tooth, he strolled out, pipe smoke flowing behind him.

Dax was mashing his mouth together, fighting a smile. "You're bringing me to all the hot spots, aren't you?"

"You know it." She started walking toward the back. "I'm curious about the blue fish."

"No shock. Kin like a visit when you're in town."

"Har-de-har-har." She stepped over a red plastic duckie protruding from the ground and pointed it out to Dax. "The fish must have happy hour back here. A few of the bars out this way put ducks like that in their drinks."

"My kind of place." When they reached the sign that said African cichlids, Dax set his hands on his trim hips. "Makes me think of *A Fish Called Wanda*."

"Classic film." She spied the bluish bodies with the bluish purple tails along with the ones with the yellow heads and tails with a main color of bright blue. "One of those movies guaranteed to make you laugh even on a bad day."

"They probably couldn't make it now, what with Kevin Kline's character eating pet fish to squeeze the confession out of the bad guy, but God, it's hilarious stuff." He peered into the tank, leaning over, making her aware of the muscles in his back when his shirt stretched with him.

Yum.

"My favorite is when Jamie Lee Curtis' character informs Kevin Kline's that the London Underground is not a resistance movement."

"We should watch it tonight," he suggested, standing up and sending her an inviting glance with a raised brow. "We can put your new wig on the TV to class up the joint. God, I still can't believe they're insisting you do something with your hair. It looks beautiful to me, if you don't mind me saying."

She had the girlish compulsion to lift her hand to the ends. "If I were in college, I'd suggest we play wig pong instead of beer pong, but I don't drink like that anymore."

"I love that idea! We could change what we play for."

Kisses came to mind. *Hang on, Ariel. Take it easy. Let things take their natural course.* That they were going to kiss wasn't in question for her. The only question was when. Would hanging around a fish tank be a good place for a first kiss? She wondered if the fish would jump out of the tank.

"Chocolate would work," she said slowly. The mere thought of dark chocolate melting in her mouth along with Dax's kisses was enough to heat her cheeks.

"I'm good with that."

His gaze slid to her mouth, making her flush harder. When heat lit his gorgeous green eyes, she decided to call it out there. They were both staying through Sunday because Tiffany had wanted a post-wedding brunch. Today was Monday.

"Would you—"

"Are you—" he asked at the same time.

She almost gave a girlish giggle. "You first."

He leaned closer, so close she could feel his body heat. "I was going to say... Are you thinking what I'm thinking?" His voice was a touch deeper and a little gravelly in a way that made her belly tighten.

She liked that he was giving her the power to answer. They both had a job to do—neither of them wanted to screw it up. "That we might play for kisses?"

He moved a little closer, blocking the sun out with his height. Those heated eyes told her all she wanted to know and then some. He wanted her as much as she wanted him. "Might be the best game of my life. When is that wig appointment again?"

Her mouth went dry. "Two o'clock."

"Too long." He heaved out a sigh and stepped back. "I'll

be counting down the hours until we have that wig. You ready to head back?"

She put her hand on his chest hesitantly, desire pouring into her when his muscles leaped under her touch. God, he was built, and heaven help her, she loved strong men. "I think you're right. Two o'clock sounds like next month right now."

His luscious mouth tipped to the side in the sexiest smile on earth. He could have anything he wanted from her with that look. "We can't have that, can we?"

He moved closer, pressing his hand lightly on her waist. She lifted onto her tiptoes—because he was so much taller— and loved watching his head descend, his gaze never leaving hers.

Sherlock gave a staccato of warning barks out of nowhere. She came back down on her heels immediately. "Something's wrong."

Dax went on alert. They both looked around.

And then she heard the slither...

She froze. That sound was one she knew from childhood. Putting a hand on Dax's arm, she felt the tension in his muscles. "Gator."

"Shit," was all he whispered before taking a protective step ahead of her. "Stay behind me."

"We don't know where it is." She craned her head until she spotted it near the rusted-out car by the edge of the marsh—a solid distance from where Sherlock was poised at the edge of the backyard, tail pointed in the air, but not moving. He knew better than to mess with wildlife, but he would defend her if it came to it. He was that kind of dog.

"Eleven o'clock."

"I see it."

Her insides cringed at the sight. Seven feet to her mind.

Beady eyes. Big, scary body. "Head back to the house. No sudden moves."

"You mean I can't invite it for a beer?" His voice was calm, but then again, he flew military jets for a living. "I want you to go ahead of me. If it takes off for us, run to the house for Scooter and get Sherlock out of here."

Like she'd leave him, but she appreciated the knight in shining armor act. "Let's go. Slowly."

She kept her gaze on the gator, not fighting with Dax about the way he was keeping himself between her and the reptile. When it didn't follow them, she breathed a sigh of relief. When they neared the house, Scooter slammed the screen door open as he came out, making the gator hiss and the hairs on her arms stand straight up.

"You've met Bumper, I see," Scooter commented in that agreeable drawl. "Don't worry about him none. He's just saying hello."

Saying hello...

Tell that to her poor heart and her dog.

"Bumper, huh?" She and Dax traded a relieved look. "How'd you name him that?"

"Found him under my bumper one day when I got home from watching the Cocks up in Columbia."

"Cocks?" Dax mouthed to her.

"Football team," she mouthed back, pretending to throw a pass, which he mimed catching.

"Bumper there wouldn't come out when I looped a gator hook around his neck. Tore off the side of my bumper in the tussle. I finally caved. He's been around ever since. Normally, he's pretty docile, but his blood is up. It's mating season right now, and he's got a lot of alligator misses to impress. You might have been part of the show."

She looked around for potential suitors and spotted

another gator partially hidden behind the shed. "What we do for love," she joked, wondering what gator courtship looked like. Lots of teeth preening? Did they worry about whether their skin was scaly enough?

"Sounds like my courtship with my high school sweetheart," Dax added dryly. "You got that invoice written up, Scooter? Because I'm going to need to find myself a drink after this."

He pulled a crumpled piece of paper out of his overalls and thrust it out to her. She gave him a weak smile. "Thanks, Scooter. We'll see you Saturday morning."

"Please tell your missus and Bumper goodbye for us," Dax added, patting Scooter on the back. "It was a pleasure."

Sherlock was waiting for them at the edge of the house, his gaze trained on Bumper. She gave him a good rubdown when they reached him.

"Good boy," she crooned.

"Yeah, Sherlock, thanks for the alert." Dax glanced back at the gator. "Tell me you don't have any gators at your grandma's house."

"No big bad wolves either," she quipped.

His smile had the icky feeling in her stomach subsiding. "Clever. Count me relieved. I really like you, Ariel, but worrying about finding a gator under my car every time I came to visit might have been too much for me."

She knew he was only kidding. But she liked the allusion to him visiting her. Was he thinking they might have more time in them after the wedding? She could certainly see that. Except she cautioned herself. They'd only truly met yesterday.

They crowded into the golf cart with Sherlock between them. "You know," Dax said, "that gator is lucky I'm a peaceful kind of guy. He interrupted a pretty serious moment back there."

She turned her head to see him watching her with that heated glint in his eyes. "I know what you mean. I know a place that serves gator bites if you'd like to exact some revenge."

His laughter rang out as she started the golf cart, making her want to join in. Her family trials might be upon her like the plague of locusts on Egypt back in the day, but even after running into a gator, there was nothing about being with Dax that remotely resembled a trial.

SIX

Having a gator interrupt his first kiss with Ariel had Dax wondering if her family's beliefs about wedding curses were catching.

He'd always been lucky, from when he'd won a set of tickets to the Austin zoo through a school raffle at the age of six. He'd brought home a new stereo after being Caller Number Five on the radio one fine spring day. The only girl he'd wanted to go to the prom with—the most sought-after cheerleader—had agreed. His high school basketball team had won the state championship. The Naval Academy, his first choice of schools, had made his life when they'd accepted him. He'd been top of his class at Top Gun, as much for his technical abilities as his creative flying. He could go on...

But having a kiss interrupted by a gator named Bumper? That seemed totally outside the normal, and it sure as hell wasn't something Dax wanted to happen again. Especially since he so desperately wanted to kiss Ariel. Not only was she as cute as a button and sexy as hell, but she didn't scream or run in the face of trouble. Some women would have fainted dead away at the sight of that gator back there. She'd been rock solid, but then again, she did search and rescue. He had a feeling he could take her up in the air and do barrel rolls and she wouldn't flinch.

Shopping for a wig was another matter...

The two margaritas she'd had at lunch wouldn't be near enough to get the poor girl through that. Especially since her mother had already picked out her hairpiece. Shocker. The very sight had made his nose scrunch up, to be honest, and Ariel's entire face had bunched up like she'd smelled something rotten.

"I'm sorry, ma'am, but are you sure this is what my mother selected?" Ariel asked, her voice raspy.

Dax pressed his hand to her tense back as they both stared at the long, wavy dark blond wig more suited to a beauty queen contender than the sassy woman standing close to him. Why was it dark blond and not brown? Had her mother wanted her to be a bottle blond like her sisters?

He had the urge to protect Ariel from her family. Hell, even from the shop owner. She closely resembled Cruella de Vil with her almost feral gaze and her pointy chin, white and black muumuu, and loads of costume jewelry. Ariel kept saying Charleston had characters, and this here was definitely another.

"Yes," Cruella answered, petting it like it was a miniature dog. "Your mother and I had a consultation first thing this morning when she called. She assured me this wig would be perfect for the wedding."

Not Ariel, Dax observed. The wedding...

God, he'd never been more glad not to be a woman.

Ariel cleared her throat. "I see. Well, I'm not sure this wig is going to suit me, what with me being so petite."

"Don't dismiss it yet." Cruella moved toward Ariel, gripping the atrocity in her hands, looking ready to bowl her over and wrestle it on her head. "It's called Longing for Locks, and it's one of my bestsellers."

There were wig bestsellers? He was in a new universe. Get him out! Still, Dax stepped in front of Cruella to block her from reaching Ariel and gave her his best shit-eating grin, one honed for the older ladies at church who used to pinch his cheeks abominably and try to set him up with their daughters.

"Ma'am, I have to agree with Ariel here. That wig looks more appropriate for an Amazon than a pint-sized sweetheart like Ariel here. How about this one?"

He pointed to the display shelf to distract her, almost laughing at himself. What the hell did he know about wigs? Then he shoved that thought away. He knew women. Spotting a cute little bob in Ariel's actual hair color, he walked over to the freaky head displaying it with the penciled-in brows and glassy green eyes. God, he was going to have nightmares about this place. Styrofoam female heads wearing bad wigs were going to haunt him in his dreams. Ask him big questions like *What did he want out of life?* or *What did he look for in a woman?*

"A woman Ariel's size would be swallowed up by that much hair." He made himself lean in to Cruella confidentially, like they were besties. "This little brown bob would suit her delicate features better, don't you agree? I imagine it will also showcase her bridesmaid's dress better, something the bride must be proud of selecting."

God, he was grasping at straws here. Ariel slipped behind the woman and made a show of clapping silently, her tense mouth fighting a smile now. Good. Mission accomplished.

"Ariel's mother was very insistent on the wig I showed

you." Cruella's tone was syrupy yet tough as nails. "If she'd try it on, she'd see why."

Dax wasn't putting her through that. Sure, she intended to lose the wig anyway, but that didn't matter—what mattered was ensuring she enjoyed herself. He plucked the wig he'd chosen off the freaky head display and strode over to Ariel. Eyes pleading, he fitted it as gently as he could, wincing as she fought laughter.

"Here now, wait!" Cruella slapped his hand like he was a bad schoolboy. "You need a wig cap. Land sakes, you men are about as useful as tits on a bull."

God, when was the last time he'd heard that one? From one of the cheek pinchers probably. Cruella huffed but she brought a wig cap over. First time he'd ever seen one of those, but Dax politely plucked it from her hands after giving Ariel the wig to hold.

"Allow me." He flashed her a winning smile. "I'm told I have magic hands."

"I'll bet, but not in this fashion, young man." Cruella cut him a terrifying glare, making him wonder if she'd been the model for the freaky female heads on the shelves.

Ariel let him do his best to put it on her. The wig cap made him wonder about the torture women endured for beauty. His mother and sister liked to look nice, and they went to the beauty parlor and had their nails done. But nothing too extreme that he knew of.

Of course, he'd heard old girlfriends talk about things like sugar hair removal—his untutored male mind imagined something as a clear pancake syrup—and fish-eating pedicures, which were straight-up terrifying. He couldn't imagine paying to stick his feet in water with pedicure-focused piranhas. He'd live with calluses.

Thank God the wig cap only rated about a two on the

beauty torture scale. Between the two of them, they got Ariel's hair tucked into the darn thing within seconds. He tried to ignore how soft her hair was and how pretty she looked up close. Her nose was a sweet little accent to her oval face, but it was the rapid rise of her chest from her accelerated breathing that had him getting a little hot under the proverbial collar.

Ariel handed him the wig, biting her lip, trying not to laugh. Good. At least that pale, horrified expression had faded. Dax couldn't imagine anyone in his family doing anything like this. He did his best to fit the wig, only to have Cruella ram her elbow into him to push him aside.

"You're doing it all wrong." She tugged on the wig, making Ariel wince. "There. That's better."

Dax didn't care for the wince or the way Cruella was eyeing Ariel, so he walked over and lifted up her chin. Her blue eyes were enormous and sad, the expression almost like Sherlock's. "Shall we amble over to the mirror and see what you think?"

He already knew. She was beautiful—with or without the wig.

At the mirror, she made a face before touching the wig and adjusting it herself. "This will be fine."

Cruella made a *tsk-tsk* sound and came over with Ariel's mother's choice in her skeletal hand. "We should try this one on as well."

"But—"

"Your mother *did* choose it, dear," Cruella interrupted, pulling the wig off and beginning to fit her with the other. "And mothers always know best."

Dax wanted to gag and respond, *Not this one,* but he figured the quicker they finished this fitting, the faster they could leave.

Once Ariel had the other wig on, Dax gave in to his impulse and started laughing. "It's horrible," he sputtered. "Ariel, where are you? I can barely see you."

Ariel sashayed her head, making the hair swish around her like a mass of blond seaweed. God, the story behind her name had to be the reason he'd thought that up.

"You can't see me?" She piled the hair over her face and then used her hands to part it down the middle. "Peekaboo."

He chortled.

Cruella mashed her lips together and marched forward, yanking the wig off. "This is not a laughing matter. Wigs are pieces of beauty. Art even. Not the butt of jokes, I can assure you."

Dax turned to her and gave her his best Captain Cross look. "How about this? We won't tell Ariel's mother how bad it looked on her if you tell her you agreed this wig was more flattering on Ariel. Especially for the wedding photos."

Cruella gripped the blond wig in her hands, and for a moment, Dax worried she was contemplating strangling him. He was ready to shout, *Run, Ariel, she's going to smother me with a wig* when Cruella nodded. "Fine, but only because I stand by my product. When someone compliments your hair at the wedding, Ariel, I want you to tell them where you bought the wig."

She glanced over at Dax, and he could hear her thinking *No problem since I won't be wearing it*. "I'd be happy to do that, ma'am."

By the time they left the store and started walking to the golf cart, both of them were hanging on to each other, fighting laughter. "Don't bray like a donkey yet," he told her. "Cruella is probably still thinking of smiting us from the window."

That had her clutching his bicep, and God help him, he wanted to take her in his arms that minute and kiss her senseless.

"Bray like a donkey?" Her laughter reminded him of the sputters his old Honda gave when it backfired. "I'll have you know I sound adorable when I laugh."

"You sure do." He put his arm around her waist as Sherlock lumbered out of the golf cart, stretching the leash Ariel had secured to it—because dogs in wig shops with all that hair would be a foregone disaster, Ariel had told him. "I'm mostly talking about myself. God, Ariel. It was like a horror movie in there. That woman. The wigs. Those freaky fake heads wearing human hair. I might need you to hold me tonight so I can fall asleep."

"Oh, you poor baby," she crooned like she did with Sherlock. "I'll make you some warm milk and tuck you into bed."

He thought they were joking—at least about the warm milk. "You can tuck me into bed anytime. First, Bumper the gator and now Cruella the wigmaker. Who's next? Please tell me it's someone normal."

"Honey," she drawled, "this here is Charleston. Like I keep telling you, we adore our characters and eccentricities. Or did you not point out earlier the joint taxidermy and leather goods shop?"

He tapped her cute little nose because she looked downright adorable standing there on the street, petting her trusty bloodhound. "I did. Do you need a purse for the wedding? A newly killed dead animal purse would go great with your wig of real human hair."

"Eww."

"Exactly! I got creeped out when Cruella started

describing how all her wigs come from natural subjects. It made me think—"

"Some wigs come from dead ones," she finished with a grimace. "I know! I thought that too. I mean, I know there are tons of good reasons people wear wigs, but if they have to deal with Cruella, I feel awful for them. Of course, you outdid yourself in there, Captain Hotpants. Thank you."

The way she was looking up at him—like he was dark chocolate and sunshine all wrapped up in one—had him touching her cheek. "You don't need to thank me, Ariel. I'm only sorry you had to go there in the first place. Besides, I told you that I have your back."

She laid her hand on his chest, and again, his heart started to pound faster. Yeah, they were going to have to tuck each other into bed and soon. The heat between them was as sweet as it was scorching.

"I know you do, and I appreciate it." She lifted the shopping bag as her hand fell from his chest. "Well, we have the wig. Are you ready to run a few more errands before we head back to the resort?"

He thought about Rob and wondered what he was up to. Maybe he should check in. But after this morning, he wasn't eager to reach for his phone. That totally sucked, but he wasn't sure what he could do about it. Rob had set a line in the sand, so to speak, and things were different between them now. He knew that happened when a guy knew his friends didn't approve of his woman—more often than not, he distanced himself from the friends. It had just never happened with him. Still, he'd be there if his friend needed him. "Let me check my phone and see if I have any word from the groom. But as far as I know, the only thing I'm supposed to do is help you. Although if you must know, I'm mostly here to spend time with you."

"I like that," she said softly, her small hand resting lightly on his chest. "When you're around, I feel better about getting through the day."

He gave in to the urge to stroke her cheek again, holding her gaze a moment longer, before pointing to the golf cart. Downtown was filled with tourists and other people walking by, but he only had eyes for her. "Come, our carriage awaits."

"You shouldn't joke like that too loudly around here." She started the engine after she stowed the wig in the storage box in back and plunked down in the driver's seat. "One of the carriage drivers might hear you and offer you a ride. Charleston is famous for its carriage rides, you know."

He petted Sherlock under the ears when the dog rested his head against his side. "Is Cruella's shop on the tour? I wonder if the wig heads in the window stare at people as they go by. Like the Mona Lisa's eyes following you wherever you go."

"Well, Charleston does have a famous ghost tour, but I don't recommend it for you if you got creeped out by the wig shop."

"Lord, I swear this city is looking better and better to me."

She was laughing as their eyes met and held. "Good. Because as far as I'm concerned, it looks really good on you."

That had him wanting to puff out his chest. She sent him a wink as she dug into her purse for her phone. He did the same. He had nothing from Rob, but he had a text from their buddy and fellow groomsman.

CARSON

> Heard you've given my room to Ariel and the two of you are getting cozy. Told you she was hot. 🔥 Let's not forget brave and smart. You go. I'll be bunking with Perry since it sounds like you two might need your privacy. We've agreed to buy all your drinks when we arrive since you're pulling most of the groomsmen duty. Rob is being a dick. Like he doesn't know how cool it is that you're into a girl like this. Have fun! 👧🍗🍺

> Rob is being a dick, sure, but we won't hide his parachute. Yet. 🪂 Thanks for bunking elsewhere. She IS hot. Cute. Funny. I could go on. 😊 But then you'll have more ammo. See you soon.

Dax was kinda glad his buddies weren't showing up until Thursday. Their work schedules didn't allow them to come earlier like his had. He kinda felt bad about not telling his buddy what had happened with Tiffany, but Rob had made his position all too clear. Still, he wished there were a way to warn Carson and Perry not to be alone with her. God, that sucked. To pull himself out of those shitty thoughts, he opened up his family group text.

> Hey! Checking in. Having a ball with the maid of honor while getting ready for the wedding. Wanted to tell y'all how awesome you are. I don't say it enough. Some families are crazy. Thanks for not being one of them. Talk to y'all when I wrap up here. 🖤

He got a few hearts back and some *Ahs...* before pocketing his phone. When he turned to look at Ariel, she was biting her lip, her brows smashed together. "What now?"

She made her eyes cross before shoving her phone in her purse and starting the golf cart. "My family has micromanaging down to an art. My mother checked in about the new wig I chose with some very severe language. Cruella apparently called her the minute we left her shop. Then Tiffany wanted to see pics of her koi. You know…"

"We should have taken a pic of Bumper and sent it to her."

"With a koi photoshopped in his mouth." She gave a snarky laugh. "She'd freak. I pretty much sent a thumbs-up back to all the texts. No point in answering them. It only encourages their interfering. Let's keep going. We have more fun ahead."

At the next errand, she got all serious with the wedding setup contractor, running through tables, chairs, silverware, and everything else including posh trash bins, intended to not distract from the day's beauty.

Upon leaving, he made a face at Sherlock who gave him a soulful look as they climbed back into the golf cart. "I had no idea there was so much to a wedding. I'd always wanted a small one, but now I'm thinking of eloping. The trash cans sealed it for me."

Her melodic laughter had him wanting to lift her onto his lap as they cruised through the downtown streets filled with Charleston's charming shops. "They're called disposal units, *honey,* and they were new to me too. Also, I agree on eloping—if that ever happens."

"You mentioned thinking you fail to entice men, which I definitely don't believe." He motioned to himself. "Any other reason you sound so pessimistic?"

That greenish tint returned to her cute little face. "Let's just say that right now I'm of the mind that there's truly nothing a good vibrator can't fix."

He choked. *"What?"*

"You heard me." She batted her eyelashes at him playfully. "Relationships are messy, with one or both parties not often fulfilling their end of the bargain."

The edge in her voice made him observe, "Sounds like experience talking."

"It is—in the form of a canceled engagement." She merged onto Broad Street, wind playing with the ends of her hair. "I was in my mid-twenties and thought I could have it all. He decided once we started living together that I traveled too much for work."

Yeah, he'd heard that comment after he'd graduated from the Naval Academy and started his career in the Navy. "I know what you mean. I had complaints about how much I was away. Made it hard to do any long-term dating."

She pushed the gas pedal as they sailed through a yellow light. "I'll bet they didn't ask you to find a different job."

He muttered a curse word under his breath. "No, they didn't. They might have complained, but they liked the idea of dating a Navy pilot."

"Women like a man in uniform." She sent him a thorough once-over, smiling as she made his blood heat. "Understandable. My ex didn't find my job that enticing, and he certainly wasn't reasonable when I explained disasters don't work that way. We broke it off. I haven't met anyone since who understood my profession. It's a calling."

"Like how I love to fly." He put his hand on Sherlock when the dog gave an enthusiastic ruff as they passed a horse-drawn carriage. "Look, some guys are jerks. I say that as a guy. But not all of us are."

"I know that. I work with terrific guys, but they're like

me, you know? When you find your tribe, it makes things easier."

He thought about his next question before deciding to go for it. They were getting to know each other. She'd opened up this line of talk. And they were heading to something more than friendly. "So you haven't met anyone in that tribe you wanted to be with?"

"Temporarily, sure. But we don't always hit the same disasters. Also, when you work together, the work comes first. We're on a clock to find people. No time for messing around when people's lives are at stake. None of us would mess that up for a fling. Even after things settle down some."

Practical to the core, but he liked that. You knew where you stood with Ariel. "Your work is harder that way. Most of the people I work with in the Navy are men obviously, despite our branch having more women than the others. We're still at twenty percent."

The wind was riffling her short, curly hair when she glanced his way knowingly. "But not in the aviator ranks, I expect."

He gripped the grab handle tighter as she turned left. "No, that's about ten percent, and trust me, my mom and sister ask me about that all the time. They think it's a shame there aren't more women in the skies. They're fond of saying women look good in dress whites too. My very funny brother agrees."

She zipped around a car attempting to parallel park and turned right. "You have two siblings?"

"Yep. Both younger. Laurie is the middle one. A family practice doctor. Drew is the baby and milks it for all it's worth. He's a small business loans specialist."

"Sounds like your family likes to help others." She

coughed along with him when the car in front of them puffed out a dark cloud of exhaust, one of the drawbacks to driving in a golf cart. "What do your parents do?"

"Mom was a social worker and now volunteers at a food kitchen. Dad is a criminal defense attorney, working mostly pro bono cases now. So yeah, we were raised to believe in service."

She pulled into another parking lot and parked in the front; he was grateful to be away from someone who clearly had failed their emissions test. "Do they have any concerns about you becoming a cushy corporate pilot?"

He uncurled his long frame and joined her as they walked into an unremarkable brick building with no signage, Sherlock remaining in the cart. "It's kinda breaking the mold, but everyone has been supportive. It's not like I'm changing who I am. I'm hoping to do some Big Brothers work and the like now that I'll have more control of my schedule. Be active in my community. I like being a part of something bigger than myself. You understand that. Not everyone does."

She shot him a sexy smile and held out her hand for a fist bump. "We're weird that way, I guess. Now put on your best serious look. This place doesn't do loony."

She was kidding. She had to be. He'd finally spotted the sign for the business in the lobby: Paradise Ignites. "Tell me this isn't a place where you rent strippers."

She snorted. "You should be able to guess. Take a whiff of the air."

He looked at her oddly before sniffing. His mind clicked. "Gunpowder?"

"Welcome to the best wedding sparkler displays in town." She had the door open before he did this time, but didn't go in. "Charleston doesn't allow fireworks at weddings, but this is people's workaround. Wait until you see the size of their displays."

"*Sparklers?*" God, he was getting a college-level education in weddings.

"That's right." She slapped a hand to her forehead. "I told Tiffany these things could start a fire, especially given our family history, but she insisted. Rob loved the idea too. They created a his-and-hers display. Also, because we need more fire, every guest will be given a handheld blue sparkler because Tiffany *loves* the color of Rob's eyes."

He made a gagging sound. "Oh God, he's my best bud, but I think I just threw up in my mouth."

"Ditto." She put her hands to her throat playfully. "I should think it's sweet, but I missed the schmaltz gene."

He grimaced. "So did I."

"Hey there," a deep booming voice called before a giant man appeared in the doorway, filling it from end to end. The guy was easily six foot six and weighed over three hundred pounds. He had a brown beard down to the middle of his chest and what looked to be fireworks tattoos up both arms before they disappeared under a camouflage shirt. "What can I do for y'all?"

"Are you Bubba?" She gave her signature polite smile. "I'm Ariel Holmes."

"You're the one organizing the wedding this Saturday, yes'um." He trudged over to the counter and flipped open a huge leather-bound book. "We're ready for y'all."

"Good. I wanted to make sure I talked with you before setup to make sure you have all the information you need."

He ran a scarred finger down the ledger. Had it been burned in the execution of his professional duties? "Looks like we're good. We provide a fire extinguisher for each sparkler display. The only thing I wanted to go over with y'all was water receptacles for the twenty-inch sparklers."

"What do you suggest?"

He leaned his elbows on the counter, taking up near the entire length. "We can provide you with some tin buckets for the guests to drop them in, but some brides don't find them fancy enough."

Dax almost snickered, thinking of the posh trash bins Tiffany had wanted.

"Right." Ariel took her phone out and started typing in a note. "No offense, but my sister is particular. Thanks for that reminder. We'll figure something out."

His huge head barely moved when he nodded, making Dax wonder if he had a neck. Then he noted his hands. They were like giant bear paws. "You ever play football?" he asked.

The old wooden floor shook when Bubba dropped down into a defensive stance. "Way back in the day. For the Gamecocks. Tight end. Although my missus says it's less of a tight end now and more like a plentiful tush."

When he grabbed his backside in both hands, Ariel squeaked out a laugh. "Go Cocks."

Bubba made a fist and extended his thumb and pinky before waggling it a little. Ariel did the same and they shared a smile. She turned to Dax and said, "That's 'Spurs Up.' We fans love our Cocks."

God, the jokes he wanted to make. But he lifted his hand playfully and mimicked the gesture. "I'll get the hang of it."

"You planning on doing anything for the Cocks at the wedding?" Bubba's massive jaw transformed when he grinned. "I had a few buddies get a Cocky cake for the groomsmen's cake. Nothing like having our team's mascot present when you're getting hitched."

"Unfortunately, the groom is from out of town and my sister doesn't follow sports, so no, we're missing Cocky at the wedding," Ariel told him. "It's totally our loss because Cocky is awesome."

"Betcha." He scratched his beard. "Hang on a sec. I've got something for y'all."

He disappeared into the back, and Ariel looked over and batted her eyelashes at Dax. "How're y'all doing over there?"

He gave her his best eyelash batting technique, hoping it didn't trigger an eye twitch. "Mighty fine. Yourself?"

"Stupendous." She tucked her curls behind her ear. "Any idea what a posh water can looks like?"

He tapped the side of his jaw. "Would those cute watering cans women like to water their plants with work? My mother has a couple from a flea market."

"Good one!" Ariel plucked her phone out of her pocket again, prompting him to take another slow inventory of her legs. She had nice ones, the color of warm honey. He couldn't wait to run his hands over them.

"That might work." She tapped on her screen, her brows knitting together. "We're at the budget ceiling for incidentals, but we need something to put the sparklers in. I should probably buy aloe vera or burn cream and some Band-aids too in case of any issues. But God, I really hope nothing happens."

So did he. The last thing anyone needed at a wedding was a medic. "You've got lighters or something to ignite them, right?"

She nodded, still typing. "Ah...I was hoping you and the other groomsmen would be amenable to lighting them and handing them out. I need responsible people in charge of the sparklers. The Three Tornadoes actually suggested putting my nephews in charge of that."

Dax started laughing. "Do they know nothing about young boys? When I was that age, we used to fire bottle rockets sideways. Hell, one time my cousin and I took down a pegboard from my dad's toolshed and stuffed the holes with about twenty rockets. Dropped them onto a bonfire and boom. Everything exploded. Idiots."

"Boys," Ariel summarized. "Sounds like fun."

"You a tomboy back in the day?"

"In secret." She put her finger to her lips and went *shhh* in the sexiest way. "I was the girl in the pretty dress running off to climb trees and bait fishing hooks so I could catch something."

"A closet tomboy." He gave her a considering look. "Sexy."

"I try." She wiggled her hips with a little flirtation in her eyes, making him want to take her by both hands and kiss her soundly. When they finally got around to it, their first kiss was going to be out of this world.

"Maybe you can show me how you bait your hook sometime. I'll need a new fishing buddy."

Of course he could go with his Navy buddies, but he also liked the thought of going with this sweet little woman who'd captured his interest. Good way to get back to fishing. Plus, they could pack a picnic. Have a little romance on the side.

"I'd like that." She turned her head toward the door when heavy footsteps sounded, signaling Bubba's return.

The giant man came through the doorway with a black T-shirt in his hands. "Here. I want ya to have this. I thought it would be fun to have some made up. Cocky and sparklers go together in my mind. Might be a bit large on ya, but you can wear it as a nightshirt."

He held out the black T-shirt and handed it to Ariel. There was a cartoon rooster on it with giant yellow feet with the words STAY COCKY and giant fire sticks exploding outward. She fitted it to her body, and sure enough, it ran to her knees. But she was grinning, and Dax had a strong urge to see her in that and nothing else. Perhaps later…

"I love it!" She clutched it to her heart. "Thanks, Bubba! I'm hoping to get to a game this fall, and trust me, I plan to wear it."

"Does me proud to hear it." He tapped his chest, ruffling his beard. "I'll see y'all Saturday morning to set up. Holler if you need anything else in the meantime."

"You betcha!" Ariel gave another one of those Spurs Up gestures, which Bubba returned, and then they were heading out the door.

Dax only gave a wave. "You're really good with people."

"You say that now." She slid into her seat, tugged down her skirt unfortunately, and patted Sherlock before starting the golf cart. "Wait until you see me crash and burn with my family. Which we're about to head on back to. You ready?"

"Is there a choice?"

She gave a scary laugh that would have made even good ol' Cruella the wig lady's hair stand up on end. "Gird yourself, Stephan. We're about to return to talk to the bride about watering cans."

This was best man's duty?

Yeah, he was so eloping.

SEVEN

Was she a terrible person for wanting to be alone with Dax tonight?

Probably. But as they arrived at the resort and he came around to her side of the golf cart after Sherlock jumped out behind him, hand extended to help her out, she realized she had a serious chance to have fun with a great guy this week.

She was not going to let this opportunity pass her by.

Then she spotted her mother's husband coming toward them with his golf clubs. He was wearing blue and white checkered pants with a blue polo and a matching golf visor over his perfectly dyed blond hair. Trey inclined his chin. "Hey, Ariel! Your mother said you were getting a wig today because your haircut is so unfortunate. You still doing that weather girl thing? That's the perfect golf cart for a spot on the news."

She gritted her teeth as Dax froze beside her.

"Hi, Trey! Yes, you can see me on the six o'clock news every night."

Dax swung his head her way as Sherlock gave a low howl. "What the—"

"Just smile," she said through clenched teeth, grateful when he continued past them toward his Mercedes. "My mother's current love interest. I don't know how he got it in his head that I'm the weather girl, but after correcting him twice, I gave up."

"That's— I'll refrain from saying what I'm really thinking. I didn't meet that guy the other night when I met your mom. So, that's Trey. All Rob said about him was that he was a big golf enthusiast."

"He's keeping my two brothers-in-law busy on the golf course this week, so I'm grateful. Morris and Bartlett are about as annoying as Trey."

"Wonderful, birds of a feather flock together, huh? Sorry, that was awful of me."

She laid her head against his strong, warm arm. "Don't worry about it. They don't help their case. I have an idea! How about we skip out and have dinner at one of my favorite spots before we have a game of wig-pong?"

He tipped up her chin, his finger giving the underside a sweet little caress. "We still playing for kisses?"

The very thought had her heart doing backflips and giving the cheer, *Yes, let's go.* "If you promise to check the area for gators so we won't be interrupted again," she bandied back. "I can't handle another aborted effort."

His green eyes turned hot. "Me either. Ariel—"

"*Aunt Ariel!*"

"*Aunt Ariel.*"

She turned as Marshall and Ripp sprinted toward them, bad intentions in their squinty little eyes. "Run. Now."

"I never abandon my post," he shot back, stepping forward and holding his arms out. "Slow down, boys. Your aunt and Sherlock just got back here after a long day. Give them a second to settle in."

"Mom says I can take the golf cart out," Marshall informed her, his punky nose sticking up in the air. "Give me the keys."

God, would these kids never learn manners? *Please* and *thank you* weren't stressed by the Three Tornadoes. When Ariel had tried to correct their rudeness, she'd been told to butt out and stop trying to parent other people's kids. That had been enough to keep her from pointing anything out when it came to her nephews. "You have a license, Marshall?"

Ripp grabbed on to the cart's overhead bars, treating them like they were monkey bars. "Ah, come on, Aunt Ariel, it's only a golf cart."

"Rules are rules." That didn't make her a cool aunt, sure, but she'd never have that rep with these boys. "And you leave Sherlock in peace. I don't want you chasing him. Understand me?" Keeping them from teasing Sherlock was the only time she schooled their behavior, but he was her dog, which was rather like a baby in her mind.

Marshall only rolled his eyes at her while Ripp pulled himself up onto the golf cart and hung from the bars. Sherlock stood at attention at her side, watching them carefully.

"Boys, your aunt is talking to you," Dax said in that military command voice she found so hot.

Marshall's chin lifted defiantly. "We heard you. Fine. We won't bother Sherlock. But can you take us for a ride?"

"Yeah, can you?" Ripp pleaded.

"This golf cart is not for joy riding." If she gave an inch, they'd be all over her for the rest of the week, being as demanding as her sisters. "Ask your parents to rent an ATV and bring y'all somewhere."

"Mom doesn't do anything but obsess about the

wedding." Marshall kicked at the ground. "I could jump in the ocean and drown, and she wouldn't notice."

Ariel laid a hand on his shoulder, knowing that probably wasn't far from the truth. She'd felt the same way about her mother. "What about asking Rob? From what I remember at Thanksgiving, he liked to be outdoors."

Marshall's mouth thinned and he pushed away from her, fisting his hands at his sides. "I'm not asking him. Come on, Ripp."

"Yeah, we know you didn't want to stay with us," Ripp called out as he jumped down from the golf cart. "You're staying with *him*."

They were running off before she could open her mouth to reply. "Wow! I...didn't expect to get judgment over my rooming options from my own nephews. Dammit, sometimes the Three Tornadoes make me want to pull my hair out. Those boys didn't need to know that. Now they think it's them when it's not... Shit."

Dax turned her toward the house after grabbing the bags from the back. "There's more going on there than you not babysitting a bunch of boys. Marshall thinking his mom wouldn't notice him drowning is alarming. I knew he was having a tough time with all the changes from what Rob had said, but that beats all. I can't imagine ever thinking something like that about my mom."

She walked quickly with him down the path, not wanting to run into anyone else. "I felt that way sometimes. God knows, I want to like those boys, but they're brats. Have been since they were little. All of them. I call them the *Lord of the Flies* boys. I wish I could say his behavior was just Marshall being upset about having a new stepfather and moving away from Pensacola and his friends."

"Yeah, Rob said his new orders didn't go over well, whereas Tiffany can't wait to get to San Diego. She thinks it's going to be posher. Clearly, she hasn't seen military housing."

Not her concern. Her goal was the wedding coming off in spectacular fashion. Marshall wasn't her responsibility either, and even if she were inclined to be more present with him, Tiffany would bite her head off for any interference. Plus, he could do no wrong. Her sisters were fond of saying, "boys will be boys." Ariel thought they took the saying too far.

They were closing in on Dax's cottage when she heard "Ariel!"

Mother. God help her, but she increased her pace, Sherlock hurrying beside her. "Let's get inside. You can say I had to pee. She's going to grill me about the wig."

Dax pushed the key card into her hand and gave her a gentle push toward the cottage. "You run this time. I'll handle her. Stormy!"

When he pulled up, she kept going with her dog, telling herself she was not a child or a coward. She did technically have to pee. When she hit the cottage, she unleashed Sherlock and headed straight to the bathroom. If she took longer than necessary and washed her hands like ten times—she had been around fish, a gator, and gunpowder, not to mention someone else's hair—it wasn't the end of the world.

"You can come out now," Dax called a few minutes later when she was soaping her hands up for the third time. "Coast is clear."

When she emerged from the bathroom, her fingers were tingling from her little hand spa moment. She found him in the open kitchen pouring water into two glasses. He handed one to her when she joined him.

She winced as she lifted her glass. "How did it go?"

He bared his teeth, grimacing. "Well, knowing your mother wants to entice me because I'm a man gives me the upper hand."

She choked on her water.

"So when I assured her this wig looked so much better on you in person than the other one, she gave me that slow smile of hers and patted me on the arm. I said you had a wedding contractor you needed to call before six, so she said she'd catch up with you later. I hated lying, but we're in enemy territory. If you don't mind me saying so."

"Yes, Captain, we are." She pressed the cold glass against her hot forehead. "Do you still want to get out of here?"

"Like now?" He drank the rest of his water down. "Sure. I should drop by and check in with Rob. Don't really want to, but maybe I can make things easier for both of us. Is there anyone I can say we're meeting tonight as cover?"

"Satan," she quipped. "Oh, wait. He's probably around here somewhere."

Dax snorted out a laugh, tipping her chin up. "God, you're a riot. I didn't know that before. Probably a good thing. I would have thought about you even more."

She felt her mouth slowly fall open. "You really thought about me before we met?"

"Sure. I imagined meeting you and what you'd be like." His finger grazed over her jaw, lighting a trail of fire. "How you'd smile. What we'd talk about. I suppose I should have guessed you'd be funny after you made that garlic comment, except now I know it wasn't totally a joke."

She shifted a little closer to his warm body, aware of the broadness of his chest under his white T-shirt. The smell of warm man reached her, making her give a little sigh. "Right.

Thanks for the reminder. We should buy garlic tonight. I think it's our duty, Stephan. To save the world."

He cupped her cheek, and she rose onto her tiptoes with a smile on her face, sensing what was next. God, she was more than ready.

"Whatever you say, Elizabeth." His husky voice liquified her bones. "Whatever you say."

His head descended, those brilliant green eyes never leaving hers. She laid her hand on his chest, feeling the strength there, the heat. His arm came around her waist, making her belly tense. God, he was taking his time watching her, heightening the desire growing between them. She kept her eyes on his, watching him right back. The heat and promise she saw there had her biting her lower lip. Her pulse went erratic, and her thighs clenched.

Kiss me, dammit!

Sherlock barked. Ariel jumped back, nearly stumbling. Dax's hand caught her. Muffled laughter reached her ears, making her look around.

Dax's mouth twisted as he jerked his head to the right, peering out the window. "Ten o'clock. Jesus, we're going to need to close the blinds."

Spotting the little Peeping Toms, she reached for patience. They'd almost been caught kissing by her nephews? How great was that? "Privacy isn't respected in my family."

"I'll make sure to lock the doors even when we're tucked in the house. I don't usually keep my doors locked. Maybe it's being on base or a carrier, but I'm not used to it."

"It's good to be a guy," was all she said as she heaved out a frustrated breath.

Dax strode over to the window where the boys were

peering in—Marshall and Ripp pressed near the front of the group. "Boys," he called through the window, "last I heard, spying into people's houses was illegal. Y'all move along. *Now.* And don't let me catch you doing it again."

She crossed over and watched them run off, yelling like banshees. "Why do I suddenly feel cornered?"

He lowered the blinds and closed them. "Because you know they'll talk. Now, I'm really ready to get out of here for the evening. I'll text Rob and check in."

She pressed her hands to her temples while he did that, where a dull throb was starting. "If I thought we could get away with staying at my grandma's house on Folly Beach, I would have us both pack up and leave now. But I need to be on-site, according to Tiffany, and traffic can be a nightmare."

He set his phone down and put his hands on her shoulders, massaging the tension there. "We'll get through this, Ariel. I promise. Don't let those boys bother you."

She made a face. "I actually miss Bumper."

"Me too." He grabbed her hand and tugged her toward the front door. "But don't worry. We're going to kiss. When I set my sights on a target, there's no stopping me."

Oh, that was so sexy. She liked the shift in conversation. "Am I in your sights, Captain Hotpants?"

"You'd better believe it, honey. Now grab your purse and anything else you need. What about Sherlock? Does he need to be fed?"

Ariel glanced over at the bloodhound. He was standing at attention, peering at the door. Playing guard dog after the boys' peeping. "I always carry something for him in my purse, but where we're going, he's going to be well taken care of. Just you wait."

Dax flashed her a grin. "Race you to the Bronco."
"You're on."

With Sherlock in the lead, they made it there, both of them breathless, but since she hadn't seen any of her family on the way, she was feeling great. Revived. As much from the way Dax was looking down at her as from the short run.

The pull between them was palpable, and all she could think of was their two aborted kisses. No way she was coming back here unkissed. She'd let things take their course, but if it hadn't happened by the time they headed back to the resort, she was taking him to a romantic spot along the water and getting it done. She needed his mouth on her. Stat.

"Let's get a move on." His usually deep voice was rough with desire. "If we get caught again, I might lose my mind."

"Me too."

She caressed his bicep before he opened her car door and the back for Sherlock. She hopped inside and was still buckling her belt when he joined her. Sherlock gave a low ruff, gazing out the windshield. "Where we going, honey?"

Oh, how his sugary endearments lit her up inside. "To a little shack along the water that serves up the best fried food around. You like fried okra, *baby*?"

Her equally teasing drawl had him skimming a hand on her bare knee as he turned the car on and put it in reverse. "As much as I like shrimp and grits and cornbread. I don't eat fried food all that often, but when it's around, you won't find a happier man."

She rubbed her hands in delight. "Then you're going to love Kaz's."

When they reached the old blue and white shack with the expanded outdoor porch along the water, she felt her shoulders come down from her ears. Here she could relax.

Dax hurried around her side of the Bronco to open her door, but she was already opening it.

He gave her a pointed look as she sat back down. "How about letting me be the gentleman and treat you right? I know it didn't come together like a date, but I'd like to officially change that."

God, could he be any cuter? "I'm up for that."

He cleared his throat and held out his hand gallantly. "Elizabeth, would you like to go out with me?"

She fanned herself theatrically before taking his hand. "Why Stephan, are you asking me on a date?"

The waning sun shot rays of gold into his sandy hair, making him a dreamboat in one of those old beach movies she loved to watch on late night. "Yes. Would tonight work? Kaz's?"

"It's one of my favorite places." The strength of his hand had her curling her fingers in his. "Seven?"

He checked his watch. "Perfect. I'll pick you up."

Then he shut the door on her with another sexy wink, and she laughed as he disappeared from view only to reopen the door again. Sherlock gave a quiet ruff as he watched them, his head swiveling to take in their theater. Okay, they were being silly, but it was fun. Plus, all her trials seemed far away. Like as far as Bali.

"Here we are." He gestured grandly to the place as he helped her out of the car before letting Sherlock out. "Would you like to sit outside or inside on this fine night?"

She could already feel the humid air on her skin and smell the ocean. "Outside."

"Perfect."

He was the one who looked perfect with the stubble on his jaw and the way his shoulders seemed to go on forever. Then there were those endless eyes taking her in...

"By the way, you look beautiful, Elizabeth."

His deep voice practically pulsed with intimacy, making her pluck at the fabric of her skirt. While she was more than presentable for a place like Kaz's, she wished she'd dressed up a little more for their date. "Thank you, Stephan. So do you."

"My beauty routine is legendary." Turning, he pointed to his backside. "Like my buns."

She sputtered out laughter but truthfully wouldn't mind if he kept modeling that fabulous ass all night long. "I can see why. My goodness, what it does to this little heart of mine."

He snagged her arm, laughing himself. "Come on. Let's get a drink and some chow."

At the door, he did the whole gentleman thing again. Once inside, she took a deep inhale of fried food, onions, and beer—all homey smells.

The waitress with the stringy gray hair slapped the menu she was carrying against the counter when she spotted them. "Why, Ariel Holmes! I heard you were in town for Tiffany's wedding. How are the Three Bitches treating you?"

She hugged Maybelline hard as Dax choked out a laugh. "It's the Three Tornadoes, as you well know, and about like always if I'm being truthful. They're even insisting I wear a wig for the wedding."

Maybelline touched her hair softly, gray brows slamming together. "Why in God's name would they do that? You have perfectly beautiful hair."

"Too short for them." She pointed to her chin and ears. "These horrible things might also show in the wedding photos."

"Land sakes." Maybelline pressed a hand to her forehead before shaking her weary head. "That sounds like Stormy talking. The original bitch. You're missing your grandma, I expect."

A blast of emotion rolled through her as Dax took her hand and squeezed it. "Hard not to. She was a great lady."

"Yeah, she sure was." Maybelline reached down and gave Sherlock a good rub behind his ears. "We miss seeing her around here too. This your fella?"

Ariel glanced up at Dax and punched his shoulder playfully. "For tonight."

Dax didn't miss a beat. Grinning, he said, "Maybe even tomorrow if I'm real good."

Maybelline's laughter was like gunfire. "I've been married for thirty-two years and I still tell my hubby there's no guarantee he's going to get lucky. The key to a happy marriage is keeping them on their toes. Men want to work for it. Hi, I'm Maybelline."

She thrust her hand out to Dax, and he let go of Ariel to shake it. "Stephan. Nice to meet you."

His use of his fake name had her fighting laughter. "Maybelline, we need a drink. And then some hush puppies. Outside if you please."

"Make sure you use some bug spray on yourselves." She grabbed a well-known brand from behind the counter. "The skeeters are out tonight after the rain we had. Come on. We'll find you a nice table and then get you that drink. After hearing about the wig, the first round is on me."

"You're the best." She followed Maybelline out to a corner table and plunked herself down. "You still making the same watered-down margaritas?"

Maybelline leveled her a glare even though her mouth was twitching. "Don't go insulting me so early, missy, especially before you order food. Gator bites might end up being in your fried chicken by mistake."

"Poor Bumper," Dax said mournfully as he sat across from her at the wooden table, the light from the water bringing out the gold in his hair again.

Sherlock plopped down at his feet as she held back her laughter.

"What do you want to drink, Stephan?" Maybelline asked him.

"Got any Chardonnay?"

"Chardonnay, huh?" Reaching down, Maybelline tugged lightly on Ariel's curls. "Ariel Holmes, sometimes I think you have a screw loose."

"He's kidding, Maybelline."

"I hope so for your sake."

Laughing, he said, "I'll settle for a beer."

Maybelline set the bug spray on the table. "Be right back with those and some water and a treat for your sweet dog here."

Ariel began spraying her legs before turning to her arms because God knows what treatment her mother and sisters would insist on if she came back riddled with bug bites. Her future would be full of ice packs and gallons of calamine lotion. "Want some?"

He grabbed the can and sprayed his long, muscular legs and then his powerful arms, the sight of his muscles making her heart race. "So this is a comfort spot. I can see why. The view is incredible. Maybelline seems to know your family well. Nice to have an ally of sorts."

Ariel ran her hands over the rough wood table as she gazed out across the shimmering water. Boats were out. The tall grasses around the edges were swaying in the breeze. Everywhere she looked, it felt like home. "I've known

Maybelline since I was taking my first steps when we visited my grandma. I think she gave me my first hush puppy."

"Makes sense. You probably didn't have any teeth. I'll bet you were adorable."

She struck a pose, wishing her mother had thought so. But no, her mother had kept a knit cap on her, thinking her ears stuck out. "Adorably adorable. That was me. All right, enough of that. Let's get down to brass tacks, as you soldiers like to say."

"Says who?" he bandied back, looking every bit a relaxed and *hot as hell* man.

All she wanted to do was stare, but her stomach rumbled. Picking up the menu Maybelline had left, she thrust it out. "I've had everything on this menu more than once. Some things are better than others. If you promise to be a sweetheart tonight, I'll tell you my faves."

He made the show of crossing his heart. "Scout's honor. So what makes your taste buds sing?"

She thought about kissing him. That would certainly make her taste buds sing. Later. Please God. "In this order. Fried okra. Fried pimento balls—"

"I've never been sure about those, to be honest."

She could already taste them. "Trust me. They're freaking delicious. Pimento cheese spread is part of the food pyramid in Charleston. You'll see it everywhere."

"I'm game." He leaned his elbows on the table, his complete attention on her. "What else?"

"Fried oysters. Fried chicken. Fried flounder."

He gave a studious look, stroking the sexy stubble on his jaw. "I sense a theme. So you're suggesting anything fried."

"You bet your cute little buns, I am. Fried is the way to go here."

A splash came from the water below, and Dax turned to

look down as Sherlock rose up and wandered over to check things out, tail up. She knew what that meant.

"I believe Bumper's relations have come to visit." She peered over the deck and raised her hands in a theatrical show of horror. "Quick. Say 'gator bites' three times. It usually makes them go away."

He snorted but eased his chair farther away from the railing. "Does not. If a gator isn't going to respect the moment when a man wants to kiss a woman, he isn't going to run from hearing 'gator bites.' Probably because it's what he does. Gator bites. Not really intimidating."

She choked on a laugh. "You're completely right. Whoever named that dish was an idiot."

"Exactly." He turned back to her, leaning on the table, clearly flirting. "Now... Since we're on a date, shall we go through the requisite questions?"

She clapped her hands. "Yes, please. Give me your best."

He looked off into the setting sun, gold washing over his chiseled profile. "Do you prefer a long walk on the beach or a cozy book?"

"Both."

His head swung back to her. "So that's how it's going to be. No either/or for my beautiful Elizabeth."

"Why choose?" She smiled as Maybelline set Sherlock's water on the floor before putting their drinks and steaming hush puppies down on the table. "Thanks, Maybelline."

"You're welcome, honey. Y'all decided what you want to eat?"

"Everything with the word fried on it," Dax answered. "I've heard it's the best on the menu."

Maybelline waved as a squawking seagull flew overhead

and landed on the roof. "Everything, huh? Honey, you know that's a whole bunch of food, right?"

He patted his flat abs, ones Ariel knew resembled a washboard. "I can handle it, and my date here doesn't like to choose when she can have it all."

She grinned at him. "What can I say? A girl likes what she likes."

"Oh, good Lord, I'll let you two do...whatever it is you're doing." Maybelline backed up with her hands up before turning around.

"It *is* a lot of food." She leaned closer, and he did the same, giving her his spicy, manly scent. "But I thank you for the buffet of flavors."

"You're quite welcome." He folded his hands on the table, his concentration on her complete. "Now, what's your best date question for me?"

She thought about it for a moment. "Boxers or briefs?"

He gave a mysterious grin. "Neither."

Her belly tightened and a moan tried to rise up her throat. "Oh, so *that's* how it's going to be."

"You asked." He snagged her hand from the table and clasped it in his own. "I figured you should be prepared. In case you're the fainting type. A woman named Elizabeth strikes me as such."

She ran her thumb over the back of his strong, muscular hand, laughing. "You are too funny, but let me assure you of one thing."

He leaned closer. "What's that?" The heat in his eyes only outmatched the twinkle. Oh, how much more could he make her pulse race?

"I don't faint, Stephan, and this girl can handle whatever you want to show me."

His brows inched up. "Noted. Let me equally assure

you that I'm the same way. You could ask me to skinny-dip tonight, and I'd go."

"Forget it!" Her cry had another table glancing over. "There are gators out there."

His powerful shoulders shook with laughter. "How about a late-night swim in the ocean?"

She blew out an aggrieved breath. "Unfortunately, the beach ordinances here are serious. No swimming after ten o'clock. I have a feeling skinny-dipping is illegal. The fines would be substantial—"

He lifted her hand to his mouth and kissed the back of it, making her feel very much like an old-fashioned Elizabeth. She rather liked it.

"I knew you were a rule follower from the moment I met you. We have that in common."

"Guilty and not ashamed to admit it. But don't worry. I know when to follow the rules and when to improvise. With you, I feel a compulsion toward the latter."

Weren't they talking like idiots? But it was so much fun. And she loved using their nicknames. It felt liberating somehow. Because Elizabeth wasn't "The Runt" or the kid who didn't seem like Stormy Deverell's daughter. Or the sister of the Three Tornadoes, even if they only shared half-blood.

Elizabeth could be whomever she wanted to be.

And what she wanted, she decided, was to stretch her hands up to the deepening blue sky and *dance*, because she felt *that good*. She'd put Dax's hands on her hips and rub herself all over him. Look up into his deep green eyes and know what was going to happen between them.

Because it was so going to happen...

She didn't know where it would lead, but she didn't need to. She'd learned to take life as it came. Dax was in her life right now, and she planned to enjoy the hell out of him.

"You know..." He gave the back of her hand a wicked little stroke that ignited more fires in her already achy belly. "I'm pretty good at improvising too."

Their eyes locked. She could see the heat flash in his intense gaze. Maybe it was time to take down some of her walls, the ones she'd put up because so few of the people she'd come across had bothered to take a second look at her. So she consciously unstacked the bricks and peered out at him—and he seemed to notice.

His flirtatious smile changed. While it wasn't as bright or wide, it was more intense. Her own mouth shifted as she let him in a little more, inviting him into the private little space inside herself. Then his mouth tipped to the right, and a new light entered his mesmerizing eyes—one she hadn't seen before—and she felt like she'd gained something special.

He tightened his grip on her hand. "You really are beautiful," he said, his voice strong and true in the breezy evening. "Thanks for coming out with me tonight."

She went with pure honesty, the kind she only gave when she felt safe with someone, a rare feeling. "I didn't want to be anywhere else."

His chest lifted, and he leaned back, almost as if to give them room, before shifting closer to her and tucking her hair behind her right ear. "Me either."

The sun was setting, casting a soft glow on his face, which was already becoming both familiar and dear to her. She took in more details of it now. The elegant line of his straight nose. The strong, deep-set brow. He had a tiny scar under his jawline, and his earlobes were the kind that partially attached. His green eyes had flecks of gold and black in them, making her think of panning for gold in the days of the Gold Rush, maybe because of how strong he was. A man clearly made of courage. One who loved adventure. One who made his mark in life…

The moment stretched as they continued to study each other in the waning light. She heard the easy cadence of his breath and leaned closer to catch more of his spicy scent. He did the same, and then he was cupping her chin gently in his big, warm hand and guiding her face toward him. Their gazes locked a moment before their lips met, the touch light but still shocking. The jolt from touching him rocked her back. His hand curled around her nape, keeping their mouths joined as they learned each other in soft, easy passes with an undercurrent of urgent longing.

She couldn't say how long the kiss went on. All she knew was that his lips were warm and firm and that he kissed her like he'd been waiting to do it his whole life. Even then, there was no impatience in his touch. It was perfect, and she found herself wishing there wasn't a table between them.

Sherlock gave a low ruff, and she eased back. Maybelline was coming toward the table with a platter of steaming fried food and a few treats for Sherlock.

"Sorry to interrupt, but I thought you'd prefer your food hot." She set both plates down. "You can always smooch later."

The waitress cackled as she walked away after patting Sherlock's head and giving him a soup bone, leaving them staring at each other.

"Well, Elizabeth…" His voice was rough and deep and made her thighs clench.

"Well, Stephan," she answered because she didn't know what exactly to say.

How did one make sense of a kiss that seemed to make the world brighter? She'd never experienced its like before.

"Shall we eat?" he asked, handing her a table setting.

She took it, knowing he'd seen the shaking of her hands. Channeling her alter ego, she found the right response. "Eat? No, I say we feast tonight."

The word seemed appropriate.

For once in her life, Ariel Holmes had everything she could ever want, and she was going to savor every minute.

EIGHT

They were in the car, but he didn't want to go back to the resort.

Sometimes he felt this way when he was up in the air with nothing but beautiful blue skies and white clouds before him. The whole world looked perfect up there. No petty squabbles in the mess hall. No difficult orders to execute. No power-hungry three stars trying to show everyone who had the bigger dick.

Ariel was like that blue sky. Enveloping. Fun. Easy.

He'd known right away that he liked her.

He'd known he was attracted to her.

He hadn't expected to start falling for her so fast.

Then again, his whole life was governed by how fast he could do something. It had been that way since Top Gun. He made lifesaving 180-degree turns when necessary. He lived minute to minute. Second to second. Had to, as a pilot. He knew when things were lining up to hit the target, and tonight, here, everything was lining up. He could see their interactions almost like a flight checklist before he took off.

Attraction? Check.

Shared values? Check.
Fun factor? Check.
Friendship? Check.
Partnership? Check.
Trust? Check.

So often on dates, he'd felt like he wasn't getting the full story. The woman across the table from him was too packaged. Like wearing dress whites on special occasions. Not the everyday wear of life. He hadn't liked the feeling of disconnect. But Ariel was straight up and straightforward.

Yes, she was something really special.

He glanced over as she started singing a Miley Cyrus song quietly from the passenger seat—rather badly, which only seemed more endearing—and couldn't help but join in.

When they arrived at the resort, she broke off singing, and he noted the reason immediately as he gazed through the windshield. The Three Tornadoes were bearing down on them from the lobby, dressed in yoga pants, attitude in every exaggerated catwalk stride.

Sherlock gave a rare whine. Dax couldn't blame him.

"Were they staking me out, sitting on the lobby's front porch?" She groaned and gave Sherlock's angular head a good rub. "God! You'd better get on to the cottage. I might be a while."

He didn't like the way they were scowling at her. Maybe it was all the garlic references—they hadn't stopped for any despite the joking—but he wondered if her sisters went to secret vampire meetings. "I'm not leaving you alone with them."

She turned her head, her mouth parted slightly. Yeah, even he was surprised by the sour note in his voice.

"I'll be all right, Dax." Her reassuring hand was as

heavy as her voice. "I've been handling them my whole life."

That didn't make it right. "But I'm here now, and we're in this together."

Because while he'd come here with a clear mission—to get his best friend married—his new mission was her.

Someone knocked on the window, making Ariel jump in her seat. "Hey, y'all!" Terry called, waving crazy hands. "Are you getting out?"

Tiffany stood at the end of the hood, hands at her hips. Okay, she wasn't so much the vampire society member as she was Frankenstein's Bride come to life, he decided, what with her face stretched with tension and her platinum blond hair big and crazy in the breeze. Her mask was clearly slipping, and he wondered if Rob had noticed. Then again, his friend had been drinking more than usual, and that meant he was using alcohol as escapism, a habit that went back to his teenage days when he'd run wild before deciding to up and join the military.

"Get out of there!" Tricia knocked on the window, making Sherlock give a loud ruff.

"Want to speed off and never come back?" he asked.

"You have no idea how bad," she told him with a sigh, "but duty calls." Opening the door, she said, "Hey there! How was dinner at the chophouse?"

"Good!" Tricia hugged her, practically hanging on to her, likely from drinking too much. "I know you hate eating there because it's so fancy, but you should have come. Mother told us all about your new wig. We want to see."

"Yes!" Terry echoed as Dax got out of the Bronco. "Mom says Dax picked it out."

"Yes, this we all can't wait to see." Tiffany was looking

down her nose at him. "I didn't know you were an expert on wigs, Dax."

"We naval captains have to be experts in all sorts of things." Inspiration struck. "Wigs are part of disguise training. If we're ever downed in enemy territory, we have to know how to blend in. So I was the perfect person to select it. Plus, I'm a guy. I know what looks good on a woman."

Tiffany hummed sensually. "Is that so?"

His gut immediately cramped like they'd eaten bad flounder, which wasn't true. No, this was what happened when your best friend's fiancée treated you like a piece of meat.

"I know I love a man with confidence," Terry finished in an equally flirty tone.

"Ariel," Tricia cried, "we've just *got* to see this wig."

She gave a heroic smile. "I need to let Sherlock do his business, and then I'll come find you. Will you be in the lodge?"

Tiffany strolled over and took her arm, her smile tight. "We'll come with you. You remember our deal, don't you?"

Her entire body went eerily still, making him wonder at the subtext. "Of course I do."

"Well, then, we'll come along. Don't want you to get lost in the dark."

"I have a flashlight." She grabbed Sherlock's leash as she let him out of the back and clipped it on. "Dax here had a long day. He hit every errand with me. You got my email update, right, Tiffany?"

"Yes." Her sister didn't let go as the group of women led Ariel along the winding path to their cottage, Dax following behind them. "I also got your suggestion for the watering cans for the sparklers, and I think that will work. Better than ugly tin cans."

"That's what I thought," Ariel replied, stopping when Sherlock paused to take care of things.

Her sisters' noses wrinkled up as she pulled a waste baggie out of her purse and cleaned up after her dog. Dax almost laughed. Bitchy *and* squeamish. He'd have to remember that. "I'll run ahead and grab the wig."

The faster these women saw it, the faster he and Ariel could move on to other things. Like some serious necking on the couch. Or wig-pong for kisses.

He sprinted the rest of the way to the cottage, hoping to grab the wig and be outside before they arrived. If those women got inside, he had a feeling they were going to be impossible to dislodge. God knows what they would ask Ariel next.

They arrived at the cottage as he came back down the front steps, wig box in hand. "Here you go. Prepare to be dazzled."

Tiffany rolled her eyes as she grabbed the box. Ariel stepped back until she was standing beside him. He rubbed her back, feeling the tension there. The Three Tornadoes clustered around as she opened it. Terry gasped as Tiffany held it up.

"But it's still too short!" Tricia complained.

Tiffany drilled Ariel with another bridezilla glare that would have made a puppy piddle. "The whole point of getting a wig was to have your hair be long for the wedding. Like ours. So you fit in with everyone in the photo."

Ariel straightened her shoulders. "But I don't fit in, Tiffany. Why pretend?"

All three women turned to her with shocked expressions before their gazes hardened. Dax stepped in and held out his hands. "Ladies, we tried on the long wig, and let me tell you the God's honest truth." Because he had to sell it and hard. "She looked like she'd been attacked by wolves. In a fantasy movie. It. Wasn't. Good."

Ariel sent him an endearing look, one that made him remember how sweetly she'd clutched him while he kissed her.

"She would break the camera with that wig," he continued, seeing Terry's and Tricia's expressions shifting. What he was saying was working. "Worse, her hair was so big and wild she'd stick out in the wedding photos. Tiffany and Rob are supposed to be the standouts, right?"

Tiffany put the wig back in the box and closed the lid. "Correct. Fine. If that was how it looked…"

"It was." Ariel took the box back. "Do you remember that horrible yellow gingham dress with the ruffles Mother put on me with the bonnet for Easter?"

Terry pressed a hand to her chest. "That bad?"

"Yeah," Ariel declared with a nod. "Nightmare quality."

"Thank God Dax was there to avert *that*," Tricia cried out. "Mother cut you out of the Easter photos that year when she was scrapbooking."

Stormy had cut her own daughter out of the photo? Jesus, who were these people?

"We'll make sure my hair and makeup people give you extra time," Tiffany announced.

Sherlock gave a low howl. Dax wondered if the mournful sound mirrored how Ariel was feeling. Extra time? He was getting pissed.

"Tiffany, I know you want everyone to look their best," Ariel said quietly, "but I've had my hair and makeup done at all the other weddings, and it's never worked. I look terrible."

Tricia put a companionable arm around Ariel's shoulder. "I have to agree. When I was putting the matting on my wedding photos to hang them in the family room, I was grateful Ariel had been at the end of the row of bridesmaids. The mat kinda covered her up."

Dax could feel his blood pressure rising.

Ariel walked over to Tiffany and laid a hand on her arm. "Let me do my own this time, and yes, please put me at the end of the line. Easier to cover me up."

"Or cut her out, if she doesn't look right," Terry added quickly with a hand to her mouth. "I hate to say so, but wedding photos are important. Sometimes drastic measures must be taken."

Dax bit the inside of his cheek. How dare they talk to Ariel like this! Or anyone else for that matter. Why did family think they could say things like this that they'd never say to strangers? Hell, then again, her family might. He desperately wanted to give these women a piece of his mind. "I can't imagine Ariel ever looking bad," he said tightly, gazing down at her. "She's one of the most beautiful women I've ever met."

"That's so...sweet." Tricia looked at Terry, as if confused. Terry shrugged.

Tiffany only smiled with so much fakeness, he was sure something inside her must be cracking. "Sweet, yes, but you've spent a lot of years on a carrier with mostly men, so you're no expert, Dax."

He stared her down, unable to keep his outright dislike of her and everything she stood for out of his gaze. She only stared back with flinty, feminine arrogance.

"I have some more wedding things to take care of tonight," Ariel broke in, crossing to them and bussing cheeks with each sister. "I'll email you an update in the morning, Tiffany. Good night."

Turning from them, she took Dax's arm and walked him

up the porch steps. Sherlock ran after them—fleeing the scene, Dax imagined, because how did anyone take that kind of bullshit?

He shut the door and locked it, then made sure to close every curtain and blind. The last thing they needed was another Peeping Tom moment. Sherlock plopped down beside the fireplace on his makeshift bed. Dax looked over at Ariel, standing still as stone. "You all right?"

"I'm used to it." She rubbed her forehead however, her shoulders slumping. "Your bit about the wig was terrific, though. I almost bought it."

"They're a hard sell, your sisters." Satisfied they had complete privacy, even if those little *Lord of the Flies* brats had seen them come back, he walked over and put his arms around her. "I wanted to give them a piece of my mind for talking to you like that."

"I try not to take it personally. Barbie was perfect, and even she got her hair cut by them and was re-accessorized constantly. She was never good enough. How could I ever hope to be?"

When she gestured to herself, Dax's heart broke. "Ariel, I never imagined people being so mean. Especially to family. They're your sisters, and don't tell me the half makes a difference. It's cruel."

She wrung her hands together before letting them fall to her sides. "And yet, that's how it's always been. It's not like they don't love me. They just don't like me."

Her sigh was harsh, and Dax wished he'd never brought it up.

"The worst part is that I don't like them either." She patted Sherlock when he rose and walked over to her. "I can remember fun times together when we were younger. Back then, I think Mother was trying to get us to love her, but then something broke inside her, and she stopped trying. To a kid it was a joy ride. Giant popcorn fountains for snow as a kid at Christmas. A birthday with pet rescue puppies. Disney Princess days."

He couldn't imagine any of that now. At the same time, he recalled Rob telling him about all the stuff he'd done with Tiffany—over-the-top picnics, race car night, and a last-minute trip to Vegas. She'd clearly learned at her mother's knee.

"They're diabolically fun when they want to be. That's their charm and the reason I felt lucky to be their sister. Everyone wanted to be their friend. All my life, I've wanted to be one of them. But every time I get invited to join them—like now—it's never the kind of good time I hope for, and part of me doesn't know what to do."

She lifted those big baby blues to him, and his heart clutched at the agony he saw there.

"It's not like you can quit your family," she added softly. "They're the only people who can't turn away from you, right? Maybe families are like gasoline tanks, and when your relationship with them runs low, things are just harder."

There were a million retorts on the tip of his tongue, like how a car could run the same on the top part of the tank as at the bottom. Maybe the problem was her sisters syphoning off gas from her tank and draining her. Or maybe no one was contributing to the family tank, so it was going dry. His family's tank was healthy because everyone contributed.

"You're quiet." She scanned his face. "Have I made you uncomfortable?"

He bit his lip. Should he say it? Fuck it. He couldn't stop himself. "No. I hope you won't think I've gone too far saying this, but your family seems to have already turned away from you, calling you bad things like that. Ariel, they've cut you out of *family* photos. If that's not turning away from someone, I don't know what is."

She pursed her lips, obviously fighting emotion. He didn't know what to do. He started by pulling her to his chest and rubbing her back.

"I hear what you're saying, and God knows, I've gone over this a million times. Jeffrey's concluded no family is perfect and you make the best of what you have while getting professional help. And using alcohol when necessary. He's not exactly accepted either, but being gay, he likes to say it's his cross to bear. He's not accepted a lot of places."

If that didn't make him grit his teeth. He'd never understood why race, sex, or labels mattered. People were people. Good and bad. And everyone deserved at the minimum a basic level of respect. "Well, I can't wait to meet Jeffrey. What do you want to do now? Watch *A Fish Called Wanda* or something else? Wig-pong?"

He rubbed her back briskly, trying to infuse good feelings back into her. But she stayed rigid in his arms.

"I was hoping we'd come back here and make out more," she confessed, "and I hate that I'm not in the mood now. I feel like they've ruined something else for me. Something special."

He tipped her head up and caressed her cheek. "You're entitled to your bad mood. But I don't think you should go to bed like this. I'd like to help you feel better. If you'll let me."

Because she had to want it. Despite having the fix-it gene, he knew a person had to make the choice. Be responsible for themselves and their emotions. He waited to see what she would do.

When she made a face at him, crossing her eyes, he smiled in relief. "I like that look on you." He gave her one right back, scrunching his face up so tightly he felt like his eyes might get stuck that way. "What about this?"

"I'd keep a photo of you making that face." She pressed a soft kiss to his chest. "Heck, I'd make it the screen saver on my phone."

He felt like he had leaped out of an airplane, tumbling down through the air—the best sensation on earth other than being in the cockpit. "How about we take one together? Because I want to put it on my phone too."

She gave him a considering look. "Talk like that only makes me like you more, and Dax... I already like you a hell of a lot."

He tapped her nose because kissing her again didn't feel on the table quite yet. "Ditto."

"I like a man with brevity." She smiled more easily and left him to grab her phone before pressing close to him. "Okay. Give me your best face. One, two, three. Cheese!"

Stretching his mouth wide and tipping his head to the right, he was sure he'd delivered. She went with strongly clenched features and an open mouth to the left. After she took the photo, she lifted it so both of them could see.

"Hideous!" she cried with delight. "I love it! High five."

He smacked his hand to hers as he watched her put it as her screen saver. Speaking in a British accent in the hopes it would make her laugh, he said, "Text it to me. I need that, Elizabeth. Its immortal quality will always speak to me."

"That's a terrible accent," she said as she sent it to him. She was laughing—a miracle. He'd roll out a dozen awful accents if they'd make her laugh. "When did Stephan become British?"

He felt his phone vibrate in his pants and dug it out. His

mood deflated a bit, seeing no text from Rob. He shouldn't be surprised. It was weird between them right now, and they both knew it. "Stephan was imitating that British guy all you chicks love in that Jane Austen flick. What's it called? *Pride and Penetration?*"

That had her erupting in gales of laughter. "That's a good one. You're thinking of a different version of the movie. I think we'll go with the Keira Knightley version. Yes, you know what? Good call. I think that's our movie choice tonight."

He groaned. "Oh, no! You're not going to do that to poor ol' Stephan."

She gave a sexy saunter as she walked over to the entertainment center. "You bet I am."

He didn't argue, and that's when he knew for sure.

He'd fallen for her but good.

NINE

Ariel groaned as she looked at her phone calendar, still tucked in bed. God, how could it only be Monday? And why did family time seem to take so much longer? It was like all the baggage everyone was carrying ground time to a freaking halt.

She didn't know how she was going to make it to the wedding, let alone through it.

Then she heard someone moving around in the hallway, clearly trying to be quiet, but there were a couple of squeaky floorboards, and he'd stepped on one.

The thought of Dax was like a fire burst or a bite of saltwater taffy on a perfect summer day.

"Good morning, sunshine!" she called out, feeling the weight of eternity lift as she flung off the covers and flew out of bed, opening the door. "How about chicken and waffles to start the day?"

He leaned against her doorjamb, his shoulders taking up the whole space. His Navy T-shirt was damp with sweat, suggesting he'd just returned from a run. He looked hot and vital and smelled like man, nature, and spice. Another bonus. He hadn't shaved yet, and goodness, did he look good enough to eat. Add in some maple syrup, and she'd never want to stop.

"Good morning to you too," he answered with a grin, "and that sounds perfect. I need to shower. Five minutes?"

"Terrific." She tugged his shirt into her hands and pulled him close until his head was inches above hers. "Also...thank you for last night. I know it wasn't *Pride and the Pickle Jar*."

His deep rumbling laughter had her bare toes curling. "Did I say that? Hmm... Mine involved penetration, I believe. Yours sounds like a mystery by Agatha Christie."

Penetration. That might be the sexiest word in the entire English language, she decided, breathless now.

"Oh, honey." She swatted his chest, feeling happy and daring. "Come here and give me a proper good morning."

He leaned down as she rose up onto her tippy-toes. When their mouths met, she sighed in delight. *Yes. This.* Time stood still for another reason this time, and the eternity in this kiss was something she didn't want to end.

When he lifted his head, he was grinning. His green eyes twinkled with flirtation, a really good look on him. "You're peppy this morning. I like it. See you in a few."

With one last swift kiss, he headed off toward his room, whistling. She closed the door and leaned back against it. Closing her eyes, she took in the moment. The feel of his lips moving over hers. The way she could taste his desire for her and his happiness at seeing her. She ran her fingers over her still-tingly lips.

They were going to have a good day.

She was not going to let her family mess this up.

As she dressed, she checked her texts. Her mother had texted that she and the Three Tornadoes were going to the beach for the day with the boys while the men went golfing. Which meant they'd be going to her grandmother's house.

Her stomach flipped.

She pressed her hand to it. That was why she was doing this. Forget the insults and the gas tank analogies—God, what had she been thinking? She needed to focus and do her job. Stop letting anything else bother her. Because Tiffany's reminder about their *deal* last night had chilled her to the core.

With that pep talk done, she went to take Sherlock out, only to have him stand unmoving beside the fireplace.

"Oh, Dax let you out, didn't he?" She gave her dog an affectionate rubdown as she noted he'd had his breakfast too. "Isn't that nice? We like him, don't we, boy?"

He gave a resounding ruff before she retraced her steps to her room and grabbed her things. Dax came out of his room as she emerged.

"You look nice." His drawl was as lazy as the once-over he gave her, speeding up her heart.

"You're not too bad yourself," she quipped, knowing he was checking out her legs.

Yes, she was wearing the same jean skirt as yesterday, but she didn't think he'd mind. She wanted to look a little sexier, and shorts weren't going to cut it.

"So before we leave, I have something very important to tell you."

He stilled and clasped his hands, immediately serious. "All right."

She bit the inside of her cheek to hide her smile. "Nothing to worry about, but the place I am taking you to will ruin you for chicken and waffles forever. I need to know if you're good with that."

His chortle was spontaneous and short-lived. "Is that all? Elizabeth, you had me concerned."

She waved a hand in the air and headed toward the door. "We're not doing 'concerned' today. We're taking the day off on that one. And you're driving."

"Hallelujah. Because we can outrun your family faster in my Bronco."

Still, she opened the door a crack and peeked out, making sure no one in her family was waiting on the front porch.

"Is the coast clear?" His enticing whisper tickled her ear.

"Yeah." God help her, she could feel her knees going weak in relief. Or was that Dax's hot breath against the side of her neck?

"Whew!" He was nuzzling her in the most moan-inducing way. "I was afraid I was going to have to ignore the law and drive my Bronco onto the beach so I could pick you up out back."

"You'd do that for me?" She turned her head and patted his cheek sweetly as he nodded with a lazy grin. "Come on. We're still going to need to run for it."

She was out the door in a flash, Sherlock racing ahead of her. Dax's pursuit sounded in her ears, kicking up her heart rate. Another fun moment. They were stacking them up like blocks in Jenga.

He beat her to her car door and opened it for her grandly. "If I may..."

"You may indeed." She felt the compulsion to kiss his cheek, so she leaned over and did it before he could close the door. When he returned the gesture, she clasped his face in her hands and gave it her all. He was groaning when he broke free, and she had trouble fitting her seat belt into the buckle.

After running around to his side, he had them on their way.

When they entered her favorite place, Sherlock at her side, the three college-aged employees chatting behind the hostess station barely said hello. Usually when you entered a place in Charleston, you heard, "Welcome. We're happy to have you. How y'all doing?"

She turned to Dax as one of the girls led them upstairs to their table. "Do I have a dark cloud over me?" she whispered.

"No. That's all her, honey."

Her smile was forced as the server seated them, but the waiter appeared with a smile and a welcome for everyone, including Sherlock. He wasn't a college student, and when she asked, he said he was Charleston born and raised, which had her thinking maybe the college girls didn't understand Charleston was all about hospitality. But surely this would have been mentioned in their training.

She knew her grandma had strong views about outsiders moving in and not getting into the "spirit" of things, but seeing the lack of hospitality made her sad. She planned to make a home here. She wanted to feel that spirit as much as she gave it.

"You're frowning." Dax leaned across the table after the server left with their order, the scent of his understated cologne making her olfactory senses cheer at least. "Hey... Do we need to start bringing your flask with us?"

"Now that's an idea..." He'd love her garter flask, and they were at the point where she'd let him reach under her skirt and find it. "Maybe we should have a mimosa."

An indulgent smile played across his lips. "You can. Even if I weren't driving, that's too sweet for me."

Right. Guys drinking mimosas was rare, except for Jeffrey, who adored them. But Dax did groan when he took his first bite of chicken and waffles, and that deep sound pinged something low in her belly.

She wanted him groaning like that with *her*. "Good?"

"You're right." He closed his eyes in pure bliss, so manly, she wanted to leap across the table between them and launch herself at him. "I'm ruined for them elsewhere."

Or he could come back here with her…

Was it crazy to start hoping he might actually want to relocate here? Yeah, but crazy ran in the family. "Another thing to love about Charleston."

Seed thrown down.

"Honey, you're the best thing about Charleston. Chicken and waffles are like here." She watched as he set a reasonably high bar in the air before he raised his hand over his head. "You're here."

Her heart fluttered. "That's mighty high praise. I'd say the same about you, and I really love me some chicken and waffles."

The way his mouth curved as he forked another bite had her clenching her thighs. Goodness, this man was hot and she wanted him like a plate of chicken and waffles. With butter and syrup on top.

"You're not eating."

The implication was in the rough edge of his voice. *You're watching.*

Her inner reply was immediate. *Yes, Captain Hotpants, I am.*

"I'm anticipating." She drew out the words, enjoying

the way his green eyes sparked with heat. "I know the taste is going to be out of this world."

He seemed to lick his lips as he finished chewing before tearing off the end of another chicken tender and holding it out to her. "You're damn right it's the best you're ever going to have. I guarantee it."

Good Lord! She was going to die right here. Leaning forward, she let him feed her, not breaking their stare once. The green in his eyes darkened from the heat he found in her gaze, and she was grateful she had a full water glass because once she finished chewing, she was going to be downing half of it and crunching some ice cubes to cool down.

By the time they finished their meal, she was sure her face and neck were flushed. Sherlock was even looking at her oddly with his expressive eyes. She wanted to explain. *I'm in heat. For this man. You remember what mating season feels like, right, buddy?*

After Dax paid the check, his hand settled on the low right side of her back. Close to her waist. His hand was hot. She was glad she wasn't alone.

When he opened the door and helped her into her seat, he leaned in. "Excuse me, but I can't wait another minute."

His mouth covered hers, hot and searching. She lifted her hand and threaded it through his sandy hair. She had the taste of maple and fried chicken along with Dax in her mouth. And when his tongue slid through the seam of her lips and rubbed against hers, she gave in to a soul-deep groan.

He answered, the reverberation rolling through her, as he pressed her back into the seat. His mouth slanted over hers, changing the angle, making things hotter until he was pulling back, breathing hard. "We're in the middle of a parking lot."

"Kissing in public is probably against the law," she replied hoarsely with a laugh. "I think spitting is still illegal for women. You know those old laws."

"Damn, because I'm a rule follower." His mouth looked absolutely luscious when he grinned. "Law-abiding citizen and all. Although I'm relieved to know they temper women's spitting, I won't lie."

She swatted him. "Men are the gross spitters with all that..." Her attempt to mimic a man coughing up a loogie made him chortle.

"You're terrible at that. Here, let me show you."

"No!" She put her hands on his shoulders, like that would stop him.

They both started laughing so hard they were wheezing. A car pulling into the space a couple of cars down had them sobering up. Dax tucked her into her seat, fixing her seat belt for her.

She hissed as his hand slid across her belly in a sexy caress. "Stop that! I'm so hot I might..."

His brows edged up and a satisfied smirk appeared on his face. "Good to know I'm not alone."

With that, he walked around to his side and let himself in. "Where to next?"

He gave her the same attention he would a fellow poker player, watching for a tell. Intense. Connected. All-consuming. She liked it. Men who listened were sexy. She'd never had her head turned by a pretty face alone.

She thought about her list, telling herself she should have brought a to-go cup of ice water with her. "We're heading to Home Depot."

When he took out his phone to plug in the directions,

he smiled at the photo of them. "Awesome! Now that's my kind of place."

"Excellent!" She kicked her feet out with the hope the action might release some of her trapped sexual tension. "Because I'll need you to haul a few things."

A lock of his sandy hair flopped onto his wide forehead as he turned and flexed his incredible forearm. "Me and my muscles are entirely at your disposal."

Her already heated blood turned white-hot. "Good, because we need to buy some sand."

"Sand?"

Yeah, that's what she'd thought when she'd first read about it. "Yes, because it might be windy, and we'll need to anchor the outside flower arrangements so they won't topple over."

He pulled out of the parking lot. "The details you're juggling blow my mind."

Indeed.

They bought sand, probably her favorite errand of the day because it involved watching Dax's muscles flex. Yum! And he had no trouble throwing it over his shoulder. Goodness, that man was strong. He didn't seem to mind it either.

When they went to the printer, though, Dax started tapping his foot on the floor. Boredom, she knew, but they had to go over every printed place card and sign to make sure everything was correct. Even her eyes were crossing as she studied the list. The truth was he didn't need to accompany her to all her errands. They were having such a good time together, but even she had to call it.

"Why don't you head back to the resort?" she asked when the woman went for another round of beverages.

He put his hands on his thighs, looking very manly in

the pale green office with fake orchids adorning the gold-leafed tables. Like a large jungle cat let loose in a tea parlor. "If you can take it, so can I."

Oh, she wanted to tell him how she could take it...

He seemed to know because his sandy brows rose, but then the woman was returning, clearing her throat as if she knew something was going on.

The moment didn't last long. She began checking her names, as did Dax, and was grateful they only caught three errors. Except they needed to wait for those to be reprinted, of course.

By the time they were finished and headed back to the resort, Ariel had a low-grade headache. "All I want is a margarita," she practically moaned.

He had his arm resting on the open window, and the breeze felt good. "Well, I need a whiskey, and I *never* need a drink. Why in the hell do people do this?"

"Get married?"

He choked before laughing. "No, this! The whole printed cards and sandbags for flowers shit."

She tried to remember the reasons she recited to herself when the spreadsheets seemed to blur and the budget lines made her eyes widen. "Beauty. Immortality. Giving themselves and their guests a day to remember fondly."

"I would think remembering your wedding day would be pretty easy." The way the wind ruffled his sandy hair was downright sexy as he glanced over. "The moment you first wake up and know you're getting married today. The first glance of her coming down the aisle in her wedding dress, looking so beautiful she takes your breath away. The way her eyes soften when you put your ring on her finger and say your vows to each other. The first kiss that seems so new and different, even though you've done it a million times. And then holding her hand as you smile at your friends and family because they know you're the luckiest man in the world because now she's yours forever."

She fell back against her seat, stunned. He thought that? She turned to him. "Oh. My. God. You're totally a romantic."

His brows slammed together. "No, I'm not."

"You are!" She watched him shrug and ruefully shake his head. "See—I knew you'd watched *Pride and Prejudice* before!"

"That was below the belt, Elizabeth." His brows drew together suspiciously. "Jesus, did you pick that name because of Elizabeth Bennet?"

"Not consciously." She rolled her window down and let the fresh air cool her head. "Trust me, the last man who'd entice me is a pompous ass like Darcy is in the beginning. I wouldn't stick around to see if there was a nice guy underneath it all. That's why I liked you right away, Captain Hotpants. From the minute I got your text and looked you up, I knew you were a great guy."

And hearing him talk about his wedding day like that had lit a new longing within her. She wanted the man she married to feel like that on their wedding day. About her. If she ever found someone she wanted to walk down the aisle toward...

"Let's change the subject, shall we?" He pulled into the parking lot at the resort and cut the engine. "I'm just a regular guy who does his duty to his country and loves his family. People like to make us out to be heroes, but all it involves is showing up. That's what a true hero does."

With that statement—another that left her reeling—he exited the vehicle and came around to open her door. She put her hand on his meaty arm as she alighted from the car. She could tell he didn't want to meet her eyes. He was embarrassed, which only made him more endearing. "I feel like that when people call me a hero too. I'm not sure how Sherlock feels."

He snorted at that.

"But I agree with you about showing up. However, I do want to insist on one thing."

"What is it?" he asked, putting his hand on the car near her head.

"You *are* a great guy." When he rolled his eyes, she tugged on his T-shirt. "For that I want to thank you. I needed someone like you to remind me why people do things like this."

Now she was a little embarrassed herself, so she ducked under his arm and opened the back door for Sherlock. He jumped out after she clipped on his leash. Her nephews were chasing each other with bloodcurdling cries, spraying each other with water guns. When they saw her coming, they headed her way.

She held up a hand. "Don't you dare."

"What she said." Dax suddenly pushed her behind him. "I'll toss all of you in the ocean, and that's a promise."

Marshall extended his gun toward them but didn't fire. Ripp ran off along with the rest of the boys. After a flinty stare-down, Marshall turned and followed.

"He's an angry kid," Dax commented as they continued their way to the cottage.

"I remember feeling that way, but it doesn't justify some of his actions." She let herself inside after Sherlock raced in and held open the door for him this time, aware he was watching her.

When she turned the lock, his hands were on her shoulders. "I hope you don't mind, but I need your mouth right now."

She lifted onto her toes and pulled his head down. The first kiss rocked her back into the door. His body pressed into her as the kiss went wild. The wall of heat pressed against her had her moaning into his mouth. This was no time for discovering or feeling things out. After the desire that had blossomed between them today, they were both ravenous. She opened her mouth when he pressed in deep and rubbed her tongue against his. Her hands went to his waist and slid under his T-shirt. The feel of his hot, sculpted muscles had her heartbeat pounding in her ears.

"God, Ariel," he whispered, kissing her neck softly.

She could feel another moan at the back of her throat, the loud kind, the kind that would travel across distances.

Grabbing his hand, she dragged him deeper into the house. When she was at the entrance to her bedroom, she stopped. Dax halted beside her and looked at her, breathing hard now. His green eyes were dark with need. She tuned in for a moment.

Her heart already knew the answer.

"I know it's early, but I want you." She could feel a little tinge of vulnerability creep into her, likely from the cracks in her heart that had come from past hurts and disappointments.

"I want you too." His voice was a shade deeper but filled with the certainty she'd come to expect from him. "It might be early, but time doesn't seem to matter sometimes. You know when something is right, and this is more than right. It's perfect. But I want you to be sure."

She touched his jaw, feeling the stubble there, wanting it against her skin. "I'm sure. I know when something is right too, Dax. Come to bed with me."

He took her hand and led her inside, locking the door with a flirtatious wink before closing the blinds. There was still light seeping into the room, and she had no trouble seeing the heat in his eyes as he stripped off his T-shirt and kept coming. She couldn't take her eyes off the hard line of his chest, decked out with ridges of muscles that flowed into washboard abs. God, he was beautiful, and right now he was all hers.

When he reached her, he picked her up in his arms and lowered his mouth to hers. They kissed, taking it slower this time, knowing they'd get where they'd wanted to go all along.

He slid his hands under her shirt, caressing the skin at her waist, making her arch into his touch, before seeking her breasts. She wanted to feel his hands on her, so she reached back and unsnapped her bra. He helped her at the last moment before running a smooth finger around her side until he reached her breast. Giving it a slow caress, he watched her, and she could see the kindness, the arousal, and the thing that made him Dax. There was goodness and awareness and a desire to connect with her as much as touch her, and she fell deeper under his spell.

"You are so beautiful, Ariel."

All the other words she'd been called rose up in her mind, ones that were anything but beautiful. She hated that, and she lowered her head, trying to force them back. He only tipped her chin up and kissed her slowly.

"Don't listen to that chatter in your head. Listen to me. I know what I'm talking about. You. Are. Beautiful. I don't think you know how much."

She ducked her head, kissing his chest, trying to take his words into her, because they were precious, and now they were hers.

"Look at me now."

She looked up and found his warm gaze resting on her. When he touched her cheek, she could almost hear him saying the words to her. *You're beautiful.* When he touched her neck, the words were there too. *You're beautiful.*

But it was when he tucked her short hair behind her ears and gave her a heart-melting smile that she finally believed it. A profound calm filled her, running through her already heated blood. She wasn't feeling any urgency now. There was desire, yes, but also peace she'd never known with anyone else.

When his hand explored her more deeply, she arched into him, closing her eyes, giving herself up to the moment. When he finally laid her down on the bed and helped her off with her shirt and the rest of her bra, she was ready for the skin-to-skin embrace. The heat of it had them both groaning as they pressed together. He dipped his head to press soft kisses to her neck and shoulder while she gripped the hard muscles of his back.

His hands slid under her skirt, palming her butt. She tilted her hips toward him, loving the feel of his strong, warm hand. She was unable to smother the gut-wrenching groan that fell from her lips. He teased the edges of her panties, making her open wider for him. Running his fingers along her core, he gave her an open-mouthed kiss that left her shaking.

Needing more, she popped the button to her jean skirt and pushed it down with help from him. It dropped onto the floor, and he rose to strip off his shorts before pulling out his wallet and drawing out a condom.

She smiled like a woman who knew she was about to be well satisfied. "Good idea. I was getting there."

He threw it on the bed and pulled her onto his lap, his

arousal making her body clench with need. "Baby, we're already there."

The husky way he said that had her grabbing his nape and pulling him down for another kiss. They rubbed. They took. They gave. They whispered incoherent things to each other she wasn't sure either of them could make out but they still somehow both understood.

His skin was so hot, but she only wanted more, and when he finally slid his fingers toward her core under her panties, she gave a loud cry and opened to him. His first touch held a certainty, a knowing, and she pressed into it, wanting more. He took her there easily the first time, and she was panting when she finally opened her eyes.

He was leaning over her on his elbow, his green eyes smoldering. "Okay?"

"Better than okay." Her voice was hushed and low, and she smiled at the realization that she sounded rather sexy. "Pretty perfect actually, Stephan."

He leaned down and kissed her slowly, his tongue dancing lightly before he leaned back. "Oh, Elizabeth. We've barely started. Let me show you."

Pushing her onto her back, he slid her panties down her legs, tossing those aside too. She had no vulnerability now as he studied her, widening her so he could give her a deeper caress. One finger. Two. Soon she was lost in a sea of sensation. Her eyes closed again, only to open wide when she felt the first press of his hot, wet mouth on her core.

"Oh, God!"

"That's right. Come for me, baby."

She did. And then she did again when he slid his tongue deeper inside her. Making her keen and press up into his hot, clever mouth.

"Dax!"

"Right here."

She reached out blindly and found a shoulder. "Condom. Now."

"Yes, ma'am," he drawled roughly.

Wanting to touch him, she rose onto her elbow and gave him a feather-like caress. He was beautiful and he was hot and hard and silky to the touch. He covered her hand with his own and then drew it away so he could fit the condom on.

"Have mercy, honey. I've been like this most of the day. All I've wanted is you. Let's *try* and take it slow the first time."

That had her snorting out a laugh. "Okay. We can try, but I can't make any promises."

He covered her and pressed into her with the same careful, methodical deliberation she expected made him a great pilot. When he was seated to the hilt, they were both breathing hard. Their eyes met. Their hands reached for each other at the same time, their fingers curling around each other.

"Ariel."

She knew it was a benediction, and it made her heart pulse with feeling. Yes, this man. Right now. *"Dax."*

"You're perfect."

His hands tightened on hers as he withdrew slowly and thrust again, setting the pace. She could feel her muscles clenching around him and knew it was destroying him, but he set his jaw and kept that delicious, pulse-quickening rhythm until she thrust up hard to him.

"More. I need more."

His forehead pressed to hers, their sweat mingling. "God, so do I."

And then he was thrusting hard and deep, making them both groan and moan and give in to their full desire. He pistoned his hips and she met him the whole way. When she could feel herself screaming for release, she grabbed his hands tightly and took him under with her.

She heard his shout along with her string of cries as she came and came and came, the sensations taking her to a place she'd never been. Her heart glowed. Everything pulsed. There was peace and a warmth inside her that she never thought would end.

She was aware of him pulling them onto their sides and moving for a moment before he fitted his body back to hers, woven together. She couldn't open her eyes, but she didn't want to leave this place yet. It was complete. A place where there was everything she'd ever wanted. No thoughts. No worries. No fears.

When she felt a tender kiss at her neck, she nuzzled him back to let him know she was there with him. Her heart continued to pound, but slower now. She could breathe deeper. She could open her eyes. He was there, waiting for her, the light in his green eyes dazzling.

"Hey," was all he said, and yet it contained everything.

"Hey, yourself," she answered, feeling an answering smile touch her lips.

He leaned in and kissed her, and she him, and it was just as slow and smooth as the first part of their joining.

When he leaned back and pulled her onto his chest, she knew he'd shifted from repletion to joy. "So that was pretty awesome... You remember my bar for you earlier with the chicken and waffles. Well, honey, I'd have to fly my plane up to the highest stratosphere I could find to show you where you stand now. Ariel..."

When he met her gaze again, his smile shifted. The light in his eyes grew brighter. She touched his jaw.

"Yeah..."

He grinned. "I'm good with a profound 'yeah.'"

Funny. So was she.

TEN

Waking up with Ariel was up there with getting his wings.

Dax was good with that. Sex for him had always been a meter. When it was really great with someone, it foretold good things. And so forth...

With Ariel, he'd never burned hotter. Never come harder. Never felt such peace and happiness afterward.

That last part had him smiling. His parents had talked about that kind of thing a time or two when they'd first told him about sex, saying the emotional side was as important as the physical connection, and when the two were both out of the park, you knew you had a winner.

He tucked Ariel's short, curly hair back from her face. She was sleeping on her stomach, mostly on top of him. She wasn't a spooner so much as she was a face-to-face kind of girl. They'd taken each other again twice more after that first time, and both times they'd peered into each other's eyes. The intimacy had been off the charts, but he wasn't freaked. Nope. He was looking forward to her waking up, showing him those beautiful baby blues he was beginning to set his day by.

He couldn't wait for her to get up.

Funny how quickly she had become part of his routine. He liked knowing she was in the cottage with him and that he'd see her before he went to sleep and when he awoke. He liked knowing she'd be there when he got back from his run, working on her phone, and that she'd look up and smile.

This morning, he hoped she would stretch and then languidly smile as she felt him beside her. Open her eyes with a little smoke in them. Because he wanted to make love to her again, and she'd be feeling that. His desire. The heat between them. The skin-on-skin friction.

Hot. As. Fuck.

Yeah, he was the luckiest guy out there.

He thought about Sherlock and wondered about letting him out. The bedside alarm clock said they'd slept in; it was 7:07 a.m. He never slept that late usually. Good sex would do that to you. When she gave a little chuckle snore, he realized she was still out. He decided to slide out of bed, put some shorts on, and see to Sherlock.

When the dog spotted him coming, he padded to the door immediately. "Yeah, I thought so. Look at me taking care of you while your mistress sleeps."

Clipping on the leash, he inclined his head to the back door that led to the screen porch with steps down to the beach. He didn't want to encounter anyone this morning. Sherlock followed as Dax grabbed his phone, and they stopped when they reached the sand. Dax didn't like the dread he felt when he saw Rob's text.

ROB

> You up, dipshit? I'm going for a run. 🏃, Heard you and Ariel went out for dinner alone last night.

> Since you didn't answer, I'll assume you aren't up. Ran by the house. Closed up tighter than Rambo's headband. Which means you got lucky. This is me being pissed. 😠

Dax stared out at the ocean. He wanted to text his friend back a simple *WTF*, but that didn't seem like a great idea. Sherlock had handled business and was standing tall, his sad expressive eyes looking up at Dax.

"Any idea why friends can up and become assholes?" Sherlock only continued to stare at him. "No? Me either, buddy. What to say. What to say. Okay, I've got it."

> I'm up now. You need something, princess? Because I hauled a buttload of sand for your wedding yesterday and I need a good shoulder rub.

His friend's response was immediate.

ROB

Dax didn't laugh, but he was glad for the smile he felt touch his lips. "Now that's how best friends talk to each other."

He would ignore Rob's asshole comments about Ariel. Unless they got out of line. He would finish his duties as best man and get out of this looney bin.

The thought blindsided him. He didn't want to leave Ariel. Not yet. Maybe not at all. Yeah, they'd only just met, but he wanted to see where things could go. He needed to think about making some plans.

With that in mind, he decided to text his new boss, former Naval Captain Jim Kennedy. While Dax's general discharge had been accepted, he was still going through the routing process. That was the Navy for you. Discharge could take anywhere from thirty days to six months. As of today, he was technically at one month out. He appreciated Jim's flexibility, but as a former naval officer, he knew the deal. He had no trouble waiting for good pilots.

> Hey Jim! Checking in from Charleston. Ever been? So far so good. Look, I haven't checked the airport out but wanted to add this to my list of possible plunk-down sites. I know you wanted my thoughts.

He saw ellipses right away and counted himself lucky.

JIM

> Know Charleston well. My wife's family is from there. Good airport. Good people. My wife's sister is in real estate if you're looking to rent or buy. She'd take good care of you. Just saying. Have a good time. Check in when you hear back from those paper pushers. I don't miss that one bit.

Dax lowered his phone in a daze and glanced down at Sherlock. "Well, I'll be damned. My new boss' sister-in-law is in real estate! How lucky can one guy be?"

"Pretty lucky," he heard a familiar voice say. "I heard you got laid last night."

He spun around. Ariel was walking toward him in nothing but little denim shorts and a white tank top, her hair mussed, her lips a little swollen. "I did, and it was pretty spectacular. Good morning to you too. Don't you look absolutely delicious."

She struck a pose, her bare feet already coated with fine sand. "Maybe not the chicken and waffles of your dreams but at least blueberry pancakes."

Sneaking a quick hand around her waist, he pulled her against him and kissed her soundly before gentling the touch. "Do I need to show you the Ariel bar again?" he whispered huskily. "I'd have to stand on a ladder after last night."

"A stepladder, right?" She had both her arms wrapped around him, her cheeky smile contagious. "Because it *was* really good."

He chuckled naughtily. "It surely was, and it's going to be really good again. Beat you back to the house."

She gave him a playful shove and started running. "Not if I beat you first."

She beat him, but he didn't care. In the end, they both won.

After they'd showered together, enjoying a new place in the house, he made them some coffee. They were both in the kitchen when someone pounded on the door.

Wincing, she ducked low in her chair. "Do you think we can pretend we aren't here? Is it terrible to say that?"

"I'm thinking the same thing, but I have a feeling they aren't going to stop." The pounding grew more insistent, so he headed to the door. "I can tell them you're still asleep."

"They'll never believe you. I never sleep in."

"Me either." He sent her a wink. "Unless there's good cause. All right, put on your game face and let's continue with our mission."

She batted her eyelashes at him. "I really like it when

you go all naval commander with me. Should I say, *yes sir* too?"

He puffed out a laugh. "Maybe later. On three. One. Two. Three."

With a flourish, he opened the door. Tricia stood on the porch, breathing hard, her strawberry blond hair as wild as Medusa's snakes.

"Where's Ariel? We have a crisis. I need her. Right now."

Ariel came running. "What's wrong, Tricia?"

"Tiffany can't fit into her wedding dress," she blurted out.

Shit. That can't be good.

Dax stepped out of the way as Ariel rushed onto the porch. "I thought you were going to the beach. Never mind. What happened?"

"We don't know!" Tricia wrenched her hands. "Tiffany decided she wanted to try it on before it went out for pressing and steaming. When it didn't fit, she came running from the bridal cottage. We don't know how this could have happened. She's been working out. She's been on a strict diet. No carbs or sweets."

Dax uncharitably thought tequila clearly wasn't on the list.

"Okay, we'll figure something out." Ariel spun around and looked weakly at him like she had no clue what to do.

"Maybe someone can alter it?" he suggested.

"Not if she can't fit into it!" Tricia threw her hands up in the air. "It's the first sign of doom, Ariel. Tiffany is beside herself."

Okay, that he could help with. "Have you found Rob? He's good in a crisis."

Tricia gaped at him and threw her hair over her

shoulder with a giant huff. "Rob cannot know about this! He's not even supposed to see her in her wedding dress before the wedding."

But if she couldn't fit into it, he wouldn't see her in it at all, would he? But that insight probably wouldn't be welcome.

Ariel ran a hand over her brow. "Tricia, let me grab my wedding master. I'll meet you."

"We're at the bridal cottage. Your old place."

He couldn't help but think it seemed fitting revenge for stealing it from her in the first place. Not that Dax wasn't happy with how it had worked out, but boy, was he pissed at her sisters for the way they treated her. Especially since they leaned on her whenever there was a crisis.

Tricia ran off. Ariel rushed inside. "God, it's happening again. I swear. I'm a fully functioning adult with common sense, but this kind of stuff makes me believe the wedding curse is real."

She was breathing shallowly, so he held out his hands to her. "What can I do to help?"

She rubbed Sherlock's head when he pressed his face to her side. "Can you watch Sherlock for me?"

"Happy to."

"Thanks. God! What a disaster. Maybe we really do need garlic."

She meant it as part of their ongoing joke, but hell, why not? "I'll pick up every bulb I can find."

A hoarse laugh sounded like it had been squeezed out of her throat. "You'll laugh but I saw someone make garlic into a wedding wreath. They were Italian and talked about garlic being part of the heart of the home. Like that scene in *It's a Wonderful Life* where Jimmy Stewart and Donna Reed's characters give their new tenants salt and bread to bless their homes. God, I'm not making any sense."

Walking over to her, he put his hands on her shoulders. "Take a breath."

Her inhale was as fierce as her exhale. "How are we supposed to get Tiffany into a dress that no longer fits?"

He patted her shoulder awkwardly. Like he knew. "You'll figure something out. How about I pour you some coffee for the road?"

Her blue eyes were a little unfocused. Shock? Overthinking? Sherlock helped by nudging her. "Yes. Coffee. Maybe a tranquilizer for Tiffany. Just kidding. Okay, if I'm not back in two hours, pack up and run away, Stephan. Take Sherlock with you and go to Bali or something."

He smiled at her. "Elizabeth, no one is running away. Least of all me or your awesome dog here."

A goofy smile appeared on her face. They stared at each other for a moment before Sherlock gave a gentle ruff as if giving his two cents.

"That's my cue to go." She tugged his shirt and gave him a scorching kiss. "That's for me." Another tug had his mouth back on hers, moving sweetly. "That's for you. For being such a nice guy."

"I'll take it."

He smoothed her hair back and then headed over to see if there was a to-go cup anywhere in the kitchen. Her footsteps running to the back of the cottage sounded behind him. Opening the cupboards, he was happy to find a glittery purple to-go cup. He wouldn't want his coffee in it, but maybe it would pep her up. He had it waiting for her when she ran back to the front.

"Okay, I'm off. Wish me luck."

"You've got this." Another kiss and she was out the door.

Closing the door, he went to finish his coffee and then buy some garlic.

When she wasn't back after two hours, he started to worry, a rarity for him. But they were in enemy territory and he didn't have complete information or a good sit rep. Since he wasn't sure if he was supposed to mention this to his buddy, he didn't text him about where to find the women. Since Sherlock was taking a nap, he headed alone to the lobby and asked where Tiffany's new wedding cottage was located. Cruising through the winding path toward its spot directly on the beach, he spotted the *Lord of the Flies* nephews chasing egrets and pelicans at the shore.

"Wild savages," he muttered as one threw a rock at the funny-looking little white bird pecking in the sand for his next meal, making it squawk and fly off. "Stay out of it, Dax. Nothing good comes from shouting at other people's kids."

He increased his pace.

"Hey!" Marshall was chasing after him, Ripp running in pursuit. "Hey! Can you take us for a ride in your Bronco? I think it's awesome. My mother is acting nutso over her wedding dress not fitting because she's too fat. Her mascara is running, and she's moaning about there not being a wedding if there's no wedding dress, which is okay with me, but it's driving me crazy."

Was it horrible that he didn't want to stop and converse? The kid had just called his mother fat—hopefully something he'd overheard someone say—and suggested he was fine with the wedding not happening. Dax would chalk that up to the kid thinking he wouldn't have to move and leave his friends if the wedding didn't go off. Honestly, he couldn't blame the kid for that. He reached for patience. This was going to be Rob's stepson. He'd see him when he visited. Maybe he should make an effort.

"That's because it's a serious situation, Marshall, but one they're handling. Where did you want to go?"

"Anywhere but here," the kid told him, throwing another rock toward a bird flying overhead.

"Understandable." Dax leveled him a look when he threw another rock with pretty good accuracy, making the bird veer to prevent getting winged. "You know...that bird didn't do anything to you."

The kid looked at Ripp before shrugging. *"So."*

"So," Ripp echoed, cocking his head defiantly.

He studied Marshall. He was tall, thin, and bony while Ripp had a rounder look to him, freckles spotting his equally round face. They didn't do smiles, and as Dax thought back, he didn't remember seeing any. Wasn't that weird? He remembered being happy as a clam as a kid, playing outside, hanging with his friends.

Maybe these boys' lives were like Ariel's childhood.

Maybe he needed a little more compassion.

"All right. Let's go."

He had no idea where to take them, but the boys let out a whoop, so he figured it probably didn't matter. They ran off, giving him time to knock on the bridal cottage.

No one answered.

Marshall reached him along with the rest of the boys when he was coming down the steps. "They're all gone because Mom is too fat for her dress."

"Hey! Language!"

"Fat isn't language," Ripp informed him with his brand of kid-like cockiness. "Fuck and shit are."

Dax shot him a hard look. "Calling someone fat isn't nice, so in my book, it counts."

"Whatever," Ripp answered, the rest of the boys nodding their agreement.

God, he felt old, and he never felt like that. Was it his age that had him thinking these kids were brats? Of course Ariel had said they'd acted like this since early on, which was sad really. Normally he liked children. His sister had two great boys. His brother had a little girl with curly blond hair who'd just gotten her front teeth. They played games and hugged him every chance they got when he was home.

These kids? He had a feeling their motto was simple: try to hug them and die.

"You think you've got it pretty tough, don't you?"

Marshall lifted his chin, glaring at him. "What do you know? You think you're so perfect with your Navy uniform and your hot plane like in that *Top Gun* movie. Everybody loves you."

"Yeah, people kiss your ass wherever you go," Ripp broke in, stepping closer to his cousin. "Women throw themselves at you. Like Aunt Tiffany."

He closed his mouth in shock. Not only had they taken his question totally wrong, they'd confirmed Tiffany had made a pass at him. Holy shit! And when all he'd done was try and be nice to them...

"You don't know nothing about me." Marshall's face scrunched up in pure dislike. "Just like your stupid friend, Rob. I wish my mother had never met either of you. We were better off before."

He started running. Ripp spat on the ground for emphasis before following. The other boys—God, he couldn't remember all their names—ran off too. Rubbing the back of his neck, he stared out at the water.

He wanted to be anywhere but here, and that meant they had something in common. They were pissed off little boys. Maybe the neglect had turned them mean and disrespectful early, but there wasn't much he could do about it.

Not his circus. This was going to be Rob's life, though, and what sucked was Rob already had it tough. Dax started walking back to his cottage with a heavy feeling in his chest.

This whole family needed to be Roto-rootered of all their shit.

"Hey, dipshit!"

Steeling himself, he turned around to face his friend. Rob looked rough from a couple days of not shaving, and his face didn't have the usual *good to see you buddy* look Dax was used to. His probably didn't either. Not after the altercation with Rob's future stepson, who had major anger issues and way too much on his shoulders for a kid.

He punched up a smile. "Hey, asshole! How's it hanging?"

"Pretty good. *You?*"

He heard the leading edge in his friend's voice and knew what he was talking about. "You don't want to go there."

Rob jerked a shoulder. "Fine. I hear Ariel left you behind today when all the women went on some errand."

Well, that answered Dax's question. "There are a lot of errands."

"You're telling me. Tiffany is so stressed that I'm trying hard not to be concerned about her."

Dax nearly sighed. Rob must really love this woman, or he wouldn't be concerned. All he could hope for was that she didn't break his friend's heart. "Weddings seem to cause a lot of anxiety."

"No shit. I don't think my blood pressure would pass medical right now. So with the women gone, what the hell have you been up to? Tell me it's something interesting. Because I'm losing my mind."

He said it playfully, so Dax inclined his head toward the

cottage. "Why don't you come see what I picked up? You've got Italian blood on your mom's side, right? Ariel heard a garlic wreath symbolized a happy home and good home cooking—or something like that."

"Tiffany doesn't cook." Rob's frown couldn't be more sour. "Especially lately."

Dax didn't ask why that was a sore point. If Rob wanted to talk, he'd talk. But they needed to get back on good terms. Dax swung an arm around his friend's shoulders. "Well, princess, you're going to help me make this fucking wreath."

Rob shoved him away. "No way, man!"

Dax snagged him into a neck hold and marched him to the cottage, the kind of prank they'd pulled on each other hundreds of times. "You so are. I got all the necessary items. Think how it will impress Tiffany. Because it's not like you've contributed much to the wedding."

"I'm here, aren't I?" he bit out. "I just want to marry Tiffany. I didn't know how important all this stuff was going to be to her."

Dax let them inside, smiling as Sherlock looked up from his place by the fireplace only to put his paws over his head. "Ah, don't bitch. Think of how much this will mean to her."

Rob planted his hands on his hips and glared at him. "Fine, but I'm going to need some fucking whiskey. Jesus, the things you do for love. Clearly, you're in deep like if you're taking care of Ariel's dog here."

He didn't want to talk with Rob about any of that because he didn't feel good about where it might go. "Let me call the front desk and get us a bottle," he said, not that he was going to drink and Rob knew it. "Too bad Carson and Perry aren't here to help."

The middle finger was his answer, and Dax smiled.

He'd finally figured out a way to do his duty and rebuild their friendship.

They watched DIY garlic wreath videos on YouTube and bitched and moaned the whole time. When Dax lifted up his first braided garlic attempt, Rob said, "That's pathetic, man. Your braids are totally uneven."

Dax responded with a pout. "You want to braid this into a heart?"

Another middle finger and more insults to his manhood made Dax grin.

They were back on track.

ELEVEN

She was in hell.

Make no bones about it.

"Oh my God!" Tiffany pressed a hand to her forehead, shock making her unusually tanned face pale as she stood in front of the shop they'd just left. "That's the second seamstress who's said there's no fixing my dress! Ariel, do something!"

All of Deverell women turned and looked at her, their eyes as panicked as a deer frozen on an interstate. She had to tell herself yet again not to clutch the garment bag that contained Tiffany's wedding dress. Because it was time to get real. If Tiffany didn't have a wedding dress, she wasn't getting married. Ariel wouldn't get her house.

The end of the world was nigh, and that woman who'd cursed the Deverell weddings was having yet another last laugh.

Still, she was a professional. She knew how to talk reasonably in chaos and focus on fixing things. "Let's all calm down. There are more people on the list I found online who do alterations. We've only visited two. I think we should take a break, eat, and get y'all a drink—"

"I don't think so." Mother smoothed her white blond hair back, a gesture of outward cool that she always rolled out when agitated. "Clearly the last thing Tiffany needs is food. God help us if Terry and Tricia can't get into their dresses."

Her two sisters clutched each other with little care for the state of their sundresses. Tiffany stutter-stepped over to Ariel and slumped against her side, more tears in eyes. Ariel put an encouraging arm around her. *Not helping, Mother.*

"Ariel is the only one who looks to have lost weight," her mother commented, her motherly appraising eye falling to her waistline. "Nice job, honey."

"Working tornado sites will do that to you," she answered dryly. "Let's keep focused. I still think a break would do everyone good."

"Tea, then." Mother crossed her arms stiffly over her navy cotton dress, her knuckles white as she clutched her white purse. "No food. Not until dinner. You're going to have to do a crash diet, Tiffany. You other two should join in. But not too much because then your dresses might not fit well."

Terry and Tricia only bleakly nodded while Tiffany gripped Ariel. She wanted to shut her mother down, but she knew distraction was the key rather than a direct offensive. Whatever it took, they were not going to get distracted by the body-shaming or the diet talk. "Let's get that tea while I make some more calls."

She guided the walking wedding dress mourners to the next coffee and tea place on King Street. Everyone dutifully got a tea. Mother paid. Ariel didn't bother to say she wanted a chai latte or that the wedding dress was starting to get heavy. Mother had already complained about her setting it down. Like wrinkles were their enemy right now. Still, they were in serious *don't rock the boat* waters.

God, she needed some aspirin. Or Dax.

While she sipped her Earl Grey from the corner of the coffee shop, she called two other alteration shops on the list, balancing the garment bag against her side. Both said that even if they could help, which they doubted after hearing Ariel's details, they couldn't alter it in time for the wedding.

Yeah, time was against them.

As her mother was tossing her tall English Breakfast tea into the trash, Ariel finally reached a seamstress on the list who said she had an idea that might work. Closing her phone, she gathered their depressed group huddled together around a round café table.

"I found someone who says she has an idea." She hefted the garment back up, wishing one of her sisters would offer to help, but no...

That would be wishing on the moon.

"Let's go, then." Mother rose and headed toward the door at a brisk clip in her white heels.

Tiffany looked at her with bleak eyes, the very image of a woman in a horror movie, what with her yellow sundress and shocked raccoon eyes. "Do you think it will work?"

Ariel took her by the arm and led her out, sending Terry and Tricia pointed glances as they followed, hoping they would be supportive. But they were in their own world after Mother's comments about their figures. Everyone had had a fitting two weeks ago—even Ariel—and there hadn't been any issue.

"Maybe Terry and I should go back to the resort and try on our dresses." Tricia put her arm around an equally rumpled Terry. "We're worried we might need a seamstress too."

This was getting out of hand. "One thing at a time."

"But if we need our dresses altered, wouldn't it be better to know sooner?" Terry asked, nervously making circles with her finger in her blond hair. "Besides, I can't stand not knowing."

"Me either!" Tricia practically wailed.

Maybe sending them back to the resort wasn't such a bad idea. It would reduce the drama by fifty percent.

"Girls!"

They all faced toward Mother's voice. Ariel almost wilted under her steely glare.

"We're coming." She hurried toward her, lugging the dress. "Terry and Tricia think they should go back to the resort and try their dresses on—"

"Fine!" Mother opened her purse and proceeded to touch up her lipstick. "You two head on back. If they don't fit, call Ariel. And then do some Pilates and have the resort make us some juice. Especially pineapple or pomegranate."

"Yes, Mother," they both said at the same time.

Tricia grabbed Ariel's arm, so tight she was going to leave a mark. "Ariel, can you find us a taxi?"

She had to swallow her retort. *Can't you hail one yourself? This isn't hard.* Instead, she smiled. "Sure thing."

After she located them a cab, she directed her mother and Tiffany back to her mother's BMW. She drove, because Mother was too upset, and Tiffany rode in the back seat with the garment bag in her lap, looking as if she'd been whipped.

When they arrived at the seamstress' bright blue house, Mother turned to Ariel. "If this doesn't work, we might have to consider looking for a new dress."

Ariel had to work hard not to be relieved. She wanted her house, and she would need Tiffany to be on board with wearing a different dress if it came to that. It was good her mother was the one who'd brought it up.

Tiffany's anguished crying filled the car a moment later. "But I love this dress!"

Mother turned in her seat to look at Tiffany. "I know you do, but if you can't get into it, there's no other option."

"I spent six weeks looking for the perfect dress, Mother!" More tears spilled down her wan face. "How can I find something special in three days? And that doesn't even account for the pressing and steaming…"

The bile in Ariel's stomach was starting to burn her throat. "Let's cross that bridge when we get there. Tiffany, let's think good thoughts."

Her sister got out of the car and handed the nearly limp garment bag to her. "I want to, but it's so hard right now. This wasn't supposed to happen. I thought I was safe after the fitting. That the—"

Her face blanched, and she hurried toward the little house. Ariel followed, feeling the storm brewing behind her. Mother on a tear. Shaming everyone.

God help them all.

It had been a sad scene back at the bridal cottage—Mother had tried to shove Tiffany into the dress, and her poor sister's skin had gotten caught in the zipper, even with Terry and Tricia pulling the sides together.

What now?

Somehow Mother beat them to the door. Her knock held a *don't mess with me* quality Ariel remembered from their childhood.

The door opened, and an elderly woman with a nice round face in a simple green dress gave them a compassionate smile. "Come in. I'm so sorry for your troubles. I can't imagine how upset you might be. I'm Paula."

"Hi, Paula. I'm Ariel, and this is Tiffany, the bride, and my mother. Thanks for agreeing to see us on short notice."

"It's my pleasure, dear. Sounds like you have the worst nightmare a bride could face. Let me see what I can do."

Ariel handed her the dress, thanking the wedding gods they'd found someone kind. The first seamstress had looked at Tiffany's waistline after she'd pulled on the dress and declared it was impossible. The next woman hadn't been much nicer.

But Paula's charming little house conveyed a comforting aura, from the lace curtains on the windows to the cheery yellow paint on the walls.

"What a day you must be having." She patted Tiffany's arm when her sister weakly nodded. "Come on to the fitting area with me. Let's see if we can figure this out."

Ariel shot her a thankful smile as they walked through an ocean blue doorway into another room. "Mother, I'm going to do a little more research on this problem. Would you go on with Tiffany? I'll be there as quick as I can."

Her mother came over and bussed her cheek, surprising Ariel enough that she almost dropped the phone she'd taken out onto the worn hardwood floors.

"You're doing a wonderful job, Ariel." Mother squeezed her arm for emphasis. "I don't know how Tiffany could let this happen."

"She didn't mean to—"

"It was downright irresponsible of her to gain this kind of weight before the wedding." Mother patted Ariel's hair as if trying to make it more presentable. "She admitted she's stress eating again and hiding it."

Ariel knew she couldn't refute that. Tiffany had started

those habits as a teenager when Mother's body-shaming had kicked in. "Let's hope Paula can help."

"God help us if Terry and Tricia have gotten a little chunky too—unlike you." Mother stroked her cheek before heading to the doorway, heels clicking on the hardwood. "Finish your calls as quick as you can, dear."

Dear.

Suddenly, she was the favorite daughter. All because her mother approved of her weight. Ironic. As a young girl, her mother used to find fault with how bony her knees looked in a dress. When her breasts had come in, Mother had despaired of them not being big enough. A B-cup wasn't enough to entice a man, to her mother's mind. Then there was her lack of hips. She was still rail thin.

Mother had finally given up, only bringing out a suggestion for a butt or breast enhancement every couple of years around the holidays. Something she would pay for, of course. Because Mother believed in putting her money where it was needed when it came to her daughters' looks. They were supposed to be her pride and joy, after all.

Ariel had always failed there. Until today. Too little, too late.

She let herself out onto the porch, her heart heavy. She needed to vent.

> Jeffrey! I can't wait for you to get here. 😬 Tiffany can't fit into her dress, and it's a MESS. I'm contemplating throwing myself in the ocean or running into the marsh and letting a gator get me. 🙍‍♀️🐊 Because you know what that means for my house… 😢

BEST BROTHER EVER

> SHE CAN'T FIT INTO HER DRESS? OMG! The curse is hitting hard. Hang in there. I'll be there soon. Cling on to Captain Hotpants like he's a safety float. Anything to survive. We will get you that house! So don't let that gator get you. 🐊🚫 I love you too much for you to die from Deverell drama. 🖤

> LOL. It's worse than that. Mother thinks I'm the best because she approves of my weight. For once. It kinda broke my heart. You know? 🖤

BEST BROTHER EVER

> Ah, sweetie pie. 😢 That's awful. What a bitch. She insisted on a wig and now she's being nice? That's the Stormy I remember. 😢 Stand tall. You know who you are, and who you are is perfect. I'm coming. God, I need to think about what to do to fight this curse. Ariel, girl, we're going to get you granny's house if we have to boil frog's eyes or something.

> Yuck. But appreciated. I love you. 🖤🖤🖤

She clutched the phone to her heart. Right. That was her goal. But God, right now it seemed like there'd be a lot of collateral damage. She closed her eyes and took a couple of cleansing breaths, reminding herself she could get through this. She'd gotten through every other family disaster. She'd survived not finding victims in the wreckage in time.

But by God, old wounds could still bleed. She'd thought she was beyond the desire for parental approval, but the look her mom had given her while patting her cheek had affected her. There had been love there.

Yeah, it was fucked-up love, because she should be loved for who she was. But she couldn't deny she still felt the love and also the pull for more of it.

She almost laughed at herself. Not in this family.

Heading inside, she found everyone in the fitting area. Tiffany was crying uncontrollably now, makeup smeared beyond repair. Mother had her hands crossed stiffly over her chest, purse clutched tightly to her side. Paula was fussing with the one-inch gap in the back where the dress wouldn't zip.

"What's the verdict?" she hesitantly asked.

Mother turned to her, her brow line not moving when she gave her a disgruntled look. "Paula can rip out the zipper and fashion something like a bustier."

"With strings!" Tiffany's voice held an unnatural pitch, grating to the ear.

"I can sew in a matching piece of fabric, or as close as possible, and then use the strings for a closure," Paula added calmly like she was used to bridal meltdowns, never taking her gaze off the back of the dress. "It's not going to be an exact match, but it will handle the issue. On short notice."

Tiffany was blubbering something fierce, and the dress was in imminent danger of getting snot on it.

Ariel spotted a box of tissues. After she gave a few to her sister, Tiffany blew her nose as loudly as a goose—not her usual ladylike puff—and handed the used one to Ariel.

God, what was she? A kindergarten teacher? Still, she took the tissue and tossed it in the wastebasket.

"Ariel, what do you think?" Tiffany grabbed her arm, eyes wild, breath shallow. "Will the corset strings will make me look like a slut? Because I don't want anyone looking at me like that on my wedding day. I had that the first time around. This time was supposed to be different."

Ariel sighed and gave in to the urge to comfort her sister. Tiffany had married Marshall's dad after she got pregnant, and a few of the Deverell relations had commented on her showing at the wedding. Ariel hadn't been surprised by their cruelty, but she'd wanted to push them into the punch bowl.

Tiffany had sworn up and down that day like Scarlett O'Hara with her fist in the air that she would never show up pregnant to another family event. She'd been true to her word, avoiding Deverell get-togethers until Marshall's baptism and the party Mother had thrown thereafter for her first grandchild.

"Tiffany, pull it together." Mother's order was like a harsh blast of cold wind. "You should have thought of all this before you started stress eating again."

Her hand flew to her throat. "I—"

Ariel's throat tightened as her sister's already tear-streaked face crumpled like a dry muffin. "Come on, Tiff. Everything's going to be okay. I think Paula's solution is brilliant. This way you can keep your dress. Because it really is so beautiful. Truthfully, I think your veil will cover the back."

"Not at the wedding reception." Tiffany was crying jaggedly again after Mother's reprimand.

"I'll bet Rob will think the corset design is hot." Ariel tried to give her a winning smile. "No one is going to know it was supposed to be different. Besides, I bet you'll be more comfortable with the strings."

God, she was reaching deep for positives. Next up, fairies and unicorns?

Tiffany wiped her nose and handed Ariel another tissue. "All right. It's not perfect, but what choice do I have? Ariel, everything else has to be perfect, okay?"

The weight of that demand nearly crushed her. Suddenly she wished Sherlock was beside her, giving her one of his soulful looks.

Or Dax.

She could really use one of his smiles now.

"I'll do my best, Tiffany." She threw the tissues away and turned. "Okay, Paula. Sounds like we have a plan. Let's talk some more details."

When they left the little house, Ariel felt a little better. Paula wasn't taking advantage of their plight by charging something unreasonable, and she'd promised to have it ready for pickup on Friday morning.

"Ariel, are you sure that's enough time to have it pressed?" Tiffany asked, her face splotchy from crying.

"We'll get it done," she said with an authority she didn't completely feel.

She needed to call the steaming and press service next. She'd given them two days for the appointment. Now she would have to see if they could do a rush job because of this disaster.

If they couldn't handle it, she would find someone to steam and iron it by hand, God help her.

Her phone chimed, signaling a text. Helping Tiffany into the back of Mother's car, she checked it as she walked around to the driver's side.

> **TORNADO #2**
>
> Our dresses fit! Tricia's opening a bottle of tequila. Tell Tiffany we have a bottle of silver waiting for her since it's her new fave.

She'd noticed the silver before. When had Tiffany started drinking silver? She'd always been a gold girl. Maybe it was Rob's influence? Didn't matter. She pocketed her phone, trying to be grateful they had the wedding dress taken care of.

Disaster averted. Her house was still on track. Whew!

Entering the car, she was aware of the tension hanging in the vehicle. Harsh words had a way of doing that. "Good news! Terry's and Tricia's dresses fit."

"Well, that's something at least," Mother commented, picking at her manicure after putting her designer sunglasses on.

Tiffany didn't say anything but only swiped at a lone tear as she looked out the window, a study of a pale woman in complete desolation. Ariel didn't know what else to do, so she started driving them back to the resort.

She'd always hated being left out. The different one. But in some ways, the silence in the car right now was worse. When her mother and the Three Tornadoes turned on each other, the wreckage was the worst kind.

Usually, it portended more disaster.

TWELVE

The whiskey was almost finished, the garlic wreaths nearly done when footsteps sounded on the front door porch.

Sherlock gave a welcome ruff. Dax felt a silly grin spread across his face. He and Rob had spent the afternoon shooting the shit. Back on track. Now his girl was home...

His girl? Yeah, that's how he was thinking about her.

"Hide the wreaths!" Rob hissed.

Dax pulled them out of his reach. "Why?"

When Rob made another grab, Dax held them behind his back. "Because I'm about to lose my man card here."

"Aren't you telling Tiffany you did this?" Dax asked as Rob made a strategic lunge.

"Yeah, but I'm going to swear her to secrecy after."

"Seriously?" Dax evaded Rob again. "Who are you going to say made them?"

Rob gave a wicked grin before making another attempt at them. "You."

"Funny! But you're not getting them..."

"Ah...hi there!" Ariel stopped short at seeing them. "I didn't know—"

"That we were going to make the garlic wreaths you suggested for the wedding?" Dax shot Rob a look as he held up his pride and joy, modeling it in a way that would have done Vanna White proud back in the day. "This is mine. Rob's is—"

"Traitor." His buddy picked up his mostly empty drink, knocking it back like he had most of the bottle. "Only Tiffany is to know I did this. Got it, Ariel?"

She gave a polite cough of suppressed laughter. "Of course."

"Thanks, Ariel." Scowling like a thunderhead, he pointed to their craft project. "Mine is a piece of shit."

"Which is why I am donating my wreath to you." Dax handed it over like he was presenting a king a new crown. "You can even say you made it."

"Go blow yourself." Rob hid a raised middle finger behind his large palm. "So Ariel... Is everything good with my honey now? I could tell she was really upset earlier, and you gals were gone a long time. Where did you go?"

She was suddenly as pale as the glue paste Dax had seen in one of the many wreath videos they'd watched. "Yes, we got our errand finished. Wedding rules. All I can say is that you might want to go find Tiffany."

Rob gave a dramatic wince. "That bad? Good thing I'm fortified. But I'll take the bottle if you don't mind."

Maybe what he'd told him about Tiffany hadn't gone unheard, after all. Dax held it out. He knew Rob drank more when he was stressed, and while he didn't like it, there wasn't much for him to do. Rob blasted him whenever he said anything.

"I'll keep the wreaths here so it will be a surprise." Dax

clutched his wreath playfully to his chest. "I'm always going to treasure them and the time we spent together making them."

"Maybe take a pic and send it to your mama." Rob snorted as he strode to the front door with the kind of determination Dax was used to seeing from him when they were on an air carrier heading to their planes. "I'll bet she still has that stupid little paper plate art that you made in kindergarten with all the glitter."

Rob loved Dax's family. God knew how many holidays he'd spent with them, so normally Dax would think his friend was joking. Except there was a hard edge to this barb. He decided to answer anyway. "Mom does, actually. She keeps her favorite things we made as kids in her bottom drawer beside her bed. We tease her about it sometimes, but she says it makes her happy to open it up from time to time and remember how far we've come."

Ariel gave a strangled sigh. "How sweet."

"And that's what makes Dax the luckiest son of a bitch when it comes to family." Rob's dark eyes went flat. "Man, I'll catch you later maybe. Tiffany has some sorority sisters coming tonight and she's told me she'll probably be partying with her girls. That's still on, isn't it Ariel?"

She shrugged. "Probably, but you should check with Tiffany."

Dax studied Ariel. She was biting her lip, mostly frozen in place with Sherlock beside her. He doubted she'd be included in that party. Not that she probably wanted to attend, especially after today. "I might have plans, Rob, but text me." Because it looked like Ariel needed him more right now.

"Aye, aye, Captain." Rob gave him a cocky mini salute. "See you later. Ariel."

He was out of the cottage in a blur, the door shutting hard behind him.

The silence in the cottage was potent. Ominous almost. Sherlock hadn't left Ariel's side yet.

"How bad was today?" He came forward until they were a yard apart, wanting to take her in his arms and hold her until she leaned on him. "Or don't you want to talk about it?"

She rubbed her forehead like she had a headache. "Bad. We went to three seamstresses in Charleston and finally found someone who could alter the dress—but Tiffany is worried about how it will look. I feel terrible for her. And Mother— No, I'm not going there. All I want to do is take a shower and wash the day off. Is it only four? It feels like it should be midnight."

"I'm sorry." Even he knew a dress incident had to be like the worst wedding disaster ever. "What can I do for you? Start your shower? Rub your back? Get you an aspirin?"

She walked over blindly and touched the garlic wreath on the table. "You did it." Her voice was whisper-soft and rough as hell. "You actually did it."

He could feel heat rising up his neck. "Honey, it was nothing. I had time. I thought Rob and I needed something to focus on. We're used to going all the time. When speed is your best friend, you have little patience. Plus, we have to break this curse, don't we?"

He only said it because he wanted her to know he understood the severity of the situation. If they could still joke about it, they could defeat it. Even if it was only in people's minds.

Her face lifted, and there was so much sadness in it, she could have beaten Sherlock out in a sad eyes competition.

To make her laugh, he held the wreath up to his chest and wiggled it.

"Is this enough garlic, do you think? Or do we need more?"

An errant laugh came out before she pressed her hands to her face. "Sorry, I'm just tired. I was fine until I started walking back to the cottage, and then it hit me. It's like they sucked all the energy out of me. I need a shower and something to eat. Mother wouldn't let us have anything because, and I quote, 'Tiffany obviously does not need to eat.'"

"That's terrible." What a bitch. Sending gratitude to his mom, he set the wreath aside and pulled her to his chest. He caressed her back softly, hoping to infuse her with his strength. If only he could share his mom with her. His mom was going to love her. "I wish I could make all this better. For everyone. Because Rob isn't right either somehow. I finally saw it today even though there's nothing really that I can do."

She squeezed her arms around him tightly, like he was a lifesaver in a turbulent ocean, while he rested his chin on top of her head. "Stress and weddings in my family go together like raccoons and garbage cans."

God, he hoped he wasn't projecting. "I grant you the point. It's valid."

Maybe she was right. Except he knew Rob. Something was wrong, and he wanted to get to the bottom of it, even though he should probably leave it alone. Lots of people were involved—and he cared deeply about two of them.

"I missed you today," she whispered against him, pressing her face into the center of his chest. "Sherlock, I missed you too." She held out her right hand to the dog and gave him a good rubdown.

"Hey! We missed you too, didn't we, Sherlock? Come

on. Let's get you into the shower. I'll rustle up something for you to eat."

She pulled back and touched his jaw. "Thank you, Dax. I won't be long."

"Take as long as you need." He cupped her cheek, noting she wasn't as pale. "If you think of anything else I can get you, I'll get it. Ice cream run. Ride to the beach so you can walk this off. Anything."

Because right now she was hurting, and he'd do anything in his power to make it stop.

"You're so sweet." She reached up and pressed her face to his cheek. "Thank you for being so nice to me."

God, she might as well have gutted him. "Ariel. *Honey*. Being nice to you is a piece of cake. Best part of my day. Come on. Go wash it off, and then we'll make it better."

He wanted to kiss her, softly and slowly, but she needed to settle a little more.

She gripped his forearms, trying to smile, as much for him as for herself, he imagined. "There are some days when I wish you really could kiss it and make it better. This is one of them. God, forget I ever said that."

Turning quickly, she hastened from the room, leaving him and Sherlock watching the space where she'd been. "She's in a bad way, buddy. But I'll bet you've seen that before. Go to her. I'll find her something to eat."

Sherlock's expressive eyes blinked, and then he was trotting after Ariel. Dax decided to put the garlic wreaths out of sight. The last thing she needed right now were reminders of why they needed garlic in the first place. He decided to jog over to the lodge and see if he could pick her up something like a piece of fruit or another snack. Maybe she needed some air. She loved the beach. He'd suggest they go for a walk if she was up to it.

She was up for it, he discovered, when she returned from her shower. He was glad to see her polish off the banana he'd found in the snack area, along with two mini bags of Cheetos.

"Mother would yank these bags out of my hands if she saw them. She'd tell me I was playing with fire. Right now, she approves of my waistline, but after eating this? She'd chide me something fierce."

He could feel his jaw crack as he clenched his teeth. How could anyone say that about their own child? He knew it happened. Rob and plenty of his friends had come from families that hadn't treated them right. But it didn't compute. How could you not be crazy about your own kid? "Well, I think you're perfect."

She only managed a stricken smile before agreeing to his adventure on the beach so she could get some air.

"Turn right," she called as they reached the end of the road leading to Folly Beach. "There's a place to park where we can hit the beach right past 9th Street on the left."

He followed her directions, noting the golf carts parked out front and the brightly colored houses on stilts.

"Can you turn into the next driveway on the left?"

Puzzled, he pulled into the gravel driveway of the two-story white house with green shutters. It was built on stilts like the rest of the ones they'd passed. Flooding measures, he imagined.

When she put her hand on his arm, he already knew what she was going to say by the way she seemed lit up from the inside. "This is Grandma's house. I wanted you to see it."

He cupped her cheek. "I'm glad you brought me here, Ariel."

"Me too."

He stopped the engine and went around to open Ariel's door before letting Sherlock out. She had another heart-tugging expression on her face as she left the car, one he wanted to fix but knew he couldn't. Grief. He got choked up like that whenever he thought of his grandpa.

"It's a really nice house," he commented softly as she walked over and touched the palm tree in the front yard. "I like the flamingos the most. She must have been a cool lady."

Pretty determined too, he imagined, since there was only a wide wooden staircase in the middle. He wondered how a little old lady had climbed it, because he didn't see a ramp or anything. None of the houses they'd passed seemed to have anything but stairs, yet many of the people he'd seen in the area were older.

Sherlock was pressed against Ariel's side now—his favorite place. "She was the coolest, and yeah, she loved her life-size flamingos. Said it told anyone passing by she was a fun bird who wasn't afraid to stand out. Plus, she loved shrimp. God, she could eat a pound by herself. But only in her later years when she relaxed some about that kind of thing."

Her voice was raspy, and he had a moment. Was it a mistake for them to come out here? "Is this bringing back too many tough memories? Because Ariel, we can do this another time."

She shook her head. "No, I wanted you to see. Plus, there are good memories here, even though I miss her hard. I tried to shimmy up this palm tree once. Failed miserably. And see that white shell wind chime? I made that when I was eleven. I spent one whole summer scouring the beach for the best shells and then found some old fishing wire in the tackle box and strung them. I gave it to her for her birthday. She loved it."

He went over to her and put his hands on her shoulders, feeling the tension there, but worse, the grief. Sherlock gave a sad whine as they looked up at the house from the ground.

"I love this place," she whispered, pressing her hand to her chest. "When I need a happy thought—besides you—I think of this place. That's how I got through today, and that's how I'm going to get through this wedding."

He could hear the resoluteness in her voice. "It's a beautiful house, Ariel. I can see why you love it so much."

She slid her hand into his, as if it was the most natural thing in the world to do. He clasped it, and when she looked up at him, her heart was in her beautiful baby blues. "I'm glad. I wanted you to understand. She'd have liked you a lot. You're what she'd have called a fine fella."

He traced her cheek with his free hand, deeply moved. "I'm glad you wanted to share it with me. Her memory too, because I know how precious those are. You don't just share them with anyone. Only people who will treasure them. As I look around, I see a lot to treasure. Besides you, there's the smell of sea in the air. The way the flamingos brighten up the front yard and how your shells blow in the breeze. I like seeing something that means so much to you. Because Ariel, I want to know everything I can about you."

Her smile was soft and sweet and almost heartbreaking as she gazed up at him. "I like hearing that, and Dax, I feel the same way. Let's do more speed dating questions when I'm up for it. But first, I'd like to take that walk on the beach."

They headed there holding hands and didn't let go the entire length of the beach and back as Sherlock walked with them. Neither one of them said much. They didn't need to.

The rush of the tide and the call of the seagulls was its own soundtrack, along with the sound of nail guns and electric saws from the surprising amount of construction taking place on the homes lining the beach.

When he caught a few porpoises playing out in the deeper part of the ocean, he pointed them out to her. She had wonder on her face as she gazed out at them—and with the setting sun on her face, making the gold highlights in her hair come to life, she looked so beautiful he stopped breathing.

Yes.

Her.

This moment.

They'd had a few of them, and this one seemed significant because of its lack of talking. There was an easy camaraderie between them, one that didn't need to be filled with chatter or questions. His other interactions with women hadn't been like this, and he liked knowing they could be like this together. He knew it was another item checked off on a long-term relationship list somewhere.

When they finally came back to the car, Sherlock went over to sniff at the bushes while Ariel lifted her gaze to the cute little white house again. "I have something I need to do. It's a Charleston tradition to bury a bottle of bourbon in the ground to be dug up for the wedding. Rob loved the idea so I put one in the ground when I was here not too long after they got engaged. Tiffany didn't seem inclined to want to dig it up with Rob, saying they had better things to do. I might as well do it now."

"If you grab a shovel, I can do it for you. My muscles need a little workout after all that wreath-making."

She gave a sputter of a laugh—not a full one yet, but a

start. "You still look pretty good, but I'll help your muscles out. Be right back."

He stayed in the yard, gazing around, taking in little details. The railing at the bottom that could use a touch of paint. The way a couple of the paver stones could use some leveling. Little things. House details. Ones that made his hands itch to be useful.

"Here you go, Stephan." She appeared at his side with a sturdy shovel with a green metal edge. "Or is this a Captain Hotpants' job?"

"Probably not Stephan's," he told her, grabbing the shovel. "Now let's dig up this buried treasure."

Her rich laughter filled the air, lifting his heart. Yeah, she was feeling better. And he'd liked helping her get there. When she pointed to the area beside a garden gnome with a blue outfit and red hat, he had her move it aside and started digging. Carefully. When they unearthed the bottle, he rubbed off the sandy dirt and made a humming sound.

"Buffalo Trace. Rob's fave."

"Tiffany might not have wanted anything to do with the digging, but she thought of that." She reached for the bottle and made a face. "I'll have to clean this up. Here's hoping it will add some extra luck because we need all the luck we can get."

Understatement of the century. "Hey! No one else dug up the bourbon so that's pretty lucky, if you ask me."

She nodded before grabbing the shovel and heading back to return it to where it was stowed. When she returned, her gaze scanned the house. Longing filled her eyes.

"Do you want to go inside? We aren't on a schedule, you know."

She laid her hand on the end of the staircase, rubbing

the wood absently. "No, I'll go in when I'm packed and ready to move in. I'm going to bring a bottle of champagne with me to celebrate. Grandma always did love the bubbly. If you're around maybe, I hope you'll come with me to toast."

He took her hand and lifted it to his lips, kissing it softly. He planned to be there. He was glad she knew it. "Count on it."

Their gazes locked, and he finally gave in to the urge to kiss her. On the beach, she'd seemed to need time for reflection. But now she lifted onto her tiptoes to meet him halfway and curved her hand around his nape. The first touch of their lips rocked him back. She was hot and sweet and so giving it nearly brought him to his knees. He gave her back everything, knowing she was searching for something in the kiss and hoping she found it.

When she finally drew back, her smile spread across her face, and then he knew.

Whatever she'd been looking for, she'd found.

He ran his fingers over that smile and knew he'd remember this moment until the day he died.

Her breathing was still coming hard, but so was his. He nodded to the palm tree. "I could give you a boost if you wanted to give climbing it another shot."

That had her laughing quietly as they headed to the passenger side of his Bronco. "Maybe later. Right now, I want real food. How do you feel about burgers?"

"Are you kidding? I could eat them every day."

"I know just the place."

She was true to her word. The restaurant had a beach vibe with its outside bar and seating. Twinkle lights danced above them. Palm trees swayed amidst yellow tables and chairs situated in a green-like jungle. Paradise Bar was a good name. He'd felt like he'd arrived in paradise, with the best girl in the world at his side, and the pretty damn best dog too.

He had the smash burger, she a buffalo blue. They plucked fries from each other's plates and fed each other a morsel to try. Her two blue Curaçao margaritas made her lips and tongue turn the same color, and he leaned across the table at one point and whispered, "I can't wait to see how you taste."

Her blue eyes heated, and under the table, her hand caressed his thigh under his shorts. They stared at each other after that, waiting for the check with increasing impatience. Usually he liked hearing bands, but the one setting up in the corner couldn't tempt him tonight.

He wanted to be alone with Ariel, and Ariel alone.

When they got back to the resort, Sherlock headed to his makeshift bed beside the fireplace as Dax quickly closed all the blinds and curtains. Ariel grabbed his hand the moment he was finished and led him in a rush back to his bedroom. Her blue eyes were filled with light and heat when she said, "I thought we could try out your bed tonight."

"Have at it, honey. *Mi casa es su casa.*"

She was laughing as he took her mouth in a deep kiss. The impatience from before had them tearing at each other's clothes. He couldn't get to her warm skin fast enough. She clearly wasn't in any mood for slow because she tugged his shorts down immediately and took him into her sweet little hand, milking him until he had to stop her or die.

"Have mercy, honey."

She pushed him back onto the bed, getting the rest of his clothes off, and slid a condom on him before undressing herself. "Not tonight."

When she straddled him, he was ready for her. She didn't want any preliminaries, and when he touched her core, he understood why. She wanted him in a way that made him even more desperate. Fitting himself to her entrance, she lowered herself down onto him, and then everything went wild. He bucked under her as she arched back, and they drove each other on until their cries mingled, releasing them from the sweet torment they'd endured. She collapsed on top of him, and he was more than fine with that. He handled the condom and fitted her against him, feeling like he'd died and gone to heaven.

"Was it better for you?" she whispered against his chest. "Because it was better for me, and I didn't see that happening. It was already insane."

He could barely laugh. Hell, he could barely feel his body over the mad electricity still coursing through his system. "What you said. God, Ariel."

"Oh, Dax." She squeezed him tightly. "I'm so glad we've met."

"Not planning on going anywhere, by the way." It was time to put it out there. "This is me saying I want to date you. Exclusively. I want to find a way to make this work. Are you freaked out?"

She kissed his chest and then the underside of his jaw, lingering with an assuring tenderness. "Not a bit, which is why I know I'm good. When I'm uncomfortable about something, I get a headache or I break out in hives."

She'd had a headache earlier, he recalled, but he wasn't about to bring that up. Instead, he lifted her arm and studied it. "No hives. Whew!"

She lifted her head, looking like the sexiest, sweatiest mess this side of Biloxi. "Dax, you are the best."

He kissed her softly, so sweetly he was sure both their hearts rolled over. "Ah, Elizabeth. What you do to me."

She laid another kiss over the center of his chest, and he closed his eyes, savoring the warmth, the woman, and the magic between them.

When he heard a pounding on the door, he groaned. "That can't be good."

Ariel was already rolling off him and pulling on her clothes. "What time is it?"

He turned to make out the digital clock and winced. "Almost eleven."

Another groan sounded from his girl, and he felt her pain as he put his clothes back on as well.

"You don't need to get dressed." She started for the bedroom door. "I'll go see who it is."

"Like I'm leaving you to face it alone."

He followed her out into the living room. Sherlock was at the front door, staring at it, his tail sticking straight up. Yeah, he knew they had a problem. "Last chance, honey. I can say you're asleep."

Ariel only grabbed the doorknob and opened the door. Tricia and Terry stood on the steps with two other blond women. All were clenching their hands, worrying their lips.

"What's the matter?" Ariel asked, stepping outside as he joined her.

Tricia looked at Terry before turning back to them. "Oh, Ariel. We don't know what to do."

She put a hand on her sister's arm. "Where's Tiffany?" she asked, her voice filled with alarm.

Dax could feel his stomach churn.

Terry gave a strangled cry. "We don't know! Ariel, she's disappeared."

Dax thought about going inside and putting the garlic wreath around his neck.

THIRTEEN

Tiffany was missing!

"How did this happen?" she nearly shouted before pulling herself back from the cliff.

Sherlock barked at her agitation, and Dax rubbed her back in a show of comfort she appreciated and needed.

"We don't know." Terry pressed her forehead to Ariel's shoulder, hanging on for dear life. "We were all drinking in the lodge and talking about how much Mom hates us. Alison and Presley's moms hate them too."

She sent Tiffany's pale sorority sisters a brief smile. They were leaning against each other, looking like an Oreo cookie stuck together with their black and white sundresses.

"My mother offered to pay for a nose job as my wedding present." Alison gripped Presley's hand as she whispered that horrible secret through clenched teeth. "Usually, my story makes Tiffany feel better—she loves our *my mother is worse than your mother* game. We've played it since college. But it didn't help this time. She just kept crying and saying this wasn't supposed to happen. That everything was ruined."

Tricia came closer to Ariel, her eye makeup smudged from crying. "Tiffany went to the bathroom and didn't come back, so I finally went to check on her. She'd had a lot of her new silver Patron, and I got worried she might be sick. But she wasn't there. I thought maybe she'd gone back to the cottage, but she wasn't there either."

"So Tricia texted her and ran back to find us," Terry picked up, finally releasing the grip she had on Ariel's shoulders. "We've all texted her and called her, but she's not responding."

Not good. Tiffany always had her phone on. She texted like some people breathed.

"She's not with Marshall and the boys?" Ariel asked to cover all bases.

"God, no!" Terry exclaimed. "But we did run by there and check before coming here."

"No one's seen her in the lobby of the hotel either." Tricia grabbed her hand before she could ask if they'd checked if she was with Mother, which seemed unlikely. "Oh, and her car is gone."

Asked and answered. Ariel's stomach sank. That was really bad. Drinking and drama was a terrible combination, even more so with a vehicle in the mix. "All right. Have you talked to Rob?"

Terry and Tricia exchanged a look before glancing back at Alison and Presley.

"Let me guess," Dax broke in. "He's passed out. He was pretty stressed today with Tiffany being so upset earlier."

They all reluctantly nodded, clustered together like wilted cheerleaders after a kegger.

"It's fine," Ariel told them even as her mind raced—her goal of getting Tiffany's wedding to come off was getting further away again. "We'll find Tiffany. Okay, let's think about this. It's eleven-ish on a Tuesday night. Where would she go?"

"Anywhere," Terry said unhelpfully.

She gritted her teeth. "Where would she feel comforted? Safe?"

"Grandma's house maybe," Tricia offered brightly as she twirled her strawberry blond hair around her finger.

"Good." Ariel tried to give a reassuring smile. "Dax and I will start there."

He squeezed her waist and headed back inside, likely for his keys.

"What can we do?" Terry asked in a strangled voice.

"Yeah, Ariel, we want to help." Tricia's lip wobbled. "She's our sister."

Sending them off in their cars was impossible. "I know you want to help, but the last thing any of us need is for y'all to drive right now. Besides, with my search and rescue background, I'm the ideal person to look for her."

Giant tears started to roll down all four women's faces like condensation on a glass of iced tea. "We'd never have drunk *anything* if we'd known this would happen," Terry nearly wailed, throwing her arms around Ariel. "I'm so sorry."

She was too. Tiffany could be anywhere and the more people out looking for her, the better. Thank God she had a plan.

"You *can* help." She wiped Terry's tears and gently pushed her blond hair back behind her ears. "All of you can keep your phones on. If she comes back, you text me right away. Okay? Now, I need something from Tiffany. Something she just wore or touched."

Tricia gasped, her hand going to her mouth. "You're

going to use Sherlock? Oh, Ariel, you've always been the smart one."

She repressed a wince. "Yes, I'm going to use Sherlock. Now, can you get me something she wore recently?"

They all nodded, and then there was a flash of rumpled sundresses rushing off the porch. Dax came out with his keys, two water bottles, and a sweatshirt for her. He'd already put one on that said Navy. All business. The bag he held up was the one the resort had put in their room for laundry. "I also brought a flashlight and a blanket and more water. What else do you want me to bring?"

She stared into the bag. My God! She went to a dark place, thinking about them needing a flashlight and blanket. Tiffany liked the ocean...

"You don't think something serious has happened to her?"

He shook his head crisply. "Let's not go there. No, I think she was really overwrought and needed a break. But I'm a prepared kind of guy. She's probably wearing either shorts and a tank top or a sundress. It's not cold per se, but when a person's in distress, their body temperature drops. I'm just being overly cautious. Ariel, take a breath."

She took a few cleansing breaths and then went inside. "I need to gather a few things for Sherlock. Come on, buddy, we're about to go to work. You know Tiffany, right? Well, she needs us to find her." Taking out her phone, she crouched next to him. Most people would think she was woo-woo for doing this, but she knew dogs were smarter than most people, so she showed him a recent photo of Tiffany. "The scent will be his guide," she told Dax, "but I truly believe a photo can help establish an incentive. A stake, you might say."

"I would believe that. I think dogs are awesome. Planning on getting one when I settle down."

"You'll be so good with one." She pulled up a video Tiffany had sent of her and Marshall sending a birthday greeting. "Bloodhounds are known for their sense of smell, but with their large ears, they also have good hearing. I'm giving him all the input I have to help find her."

Dax's hand landed on her shoulder and massaged it. "Ariel, we're going to find her."

She walked to Sherlock's dog bowl, indicating she wanted him to drink. When they worked, she didn't usually let him stop until they had an official break. He knew the drill. She gathered a few more treats and packed up his bag.

Noise sounded on the porch. She opened the door before Terry could knock. "We found the yoga clothes she was wearing before she tried on her wedding dress."

Which meant she was probably in the sundress she'd worn to the seamstresses. Ariel took the pile her sister thrust toward her. "Thanks. This is great. Was she still wearing that sundress?"

"Yes." Tricia worried her earring. "I hope it wasn't weird we were in there when Rob was snoring."

"He's used to people coming and going when he's sleeping," Dax assured them with a brief smile. "No privacy in the Navy."

"Right," Terry answered with an audible sniff. "Thanks for helping us find our sister, Dax. We all feel better knowing you're going with Ariel. It's late, and we don't want her going alone."

"Ladies, I wouldn't leave her for the world." He put a couple of reassuring arms around them and led them down the steps. "Now, why don't you head back to the lodge and make some tea or coffee? We'll give you updates as we have them."

Ariel appreciated him taking care of them as she did a final check on what she needed.

"I'm thinking about waking up our hubbies," Tricia said on a ragged breath. "They went out drinking too after playing golf with Trey—but maybe they're okay to look now that they've slept some."

Ariel clamped her teeth together at the thought. She wasn't surprised no one had mentioned Mother. But her brothers-in-law? They were okay, but they weren't good in crisis situations. She and Dax shared a look before he turned his star power on Tricia. "How about you let Sherlock do what he's good at? If we need more help, we'll circle back. You ladies take care of yourselves for the moment. We're going to get going. Ariel?"

"We're ready." She clipped Sherlock's leash on. "Aren't we, buddy?"

He gave a quiet ruff as they left the four women. Dax hurried beside them and had their doors open when they reached the Bronco. "How do you want to handle this since she took a car?"

"I'd like to start at Folly Beach. If she's there, Sherlock will pick up the scent."

"So we'll park at your grandma's house."

She nodded, and then they were off. When they arrived, the lights were all out and Tiffany's Honda wasn't there.

"Do you want me to stop here even though it's empty?" Dax asked, his strong profile illuminated by the dashboard gadgets.

"No, her scent will be here from the other day, and I don't want to confuse Sherlock. Let's head downtown. She won't be on the beach if her car isn't here. She's not super fond of the beach at night."

"Even if she's been drinking?" he asked as he started down the street back the way they'd come.

She watched the party lights flash by on the houses as they headed back to the main strip. "When we were kids, she stepped on a jellyfish when we were out at night."

"That would cure you. Also, what's the make and model of her car? I want to keep an eye out."

Ariel told him as they reached Center Street. "I don't have the plate number, but she has two large dice hanging from her rearview mirror. Calls them her lucky dice. Can you pull over in a space along the street?"

He zipped into an empty spot.

"Good. Now let's see what we can find here."

She found the window controls and let down Sherlock's window. She gave him the command to start his search and had him smell the article of yoga clothing again. He stuck his head out the window again and gave a quiet ruff.

"That's our boy." Ariel swung her head to Dax. "He's got the scent. Thank God. I think I know where she is."

She let herself out of the passenger side and then saw to Sherlock, clipping on his leash again. He was already sniffing the ground, moving swiftly up the street past the endless row of eccentric bars and kitschy restaurants. She heard Dax slam the doors, his footsteps sounding behind them as he caught up.

"She's at a familiar place?"

Ariel could already see the blue lights of the bar. "I think we're headed to Rusty's."

"Check out the Honda across the street. Ten o'clock. I think those are dice, right?"

She fought a heady sense of relief—a feeling she didn't

allow when she was working. But God, it was tough. This was her sister, and suddenly Ariel realized how scared she'd been. "Good eyes."

"Honey, I'm a pilot." He blew out a harsh breath. "Can I tell you how happy I am that this was so easy?"

She worried her lips as they reached the bar. The place was so familiar, with its beach shack appearance and dark blue-painted planks. A sign with Beach Living was nailed to the black door, which sported a large St. Bernard drinking a flagon of beer. "Don't speak too soon. I have a feeling the problem might not be so simple."

Thinking about what they might find, she warred with herself for a moment. Should she bring Dax inside? Or handle Tiffany herself?

Before she could decide, Dax was opening the bar's twinkly door and walking in. She started after him, almost running into his back when he stopped short.

"Fuck," she heard him hiss.

Confirmed. It was as bad as she'd thought.

She glanced over at the bar and saw what he had. Tiffany spilling over the bar top in her rumpled sundress, holding the hands of a floppy-haired bartender with colorful tattoos up and down his muscular arms.

A man who happened to be her ex-boyfriend. Fuck indeed.

Dax swung around, his green eyes narrowing, his stubbly jaw locked. "She's with someone." He'd practically spat the accusation.

"That's Bowie. Her first big love. Mother was against it, so they only had a summer, but it was intense. I know this looks bad."

"Bad?" His stature changed, transforming into soldier-like readiness. "Ariel, this time Rob can't deny the obvious."

His phone was out a second later, and he was taking a photo before she could protest. When he lowered his hand and pocketed it, she could tell he was daring her to argue. She couldn't. Suddenly the small, dark enclosure felt like it was closing in on her, the flashing neon signs of the bar mocking her.

"Look, I need to talk to Tiffany and get her back to the resort." Exhaustion rose up and swallowed her, and she had to rub her bleary eyes. "Can you take Sherlock with you? I'll drive Tiffany back in her car."

His military bearing disappeared, and when he put a gentle hand on her shoulder and rubbed, she saw the Dax she knew, the one she was falling for. He lowered until their heads were eye level. "I meant what I said. I'm your wingman. Come hell or high water. Sherlock and I will wait for you out front. If you need me, just call."

She nodded over the tightness in her throat and dug out a treat for Sherlock. "Good dog. And Dax—"

"You don't have to say it, Ariel."

"Yes, I do." She put her hand on his chest, wishing they could both unsee what they'd seen. "Thank you."

His smile was brief and short-lived before he opened the door, letting himself and Sherlock out. Ariel started walking toward the bar, the smell of fried food and hops strong in her nostrils. No one else was present given the late hour on a school night. Bowie hadn't even noticed they'd come in, but that wasn't a surprise—he only had eyes for Tiffany, and truthfully, he wasn't known for his customer service. He tended bar so he could surf. And party... He and his surfer friends had been notorious for their parties. Whether they still were, she had no idea. But she imagined she'd hear if she ever moved to Folly.

Not that getting her grandma's house seemed at all

likely right now. Tiffany was sitting cozily with her ex-boyfriend—days before her wedding—and Dax had a photo for her fiancé.

She couldn't seem to make her feet move as she took in the scene.

Rob and Bowie couldn't be more different in appearance except they were in peak physical shape. Was it their thrill-seeking that had attracted her sister?

As she studied Bowie, she could see the way the ocean and sun had weathered him. His hair was still loose and blond, now a little darker after the colder months, and he had laugh lines around his eyes. But he was still compelling. Ripped in a surfer way. And he obviously had the hots for her sister.

Worse—Tiffany seemed to be equally entranced.

For a moment, Ariel didn't know what to do. If her sister wanted to be here, Ariel didn't want to force her to leave, and she knew Bowie would take care of her. Her mother was the one who'd kept Tiffany from being with him, which had only made their love stronger and somehow more tragic.

Bowie finally looked up and flinched. Tiffany swung her head toward her and blanched, her right sundress strap falling down and leaving her shoulder bare. Ariel shuffled forward and awkwardly raised her hand in a *weird as hell* wave. "Hi! We were worried about you. Glad to see you're okay after today."

Tiffany immediately sniffed, her face crumbling. "Today was horrible. I was just telling Bowie. He always listens."

Ariel took a few more cautious steps forward, nodding to Bowie. "Thanks for taking care of my sister. Like she said, it was a rough day."

Bowie stood and started to pour a beer from the tap. "Your mother is a bitch."

When he held the pint toward her, she realized it was her favorite brand. He'd remembered. Oddly that had her stepping up to the bar and taking it. "Thank you, Bowie."

"I need to get something out of the back." He touched the back of Tiffany's hand. "Catch you in a hot sec."

She sniffed, grabbing a rumpled napkin and dotting her face. "You probably think I'm a slut for being here," she commented to Ariel.

Setting the beer aside, she took a seat beside her sister and faced her straight on. "I would never call you that. I know today was really hard and coming here was a safe place for you."

"Did Captain Hotpants come with you?" Her gaze was now looking toward the door.

"Yes, he's here." She kept her voice soft. "Sherlock too. That's how we found you."

She wiped her runny nose, a picture of pure misery. "He'll tell Rob about this. God! Everything is such a mess."

How could she refute that one? "What do you want to do, Tiff?"

Her sister started crying softly, putting one hand to her head. "I just want to get married and be happy. Ariel, I came here because I was so upset. What Mother said to me was awful. Rob was passed out from drinking when I got back to our cottage, probably because all I did when I got home earlier was cry. He doesn't like me doing that because he doesn't know how to fix it. I just couldn't take being there! I felt like I was coming apart. Bowie always makes me feel better about myself, and he doesn't mind me crying."

Ariel took her hand and squeezed it. "That's a wonderful quality in a person."

"It is." She wiped her puffy eyes again. "But we weren't meant to be. I know that. I just needed someone to tell me I'm not fat."

Her heart thudded heavily in her chest. "You're not fat. Any more than I'm unattractive with short hair. Mother...is Mother."

She dashed at her tears, inhaling jaggedly. "Doesn't mean it doesn't hurt."

Tiffany's voice sounded young and broken and unsure. Ariel hated that. "I know." She tightened her grip.

They shared an unspoken look, and Ariel could feel tears burning at the back of her eyes. For their shared hurt. For all the moments in between when they hadn't understood each other. How strange that it was this moment, this hurt, that bonded them at last.

"You've got so much going for you," Tiffany said hoarsely, turning and facing her completely. "Ariel, Mother is right. You are the smartest of all of us, and you've got a successful career to prove it. People respect you. All I have are my looks."

"That's not true, Tiff," she whispered, biting her lip as she took in her sister's complete vulnerability. "You have a great son and a really great fiancé. I don't know Rob well, but I know Dax wouldn't be his best friend if he wasn't special. You have a brand-new life ahead of you."

"I know that." Her hand was shaky as she reached for her water glass. "I just wish I was sure he loved me like crazy. Like Bowie did... Oh, Ariel—"

Her entire face crumpled, and as she reached for another bar napkin, she knocked into the water glass in front of her. Ariel caught it before it spilled right as Tiffany launched herself into her arms. Ariel held her as she cried, rocking her. Feeling that sense of powerlessness she always felt in the face of human grief, whether it be over the loss of a house, a loved one, or a relationship. She simply held on and let her big sister cry.

"I love Rob so much," Tiffany choked out, clutching her back. "I just want to feel like he really wants to marry me."

Ariel stroked her sister's hair, feeling her tears wet her skin. "Why do you doubt that?"

She pushed back and pursed her lips, clearly fighting something. Then she shook herself. "Because I'm pregnant."

Oh. God.

Not again. Especially since Tiffany had vowed to never let it happen. No wonder she was so upset. God, she'd even lied to Mother about it and confessed to stress eating, which she'd known Mother and everyone else would accept. Biting her cheek so her mouth wouldn't gape, she only did what she thought would help. She hugged her sister to her and tried to assure her it was okay. That she was okay.

"You know how it happened with Marshall, and I swore it wouldn't happen again." Tiffany's voice was hoarse as she dabbed at her tears. "Except Rob had already proposed so there's that. Maybe I have a pregnancy curse too. God, I don't know. But Rob and I had sex after I'd finished a course of antibiotics and somehow it happened. Ariel, we Deverells have the worst luck."

She was still reeling, and she couldn't exactly disagree with her sister. She could already imagine what their mother would say.

"And now my dress won't fit." She pressed her hand to her stomach, which seemed pretty flat to Ariel. "When I called my doctor today, she said it's not unusual with a second baby for your waistline to change suddenly this early on. And I have been eating more. *I'm hungry*."

Ariel already knew the answer, but she asked it anyway. "Why didn't you tell Mother? Or the rest of us?"

Tiffany took a shaky drink of ice water and smoothed her hair back from her brow. "Why do you think? The jokes about me wearing white last time were awful. I can still hear people's catty comments about me being a slut as I walked away from greeting them at my reception. I couldn't stand it again, and Mother wouldn't keep it a secret. Neither could Terry or Tricia."

How could she disagree? They both knew it was true.

Her sister's big, watery eyes turned to her then, and she clutched her hand. "Ariel, that's why I wanted you to handle the wedding. You always make things right. Even when it's a disaster."

Hearing her sister's reasoning made her feel cold inside. There it was again. Her role as the one who picked up all the pieces after disaster struck. She was suddenly sick of it. "So you blackmailed me? Tiffany, why didn't you just tell me all of this? I would have helped you, and I would have kept it secret."

"I was scared!" She turned back toward the bar and hung her head, pulling her blond hair over her bare shoulders. "I didn't want to admit I'd made another mistake. Not to anyone. For once, I wanted to be perfect. Not the bride who got knocked up for a second time. Do you know how humiliating that is? I just wanted everything to be perfect. A wedding is supposed to be the best day of your life, and I hoped that if Rob and I started out that way, then maybe it wouldn't end up like it did with Teddy."

Marshall's father.

Tiffany worried her engagement ring. "I don't want to go through that again. Divorce is awful. Being a single mom is so hard, Ariel, and Marshall is a great kid, but he's a handful. He gets into trouble at school a lot. I know Rob is going to be a good influence. A good disciplinarian. And this baby... I want it to have a happier life than Marshall and I did after everything fell apart. Can you understand that?"

Her bones felt like lead. When had her sister ever told her any of this? "Of course I understand, Tiff, but being straight about how things are going for you would help everyone understand. I think it would make things easier."

Tiffany's eyebrows flew back to her forehead. "With Mother? Not if hell froze over. And Tricia and Terry would be glad in a way. We all like to think we're the top sister, you know. We vie for Mother's approval. When one of us has a problem, it makes us feel better about ourselves. You're lucky. You don't have that compulsion. Your dad made all the difference there. Ariel, you're the only Deverell woman with any true self-confidence."

Ariel nearly fell off her barstool. Hearing herself referred to as a Deverell woman and self-confident in the same breath was too much. "Is that what you think? I've never felt like I belonged with the rest of you. The Three Tornadoes, Stormy's pride and joy. I'm never included in that. Do you know how hard that is?"

Tiffany sniffed, tears spilling over again, and she grabbed Ariel's hand this time and squeezed it tight. *"I'm sorry."*

There was real contrition in her sister's voice, and it punched a hole into Ariel's already battered heart. Ariel took a drink of her beer, reeling from everything they'd just shared. How had it come to this? Sitting in the grungy bar of her sister's ex-boyfriend, days away from her wedding, and connecting like this? "I'm sorry too, Tiff."

When her sister leaned her head against her shoulder, she put an arm around her. She caught Bowie coming back in and then immediately stepping back out. Like he was giving them more time alone.

The silence in the bar wrapped around them, and Ariel didn't want the moment to end. There was love here, and an understanding they'd never had before. For a precious moment, she knew her sister really loved her. Like from her heart loved her. Not the whole *you're my sister* or *we're family* kind of love that had never filled her heart space. She hugged Tiffany tightly one last time before finally standing up.

"I'm bushed, and you probably are too. Do you want me to drive you home?"

Tiffany looked around the bar. "Sure, but I can drive."

Ariel blanched as a thought struck her, and she pointed to the water glass. "But—"

"I lied about switching to silver," her sister answered, reading her mind. "It looks like water, and there's no smell. I take the bottle with me to the bathroom, dump it in the toilet, and then fill it up at the faucet. I haven't had a drink since I found out."

Relieved, she almost slumped onto the bar. "Smart."

"Thanks. That's a compliment coming from you. God, I'm probably being crazy emotional because I'm pregnant, and I'm sorry for that too. Let me find Bowie, and then we can go home. You're right. I am tired. So tired I could sleep right here."

She rose slowly from the bar chair and was halfway around the bar when she turned around. Ariel froze at the panicked look on her face. It was back.

"Ariel, will you promise not to tell anyone about the baby?"

Secrets were corrosive, and yet her family seemed to thrive on them. Why would tonight be any different? "All right, but what are you going to tell them about tonight? Because—"

"I'll tell our sisters that I needed some space, but I promise you that I'll tell Rob the truth about coming here. I know Dax is going to tell him anyway, so I won't ask you to intervene, but *please, please, please* don't say anything about me being pregnant. I know you two have gotten tight, but I don't want to see that judgy look in his eyes. He already doesn't like me."

She didn't want to take that on, and she certainly wasn't going to bring up Dax's impression that Tiffany had hit on him. Bottom line—she didn't want tonight to mess up what was happening between her and Dax. He had his impressions of what he'd seen, and she wasn't sure Tiffany being pregnant would change that. He'd taken a photo for Rob, and he clearly planned to show it to him. In the end, what Dax said to Rob was up to him. How Rob reacted was up to him.

Who knew how that would go? She expected Rob would still want to marry Tiffany, especially with the baby on the way, but in the end, none of that had anything to do with her.

But all the secrets and the shame and accusations made her sad. The waters ahead weren't going to be easy for anyone. Then she almost laughed. When had it ever been easy with her family?

She met her sister's wide, frightened eyes. "I won't say anything to Dax."

Tiffany grabbed her wrist in a death grip. "Promise."

"I promise."

"Good." Tiffany slumped onto the bar. "Thank you, Ariel! I'll be right back."

When she disappeared from sight, Ariel walked woodenly to the front door and let herself outside. Dax was standing on the street, rubbing under Sherlock's floppy ears, his deep baritone voice muttering encouraging words to her dog. He straightened upon seeing her. "Is she coming with you or is she staying here?"

She realized what he was asking. He wondered if she was going home with Bowie. "It's not like that that."

He heaved out a breath. "Ariel, I have to tell Rob about tonight. I can't in good conscience—"

He broke off, and it was obvious the weight of love and responsibility felt as crushing to him as her responsibilities did to her. "I know. Tiffany plans to talk to him too about tonight if that means anything. I'm going to drive her back. Can you take Sherlock back?"

A car went by, and a few stragglers came out of a pirate-themed bar a few doors down, talking loudly. Sherlock pressed his head against her side. She wanted to sink down on the ground and gather him to her. Bury her face in his fur and tell herself she was going to get through this week. Because right now, she hurt. And she didn't know how to make it stop. With Tiffany and her family. Or with Dax.

"Sure, I'll see you at the cottage." He stepped close, tipping her chin to meet her gaze. "Ariel, this doesn't have anything to do with what's between us. Let me go one step further. I don't want it to hurt anything between us."

She wanted to repeat those words, affirming them, but she found she couldn't.

As he walked off with Sherlock, she wanted to tell herself they would be okay. That her family's drama wouldn't end up causing her endless damage too. Instead, she texted her sisters that they'd found Tiffany and were bringing her back.

After she got Tiffany back to her cottage and let herself

into the one she shared with Dax, she started when he stood up from his perch at the kitchen table. Sherlock lay at his feet—a sign of fidelity that made her heart clutch.

Dax had her wedding day wig on the table, lying upside down, with a line of three ping-pong balls, obviously a recent purchase. Two beers stood in an improvised ice bucket. He'd lit a candle for either ambience or romance. She wasn't sure which.

The gesture rolled over her, making her feel way too emotional. It was his way of telling her that while he had his duty to Rob, and she'd given her word to Tiffany, they weren't on opposite sides.

She didn't want them to be on the opposite of anything. Not when they were doing so great.

Rushing across the room to him, she felt his arms close around her. They gripped each other tightly, and the abyss she'd sensed, the one she feared, seemed to close at last. "I don't want this to hurt anything between us either."

He eased back and cupped her cheek, his green eyes so tender she wondered if the ground beneath her had disappeared and she was free-falling. "We won't, Ariel. We won't."

Then he was kissing her, and she him. He swung her up into his arms and carried her off to bed, where they both showed each other how determined they were to keep what was happening between them good and true and happy.

FOURTEEN

His good morning text from his best friend wasn't encouraging.

> ROB
> You. Me. Beach. Now.

The text had arrived a minute ago. Dax had been checking his phone periodically since he'd woken up, hoping for one from Rob about going on a run so he could talk to him about last night. From the tone of his message, it sounded like Tiffany had talked to him already.

He set his phone back on the side table, his already knotted stomach tightening further, like when he was cinched into his seat belt and shoulder harness before executing a particularly challenging test flight.

Well, it was what it was. No putting it off. Besides, he was eager to put this behind him.

He hadn't been able to go to sleep after he and Ariel had made love, a rarity for him. Ariel had been out almost immediately. Sometime near four, he'd finally fallen asleep, only to feel her leave the bed when it was still dark outside.

Maybe to let Sherlock out? Somewhere in between then and now, she'd come back to bed and fallen back asleep, pressed against him wearing that funny black T-shirt Bubba had given her with the cartoon rooster on it with the words STAY COCKY with giant fire sticks exploding outward.

As a homey gesture—he didn't know if she'd meant it like that—it was reassuring as hell. They'd taken a few steps further down the path with each other last night. The sex had been raw and electric and deeply emotional. They'd both understood they could lose something precious, and they'd drawn a line in the sand.

He was about to leave the bed when she stirred in her sleep, and he leaned over to soothe her with a gentle caress, feeling the silky warmth of her skin. She smiled, and his heart turned over. God, she'd come to mean so much to him in such a short time. Whatever happened, he was glad he'd come here. He'd met Ariel, and he planned to keep on being with Ariel. Regardless of how things went with Rob.

Dax fitted a pillow beside her when he slid away. He was happy she was getting more shut-eye. She was a cuddler, and while she frowned in her sleep as she touched his pillow replacement, she still curved her body around it and stayed asleep. He kissed her forehead softly and left the bed, heading into the bathroom to dress quickly. He was used to running on little sleep and pressure in the Navy, but even he could see how drawn his features appeared. They were both tuckered out and for good reason. This morning wasn't going to change any of that.

Sherlock was standing outside his door when he was leaving, his soulful brown eyes almost humanlike with empathy. Last night, the dog had been a comfort while he'd waited for Ariel to leave the bar. Yeah, he needed a dog as special as Sherlock. He reached down and gave him a good rubdown. "You're a good dog. Do you need to go out again?"

After letting the dog back inside after a brief break, Dax headed to the beach where he and his buddy had met to run that first morning. Usually, the breathtaking view would have filled him with awe—the roll of the waves breaking near the beach, the brilliant sunrise of golds and blues—but not today. He had another view, one he knew didn't bode well.

Rob stood at the edge of the water, his hands planted on his hips, tension emanating from him.

"Hey!" he called.

Rob swung around and Dax's mouth flattened further. Rob was wearing one of his favorite T-shirts, the one with his life motto on it: *Stop crying or I'll give you something to cry about.* The young officers feared Rob for it. The brass loved seeing him running in it when they were on base. Dax had always found it funny. Now it only soured his already sick belly. He wondered if it was for him or Rob.

"At least you're not tardy, Captain," his friend ground out, his face a rigid mask of control.

"I was hoping you'd text about a run." He walked until he stood in front of his friend, battling his own emotions. "I wanted to talk to you, but from your text, I think you already knew that."

Rob inclined his chin. He hadn't shaved either, and it made him look more intimidating this morning with the dark shadows under his eyes. Not only the outcome of drinking and passing out, Dax thought. "I heard about your adventure last night. Thanks for finding Tiff. She's really sorry for the trouble she caused."

Dax could just bet how sorry. "Glad Sherlock found her."

The already rigid planes of his friend's face seemed to tighten further. "Yesterday was really hard on her. She couldn't stop crying when she got back. I don't know the full details because it's wedding related, but I heard her mother was a real bitch to her. Like crazy bitch, which Stormy excels at. Maybe Ariel mentioned it."

He wasn't going to throw Ariel into this.

His friend's mouth tightened, realizing it. "Look, man, her mother said some things I would hit a man for, and it really pushed Tiff over the edge."

Dax was waiting for the punch line.

Rob took an almost bullish stance, feet planted wide, fists at his side. "About last night... I know you think you saw something, but Tiff was only talking to an old friend."

Dax rolled his tongue over his teeth. So that's how it was going to be. Fuck. "He's her ex-boyfriend, Rob."

"Emphasis on the *ex* part." Rob's tone was as harsh as he'd ever heard it. "Look, like I said, he's a friend, and someone Tiff feels she can talk to. I was passed out last night since Tiff being so upset really bothered me, and it's not like I could run down Stormy and give her a piece of my mind. You know how I get. My temper isn't my best side, that's for damn sure."

He could feel himself grinding his teeth. "Jesus, Rob. Are you serious right now? You drinking and passing out justifies your fiancée seeking out an old flame? Come on, man."

Rob stepped closer until their heads were inches apart. Like he was about to dress him down. "Hey! Stop this. I believe her, okay?"

Dax took a step back and crossed his hands over his chest, reminding himself not to lose it. "Why?"

Rob exploded into action, punching a finger into Dax's

chest. "Because I want to, dammit!" He stalked away in a flurry of anger, crunching shells under his feet. "Because I understand why she might be acting out, and I want to be a good husband and a good father. I need to believe in the woman I love. In the woman I'm marrying, Dax."

The emotion in his voice caught Dax by surprise. "Rob—"

"No!" His shout caused the gulls to shriek and Dax's insides to further tighten. "This stops right now. I know you saw what you saw, but your conclusions were wrong. Dead wrong."

He couldn't believe what he was hearing. "That's it? I'm supposed to pretend I don't know how to read situations like the one in that bar last night? That I don't know my fucking best friend? Something isn't right with you, and you're asking me to do what? Bury this? Jesus Christ, man. You're kidding, right?"

"Dax, I want you to bury this." There was a plea in his friend's eyes, one that left Dax raw, because they both knew what it cost him: his pride.

"How can you ask that of me? I've been your wingman since we were eighteen! I know you. It's my duty—"

Rob threw his hands out. "Fuck duty, man. I'm asking you to bury this. Right now. We *never* speak about this again."

Dax let out a harsh breath, pressing his hands to his eye sockets. "You know this is the second time you've asked me that in the space of a few days. Man, you are not in your right mind."

Rob was in his face instantly, shoving him back. "That's enough. I'm fine. I'm more than fine. I'm in love, dammit. Something you don't know anything about. And I'm doing what I think is right here."

His usually iron-clad stomach somersaulted in his gut. "So am I."

They faced each other across the expanse of the beach as the tides crashed. Dax wanted to haul his friend into the ocean in the hopes a slap of cold water to the face would snap him out of whatever delusion he was in. But he couldn't. Even he knew that would be going too far. Rob was dug in, and when he turned stubborn, there was no reasoning with him.

"Fine." He knew his voice carried and was past caring. "But you get what you get. I am not going to pick up the pieces like I did with Erin."

"I knew you were going to bring that up again!" Rob stalked over to him and shoved him back. "You're like a broken record. I told you that was done."

And yet here they were again.

"I know! I helped you get *it* done. Dammit, Rob, when Erin cheated on you, you lost your shit. You almost blew your exams because you were so upset. I had to sober you up and practically pour coffee down you to get you to class—"

"Tiff wouldn't cheat on me," he ground out through clenched teeth.

"How do you know?"

Rob dug his toe into the sand and stared him down. "I just know, okay? Stop asking me so many damn questions. I said I'm cool with what happened. Because *nothing* happened. She didn't even kiss the guy. They just talked."

He'd waited until the last moment, hoping he wouldn't have to do it, but Rob didn't budge. "I took a photo of them together last night so you could see it for yourself."

His friend grabbed his hand when he reached for his

phone. "I don't need to see it, and I want you to delete it right now."

Dax ripped his hand free. "Rob, for God's sake. Take a look. It was cozy—"

"Enough!" he bellowed, giving him another hard shove. "This is the kind of thing you see good officers do when they're on TDY all the time. Talk with a girl at a bar. Trade some secrets. Because you're lonely. No. Big. Deal. Hell, I'll probably be doing something like this at some point. It happens."

An oppressive quiet lengthened between them before Dax bit out, "This is different."

His friend's scowl blackened to the point where Dax barely recognized him. "You need to get an attitude adjustment."

He stepped forward, sticking his chin out. "Or what?"

"Or I can find another best man for my wedding."

The silence between them was deafening.

"Don't make me do that, Dax."

Dax spun around, not wanting his friend to see his face right now. "Fine. But I don't want to hear dick about any problems between you two. Ever."

"Understood." There was relief in Rob's voice. "I wasn't planning on telling you anyway. You're too perfect to understand."

Dax slowly turned around, his muscles locking. "What in the hell do you mean by that?"

Rob gestured to him rudely. "Look at you. You get everything you've ever wanted. Your family is like the fucking Waltons. You graduated the Naval Academy with honors. You got the first commission you wanted and every other one since. Now you've landed a private jet gig with a signing bonus big enough to buy a Bronco. Shit, man, you came to this wedding and might have landed your one and only on the first night."

Ariel. He couldn't deny his thoughts were going in that direction.

"So what?" Dax flung his hands out. "This is about jealousy?"

Rob waved him off and started to stalk away. "No, this is about you not realizing that some of us don't have it so easy, and that when we get something good, we want to hang on to it. Even if it doesn't meet your vaunted standards."

He left Dax alone on the beach, striding off in the other direction. Vaunted standards? Was Rob kidding? Having a woman not cheat on you was an elevated view of a relationship? That was bullshit. Absolute bullshit, and they both knew it.

He picked up a shell and winged it into the sea, wishing there were bigger shells and rocks to hurl into the ocean. Because he had so much pent-up anger right now that he wanted to tear something apart.

He began to run. A few strides into it, he was sprinting up the beach, giving himself the kind of punishing run that hollowed him out and left him spent. When his legs were burning so much they were practically trembling, he stopped and bent over at the waist, his breathing harsh to his own ears. The Morris Lighthouse caught his eye. That's how he felt, he realized. Surrounded by water. Isolated from what he'd once known and valued.

God, what had they done? He and Rob had been friends since they were eighteen. They'd grown up together. As guys. As pilots. As officers. He started walking, not caring that the tides rushed over his shoes.

Should he leave? Would it be better if he did?

Except how could he leave Ariel? First, he didn't want

her to face the wedding alone. Second, he'd promised her he'd be at her side. Third, he *wanted* to be at her side.

Shit, this was such a mess.

When he grew closer to the cottages, she was sitting on the steps of the back porch facing the beach, a cup of coffee in her hand. Sherlock was beside her, plopped down with his face near his paws like he was exhausted. Dax tried to smile. But he couldn't. There was this ball of lead in his chest, one he wished he could reach inside and rip out with his bare hands.

Her mouth tightened like she understood. She lifted a to-go cup of coffee toward him. "I made you some coffee. And brought you a water. I saw Rob a while ago. He looked a little like you do."

He sat down next to her and took the coffee, scrubbing his face. "How do I look?"

"Pissed off and sad." She laid her head against his shoulder. "I'm sorry. Rob said he'd straightened you out about last night and then he thanked me—and Sherlock—for finding Tiffany and understanding what had happened."

Turning sideways, he studied her face. She was still a little pale, and her hair carried a messy bedhead look, but to him she looked both beautiful and somewhat resigned. "Am I the only one who doesn't understand?"

"No, Dax." She put her arm around his waist. "But I have a bigger scope than you, and while I understand how Tiffany ended up there last night, I'm not saying it's the choice I would have made."

Meaning going to one's ex for comfort.

"Me either." He deflated at her quiet understanding, then leaned down and kissed her softly. "I want you to know that."

She traced his jaw, her blue eyes filled with warmth and empathy. "I already do."

He kissed her again, slowly, trying to settle himself as much as assure her. This must have shaken her as much as it had him. "So what now?"

"We do our job."

His mission was her. It had to be. The rest of this was going to grind him down. "That's what I was thinking."

She rubbed Sherlock's head when he butted it between the two of them to watch a pelican fly past. "Speaking for myself, I'm going to hope that this wedding is the happy occasion Tiffany and Rob want and that they will be happy together."

Dax heaved out a sigh as he leaned back against the steps. "Do you believe they will be?"

She lifted a shoulder. "I gave up thinking about anyone's shelf life when I started going to weddings. The odds aren't so hot, and it's damn depressing."

He choked out a laugh. "God, I don't know if that's funny or tragic."

"Both." She put her arm around him, moving Sherlock to his former place, and took a sip of her coffee. "Want to start the day with wig-pong? We didn't get to it last night. I thought today should be a fun and games day. We both need to wash this out of our mouths."

"Isn't the saying, 'wash it out of our hair'?"

"I have no idea." She tipped her face toward the rising sun. "All I know is that I want to feel good today. What's done is done. The wedding will go on, and while it may be hard to believe, the details are in good shape. I don't want it to take up all of my time anymore. Let's finish some of our errands and then turn off our phones for a bit. Go to the beach or have a spot of lunch by the water. Something that would make us both happy again."

He pulled her to his side. Yeah, he didn't want to feel like shit for the rest of his time here. He could avoid Rob if needed, but he didn't need to dwell on something he couldn't change. Ariel was here, and she was right. They could have fun together.

"Sounds like a plan."

When she slid her glance his way, a warm smile touching her lips, he felt his heart swell in his chest. God, she was so beautiful. She made this trip worthwhile.

Because even though he felt like he was moving further apart from the best friend he'd ever had, he was getting closer to Ariel—a woman who meant more to him than any woman ever had.

FIFTEEN

She was going to take him fishing.

She kept her plan secret until they arrived at her grandma's good friend's place on the water—and it was worth it for the look on Dax's face when he spotted Davey loading up his fishing boat for them at the end of the dock.

Dax pulled the Bronco to a stop, his mouth moving with emotion. "God! You knew how to get me, didn't you?"

She hoped she hadn't misread him. Putting a hand on his knee, she searched his gaze. Sherlock gave a quiet ruff of concern. "Was I wrong to bring you?"

"Hell no." He blew out a breath. "For a sec, your friend there could have been my gramps bending over with his bad back, readying the boat. Grabbed me by the throat hard."

Grief. Memories. Life. Yeah, she was missing her grandma and how things used to be. They'd had some fun times on the water together, catching their dinner and then making a lowcountry perloo together.

"Come on. Let's go have some fun."

Ariel was out of the car before Dax could come around

for her, and she waved at Davey as he closed the lid to the cooler and straightened.

"Hi, y'all!" Davey drawled, hooking his thumbs in his overalls. "Fine day for a good bit of fishing. Ariel, get over here and let me meet your friend."

When she'd decided to take Dax fishing, she'd known exactly who to call. She and Grandma had always used Davey's boat and his fishing gear. The two had been friendly for years. When he'd answered gruffly and said he couldn't think of anything that would make him happier, she'd grabbed some sunblock and bottled water and directed Dax to the spot.

As they walked to the dock, Ariel could feel her own sadness well up, but she knew Grandma would be happy she'd called Davey about going fishing. When she reached him, she wrapped her arms around the tall, thin man and squeezed him as tightly as he squeezed her. Last time she'd seen him had been at Grandma's funeral, and he'd had silent tears falling down his face as they'd lowered her into the ground.

"Well, now, you're a nice sight for these here old eyes." He tapped her on the nose, his blue eyes crinkling at the corners. "I like the hair. It's spunky. Suits ya. Now introduce me to your fella."

"Davey, this here is Dax Cross, and he's what Grandma would call a good catch."

They shook hands. "Nice to meet you, sir," Dax said politely.

"Any friend of this one is prime stock with me." He tugged playfully on the ends of her hair. "Best sense of all the Deverell women, her granny used to say. Dare I ask how the wedding planning is going?"

She winced playfully. "Not if you want to keep this smile on my face."

He gave a laughable cringe. "No surprise I guess, but Lordy, those Deverell weddings are something else. I'm kinda glad your granny never agreed to let me walk her down the aisle. A chandelier might have come down or some holy statue might have fallen over. Yes, sirree, I'm rather glad my invitation got lost in the mail."

She gasped. "What?"

He tipped his head up to the sky. "With your grandma gone, Tiffany had no reason to invite me, and we both know it. I wasn't close to the Three Tornadoes. You and I were the only ones who got along, and that's fine by me. Mighty fine."

Though they'd been a couple, Grandma hadn't brought Davey around the rest of the family much, saying she didn't want to hear any of their opinions, because they surely would have them. They had them about everything, and usually they weren't good. As her mother had recently proved in spades. "It's their loss, Davey."

"You're a sweetheart." He pinched her cheek. "Now then, the day's passing and there are fish to catch. Ariel, I have your favorite rod for you, but I thought we'd give your fella here a couple of choices since you said he's a seasoned fisherman."

The three rods were standing up where Davey had secured them, and she let him and Dax get down to serious business. Choosing the perfect rod and lure wasn't exactly her forte. She liked it simple and easy like her grandma. Sherlock jumped into the boat and gave a ruff, sniffing the air, eager to go. Ariel savored the warm breeze against her skin and the swampy smell of water in the air. The marsh grass was swaying, the sound a soft rustle that called to her soul. This place was the home she'd always dreamed of, and soon she'd be here permanently.

When Dax turned around with his rod, he let out a whoop. "How about this? One of my favorites."

He grinned and patted Davey on the back with the kind of ease men had with each other. Then he drilled her with an amused look. "Davey here tells me you prefer the kind of 'chuck it and fuck it' rod that doesn't require a lot of concentration." He gave a tsk-tsk. "Ariel Holmes, I'm surprised at you."

She jerked her thumb toward Davey. "Don't pick up on his teasing. I know what he thinks of my rod choice and my approach to fishing. I like to be on the water, but I also don't want to have to work to catch anything."

Dax let out another big laugh, the joy of fishing clearly wrapping him in its spell. "This is going to be fun."

"Always is with this one, and her grandmother too, God bless her soul." Davey wiped his eyes quickly. "Now then. Dax, if you'd trust this old man, I can help you call in for a non-resident fishing license. I play poker with one of the guys in the department, and I spoke with him after Ariel rang me up earlier. He'll handle everything over the phone. Last I knew it was pretty cheap. They just need some basic information."

"You read my mind." He put a hand on Davey's shoulder. "I appreciate the help."

"We'll be right back," Davey called as they headed toward the bright green house on stilts flanked by palm trees.

Ariel looked at Sherlock. "Aren't they cute? Their heads together. Probably trading stories about their biggest catches. Oh, Sherlock, doesn't the sun and air feel great?"

The wedding drama felt miles away, and all she wanted to do was let the sun kiss her skin. She was going to enjoy this break, most especially her time with Dax. On that note, she dug out the sunscreen. She was finishing her legs when Davey and Dax arrived.

"Well, you're all set to go." Davey slapped Dax on the back. "Go give 'em hell out there."

"Are you sure you don't want to come?" she called, sensing Dax wouldn't mind the company.

"Please come along, Davey," Dax added with a boyish smile at the older man, looking years younger even with his scruff. "Those fish won't see us coming."

Davey gave a wheezing laugh and slapped his knee. "Sorry, kids. You two have fun. Being on the water with the one you're sweet on is the best feeling in the world. Enjoy it. I'll see y'all soon."

As he strode down the dock back to his house, Ariel gazed after him wistfully. "He and Grandma had a lot of what she'd call 'dates on the water.' Said it sounded better than going fishing if you get my drift. You ready, Stephan?"

He extended his hand to her and helped her into the boat grandly. "After you, Elizabeth. Although we might have to lose the nicknames for a while. I don't really see Elizabeth and Stephan fishing, do you?"

She shook her head and carefully alighted into the boat, sitting down at the front where Sherlock was standing, peering into the water. "Not really. I thought you might enjoy driving if you don't mind me giving you some directions to our favorite fishing holes."

He eased in with a quiet grace that was rather captivating, the flexing of his muscles raising her internal temperature. "Is there anywhere you aren't capable? You're good in the skies and clearly on the water. Certainly you're good on the ground."

Her question had him frowning, however, as he started the motor and set them off the dock after she'd untied their lines. "Rob said something like that to me this morning. About everything coming easily to me. It didn't sit well. I've never thought I needed to do anything differently than be how I am. Grandpa said some people like to struggle against the current like the salmon, but he thought it wiser to go with it. Sorry, we were going to get back on the happy train."

The sound of the running motor was as welcome as the warm air on her face, but hearing the anguish in Dax's voice marred the pure bliss of the moment. "I'm related to people who like to struggle. I don't. At least I think I don't. I figure struggles can crop up anywhere, and when I'm not around one, I'm like you, I try and go with the flow. I think your grandpa was a wise man, and you were smart to listen to him."

"Thank you for that." He inclined his chin toward the water ahead. "Guide me out, honey, and let's get to fishing."

She started them off in the muddy brown waters of her favorite fishing hole, casting out in the middle section between marsh grass. Dax cast in the main waters, reeling some slack in, a joyful smile on his face.

"Feels like a part of me just settled back in place." She turned her head to find his warm gaze on her, the sun turning his hair gold. "Thank you, Ariel."

A part of her own heart seemed to settle as the boat gently rocked them. "You're very welcome. I feel the same. I'm glad I'm here to witness your return to the water."

"Me too." He cast again, and she wondered if he had

done it for the sheer pleasure of doing so. "Any bets on who catches more?"

She reached over one-handed to grab the red hat she'd tucked into the pack she'd brought and plopped it on her head. "Ooh... Sexy side bet or regular bet?"

He reached into his pocket and pulled out his aviator glasses, the sight of which had her belly tightening with need. "Why in the world would I choose a regular one now that I know sexy is in the offing? Any thoughts on what you'd like?"

She felt a tug on her line and cried out, knowing she'd hooked something. "There's a place on Market Street that sells homemade fudge sauce. I want to cover you in it and lick."

"Good Lord, woman! I'm fishing here. That kind of image will have me falling out of the boat."

"Maybe the fish would like your big old pole?" she quipped, reeling her fish in capably.

Sherlock gave a loud ruff as she brought the fish in. Dax moved the net closer to her body. "Only one person I want to enjoy my big old pole. Look at you, girl. That's a nice-sized fish."

She reeled it close enough to grab the net and then maintained her balance as she tried to snare him one-handed. "Yeah, it's a flounder." She had it on the second pass through the water and hauled it in, wiggling hard.

Making sure to secure her reel—she'd lost one to the water when she'd first gone fishing as a girl—she unhooked the fish and then set it on the fish mat and ruler to check if he met the South Carolina size limits. He did. "Twenty-one inches, baby!"

"Nice one, babe!" Dax called out brightly. "If you want,

I'll bleed him for you and put him on ice. Davey said it wasn't your favorite thing. Makes sense to me. You save people for a living."

Her eyes widened at his insight. "Yeah, I... Seems hypocritical to catch it and then balk at killing it, but no, I'll happily hand that task over to you."

To her surprise, she found herself watching him as he adeptly bled the fish and handled the rest before laying it with near reverence in the ice chest. His whole demeanor was the calmest she'd seen since they'd met, outside of sex. He seemed looser. Yeah, she'd been right to bring him.

"You're up next for a big catch," she called, flashing a goofy smile.

He only picked up his reel and cast off, turning his body toward the main waters. They fished in silence, and she savored the rush of warm air over her body and the easy rocking of the boat under her. Sherlock would give an odd bark to tell her if a fish was near. Not that she hustled for it. She brought in a slimy seventeen-inch trout she was only too glad to hand over to Dax, who really did seem to enjoy the entire process. That was fine with her.

"I'm up on you, Captain Hotpants." She reached into her pack, grabbed the sunscreen, and tossed it to him. "Put some on. You're burning without a hat on. And then think about me, smearing the warmest fudge sauce all over that hot body of yours."

"Elizabeth...I love this naughty side of you." His voice was a deep, sexy rumble filled with promise. "I never knew fishing could be so sexy."

Her laughter rippled out easily like the water around them. "When I was an adult, Grandma told me she and Davey used to have all sorts of fun when they went fishing. Her eyes would sparkle, and she'd cackle a little, talking about skinny-dipping and the like. No real details. Only the kind of fun stuff that made me happy for her. They were good together."

"Can I ask why they didn't marry?" he asked as he cast again.

"Grandma said after two unpleasant divorces, she was going to stay single and have fun. While she and Davey were exclusive for the last five years of her life, they didn't live together, and honestly, she said she liked being by herself. Keeping her own schedule. Not having to keep house for a man."

She could still hear her grandma humming softly as she puttered around her house or her little flower garden. The thought of the house had her diaphragm tightening. Surely with the wedding on, Tiffany was going to give it to her. It was getting harder not to think about it. She wanted to putter in that house and plant flowers in that side garden so badly it made her teeth ache. She brought up a positive image to keep her spirits up. Maybe she'd try her hand at growing heirloom tomatoes. They would make good salsa.

"She sounds like a woman who knew her own mind." Dax shifted his long legs in the boat. "I like that in a woman."

She sent him a flirtatious smile as if to say *you'd better*. He laughed. "I think Davey wanted to get married but when Grandma turned him down and told him why, he wasn't willing to let her go. He accepted her on her own terms."

"Acceptance seems to be one of the main drivers in a successful relationship." Dax straightened when he had a tug on his line. "I've got one. Ariel, you'd better get ready for some healthy competition."

He started reeling in like a pro, and Sherlock went over to his side, his tail raised in its comma-like position.

"What's going to be *your* pleasure if you win, Captain Hotpants?"

He grabbed the net and hauled in a sizeable redfish, which he unhooked and measured at twenty inches. "You on your knees in red lace. How about that?"

She gulped, and it wasn't because he'd started cleaning the fish. "But I don't have any red lace, Captain Hotpants," she said in a playfully breathy voice.

"Honey."

The heated way he said that endearment had her thighs clenching. "Yes, baby?"

He was grinning as he put the fish in the cooler with the rest. "That can be remedied."

Suddenly, fudge sauce and her on her knees was all she could think about. He hauled two more fish in—a nice trout and another flounder—while she reeled in another slimy trout.

He was cleaning her fish when she said, "I say we call it. Both of us win. Which means I wear red lace and you wear chocolate sauce."

His grin lit her up with pure joy. "Not at the same time, however."

She puffed out a laugh. "That would be a mess."

"I like this fair and noble way of settling a bet, Elizabeth." He put her fish in the cooler and wiped his hands down with alcohol wipes. "I'm certainly going to like us both winning. Are we heading to Market Street for a few purchases after we get off the water?"

"How does that strike you?"

He smacked his lips. "Mighty fine, I must say. Are you ready to head back?"

"Are you?" He was the reason they were here mostly, and she wanted to make sure he was happy. "I know it was a big day for you."

Gazing out at the water, he laid his hands on his knees. "Ariel, this is one of the happiest days of my life. I could almost feel my grandpa thinking I'd done pretty damn well, coming back to fishing like this. With you. Thank you."

Her heart beat thickly in her chest at the steady way he was gazing at her. "Like I said, I'm glad I'm here with you. No place I'd rather be."

He extended his hand. She took it. "Me either."

"Careful," she cautioned as he pulled her to him and kissed her softly on the lips.

"I was only planning on *kissing* you." He nipped her bottom lip. "Sherlock is watching, after all."

She could hear the amusement in his voice. "Good point. Besides, I don't want to tip the boat and end up in the water. Did you see how slimy those trout were?"

He laughed in her ear, planting quick kisses along her neck. "Squeamish. I should have known. You didn't even clean one fish."

She poked him. "You offered!"

"I did." His drawl was husky. "I suppose we should head on back. If I kiss you any more, we're going to risk seriously rocking this boat."

Her belly tightened with need. "Start the motor."

She angled back to her seat as he set them on their way. The wind ruffled her short hair, and for the first time, she actually loved the feel and cut. Her former shoulder-length hair wouldn't be dancing around her head the same way. Acceptance. Maybe it was the way to go across the board. The sun warmed her face when she turned it up like she was a cute little sunflower. Laughing at herself, she heard

Sherlock give a short, delighted bark. Yeah, they'd all needed this.

When they returned, Davey helped them dock the boat. He exclaimed over their catch, and Ariel urged him to take the fish off their hands since they were still at the resort and likely not going to cook. He patted her on the cheek, his ruddy cheeks deepening with his endearing smile.

"I'm going to keep them in the freezer for you—to enjoy when you're living in your grandma's house."

She nodded past the tightness in her throat. "That's so sweet. You'll come over and we'll have our first fish fry."

"It's a deal." He jerked his head to Dax. "He's coming, right?"

Looking at Dax, she watched him pocket his aviator glasses with a grin. "If I'm invited. Davey, you should know I'm thinking I might be moving here too. I've got a new job as a corporate pilot."

The two men headed toward the Bronco, talking. Ariel was smiling as she followed them. It made her heart swell to see them getting along so well.

At the car, she gave Davey a huge hug. "Thank you for everything."

"Ah, baby girl, it's good to see you doing so well. Makes my heart happy, and wherever your grandma is—she wouldn't want me to speculate any—I'd bet she's pretty damn pleased herself. You look good, and you've got a pretty great fella here."

She kinda did. Her grin could not be contained. "See you soon?"

"If I don't see you sooner." He turned to Dax, and they shook hands warmly. "Nice to meet you too. Y'all come back now. Anytime. Even if you need to get away for a little while to escape the madness. All right?"

"All right," Ariel agreed, getting in the Bronco when Dax opened her door.

She knew Davey was pleased by the way he nodded at Dax. Moments later, they were on their way with Sherlock, and she was wiggling in her seat in happiness as she gave him directions to downtown.

Red lace.

Fudge sauce.

Best day ever.

They had fun finding her something in red lace, although it took two stores, but the fudge sauce was a piece of cake.

When they returned to the resort, people were waiting on the front steps of their cottage. She sighed. Dax sighed. Even Sherlock's pace slowed. They hadn't turned on their phones yet, and wouldn't you know, she probably had a slew of texts about the latest crisis.

"Stephan, I suddenly want to make a break for it."

Sherlock gave a dull whine and looked up at them with his sad, expressive eyes. She gave him an encouraging pat.

"Me too, Elizabeth." Dax looked down at her, his bearing becoming almost battle ready. "Should I hide our special little package here? The bag might—"

"Right." She worried her lip, telling herself she was an adult. "Maybe it would make them leave us alone?"

His laugh was as dry as the surrounding sand dunes on the beach. "Really? After everything we've experienced so far?"

"You're right." She groaned quietly. "Better to flaunt it, then. Make them wonder."

"I like that. Smile now. They've sighted us."

"How did they know we'd arrived anyway?" she hissed.

"*Lord of the Flies* lookouts likely."

She choked. "Good one. Okay, here we go."

The Three Tornadoes were on the front steps along with Alison and Presley, brightly colored sundresses flapping madly in the wind coming off the beach. Ariel noted Tiffany had used some pick-me-up regimen. Her eyes and skin were no longer puffy or red. One bonus. Thankfully her mother wasn't with them.

"Everything okay?" she asked brightly as they reached them, hoping she was wrong.

Tiffany and everyone else's gazes seemed to lower. She saw a few shocked expressions. Tricia even gasped aloud.

That's right. Lingerie and fudge sauce. Who's the lucky girl?

The shock and curiosity lasted less than the life of a fly before Tiffany strode over and nearly slumped against her, ignoring Dax. "Oh, Ariel. It's so awful. I keep thinking what's next."

She slid her arm around her sister, shouldering her weight as Sherlock gave them a wide berth. All her earlier happiness drained out of her, like she was a boat and her sister had poked holes in her all over. "What now, Tiff?"

"You need to see it for yourself." Tiffany took her hand and dragged her down the steps and then onto the path, Sherlock trotting at her side.

She could hear the herd of footsteps behind her and knew Dax was joining them. He wouldn't let her face this next crisis alone. She spotted the discreet sign on the ground pointing the way to the seaside area where Tiffany and Rob would exchange their marriage vows with the reception to follow in a tent. Following the path, she waited for the problem to become apparent, and boy, did it ever.

Stopping short, she felt her mouth gape like the trout she'd caught earlier. "Oh, you've got to be kidding!"

The usually pristine, carefully manicured green grass before her was pockmarked with pools of mud.

Bubbling pools of mud.

At least eight of them.

All situated where the wedding and reception were supposed to be held.

The Deverell wedding curse had struck again.

SIXTEEN

"WHAT HAPPENED?"

Ariel's shocked cry had Dax lengthening his strides and walking around the women. He'd been hanging back out of courtesy, but Ariel needed him. When he reached them, Tiffany had sunk down in her red heels until she was crouching near the ground, as if she couldn't stand up any longer. He could see why.

"The maintenance crew said the sprinkler system backed up," the bride-to-be said hoarsely.

Dax gazed at the wreckage before him, nearly rocking back on his heels, and he was used to watching the wreckage caused in flying incidents. "Holy shit—excuse me, ladies," he remembered to say by way of an apology.

But like his grandpa said, if there was ever a time to call a spade a spade...

Mud pits were oozing in what had been a grassy area that earlier would have made Augusta and the Masters proud. He knew they were thinking it had to be the curse, and they might be right. Or it could simply be a sign from God that this wedding was not supposed to happen. Wasn't this coming after Tiffany had disappeared last night and sought out her ex?

"Oh, Ariel," Tiffany moaned, looking up with bleak eyes. "What are we going to do? The maintenance manager said it would be impossible to fix before the wedding."

He watched Ariel almost slump in defeat. That he could not abide. He came over to join them, the other women hanging back, their dramatic whispers audible.

Ariel turned to look at him, and she nodded briefly before putting an arm around her sister. "Run us through the situation, Tiffany. Then we'll figure out a plan."

Her sister moaned again before practically throwing herself at Ariel, making Sherlock take a few steps off and plunk down on the ground. "They found it like this sometime late morning. After calling in the groundskeeper and then someone from the irrigation company, they told me they still don't even know where the leak is. They can't fix anything until that happens."

Dax knew he should feel relieved. The wedding was looking like it wasn't going to happen. Except Ariel was pale, and she looked almost as heartbroken as her sister. God, he felt conflicted. "What's the plan for finding the leak?" he asked.

Tiffany pinched the bridge of her nose. "A crew is supposed to be coming from the company with special equipment, but they said finding the leak won't matter. The ground will need to dry out, and it would be impossible for that to happen before the wedding. The resort's event manager tried to call you to explain we might need to move the wedding site—the lodge is too small—but then she clammed up and said it would be difficult to do since it's so last minute and it's high wedding season."

This is what he'd wanted since she'd hit on him, and yet there was no victory in it. "Where's Rob?"

"He went for a run after talking to both the maintenance guys and the irrigation person." She pushed her platinum blond hair behind her ear, looking pale and in shock. "He said he was going to punch something if he didn't run it off."

Dax couldn't blame him. This was a shitshow with not much to be done. He glanced at Ariel, who was biting her lip, clearly still trying to think her way out of the impossible.

"Ariel, if there's anyone who can figure out what to do, it's you." Tiffany started crying, and while Dax knew the situation was horrible, he couldn't help but think he'd never met a woman who cried as much as she did. "You know how much I wanted to get married here."

The crying grew louder. Ariel comforted her sister. Dax stalked out onto the field, stepping around mud pits, examining the problem. Sherlock followed him, sniffing the ground and making a circle, his tail pointed in the direction of their trouble.

It was bad. FUBAR bad. Why in the hell wasn't Rob here? Maybe he was taking it as a sign too? He rubbed the back of his neck. Jesus!

Ariel appeared beside him, her little body tight with tension. "Can you believe it? This kind of thing just doesn't happen to other people."

He thought of all the weddings in his family. They'd all been happy and disaster-free. Not even a drop of rain to mar them. "What are the chances of finding another venue that's going to make Tiffany happy?" he made himself ask.

Her blue eyes narrowed. "Zero, although I'll try, but that's assuming anything worth having is available. It's May in Charleston, the wedding capital of the South. Good luck there. We'd have to find a barn last minute on someone's property to rent and then..."

She left the details hanging. It was Wednesday. They were starting to set up for the wedding on Friday.

"Okay..." he said. "So that's one possibility."

"A really far-off one." She faced him and pressed a hand to her forehead. "I just have to find a solution, Dax. I have to make this work!"

He gently took her by the shoulders. "Honey, maybe this is a sign that things aren't meant to be. I don't know a lot about curses, but coming on the heels of Tiffany disappearing last night—"

"Dax! I won't get my grandma's house if Tiffany doesn't get married."

"What?"

She lowered her hand slowly, biting her lip. "I didn't want to tell you because... Oh God! Where do I start? Because you already think badly of her. Plus, how do you spin a story about your sister blackmailing you to be her wedding planner with your grandma's house? Which was supposed to be mine anyway before Mother gave Tiffany the deed and cooked up this scheme."

Dax couldn't believe this. "Wait! Your sister is blackmailing you?"

Sherlock gave a whine as Ariel nodded stiffly. "I know it sounds bad, and it *is* bad."

"Bad?" He cupped her face so she could see his eyes. "Ariel, this is awful. Like lower than pond scum—"

"I know!" She stalked away. "Tiffany thought I could offset the curse or manage the damage. And I've worked so hard on this wedding. God! I mean, if I have to pick up a shovel and start digging out this mud, I will. Dax, that's how committed I am to getting her married."

And getting her grandma's house...

The cute white one with the green shutters, the palm tree she'd tried to climb, and the shell chimes that she'd made when she was a girl.

He set his hands on his hips as he studied her. Her chin was thrust in the air, and he wouldn't have been surprised if she'd raised her fist and given a solemn vow. His heart was raw inside him, he realized, pulsing thickly, and he knew what he was going to do as he listened to its beat. What he had to do.

"Ariel, when I lost confidence in my mission as best man, I realized that you were my new mission. That I was going to do everything in my power to help you. I'm not going to deviate from that now."

Her lips wobbled slightly before she walked over and wrapped her arms around him. "You have no idea what hearing that means to me, especially knowing how you feel about things."

"That doesn't matter." He gathered her tighter toward him and stroked her back. "You matter. Because I'd do anything for you."

Suddenly, Rob's words came back to him. The things you did for...love. Whoa! L-O-V-E. Yeah. Okay. That was... Early. Very early. But not surprising. Especially given how things stood between them. On the water today, he'd looked toward the future and could envision fishing with Ariel over and over again. He knew Gramps would approve of her. His family too. That was the gold standard as far as he was concerned.

He angled back from the woman who'd brought him back to something he loved today. The vibrancy she'd had earlier was nearly gone. He was determined to bring back the light inside her, the one he loved, the one she shared so freely with others.

"You're the best." Her voice was hoarse with emotion. "Do you know how much?"

He lifted his shoulder, uncomfortable. "You'd do it for me."

When she nodded, he knew he'd made the best decision of his life. Her. Helping her find a way out of this. Putting his pride and sense of duty to Rob aside.

"The only way I see this place changing before the wedding is if we find the leak and resod the whole area. It's going to be a bitch, but it's doable with the right muscle, and you know I have the right muscles, Elizabeth."

"That I do, Stephan." She leaned up, tugging on his shirt, and laid her mouth on his.

The kiss was soft, slow, and sweet, and when she drew back, her eyes were brighter. He also could feel a new and stronger conviction that he would help her through this crisis and any other she'd encounter.

"All right, assuming they can find the leak stat," she ticked off in a practical tone that called to the military officer in him, "I'd need to talk to the resort about resodding. I don't know how many staff they have for this kind of emergency. Getting everything done in time is going to be tough."

Then she shook herself, mentally steeling herself for what lay ahead, and this was something he loved about her too. She was tenacious. He could see why she and Sherlock found people for a living. Putting a comforting hand on her shoulder, he flexed his bicep. "Like I said, you've got my muscles and a few others of the Navy's best coming. I'll bet they'll come early to help. We can be grunt labor if needed. Don't lose faith now."

Because she had to have that house—if he had to redo the whole area by himself.

"How could I lose faith when I have you by my side?" She stroked Sherlock under the ears when he returned and pressed his head against the side of her leg. "All right, I need to huddle with the event manager. The guy who trained me in disaster recovery's motto was brick by brick."

He could see her standing on the site of destruction, assessing the damage, girding herself for what needed to be done. Sherlock would be at her side. Like he was now. "Brick by brick, baby. I'll go talk to Rob about getting the rest of the Navy guys on board."

Cupping her face in both hands, he waited until she met his eyes. He held her gaze, showing her his determination and his concern for her. Then he lowered his head and kissed her lightly on the mouth until she sighed. When he leveled back, he was more settled too, one hell of an indicator about his feelings.

She enticed him.

She intrigued him.

She made him laugh.

She made him hard.

She made him calm.

She made him want to give her everything.

What more could you ask for in a woman?

He held her by the shoulders because he didn't want to let her go. "I've got ya."

"I know." She blew out a breath. "Thank God. I'll catch you later."

With that, he took off for the beach, hoping to run into Rob coming back. He spotted him about two minutes into his own jog, hampered some by his flip-flops. Rob increased his stride when he spotted him and came to a dead halt when he reached him, wiping the sweat from his brow with his forearm. He'd changed T-shirts, thank God, and seeing the simple Navy emblazoned across the front gave Dax the additional punch he needed. Teamwork. He and Rob were trained in that. It would guide them through this mess.

"Thanks for coming," Rob bit off, wiping his brow, and as a start, it wasn't bad. "You heard?"

Dax nodded crisply. "It's a shitshow, but we have a working plan. Ariel is going to talk to the event coordinator or whatever they're called. If they can find the leak ASAP, we can dig out the mud and resod before the wedding. You, me, Carson, Perry, and the staff here."

"It's a good plan." Rob rubbed the back of his neck. "Jesus, when Tiff first told me about the Deverell wedding curse, I thought she was being dramatic. But now? Shit, it's been one thing after another. I still don't even know why she was so upset before. Why she pulled the disappearing act. She wouldn't say."

Dax knew a fishing expedition when he heard it. He clamped his teeth together.

"I take it from your stance that you're not going to tell me." He turned to fully face him. "Never mind. I probably don't want to know. I only know that when I told Tiff we could get married downtown at city hall and then have a party at a restaurant somewhere, she lost her mind. This wedding..."

Dax watched his friend kick at the sand and felt his frustration.

"This wedding means more to her than I can understand, but I love her, so I'm...doing the best I can."

Dax understood that, and he put his hand on his friend's shoulder to tell him so. "That's all any of us can ever do."

He cracked his neck. "One thing I want to know is why you'd help dig out a bunch of mud—and put in fresh dirt, because we'll have to do that too—and then resod the whole damn thing for a wedding you're so dead set against."

Dax's jaw locked. Sure, he might have decided to help because of Ariel, but as he gazed at his friend, a hundred good memories flashed through his mind. Suddenly he knew he wasn't only doing it for Ariel, and that was okay too.

"Don't be a dick. You know why. Now, can we head back and get things going? You clearly need something to do, or you're going to go crazy."

Rob joined him as Dax started walking back to the resort. "Thanks, man."

He flipped him the bird.

When his friend laughed, some of the tightness around his diaphragm lessened.

Maybe he and Rob could get through this wedding and still be friends.

SEVENTEEN

She wasn't sure they were going to make it.

Ariel finished her meeting with the event manager and slumped against the wall after leaving the office. Felicity had put on her fake smile, assuring Ariel they would do everything they could. Then she'd started talking about acts of God and their contract and how this was an impossible situation, one they would make the best of, but that they couldn't guarantee anything.

Her mind had turned red at that, and she'd stood up, telling the woman the company needed to find the leak ASAP. She then outlined the plan they had in mind to dig out the mud and resod the field—with some of their own guests!—pointing out that the resort probably had another wedding the following week, right? They wanted to take care of this problem as quickly as possible, or they were going to have another irate wedding party and a blast of terrible reviews.

Felicity's mouth had thinned, but she'd picked up the phone and called the irrigation company again, demanding an emergency crew. Then she'd called maintenance. When she'd finished, she'd told Ariel they would bring in extra people to help, but the wedding party's assistance was welcome.

You betch your ass it was.

When she and Sherlock reached the cottage, she was jittery from not eating. Entering the cottage, she stopped short at the sight awaiting her. Dax was having a mint julep with one of her favorite people ever.

She gave a cry and ran across the room. "Jeffrey!"

He thrust his copper cup at Dax and stood up quickly, looking dashing like usual in a spring blue suit with a lavender Hermès scarf around his neck. Her arms were around him moments later, Sherlock giving him a nudge of greeting as well.

"I took an earlier flight, sensing you might need some support since it's been worse than we could have imagined. From what Captain Hotpants told me, I'm glad I did."

She smelled the familiar scent of the leather and citrus soap he bought from some boutique men's store and felt her heart trip in sheer joy. "You're the best! The absolute best!"

"Damn right I am." He pulled back and touched the ends of her hair. "I know you sent me a photo of your hair, but seeing it in person, I adore it! It's so Myrna Loy on you."

"Why, thank you." She hugged him again because she was so happy to see his beloved face, those deep brown eyes framed by emerald green Gucci glasses and his short layered hair combed back in perfect waves. "Now, I need a drink. I've been remiss with my flask."

"We'll work on that." Her brother took her hand and led her over to the kitchen table where an empty copper cup sat. "I made a pitcher of mint juleps after hearing about the mud pit extravaganza out back. Help yourself. They're in the fridge. Then we're about to get serious."

Ariel watched him walk toward his Louis Vuitton duffel bag, which he'd treated himself to this past Christmas. Pulling out the pitcher, she watched Dax rise and cross to her. As she poured herself a drink, he leaned in and kissed her cheek, whispering, "I've finally met someone related to you that I like."

She beamed, her heart doing its happy little Jeffrey dance. "There's no one like him."

"You two have that in common." Dax added a sprig of mint from the side tray and finished off her drink with a wink. "Drink up. Your brother has a surprise for you."

"It's for all of us really." Jeffrey brought his duffel over to the table. "Ariel, sit. You look ready to fall down. We'll have to give you something to eat too. Now, given how things were going, I went the extra mile. Originally, I was only going to bring some sage sticks to burn, but honey, it sounded like we needed more this time. Because you're going to get the house of your dreams, which was already rightfully yours I might add—"

"Let's not go there right now, Jeffrey."

"Yes, let's not go there," Dax agreed, not at all surprised Jeffrey would have known about this insanity.

They traded a look. "Oh, I love having an anger partner in this, but for your sake, Ariel, I'm holding it in and focusing on the positive." He unzipped the bag and pulled out the first item, his brown eyes twinkling. "Rabbit feet for luck. Party pack."

She eyed the giant bag of white feet he set on the table, laughing. "You think you got enough?"

He shook his head as he handed Dax a white foot, which he stuck in his pocket. "Not even close, baby sister, but it was the biggest size they had. I thought we might hand them out at the wedding for all the guests to shake in the air—birdseed isn't going to do anything. With all the new bad luck Dax was telling me about—mud oozing out of the very ground like Tiffany opened a portal to mud hell—we might need to add one to everyone's welcome bag. Tell them to walk around in the moonlight while chanting invocations to the wedding gods under the moon. Next up."

He drew out two large Mary candles and handed one to her and then Dax, who was chuckling steadily now.

"We'll light these now and won't blow them out until Tiffany throws her bouquet and rides off into the sunset with her hot pilot hubby." He dug into the bag and brought out a lighter and set the flame to the wick. "May our blessed Mother bring this wedding about with ease and grace."

Ariel was already wiping tears from her eyes but laughed harder when he drew out a vial of holy water with a label indicating it was from Chartres. He sprinkled it around the candles and then flicked some her way and then at Dax, who jumped back, laughing so hard he was wheezing.

"My God!" Dax could barely get the words out. "I could have used your help before I went on dangerous missions."

Jeffrey patted him sweetly and winked. "I'm available anytime, Captain Hotpants. Now, let's see what else we have. Palo santo sticks. The smoke is clearing like sage but very warming, the woman at the metaphysical shop told me."

He lit two, making Ariel sputter as she tried to drink her delicious mint julep through the smoke.

He pulled out a couple of white and purple sachets and handed one of each to her and Dax after he carefully put down the sticks in a bowl. "Lucky stones, I'm told. The woman said to me, and I quote, 'Keep them on you at all times to ward off the curse.' She was a font of information."

She met Dax's dancing eyes. He didn't look like the stressed soldier who'd gazed at the mud pits and flexed his muscles earlier, and she didn't feel like she wanted to throw up anymore. That was Jeffrey for you. "What else did this font of spiritual wisdom sell you?"

Digging into the bag, he brought out a packet of dried flowers. "We're to tuck these under the bride's pillow to encourage love and happiness." He picked up the vial of holy water again and flicked some on it with his usual aplomb.

"I'll let you tuck that under Tiffany's pillow," she told him, taking another fortifying drink of her mint julep as Dax handed her a power bar with a grin. "Thank you."

"Ah..." Jeffrey hugged himself. "He's already feeding you. I knew it! When I saw your picture, Captain Hotpants, my hands started tingling, and that's always a sign—"

"That someone's going to get lucky," she filled in. "Jeffrey has an inner 'get laid' meter."

Her brother cut her a glance. "I like to call it my divining rod. But I digress. I stopped short at the voodoo stuff. Scares the bejesus out of me. But this last one I could not be without. I think Dax will agree with me."

Leaning over conspiratorially, he pulled out a thumb-sized dark object. "It's a lucky piece of wood. I was like, how have I gone my whole life without it? Here, Dax, I got you one."

Dax slapped Jeffrey companionably on the back. "Jeffrey, I hate to tell you, but my wood is already plenty lucky."

Ariel put her hand over her mouth to cover another giant chortle. "I can personally attest to that," she said through her laughter.

Jeffrey pursed his lips and gave Dax a speculative gaze. "I'll bet. Well, my dears, there ends my contribution."

When he bowed elegantly, Ariel clapped, and Sherlock gave a happy bark. "Oh my God! Jeffrey, you are *the* best."

"You know it." He retrieved his mint julep and Dax's and held it out to him. "A toast. To surviving another Deverell wedding and getting Ariel her house."

She met her brother's dancing eyes before locking gazes with Dax. Amusement flickered in those gorgeous green orbs. Her world felt perfect. She wanted to bar the door and keep everything else out.

"To all that." She toasted Jeffrey first and then Dax.

They all drank for a moment before Jeffrey set his cup down. "Ariel, let's go see mud pit central. I'm going to light some sage and bring the holy water. You two grab your drinks."

They were out the door moments later, making quite the image, no doubt—Jeffrey carrying a sage stick, the acrid smoke trailing behind them. She and Dax holding hands, Sherlock trotting beside them.

When they reached the disaster site, Jeffrey's sharp intake could probably have been heard in the state capital two hours away. "Heavens, I don't think sage and holy water are going to work."

She was already depressed, seeing the endless yards of oozing brown. "So what's next?"

He didn't hesitate. "A virgin sacrifice?"

Dax barked out a laugh before biting it off.

Ariel snorted as she swept her hand around the resort. "Good luck with this crowd."

"Right." Jeffrey opened the vial of holy water and started sprinkling. "I should have bought the family-size option."

When he wandered off, stepping carefully because of his leather loafers, Dax's hand came around her waist. "See. We have muscle, and we have a spiritual guide."

Jeffrey upended the last of the holy water and made the sign of the cross with a bow of his head.

Another reluctant laugh escaped her lips. "Maybe we need a Tibetan bowl next. How do you feel about chanting? I heard it in Bali. It was supposed to do good things..."

They both started laughing so hard they were wiping tears.

"God, we're a pair, Stephan."

He put his arm around her and kissed the top of her head. "Elizabeth, from where I'm standing, it all seems pretty perfect."

She leaned her head into his side.

Funny, that's how she felt too, despite it all.

EIGHTEEN

When he'd imagined his duties as best man, backbreaking work in the mud hadn't been on the list.

Being caked with mud made it worse, and Dax had to fight the urge to scratch his skin. The temperature was up in the mid-eighties, and while the air was humid, the sun was beating down hard. He and the other men had stripped off their shirts pretty quickly after the emergency irrigation crew had found and corrected the leak. The maintenance crew had brought out every available shovel, and he, Rob, and the team members had gotten down to the tough business of shoveling the mud and putting it in wheelbarrows.

In some places, they had to dig out the mud-soaked sod, which was a bitch. The sandy nature of the soil and the invasive grass roots were the kind of adversary up there with man versus beast. But Dax wasn't complaining. Good physical labor gave him something to do to achieve his goal.

The Three Tornadoes had strong-armed the *Lord of the Flies* boys into pushing the wheelbarrows and dumping the mud in the appointed area out of sight; their fathers hadn't been willing to pass up their scheduled golf game with Trey.

Speaking of whom, the good times guy himself had waved and called out a jovial "Good luck" as he'd wheeled his golf set by, making Dax want to punch him in the face.

Tiffany and her tornado brethren were standing watch a good distance from the work area, drinking under patio umbrellas. This after the bride had enlisted Rob to pick up the incoming wedding guests this morning, one of whom included his mother. His dad wasn't coming since they'd lost track of his whereabouts long ago. Dax knew he'd been conflicted about not helping earlier, but now he was back, coated in mud and working a few pits down.

His own girl was off with the resort manager, working on bringing in dry dirt along with enough sod to fill in the area they were clearing. Afterward, the maintenance crew was going to somehow clean the area to make it look sparkling green—using mops to get the mud off any remaining grass, if needed.

Was the whole thing a little crazy? Yes.

But here they were.

Somehow, they were going to get it done. Rob would get married to Tiffany. Ariel would get her grandma's house. They would all live happily ever after.

If they didn't go crazy first...

He was digging out another mud-soaked area when he felt a light tap on his straining back. Turning, he was happy to see Ariel standing there, holding out a bottle of cold water along with some spray sunscreen. He sank the shovel in the ground, took the water, and downed the whole thing, not bothering to wipe his mouth since he'd only streak more mud on his face. "The sunscreen isn't going to do much good, you know. Not much bare skin left."

She eyed his muddy chest and winced. "True, but I

didn't know if you could get burned while covered in mud. I thought you might spray it on as a contingency."

He liked contingencies. He opened his arms. "Spray away, honey."

Her thoroughness was a sign of her character, and he loved the way her brows knit as she ran her gaze over him, making sure she hadn't missed anywhere. "Best we can do given the situation. Jeffrey is going for more holy water at a local store, you'll be happy to know."

Yeah, her brother had said he and manual labor didn't see eye to eye. His energy was better used for other things. Like offsetting this horrible curse. "At this point, more water is not what we need. Any Buddhist sacred mandala sand maybe?"

"I'll check." She smiled warmly, the sweet expression grabbing his heart hard. "God, Dax, you're a trooper."

"So are you." He held out his mud-caked hand, his expression teasing. "Want your official war paint?"

"I might not look like it, but I'm covered in sludge on the inside." She rolled her eyes toward the Three Tornadoes, all decked out in designer sunglasses and more colorful magazine-cover-ready sundresses. "If you knew what I was dealing with… I told Jeffrey I needed another lucky rabbit's foot."

He cocked his hip her way. "If you want to reach in there, honey, you can have mine."

"Tempting." Her heated blue eyes told him how much. "But I need to run a few errands."

"Take the Bronco." He spied the thunderclouds in the distance. "My keys are on the kitchen table. I don't want you in a downpour if that menace comes our way."

Please, God, don't let it come their way.

Her wince said it all. "I told Jeffrey to fling holy water at those clouds and burn enough sage to make the birds cry foul. Okay, I'm off. If you pucker up, I'll give you a kiss, but no muddy business."

He sent her a cheeky wink. "Good play on words. Scout's honor, you're safe."

Leaning in from the waist, he puckered up. She carefully leaned in and kissed him. Once. Twice. And then once more, as if the kisses weren't enough for her. He understood. He felt the same way.

When she eased back, she wasn't so pale from the stress. "See you later, Stephan."

"Count on it, Elizabeth."

He watched her walk off before he resumed his work, telling himself that what they were doing was going to work. Positive intention helped.

When he heard his name shouted sometime later, he spun around and grinned at the sight. Carson and Perry—the other groomsmen—were striding across the lawn, both already stripping off their Navy T-shirts. Behind him were two more of their buddies from the Academy. Gunner and Frank were walls of all-American muscle, and they stripped their shirts off as well, making the Three Tornadoes whoop and holler like groupies at a strip show. Dax watched Rob sink his shovel into the earth and jog over.

When Carson reached Dax, he slapped him on the back. "Jesus. What a FUBAR!"

"Amen to that," Perry said, adjusting his aviator sunglasses. "Rob mentioned some wedding curse when he called. Looks like we need one of my grandma's remedies from the bayou."

Dax thought of Jeffrey. "We already have a Minister of

Good Juju. He brought a party pack of rabbit feet and holy water and a whole bunch of other stuff."

"Looks like we're going to need it." Frank inclined his chin to the mess as Rob joined them. "You piss somebody off upstairs, Rob? Because I've been to more than twenty weddings, and I ain't seen anything like this."

Rob man-hugged everyone. "So we're special."

Dax jerked his thumb toward Rob. "What he said. You guys ready to start shoveling? Because we're going to need every able body to get this done."

Perry pointed to the gathering clouds. "Tell me I'm hallucinating."

"Ignore it." Rob's jaw practically popped. "We can't be that unlucky."

Dax fought a laugh. Sure they could. And they were...

Forty minutes later, they were hit with the kind of downpour that had coined phrases like raining like cats and dogs and coming down in buckets. The Three Tornadoes' anguished cries could be heard as they made a run for better shelter. Dax and the others worked in the rain until he heard Rob's shrill whistle, signaling a break.

The caked mud on his skin was sticky again, so Dax decided to head back to the cottage to shower. He called out to his friends that he'd be back and then jogged through the rain, his tennis shoes squelching. God, they'd be a dead loss after this.

In the shower, he reviewed their progress. They'd almost dug up all the mud and ruined sod out of the eight plugged sprinkler system areas. What it would be like after the storm, he had no idea, but worrying about it wouldn't help anyone. Dirt was being brought in later today along with the new sod. Ariel had insisted the resort bring in nighttime work lights so they could continue in the dark if needed.

But this rain could last a while...

When he finished his shower, he wrapped a towel around his waist and looked out the window. The rain continued to fall in hard sheets. Maybe it was the sheer impossibility of everything, but he could feel the ache in his back from shoveling along with a pull toward disheartenment.

What if they didn't make it? What then? Ariel had to have her house, and as for Rob... His friend wanted to get married, so Dax was going to help him.

Slapping his cheeks with aftershave as much to snap himself out of it as to clean himself up, he put his bad mood aside and went to pull on dry clothes. When he heard a knock on the front door, he detoured to it and smiled when he spotted Jeffrey with a large black mesh bag filled with brown paper sacks.

"Lunch for the working males. Steak sandwiches from my favorite place in town. I thought y'all could use some good grub."

Jeffrey had the same kind and easy way with people Ariel had, and Dax had to guess they'd gotten it from their father. "Thanks, man." The smell of grilled meat and fried onions made his stomach grumble. "Any idea where Ariel is?"

"She's checking out a couple of barns on some private properties to see if there's another last-minute option. The two I visited were disasters, the best option being a house and beach area owned by a grizzled old fisherman named Montlick who told me we couldn't have the wedding on the site where he was digging for a megalodon."

"A megalodon?"

"There are tall tales about those babies all around Charleston." Jeffrey showed his pearly whites with a laugh. "Shark teeth are a common beachcomber's item, especially on Folly Beach. Suffice it to say, Tiffany won't like any option—even if we could find a viable one last minute. The resort doesn't have a good backup, and when they desperately suggested we might cram into the lodge, after all..."

Dax whistled. "How'd that go?"

Jeffrey made a show of knocking his head against the doorframe. "Let's just say Tiffany might have turned into an official bridezilla on crack. Eyes popping out of her head. Platinum blond hair standing on end. She pretty much told them they needed to fix things and do what they'd promised, but she's always been a broken record that way. Don't get me started."

He was tempted to ask for more details. Ariel was important to him, and her interactions with the Three Tornadoes were as impenetrable to him as a conversation in Swedish or something. From the sound of it, Jeffrey's relationship with them wasn't any better.

"I need to get the rest of these sandwiches delivered." Jeffrey winced at the rain. "You know the weather forecast called for clear blue skies today."

Dax wasn't surprised. The entire area of Charleston was probably seeing its most beautiful day ever—but not here. "Apparently, this Deverell curse I'm starting to really believe in is stronger."

"It's a force of nature—like the Deverell women. I was two when Stormy and the Three Tornadoes blew into my life. My first word was help."

Dax gaped at him. "Shit, man."

"I'm mostly kidding." He gave an amused smile. "But not really. The Deverell women were all about creating scenes. Inventing drama. Making senseless trouble. They are masters of guilt and manipulation and verbal abuse coupled with sweetness. I liken them to chocolate dusted with cayenne pepper in a candy box. Ariel is the exception."

He couldn't stop himself. "How is she the exception, Jeffrey? I want to know everything there is to know about her."

"That makes me happy." He twirled his golf umbrella like Fred Astaire might before leaning on it, crossing his ankles. "Dax, Ariel is what I'd call an old soul, a special soul. You can see it in her eyes, something she and Sherlock share. If you look at Stormy and the Three Tornadoes closely, you'll notice that they're like new brass. I love to go antiquing, so let me assure you—there's a big difference."

He didn't do antiques, but he understood the premise. "I'll bet."

"As for why she's that way, I'd like to think God or the universe or whatever governs things simply knew we needed her. She was the first person I told I was gay, and truthfully, I hope she's holding my hand when I die because she's the most special person I've ever met. I know I'll die with a smile on my face, and what more could any of us ask for?"

Depressing death thoughts aside, Dax had to agree. "She does have a way of making you laugh or smile, doesn't she?"

"None better." Jeffrey hoisted his umbrella over his head with a twirl and started down the stairs. "I need to make a few more calls for Ariel. I'll see you later, Dax."

"Thanks again for the sandwich," he called.

Shutting the door, he sat down to eat, noticing how little he liked the quiet. He was missing Ariel hard. When he polished off his sandwich, he picked up his phone.

> How are the errands going? We had to break because of the rain. Glad you have the Bronco, although maybe it's only raining here in Curse Central.

ARIEL

> Yeah, I heard. No rain where I am. Blue skies all the way. Found a barn we could rent, but it's... 😅 Let's just say Jeffrey would need a party pack of holy water and sage sticks. 👻 We'd have to clean it out, and I don't think it's been cleaned since the 1800s. Not sure the attic is even safe to walk in. The "charming pond" is more like a man-made water pit dotted with gators. 🐊

> That had better mean NO then. Elizabeth, you know how much I esteem you, but I am not doing gators. 🤺

ARIEL

> When I mentioned deterrents for the gators, he asked me if I meant something other than a shotgun. 😱 Then the owner told me there are devices that emit a sound to keep them away, but they're not like the devices that keep mice away, are they?

> People could lose a leg or an arm, and I happen to like mine. 🦵 And yours... 😊 Forget the barn. We'll start digging again after the rain starts. What's our drop-dead time for wedding setup?

ARIEL

With the wedding at four on Saturday, we have until eleven at the latest. The event manager and I think we've calculated right. But this is new territory. 😅

You coming back? I'll see if Jeffrey has a steak sandwich for you. Also... I miss you. 🥺

ARIEL

Steak sounds good. I miss you too. 🥩 See you soon. If a gator doesn't get me. 🐊, 🙆

Not funny!! You've got your rabbit foot, right? 🐰 See you soon. If it's more than thirty minutes, I'm calling in the Marines. 🎖

ARIEL

Huh? But you're Navy...

Exactly! LOL 😆

ARIEL

LMAO 💋

He pocketed his phone, knowing he was grinning like he'd just traded notes with a girl he liked in junior high. Heading out to Jeffrey's cottage to hopefully find her a steak sandwich, he grabbed an umbrella from beside the door. He ran into Rob coming out of his cottage two doors down.

"Hey!" Rob called unenthusiastically and headed toward him, his brows clamped together, something clearly on his mind.

Dax headed over to meet him. "Hey, yourself!"

Rob refused Dax's offer for a little shelter under the umbrella with a frustrated wave of his hand. "Any word on another venue?"

He shook his head and filled Rob in. By the end, Rob's jaw was locked like he'd been dressed down by a two-star general.

"Shit. The last thing we need is a wreck of a barn with gators out back. We can't cut a break, can we? Tiffany is crying all the time when she's not raging at fate. Thank God my mom doesn't expect me to spend tons of time with her. She said we could talk at the welcome cocktail party tonight for the early comers."

Dax grimaced. "At the lodge, right? Seven, if I recall the schedule. Rob, we're going to need every available hour to turn around the mud pit. You should go, but the rest of our buddies and I can keep going. All night if needed."

He swore harshly, water dripping off his hair and face. "I know, dammit, but I hate leaving you again. I appreciate you guys chipping in—"

"You know it." The rain fell harder, pelting his umbrella, making him have to speak up to be heard. "We'll get it done. Ariel got the resort to rent nighttime lighting."

"Tiffany is worried the lights will keep the guests up." Rob raked a hand through his wet hair. "I told her we don't have a choice. I've laid sod before, and it can be a bitch. That's assuming we don't have a ton more mud to dig out after this downpour."

Dax eyed the never-ending rain. "We'll do what we have to. Why don't you get some rest? You look bushed."

"I'm fine." He jerked his chin up, rain peeling down his tense face. "Even if I could, I can't sleep in our cottage. Tiffany is either on the phone or complaining in the main area with her girls. God, I can't wait for this wedding to be over. See you later."

Dax watched Rob stalk off to the lodge. He'd never thought about it until now, but he didn't want to have a wedding so stressful he'd be praying for the end. And he wouldn't. It wasn't his way. With that in mind, he headed to Jeffrey's cottage.

Her brother didn't have any more sandwiches, but he'd had requests for more, so they hopped into his silver Mercedes SL and picked up another order for the masses.

"I'll have to remember this place if I end up moving to Charleston for my new job," he told Jeffrey as they left the old country market store.

Which was sitting under clear blue skies. Not a threatening cloud anywhere. Like everywhere else in Charleston but Wedding Hell. The very sight made Dax want to grab some holy water himself and shake it at the sky. How could it only be raining at the resort? Don't tell him this was a micro-climate moment.

"Ariel knows this place well," Jeffrey commented casually as they drove back to the resort. "You can always text for recommendations too. Seeing as how I think you're going to be around after this..."

"Planning on it." He kicked out his feet, enjoying the seat warmer, he had to admit—the only modern feature he was tempted to install in his Bronco besides a new stereo system. "I can pick any city in the South with the new job. Even better, my new boss has a relation here who's in real estate. Offered to set me up."

"That's awfully nice," Jeffrey drawled, turning on the windshield wipers as they crossed out of seemingly blue sky into a wall of rain as they neared the resort. "Can you believe this? It's like there's a bad luck perimeter, and we just crossed it. The negative energy here is making my hair stand up. I tell you, Dax, if I hadn't grown up with the Deverell women, I don't think I would believe it. But I did and I do."

Dax didn't blame him. This whole wedding debacle was busting up his former notions of reality and woo-woo. He'd believed angels guided his way up in the skies, sure. As a kid, he'd loved the movie *Always* about the spirit of a pilot coming back to help his successor. A few of his buddies had received a protective medal of St. Joseph of Cupertino, the patron saint of pilots, when they'd graduated from the Naval Academy, and they all knew their families prayed for their safety.

But curses? He hadn't believed in them, but now he didn't want to be near another one with a ten-foot pole.

"I'm new to all this, but even with my background in science and engineering, I'm having a hard time thinking of another explanation." He watched the wind carry a swarm of spring leaves through the air. "You think we're going to have the wedding venue back in shape in time?"

Jeffrey made a humorous face. "The forces might be stacked against you, but like General MacArthur probably said in the Pacific, I'll bet on you boys."

He coughed out a laugh. "You into military history, Jeffrey?"

"Sweetie, I *adore* anything military. I can't get enough of the uniforms, and everything is so tough and phallic. From the tip of a fighter jet to military pilots drawing giant schlongs in the sky."

Dax coughed out a laugh. Jeffrey was talking about Penis-Gate a few years back. "To set the record straight, I have *never* drawn a penis-shaped pattern with my aircraft."

"Too bad. I'll bet it would have been a good one."

Dax was trying hard not to laugh as Jeffrey pulled into the parking lot and whipped into the empty space beside Ariel's totally soaked golf cart. "It was real nice of you to offer Ariel your ride, Captain Hotpants. I did, but she insisted she'd be fine in her Barbie cart. I wonder what had her taking your offer instead of her dear older brother's?"

He wasn't going to go there because he imagined Jeffrey had a naughty answer. "My ride is better."

Jeffrey sucked in an outraged gasp. "Take that back. I love my Mercy."

He *would* use a sweet nickname for his car. "Jeffrey, I'm sure your car is superior."

Dax swung out of the passenger seat and reached for his umbrella while Jeffrey did the same. They'd just started back to the cottage when they heard their names shouted. Ariel was running through the rain with Sherlock at her side. He rushed over to cover her with his umbrella.

She tugged his shirt and drew him down for a kiss. "I needed that more than I need a drink, and I need one of those real bad. I couldn't drink since I was driving."

Jeffrey handed her one of the brown sacks. "Go take a shower and have some lunch with a drink. I'll finish up my to-do list, sister dear, and catch you two lovebirds later."

With a wink, he darted down the path through the rain. Dax's hand slid into Ariel's wet hand naturally, and they walked back to his cottage. Once inside, he dropped the umbrella on the floor and picked her up in his arms, heading to the shower. She looped her arms around his neck as Sherlock plopped down on his bed, his paws over his eyes.

He eyed the dog as they walked by. "That bad, huh?"

"Sherlock scented the gators, but I was too busy bemoaning the creak in the stairs leading up to the barn loft. I thought the whole place could come down on us. If I'd been paying attention, I wouldn't have let the owner take us to the pond. Sherlock's bark alerted me to the first gator, but he was a fast one. The owner and I had to run back to the barn."

"Good Lord!" He set her down in the bathroom and turned on the shower, helping her strip off her clothes. "We cannot unleash your cursed relatives in a place like that. Especially with food. Imagine the carnage."

Naked, eyes sparkling, she opened the shower door. "No, we can't, and the image was so horrendous that I need a big, strong handsome man to assuage my fears. Know anyone?"

"My buddy, Carson, and a couple of other guys arrived to help with the mud pit." He was already lifting off his shirt. "I could call them."

She quirked her pointer finger at him. "But I want Stephan, and no one else."

He chucked his pants off in one pass. "Good. Because as you can see, Stephan wants you."

She eyed his erection and fanned herself. "I do see. Oh my, oh my, oh my, how I see. You are bringing him in with you, honey?"

Trying to keep from laughing, he followed her into the water, savoring the heat, the steam, but mostly the woman. "Never leave home without him."

"Goody." She wrapped her wet hand around his cock, making his eyes cross. "Because I need a treat."

God, they both did, and he let her have her treat. Later he had his. When he finally could lift his head, she was sitting on his lap under the hot cascade of water, her forehead pressed to his shoulder. Her entire body was replete in his arms, and he felt the same way. Thank God the water was still hot.

"Are you asleep?" he whispered, not wanting to wake her up if she was taking a much-needed catnap.

"No, I'm just too relaxed to move." And she didn't budge even when he shifted her into his arms. "You know that moment after you've been on the go for hours and days, and you just crash. This is me."

She made a crashing noise while he picked her up and turned off the shower. Toweling them both off in the steamy shower stall, he took his time drying her, giving her a massage as he went. Her soft moans had him wanting to give her a little more TLC.

"I'm not going to be able to stand up much longer," she whispered heavily.

He set her onto the toilet lid and dried her hair. "Don't worry. I'll take care of everything."

After she was dry, he wrapped her in a resort robe and picked her up again, carrying her to his bedroom. She curled up on her side the moment he set her down, eyes still closed. He kissed her cheek. "Sleep."

Pulling the door closed, he found Sherlock outside in the hallway as if protecting his mistress. "She's exhausted. Watch over her while I go work."

The rain had finally stopped. His break was over.

Refreshed, he winced as he put on his wet, mud-soaked tennis shoes. The others were already digging up the new mud from the rainstorm. A fever of resignation hung in the air. He picked up his shovel and joined in.

Nicely dressed guests came and went, passing them on their way to the welcome party. Ariel came over at one point to check on them, but he waved her away, yelling that she looked too nice in her blue dress and should go have fun at the party. She made a face but didn't come closer. Sherlock didn't either. Smart dog.

He and the other men continued to work as the sun went down. Ariel supervised the nighttime lights being set up. Wedding guests came from the lodge after the party had broken up and watched their progress before taking off to their cottages. Even Rob's mom, whom Dax briefly said hello to. Then he was back at it. At times Dax felt like any progress they were making was sliding off his shovel like the mud he was shoveling.

But he kept going. The others did the same.

Rob came back from the party in his earlier work clothes and set to work beside them. He finally called it at two. "Get some shut-eye," he called. "We'll start at dawn."

Dax carried his shovel back to the cottage so it wouldn't rust on the ground. Ariel was inside on the computer, still in her blue party dress. "Jeez! I lost all track of time. I'm glad you stopped."

When Sherlock rose up and crossed to his side, he gave him a healthy pat since his hands were filthy. "Time for you to shut down as well." He watched her rub her eyes after closing her laptop. "How was the party?"

She was still sexy as hell despite her fatigue when she stretched. "About what you'd imagine. A lot of drama. Even though most of the guests have been to a Deverell wedding before, they ate up the mud pit incident like a helping of fried okra. I spent most of the time talking to the event manager. They're freaking out about the status of the area and what we're going to do if..."

She didn't need to state the obvious. He didn't know either. As he'd kept digging, he'd told himself brick by brick, just like she'd said. He stopped in front of her and leaned over until they were eye to eye since he was too muddy to sit next to her on the couch. "So you're calming them down too. Good Lord! Is there anyone you aren't soothing?"

"You and Jeffrey," she answered without pause, crawling off the couch. "Now, this time it's me telling you to grab a shower. Are you hungry? I made you a plate of canapés and hors d'oeuvres."

"What's the difference?" he asked as he headed back to his bathroom.

"Canapés are served with bread or pastry. Usually cold. The food tonight pleased Tiffany at least, and by that, I mean she didn't complain. God, Dax. I'm not sure we're going to make it."

He took her shoulders. "We'll make it. Me and the guys aren't going to quit until that damn field would pass for a championship football game."

Her big blue eyes were red and heavy with fatigue, but in them was a belief in him. She trusted him, and that had his heart swelling in his chest. "You're the best part of this, you know."

"So are you." She smiled and opened the shower door. "Come on, let's shower and crawl into bed. We have a big day tomorrow."

He didn't want to think about starting the manual labor at sunrise, so he stuck his head under the showerhead and let the water clear his head. She showered quickly, her whole body nearly hunched over with fatigue. Yeah, they were both bushed. When he left the shower, she was already wrapped in a towel. She touched his chest sweetly as she handed him a warm towel from the rack.

They brushed their teeth side by side, another homey little moment he savored. She'd brought her toiletries into his bathroom when he'd told her to use it since it was bigger than her own. He liked seeing her put moisturizer on her face afterward even, and then she was tugging his hand and drawing him to the bed.

He curled around her when she nestled into the covers, her eyes already closed. "Good night."

Her voice was hushed with fatigue. He kissed the side of her neck and tightened his arms around her. That they could be like this without sex somehow confirmed his conviction that they were right for each other. "'Night, Elizabeth."

The way her mouth curled into a smile had him smiling in turn.

He knew what they were facing with the wedding. Right now, the odds seemed against them. But here, with her, the entire world was at his feet.

And nothing was going to change that.

NINETEEN

She'd made it to Friday.

The men were working and ensuring the wedding site was going to be spick-and-span. Now all she had to do was drive Tiffany to the seamstress and hope against hope she loved the alterations. Because they didn't have any other choice—or so she would tell her sister if it came to it. Buying another wedding dress at this late date and getting it altered and steamed for *tomorrow* would be impossible.

"Ariel, I can't stand thinking my wedding dress won't be beautiful." Her sister pressed a can of cola to her forehead, fanning herself. "Can you turn up the air conditioner? I'm so hot."

Ariel cranked it up. She was freezing actually, but she wasn't going to argue. There were the butt warmers. "I have a water spritzer in my satchel for you."

Courtesy of Jeffrey, who was handling her Friday morning to-do list like the wonderful brother he was.

"Thanks." She dug in and sprayed herself copiously, the mist landing on Ariel's bare arms, making her shiver. "We're going to be all right with the wedding site, right? Rob told me they'd get it done, and one thing I love about Rob is that he always keeps his promises. Unlike my dad—what a joke it's going to be to have him walk me down the aisle."

She'd never liked Kevin, the girls' dad. "So why do it?" For the second time, in fact. "I know you're not close."

Tiffany gave her one of her *you're from another planet* looks, the kind Ariel had received ten times a day when Tiffany was a teenager. "Because that's what's done. It would be weird if he didn't. I worry enough about what people say as it is."

She told herself to simply drive. Offering another perspective was the path that led to hell, and they were already in it. "Look, we're here." She waved at the house. "I can't wait to see your wedding dress."

When she parked, Tiffany gripped her seat belt. "I don't want to get out. You go inside and see. If it's hideous, I don't want the image in my head."

Ariel gritted her teeth. Drama right now was so not welcome. Another reason she'd suggested she and Tiffany go alone—no mother, sisters, or friends. "Tiffany, it's going to be beautiful."

Letting herself out, she went around and did what Dax did. She opened her sister's door and smiled, offering her a hand out. Tiffany was so surprised she took it, and soon they were walking up the steps to the seamstress' pretty little house, step by step. Brick by brick, she told herself. When she pressed the bell, she shoved her hand in her skirt pocket, reaching for her lucky rabbit's foot. *Please let this go easy*.

Paula offered to make them tea when she let them in, which Tiffany turned down. "I just want to see my dress."

"Of course." Paula extended a hand toward the alteration room. "This way."

When they entered the room, the dress was on the

mannequin. Ariel made sure to gasp and clutch her heart. "Oh my God! Tiff, it's beautiful."

"Of course it is!" her sister chided. "That's the front. It's the same as when I bought it."

Ariel sent the seamstress an apologetic look and walked around to the back. "Well, I think what Paula did is ingenious, personally. But my opinion doesn't matter. Come see."

Tiffany clutched her hands. "Ariel, I'm scared. What if it's awful?"

Ariel clenched her teeth. *The woman who put in endless hours making your dress work is listening...* "That's ridiculous. It's just a little change in the back. Hey! I have a thought. What if it's even better than before?"

Tiffany edged around the back like it contained a landmine and snagged her arm when she reached her. She bit her lip as she finally looked at the dress—and promptly gave a yelp like she'd been stepped on. "It's so different... Oh God! Now everyone will know I've gotten fat."

Ariel pried her sister's hands off her arm, then gave her a one-armed hug. "Stop that kind of talk. You sound like Mother. I think it looks beautiful. Paula did a wonderful job. And on such short notice. Thank you!" She turned to the woman and hoped her smile looked grateful enough for both of them. "Let's go ahead and try this on, shall we?" Ariel said brightly, turning to Tiffany. "I can't wait to see you in it."

Her sister's facial expression was wooden as the seamstress led her into the changing room. Ariel squeezed into it, not wanting to leave Tiffany alone.

"Can you believe you're getting married tomorrow? How wonderful is that! Rob adores you, and soon you'll be living in beautiful San Diego. I've been there once. You're going to love it. Lots of nice restaurants and shops—"

"Ariel, stop!" Tiffany threw her top off and then started stripping down to her underwear. "I know what you're doing. Nothing is going to make this better. But I'm going to try it on and pretend this wedding dress is the same as when I bought it, when I thought I'd found my princess dress. So we aren't going to say anything about the back. You lace me up, and I won't even look there. Because otherwise I'll lose it and start crying, and I'm not sure I'll be able to stop."

The weight of her family was suddenly too great. Her legs felt almost leaden because of it. "Then that's what we'll do. And if you need to cry, you go on and cry. It's been a tough week."

Tiffany wiped her eyes. Ariel dug out more tissues from her satchel and handed them over. They got the dress on her, and Tiffany was true to her word. Personally, Ariel thought the seamstress had done a great job. "I know Paula will want to see you in it, but it looks like it fits to me. How does it feel?"

More tears fell. "Fine. It fits fine. Let's finish here and go back to the resort. I want to lie down. I'm getting a headache."

Ariel scooped Tiffany's hair up like she knew it would likely look tomorrow in an updo. "Don't you look beautiful. No one will be able to take their eyes off you."

"God, I hope so." Her muffled cry made Ariel's heart hurt. "My face is puffy, and my waist is bigger. I just want to be pretty. Because you're right. Everyone will be looking at me. I'm the bride. There's so much pressure. You know?"

"Yes, I know." Ariel nodded and let her sister's hair fall, fingering the platinum ends. "But you're going to get through it. You're the first of the Three Tornadoes. Who's more powerful than you?"

"Ariel, I'm not powerful." She tugged on the bodice and turned to the side in the mirror. "That's you. I'm the pretty one, who smiles to get what she wants, and when that doesn't work, I..."

Ariel's throat closed as Tiffany's teary eyes found hers in the mirror. "You what?"

Her face crumpled. "I blackmail my own sister." Tiffany turned and flung her arms around her. "Ariel, I'm so sorry! I never should have listened to Mother. You can have Grandma's house. Of course you can. I'll give it to you right after the wedding. She always wanted you to have it."

She clutched Tiffany back, shock making her mouth part. A seasoned part of her was waiting for the other shoe to drop. This wasn't the first time one of her sisters had capitulated before changing her mind. The Deverell women were mercurial by nature—but she wanted to believe Tiffany meant to sign the deed over to her. Keeping positive, Ariel hugged her back. "Grandma did, and I want it very much. Tiffany, I told you I'd help. You didn't have to go to such extremes."

Her frantic head nodding shook Ariel's frame. "I was scared you might not do your thing."

That hurt.

Pulling back, Tiffany cupped her face, soothing the hurt with the sweetest gesture ever between them. Ariel's heart fluttered at the sisterly warmth. "You always ride in and make sure everything turns out for us. You have since you were a little girl. I still remember how you reset the table after Tricia knocked it over on Terry's birthday. You cleaned up the broken dishes with a dustpan and then went to find more of Grandma's china to use. You managed to keep Grandma from getting upset over the broken dishes. And you got Grandma's promise that she wouldn't tell Mom. Ariel, you were five years old!"

It was one of her first memories. She'd tucked her hands behind her back when she'd talked to her grandma so she wouldn't see them shaking. She'd been so nervous. "I sometimes wish I wasn't that girl. That I didn't have to come in and clean things up. Make things perfect. Honestly, I'm not doing very well on the perfect front though, am I?"

Tiffany hugged her again. "Yeah, but we all knew about the Deverell wedding curse. We expected things would go wrong. You're the only one I could trust to make things right. I mean, look at the sprinkler system nightmare. The resort was going to pat us on the back and try and cram us into the lodge. You insisted they fix it. You came up with a plan. Because that's what you do. Oh Ariel! I'm so grateful for you."

Ariel thought she had a tough skin after all the years of being on the outs with her sisters, but she could feel a few of the walls she'd erected start to crumble. "Thanks, Tiff. Now...how about we step out there and let that poor seamstress see what your beautiful dress looks like on you? Once we do that, we'll pack it up and take it in for steaming and pressing, okay?"

Her sister gave her another squeeze. "Okay. Let's go."

She arranged the short train as her sister left the fitting room. Paula was looking out the window, drinking a cup of tea.

The older woman turned and smiled. "Oh, it looks really beautiful on you, Tiffany."

Ariel nodded as their eyes met in the mirror. "See, I told you."

"That's why you're always right." Tiffany reached back and grabbed her hand. "Ariel, I'm glad you're my sister."

So was she.

TWENTY

The beer Rob handed him was refreshingly cold for his hot, dry throat.

But it was the solid whack on his back that had a part of him relaxing despite the muscle ache and fatigue. They'd gotten it done, and under one helluva deadline. Their buddies were sweaty and dirty like they were, but they were all smiling as they looked at the newly sodded area, not a trace of mud anywhere. Dax let himself feel the satisfaction of getting the job done, focusing on Ariel getting her house and his buddy being happy, despite the reality that Rob would soon be marrying a natural catastrophe.

"You sons of bitches!" Rob lifted his beer to their group. "The best group of friends a guy could ever imagine having."

They all took another drink, although no one had known Rob was going to toast. Dude was getting sentimental.

"Manual labor definitely wasn't in the plan." Carson put his hand to his back and arched with a wince. "I haven't been this sore since basic training days."

"You're a bunch of wimps." Perry stomped one of the pieces of sod in further with his shoes. "I used to mow lawns for extra money in high school. Made me miss the old days."

Dax snagged him with an arm around his neck as Gunner and Frank hooted. "You've plumb lost your mind. I'd mow any lawn over digging out mud. Slides on you like a bitch."

"Yeah, but we're done." Rob tucked his beer in the crook of his arm and pulled out his phone. "Let me text my bride and let her know."

Dax eyed the time on the phone. It was 5:15. The rehearsal started at six in the lodge. "We'd better get our butts to the showers and change."

"In a sec." Rob was grinning as he closed his text. "Tiff's going to be so happy when she sees this. Jesus, I never thought it would happen."

"Me either." Dax spotted Ariel amidst a group of dressed-up women coming their way and smiled. "We have Ariel to thank for pushing the resort. I think they were going to default."

Carson slapped him on the back. "Your girl knows how to get shit done. If you screw things up with her, I'm going to jump in. She's not only cute as hell, but she's a sweetheart. And then there's her dog."

"Sherlock rocks." Frank's deep voice carried. "Makes me want a dog."

"Me too," Dax admitted. "One of my first tasks when I get my full discharge."

Carson grabbed him and punched him in the shoulder. "You're going to end up with some purse dog, aren't you?"

His buddies snickered. Even Rob. He flipped them a discreet bird because there were ladies on the scene. Turning, he watched Ariel's face transform from radiant to stern as Tiffany waved a hand in their direction. Whatever she was saying didn't please Ariel. No surprise there. Then Ariel was crossing the grass toward them. Rob must have noticed because his mouth twisted before he took a deep draw from the bottle.

"Why do I have a bad feeling all of a sudden?" Gunner muttered. "If they ask us to pick up a shovel one more time, I'm going to whimper."

"You always were a wimp." Perry snorted, setting his weight. "It's like when I was mowing lawns. There's always someone who wants to find fault with a job well done."

They all turned to watch Ariel walk toward them. Noticing their regard, she pasted a smile on her face. Dax got that pit in his stomach too.

When she arrived, he called out, "What's wrong?"

She hurried the rest of the way until she was standing among them, looking like a slice of fresh lemon pie in her yellow dress with a white shawl. "Don't kill the messenger. I told Tiffany I would confirm that there's nothing to be done about the sod lines."

Sod lines?

"You've got to be kidding!" Dax muttered before clamping his mouth shut in response to Rob's narrowing gaze.

"You mean besides the grass needing to fill in and grow?" Carson asked sarcastically. "We can't make that happen. She knows that's Mother Nature's job, doesn't she?"

She sighed heavily, her mouth twisting. "I know that, and I told her. She's concerned you'll be able to see them in the photos and videos..."

Rob swore under his breath and drained his beer. "I'll talk to her. You guys get changed."

They watched him run off. Dax wished he could slip his arm around Ariel, but he was filthy. "Let him handle it. If she can't see what a goddamn miracle we've delivered here, then she's—"

He broke off, anger churning.

"The biggest bitch this side of Biloxi?" Carson suggested, raising a brow. "Or is Biloxi your territory alone, Dax?"

"At this point, I don't care, and now I'm reeling it back in."

Gunner took another drink. "Probably best, although I feel ya."

Perry and Frank both nodded. Yeah. No one was happy about Rob's choice. Tiffany just couldn't give them a reason they should be fully behind Rob marrying her, could she? After all that work, was it too much to ask for a simple thank you?

He told himself to focus. Ariel was getting what she wanted, and while it seemed crazy to Dax, so was Rob.

Ariel was chewing on her bottom lip. "I'm sorry. I know it's beyond unreasonable. I personally think all of you are awesome. If I needed anyone to help out at a disaster site, I'd call you guys in a heartbeat."

"We'd be there, sweetie," Carson answered before Dax gave him a playful shove. "Ooh, somebody's jealous. Ariel, I told him that if he messes up, I'm going to make a play. Fair warning."

"Jeez, Carson, lay it on thick." Perry grabbed him around the shoulders and started perp-walking him toward their cottage, Frank taking the other side. "We'll see you two later."

"I mean it, Ariel!" Carson called as Gunner whacked him in the back of the head. "My feelings can't be denied."

Ariel was laughing as she regarded Dax. He rolled his eyes. "Carson's a funny guy."

"I like him. All your buddies. They're polite and serious and hardworking as well as good-natured. Exactly what I'd expect in your friends."

Dax turned at the sound of raised voices. Rob stood beside Tiffany on the path. He was pointing at the grass emphatically, his face red, while Tiffany crossed her arms over her chest and yelled something back. Rob flinched and turned and stalked off. Tiffany followed, heels clacking, calling out after him.

"They don't look very happy to me." Dax took a sip of beer, only to find it had soured for him, likely because of the scene they'd just witnessed. "I wish I felt better about this."

She gave a heartfelt sigh. "I know, but it's not our decision."

"That's what I keep telling myself." He looked down at himself. "Jesus, I need to get changed. I'm filthy."

"I'll come with you and escape the drama."

They started back for the cottage. Marshall and Ripp and the other *Lord of the Flies* boys ran over.

"Did you finish?" Marshall asked, reaching them with one shoelace untied.

Dax nodded only to hear the kid mutter a pretty bad swear word. "Hey!"

"Like anyone cares," Marshall spat back, sunburned and sweaty. "So the wedding is still on?"

Ariel leaned down and nodded. "Yeah, it's still on. Everyone appreciated your help. You guys did a great job."

"Like we had a choice." Ripp took a rock out of his pocket and winged it onto the grass. "Mom didn't make Dad help. He *had* to play golf. Like always."

"I hate golf," one of the other boys huffed out.

"It's not my favorite game either." Ariel gave them a thorough look. "You guys look pretty good, but you'd better stick to the sidewalk. Your moms are going to complain about dirt and water on your shoes and slacks."

"Who cares?" Marshall called, running off.

The others gave their own version of put-out children before running after him.

Dax shook his head. "Have you ever seen a more miserable group of kids?"

"Marshall's clearly not happy, but who can blame him? He has to move away from everything he knows with all the other changes. That's hard as a kid. I remember being angry at his age when my parents got divorced. Suddenly my whole world was upended. I wasn't particularly happy either."

He bit back a retort that she couldn't have been that disagreeable. But then he spotted Jeffrey practically dancing toward them on the path with two brown paper sacks in his hands. He'd already changed and had on something Dax could never imagine looking good in—a blue seersucker suit.

"Hey, Jeffrey!" Ariel called as they started over toward him. "You look like the cat who swallowed the canary. What's going on?"

When they reached him, he had a twinkle in his eyes. "Come with me and you'll see."

"Dax needs to shower—"

"And you'll get there in time to wash his back, I promise. This will only take a sec. Trust me, you don't want to miss this."

They followed him all the way to the edge of the beach. "Jeffrey, what are you up to?"

He handed one sack to Ariel and the other to Dax.

When the sack moved, Dax practically jumped out of his skin and dropped it. "What the hell—"

"Hang on!" Jeffrey pulled out his phone and crouched down in the sand. "I'm all set. Dax, will you please empty the sack onto the sand. *Carefully*. No peeking."

"Jeffrey, there had better not be a baby alligator in here," Dax warned, opening the sack and sliding the contents onto the sand.

A large crab took a few steps before digging its claws in, as if trying to anchor itself.

"*A crab?*" Ariel swung and gazed down at her brother with her mouth open. "Jeffrey—"

"Open your sack, sweetie." He winked. "We're about to have fun and take care of your problem."

She opened her sack and started laughing. Dax peered over and then laughed with her. Her wig was nestled inside.

Jeffrey leaned in for a closeup. "Now, put your wig on the crab, and then you're going to watch them both head off into the sunset—and the ocean—while I film it."

"Oh Jeffrey!" Ariel was sputtering with laughter beside him. "You're going to get into so much trouble."

"I don't care. Your mother was horrible to suggest a wig. I thought this would be a fitting way to have it disappear. Uncle Johnny didn't bring his beagle, so your original idea wasn't going to work. This way, I'll have a video proving the crab simply up and walked away with your hairpiece."

Dax was guffawing as the crab walked on the sand, the wig perched on its body. They were only some dancing starfish and calypso music away from being in an animated feature. "That's awesome, man!"

"I thought so." Jeffrey followed the crab's progress, bent over at the waist. "It's a special wedding memory that will always make you laugh. We can't only have horrible memories of mud pits and wedding dresses not fitting! It's time to take something back, people, and this crab is going to help us do it."

"Power to the people," Ariel shouted, putting her fist in the air.

Together, they watched the crab walk across the sand, the fake hair bobbing in the setting sun. When it reached the tide, they cheered. The crab practically flung itself into the ocean like its life depended on it while the wig floated out to sea.

When it started to come back in with the tide, Jeffrey stopped recording and ran toward it. "No, no, no. Go out! Shoo!"

Dax turned to Ariel, shoulders shaking with laughter. "Is your brother shooing your wig?"

Wiping tears, she nodded with a wide grin. In the waning light, she looked young and carefree and happy. Even covered in mud like he was, he felt the same way.

"He actually is. Oh God, Jeffrey's right. This is a memory I won't mind having about this wedding."

She took his hand despite the mud caked on it. He decided it was only a little mud, so he squeezed hers tightly, swinging it playfully in the air. "Of course I have lots of other great memories, Elizabeth."

Turning to her, he watched the waning sunlight highlight the precious angles of her face and the gold highlights in her hair. A lopsided smile appeared on her beautifully shaped mouth. "We both do."

As the wig finally floated out into the ocean before disappearing from sight, Dax realized he was excited to see what was to come—even for the wedding.

TWENTY-ONE

Ariel had been to wedding rehearsals before, but seeing Dax walking down the pretend aisle toward her with a dazzling grin on his face had her heart knocking like two cowboy boots in a good line dance.

He wore a blue sports jacket with a white shirt and camel-colored slacks with some pretty swanky shoes—certainly not the muddy tennis shoes he'd thrown into the garbage when they'd gotten back to the cottage after what Dax had fondly nicknamed Wig Gate. That had only sent her into more gales of laughter before she'd enjoyed his impromptu striptease before getting into the shower—a huge success since she'd decided she wanted him one more time before they headed to the rehearsal.

When they reached each other at the hallway point, he extended his arm to her in grand style. "Miss," he murmured in that sexy drawl of his, "would you give me the honor of letting me escort you the rest of the way?"

"I'd love that." She slid her hand into his proffered arm and enjoyed the way he clasped it with his other hand for a moment before they walked to the front to take their individual places with the rest of the wedding party at the end of the lodge where they were set up.

Before parting to stand on her side, she wanted to lean her head against the side of his strong body. It would have ruined the cadence, though, so instead she took in a deep inhale of his spicy cologne, which only enhanced his tantalizing masculine scent. Everything about him was becoming so familiar, and it made her insides light up like Christmas lights.

He'd become vital to her in the short time they'd been together. Everything was good between them—she'd enjoyed herself almost as much laughing with him over the crab video, for the third time, as she had in the steamy shower.

Tiffany had cried when she reached Rob at the end of the aisle, and they did the pretend ring exchange. Ariel was the only one besides Rob who knew she was probably hyped up on preggers hormones. She was glad Tiffany's focus was on something other than her altered wedding dress and the sod lines on the grass, because all they had to do was get through tomorrow.

Her grandma's house looked to be hers. Her new future could start unfolding here. Her gaze sought out Dax, standing to Rob's side, his freshly shaved jaw enhancing his strength and good looks. Would he really relocate here? It seemed to be in the offing, and part of her wanted to jump for joy at the prospect. She couldn't wait to spend more time with him. Maybe she could even ask him to move in with her. Was that too soon?

Even though it was super early, she really liked—okay, more than liked—playing house with him. Certainly, he could stay with her while he was figuring things out, but her heart ached when she thought about not seeing him every day. Waking up with him and going to sleep with his arms around her filled something she hadn't known was missing.

Big thoughts, Ariel. Get through the wedding first.

She was worrying her lips when the officiant described how the end of the ceremony would unfold with the whole kiss thing as man and wife. Tiffany and Rob started down the aisle, and Dax met her at the front so they could link arms and walk after them.

When they reached the end of the pretend aisle, she turned and hugged him with all the hope and spontaneous excitement in her heart. "I'm so glad you're here."

He squeezed her against his warm, solid chest and leaned down so only she could hear. "Me too. Now, let's party."

At the rehearsal dinner, held at a well-known chophouse, she practically sat on Dax's lap as Jeffrey embraced his *life of the party* persona hard. Carson and Perry were at their table, along with Frank and Gunner, and they were by far the loudest group, laughing until they were hanging on to each other as Jeffrey recounted everything from funny facts about Charleston—her favorite being that the locals started calling them palmetto bugs a couple hundred years ago because it was considered lewd to say the word cock—to his shopping spree for spiritual items designed to offset negative energy.

Their laughter reached booming levels when Jeffrey pulled up the wig video, with people wheezing and wiping tears, an awesome sight really since Dax and his buddies were all large, attractive men. She hushed them, fearing Jeffrey's wig ploy would be overheard, but no one could make sense of their comments because the men were all laughing too hard. Fighting her own mirth—because man, it really had been funny seeing the wig walk into the ocean—

she kept a keen eye on people who might not find it so amusing.

The Three Tornadoes were huddled together like usual. Her mother sat among them with a preening Trey, who seemed to be talking to her brothers-in-law about golf from the way he mimed swinging his club. Mother's slack face didn't hide her censure or boredom. She wasn't the center of attention, her worst nightmare. Ariel caught her disapproving glances a few times when their table continued to be especially loud, but she finally stopped caring. She was having fun at a family function, and that was a rare treat.

Jeffrey finally went to the bar and brought back a fine bottle of bourbon, earning him a few back slaps, which had him playfully fanning himself. Jeffrey teased Dax about what the Navy would look like if they wore dress blacks instead of dress whites, and Dax rebutted that they'd look more like priests than pilots. Carson decreed that would never work because he had way too many lustful thoughts, and when Jeffrey confessed he did too, they all started laughing again.

Ariel was so grateful they'd so easily accepted her brother, because she would have needed to punch them otherwise. Jeffrey had had enough BS from her mother's and sisters' prejudices. She smiled at her brother, even happier that he was enjoying himself this much at a Deverell event.

Which led to her joining them in drinking the bourbon. She impressed Dax's friends by how much liquor she could hold, but when Carson went to pour her a third drink, she put her hand over her glass, what with the wedding being tomorrow. He was talking to Perry and not paying attention, so he ended up pouring the bourbon on her hand and onto the table, which only had everyone howling with laughter all over again.

Rob sat quietly at the head table, nursing a drink while Trey nattered on about golf. Ariel wondered if he felt torn between staying with Tiffany and hanging with his buddies. She didn't see any reason he couldn't pop over for a bit, but there was no denying Tiffany liked exclusive attention—even if she seemed to mostly be talking to the twins and her sorority sisters.

Ariel caught him glancing their way once when she and the men raised their bourbon and shouted, "To the Navy," but he didn't come over even then. She felt bad for him. She knew his time ahead wasn't going to be an easy one.

Like she'd told Dax, it wasn't their decision.

When they all finally left the lodge to return to their cottages, it was after midnight. Her hand was in Dax's and she felt languorous and loose after all the camaraderie. His Navy buddies were humming some tune from college days off to the side, which Dax had leaned down and told her was "Anchors Aweigh."

Jeffrey put his arm around her and kissed her cheek. "You're plumb tuckered out. Why don't you give me a few more duties tomorrow morning since you're going to be crashing with the setup crews?"

The checklist she had for tomorrow needed a binder clip it was so long. She hadn't left anything to chance. "That's so sweet. I'm working with the event manager early with our vendor for the wedding tent. They want to make sure the area isn't too wet for the ground anchors to work."

"Shit!" Dax exclaimed, slapping his forehead. "I hadn't thought about that. What happens if—"

"We're not going there." She held up a hand, her brain nearly imploding at the mere thought of the tent not going up as planned. "This contractor puts up tents for a living, so I'm choosing to believe they can get it done."

Jeffrey dug out a vial of holy water and sprinkled it in the air, making her cough out a laugh. "Let's hope so. We don't need another 'Can't help you, ma'am, this here is an act of God.'"

Her stomach acid started to churn, making her feel nauseous. "Like I said. No doom and gloom. The sun is going to shine. The tent will safely go up. The wedding will come off at four o'clock in beautiful fashion, just like Tiffany imagines. All will be well."

It had to be.

"What time do you need to pick up her wedding dress from the dry cleaner?" Dax asked. "I know that's one of your main off-site tasks."

"Dax and I can go and get it for you." Jeffrey squeezed her tense shoulder. "You're needed here. Consider us on call for any last-minute emergencies."

"Did someone say emergencies?" Perry asked, as all the men stopped singing. "That's our specialty."

"We've got your back, Ariel." Carson jerked his thumb at Dax's buddies. "We didn't break our backs in the mud pit for nothing."

"Thanks, guys." She looked around the group of men as they walked to the crossroads in the path, which branched off to all of the various cottages. "I appreciate the support. I'm going to have to do some fancy two-stepping to avoid the whole hair and makeup thing. Any ideas there?"

"Maybe just say you're already pretty enough?" Carson suggested before Dax put him in a boyish headlock.

"Thanks, Carson, but that's not going to work," she said.

"Don't worry." Jeffrey thrust his hands in his pockets and rocked back on his leather loafers. "I've got my wig story. I'll come back and say I can't find it anywhere. Stormy won't buy it—neither will the Three Tornadoes—but there's not much they can do. Plus, the blame will rest on me. Better for you that way, Ariel."

She felt herself melt. "Just like old times, huh? You covered for me when they wanted me to wear that horrible Easter egg pink pinafore dress to Tiffany's high school graduation. God, that thing was ghastly."

Dax's smile flashed in the night. "What did you conceive of that time, Jeffrey?"

Her sweet big brother got a devious twinkle in his brown eyes as all the men clustered around. "I told the girl who lived next door that Ariel was giving some dresses away if she wanted them. Like a spring cleaning. When Mary arrived, I told her how good the pink dress would look on her, which it did. She was the cutest little blonde with a personality like homemade strawberry shortcake. She took the dress and a few others Stormy had gotten for Ariel, which did not suit her one bit."

Ariel felt a cold chill touch her spine, thinking about the wardrobe her mother used to make her wear. Ruffles. Caps with flowers on them. Pastels. Gag. Her baby and toddler pictures needed to be burned someday. "Mother broke two nails searching for that dress."

Jeffrey gave a dramatic shudder. "Which is the end of the world for Stormy. Nail lengths must match. Anyway, three weeks later, she spotted poor little Mary at the neighborhood block party in that pink dress and accused her of stealing it. I got into trouble, of course, after confessing—I couldn't let Mary be carted off to jail, which I feared Stormy would insist on."

"My God!" Perry shook his head, mouth gaping. "Forgive me for saying so, but I've never heard of such mean-spiritedness. What happened to you?"

Jeffrey gave a sly smile. "Stormy couldn't touch me. She and my father were already divorced by then, and I didn't live under her roof. Thank God!"

But Ariel had lived with her. She'd never told Jeffrey this, but Stormy had found a way to punish her. She hadn't allowed her to go to Folly Beach to see Grandma that summer, and it had cut her in two. For a time after that, she'd ceded to her mother's wishes. Leaving the house to go to college had helped, but her mother had never stopped trying to control her daughters.

Tomorrow, there would be a showdown about the wig. She'd take the brunt of her mother's anger—the Tornadoes' too—and tell them they had enough to focus on, didn't they? She only hoped they'd let it go. For a time at least. Because her mother was known for payback.

"Jesus!" Carson's voice held an edge. "No offense, Ariel, but Rob's marrying into a nuthouse. I've been trying to keep an open mind, but I can't say I like what I've heard here. Or from Dax."

Gunner bared his teeth in the muted light. "Me either. I love my man, but this..."

"I keep wondering what it would take to have Rob snap out of whatever spell she has him under," Carson added. "The way she acted about the sod lines really pissed me off."

Arial looked at Dax, waiting to see whether he'd tell them about the rest of Tiffany's behavior. He'd wanted to stop the wedding as much as anyone, and God knows he'd told Rob everything to no avail. But he only stood there, his body tense beside her.

Frank looked off, his mouth twisting. "I'm not from a

perfect family, God knows, but I respected my stepdad when my mom remarried. I even came to like him. Rob's not even starting on that foot, and I'm not sure Tiffany is going to help any."

"He's repeating his own family issues." Perry's tone was clipped. "Dax, did you tell Ariel? Rob had trouble with his stepdad growing up. For the five years his mom and stepdad were married, anyway."

She wanted to put her hands over her ears, especially when she thought about the baby they were bringing into the world—the one only she knew about. "I know this is hard, but we need to remember that they love each other and want to get married. We have to make this the day they want."

Because Ariel didn't like the niggling doubt still swirling in the back of her mind. If Tiffany was going to complain about sod lines, what else could she find fault with tomorrow? She wanted to trust her sister and the moment they'd shared, but she had too much evidence to the contrary.

"You mean what Tiffany wants, which you can never seem to deliver despite all you do," Jeffrey bit out. "Sorry, Ariel, I'm still really pissed that she's extorting you over your grandma's house. It's below the belt and then some."

She winced. Jeffrey might as well have poured gasoline on their already heated conversation.

"What's this about extortion?" Carson asked, flicking his sports coat open. "Ariel, honey, that's the lowest of the low. I know we're probably being way too honest here, but no one should treat anyone like that—especially family. Now I'm really concerned for Rob."

"You're telling me," Perry added, his entire face narrowing.

While Dax's jaw audibly cracked, he didn't fill his friend in, and for that, she was grateful. Her usual peacekeeper role felt like too great a task right now. She'd rather run from a gator. "Please—it's not helpful to focus on. Look, I'm exhausted, and I'm sure y'all are too after everything with the mud pit. Thanks, by the way."

Carson's gaze was downright flinty. "You're welcome, but you shouldn't be the one to say thank you."

"Hey!"

They all turned at Rob's shout. He was striding down the path, alone, a bottle in his hand.

"What in the hell are you guys doing?" He slapped Carson on the back when he reached them and gazed around the now-quiet group. "Looks like you're plotting a mission to down the enemy."

Jeffrey sputtered out a laugh before he silenced himself. "Sorry," he coughed.

Ariel sent him a pleading look.

Rob wrapped his arm around Perry and pulled him closer. "This here's a celebration."

"Is it, man?" Carson asked, brows mashed together. "Because we're a little concerned about you and how things appear."

"What the hell?" Rob spat. "Dax, did you say something?"

Dax only shook his head.

"He didn't have to," Perry continued after a look at Frank and Gunner. "We've got eyes."

Rob tapped his fingers to his temple. "Do you? Because you all sound like a bunch of babies, crying over a whole lot of nothing. I'm getting married tomorrow, dammit, and like I said, this here is a celebration. Who wants to grab a drink?"

Dax took a step forward and gripped Rob's shoulder, the action speaking of longtime friendship. Ariel wondered how much it had cost him. Carson and Perry looked as tense as statues, and Gunner's and Frank's body language wasn't much better. "All that manual labor has us wanting to up and cry like those babies you mentioned, Rob. We're going to grab some shut-eye. You should try to do the same. It's going to be a big day tomorrow. We can hang out all day and toast to your future."

Rob's eyes lowered a moment before he shoved Carson and Perry away. "Yeah, we've got all day, right? Tiffany is going to be doing the whole bride thing, starting with all that hair and beauty stuff at eight in the morning. God, I'm so glad not to be a girl."

Dax nudged him, and Rob's head snapped up as he glanced her way. "Sorry, Ariel."

"No problem." She took Dax's arm. "See you in the morning, everyone."

She kissed Jeffrey's cheek, inclined her chin to the other men, and then made herself start walking. Dax walked stiffly beside her. When they reached the cottage, she let Sherlock out. Dax was in the shower again when she came back in, and seeing her through the steamy glass door, he opened it a crack with a tired smile.

"Come on in here, Elizabeth, before you fall down."

She stripped slowly, feeling off-center and a little sad. For her messed-up family, for Rob, and for how sometimes life just couldn't be perfect—no matter how hard you tried.

The hot water was comforting as Dax made room for her under the spray. But so were his strong hands on her shoulders, massaging away the tension, and something deeper, something she didn't want to name because it would break her heart.

When his lips touched the side of her neck, she turned in his arms. "Yes. Make love to me."

She'd never said those words quite that way—even with her ex-fiancé—and while he might not know it, her heart did. It thundered in her chest. Her blood beat in sweet torment as his arms came around her and lifted her to him. Their lips met—urgent, knowing, and without any buildup. He slanted his mouth over hers, again and again, until she was digging her nails into his back. When her tongue swept in to mate with his, he groaned and pressed her against the hot shower wall, making her cry out in response.

"Now!" she whispered, kissing the underside of his jaw and then biting gently on the long line of his shoulder. "It's got to be now."

He swore as he opened the door and carried her out. They were wet when they hit the bed, him reaching over her for a condom. Sliding it on, he thrust inside her seconds later. She was hot and wet and ready for him. Wrapping her legs around him, she lifted to him and met his thrusts. Hard. Fast. Perfect. She came when he pressed his open mouth to the side of her throat, her need for him so great that she cried out his name.

He reared up, feeling her tighten around him, coming hard with a hoarse shout of his own before letting his forehead fall into the crook of her shoulder. They lay that way, breathing hard, gripping each other, still damp from the shower and not caring. The release had her opening her heart to him even more. Before, the door was halfway open, but now, it was like he was inside her, in that inner place she'd always kept closely guarded, wanting to protect what she loved about herself, what she knew to be true, what she valued. There, she could be who she wanted, who she was meant to be, and given how precious it was, she'd never shared it with anyone else save her dear brother. Not even her former fiancé.

But now there was Dax...

She kissed the side of his face, feeling the rough stubble on her sensitive lips. Her heart was still pounding, but it might as well have been four times bigger than it had been before she'd stepped into that shower with him.

She pressed another kiss to his jaw, curled her hand around his nape, and simply brought him closer to her. He rolled them to their sides and fitted her to him, nuzzling her neck, kissing her with a tenderness that made tears burn in her eyes.

"Oh, Ariel..."

The way he said her name—in his deep, assuring voice filled with a trace of awe—had her squeezing her eyes shut. "What, Dax?"

He lifted up, his green eyes glowing with light. "We've gone and done it, haven't we?"

She knew what he meant. She waited for that precious part of her to withdraw, to turn protective. But instead, her heart pulsed with something new. Happiness. She was aware of a smile spreading across her face. The act struck her with its profoundness. She wasn't scared. She was filled with joy.

Tracing his jaw, she met his eyes straight on, taking stock of his features, the ones that had become so dear to her so quickly. The way his sandy eyebrows lifted when he was amused. The glint of his green eyes when he cupped her cheek, like he was doing now. She even knew how his earlobes were attached and thought them adorable. Everything was. Because he was her Dax.

"You mean the whole L thing?" she asked, her voice hushed but strong and true.

His eyebrows really lifted then, a grin touching his sculpted lips. "The whole L thing, huh. Elizabeth, I expected a better declaration from you."

Ah, she knew the words. They were rare in the thinking, even more precious in the saying. But she knew it was right to say them now. Nothing could have stopped her from speaking the truth of her heart then and there. "How's this? I love you."

His grin had her heart turning somersaults in her chest. "As good as it gets, because I love you too. Despite it only being, what..." He checked his watch. "Nearly one hundred and sixty-eight hours since we've met. To some, that might not sound like much, but to a pilot, that's a lot of hours. Did you know that you only need forty hours of flight time to be able to legally fly a private plane?"

She started laughing. "Of all the things I expected you to say, Stephan... So that's what? Over four pilot licenses?"

"We're overachievers." He tucked her hair tenderly behind her ear. "What I'm trying to say is... Flying is one of the most profound acts of my life, and I got there in a short time."

She could feel herself practically melting into the bed. "Forty hours."

"Exactly." His fingers glided over her lips, his sweet gaze warm and pure. "So why wouldn't I do something equally profound, like falling deeply, madly in love with you, in one hundred and sixty-eight hours?"

She tightened her arms around him. "I like your logic."

"I'm a logical kind of guy." He kissed her softly then, so softly she sighed into his mouth. "And when I chart a course, I see it through."

Linking her arms around his neck, she pulled him down for another kiss. "So do I."

"Good." He gave her a swift kiss and tucked her close to his body, closing his eyes. "I'm glad we've settled that. I love you. You love me."

The words to the song "We're a Happy Family" sounded in her mind. That inner part of her did clutch then. A happy family? What in the hell was that even? What about happily ever after? People talked about wanting that all the time, but didn't it have to start with a wish or a desire to be happy in the first place? Then Dax squeezed her tenderly and she remembered. Dax knew. That would help them find the path.

Because she didn't know what in the world that looked like, but she realized she wanted it.

Bad.

"You know," she heard him sleepily say, "I'm glad we covered this."

The urge to chuckle was too great. "You are?"

"Yeah." He clutched her closer to his warm, solid body. "It will make things easier. Tomorrow."

If her reality were a building, she would have fallen down a few floors. "Right. Tomorrow."

The wedding.

Where she'd hopefully—finally—get one of the main keys to her future.

She hadn't come here with the expectation that she'd find another key waiting for her. But here he was, and she wasn't letting him go. No matter what happened at the wedding.

TWENTY-TWO

Waking up after exchanging "I love yous" had to be up there with getting his wings.

Dax snuggled up against Ariel, who groaned as he turned the alarm off.

"Did we really sleep until seven again?" she asked in a voice ruffled with sleep.

"Yes, we sure did." He kissed her neck, luxuriating in her soft, silky warm skin. "It's practically a record for me too, but since we didn't go to sleep until after three, it's understandable."

"Had to celebrate the whole L thing." Her voice was a mumble. "Now we've gotta face today."

She sounded so aggrieved, he hugged her tightly and gave her a raspberry on her neck, which only made her laugh and playfully push him away.

He rolled her onto her back and swept the messy hair out of her eyes. "Sounds like you need a little motivation and a reminder of that whole L thing we covered."

The sleep cleared from her eyes as he pressed his hardness against her softness. "What do you have in mind, big boy? Oh, wait! It's one of the poles for the wedding tent, isn't it?"

That had them both chortling as he fitted on a condom and slid inside her. Then they weren't laughing anymore because she'd lifted to him and started a gentle rhythm that had him smiling down at her.

"Do you really know how much I love you?" he asked.

He'd never imagined the freedom he'd feel, saying those words. He'd grown up saying them with his family, but with her, his whole life felt like open blue sky, the kind that had always made him feel invincible.

She clutched his hips, drawing him in deeper and arching against him. "Probably not, but I'm eager to learn, Captain."

So she wasn't going to be serious. Her sultry smile had him grinning before she tightened around him and made him groan. "So that's how it's going to be, huh? Elizabeth, prepare to be properly convinced."

He was as good as his word. Sometime later, she lay supine on his body, his hands stroking her back. She kissed his chest. "I really need to get going. The tent guys are coming soon. Think good thoughts."

"Always." He slapped her butt lightly as she rolled out of bed. "Looking good. I'll let you shower alone. If I join you—"

"We're so going to do it again." She wiggled her hips and shot him a glance over her shoulder. "How much restraint do you have?"

"You, miss, are trouble." He waved her toward the bathroom. "Go. I have to get ready to meet up with Jeffrey to pick up the wedding dress."

She crossed and dug a key card out of her purse. "Before I forget, Tiffany gave me my former room key so you guys could hang the dress in there. She's in her getting-ready outfit—don't ask me more about that—and doesn't plan on being anywhere near her dress until an hour before the ceremony. Tricia got makeup on her dress at her first wedding, and Tiffany is paranoid. I even had to get special cleaning wipes in case of a second disaster."

Dax winced. "I didn't know about all this wedding stuff until now. My sister and her husband just got hitched. Fifty people. We had a BBQ at a local ranch. No frills. My brother's was about the same."

"Sounds perfect." She handed him the card for picking up the dress and struck a pose. "Sure you don't want to try and make me late?"

He gave her a slow perusal, letting her see what she did to him by pulling back the sheet. "Elizabeth, you are playing with fire."

"Oh, Stephan," she cried, taking her sweet little bottom off to the bathroom, "didn't you know I'm a closet pyromaniac?"

He was laughing as she shut the door. Rolling out of bed, he pulled on shorts and a T-shirt. He had to pick up his dress whites from another dry cleaner this morning, along with Rob's uniform and the rest of his buddies' whites. Jeffrey had said he didn't mind swinging over there after picking up Tiffany's wedding dress.

He was making coffee when someone started pounding on the door. Sherlock trotted over and regarded it with sad, expressive eyes. Dax patted his head when he reached him. "Yeah, we know who that must be, don't we?"

Pasting a smile on his face, he opened the door. "Hey."

Rob pushed his way in and closed the door. "Hey, yourself. Look, I need you to go and get some flowers for me.

Nice ones. Lots of them. I apparently have already fucked up today."

His friend tugged on the collar of his T-shirt, a study in nerves.

"What happened?"

"According to my bride-to-be, I was supposed to have something special for her this morning. Day of the wedding present or some such thing. Did anyone tell me this? No! Shit. She got me custom cufflinks engraved with T&R and this Hallmark card that went on forever. I thought the wedding *was* her present. Oh, and the honeymoon to St. Lucia. But no... I was supposed to give her something to say I was happy to marry her."

Dax compressed his lips as Rob stalked back and forth.

His friend fisted his hands at his sides, his face tight with tension. "So can you buy me some flowers? I know she's got tons coming in for the wedding, but these are from me, and flowers are never wrong in my book. If they have a card, great. I'll look up some sappy poetry when you get back and put it on there. Jesus. I'm going to lose my mind. I need a drink. Maybe it's time to open the lucky bourbon you and Ariel dug up. God knows I'm going to need all the steam I can get."

Dax thought his eyes already looked red, so he slapped him on the back, hoping he wouldn't start drinking this early. "Go for a hard run. It always helps. I've got this."

Rob rubbed his forehead. "You're picking up my dress whites, right?"

"I'm picking up everyone's." Another solid whack on Rob's back hopefully conveyed his dependability.

Rob grunted and dug into his shorts pocket. "Fine. Now, here are the rings. Tiffany wants Ariel to keep hers until the wedding. You can keep mine. Ripp refused to carry the ring pillow. Says it's too girly. Honestly, I can't blame him. All that lace and shit. So you two are keeping them until the ceremony. I don't have to tell you not to lose them."

When he thrust the bands out, Sherlock gave an eerie whine. Dax glanced at the dog, who padded back to his bed by the fireplace and lay down. Dax had no idea what that meant, but it didn't sound good. "I'll tell Ariel. She's in the shower."

"You do that." Rob pressed a hand to the door, gripping the frame. "I keep telling myself I passed advanced flight training. I've pulled ten Gs. I'm a kick-ass pilot and a respected officer in the U.S. Navy. But Jesus, I feel like I'm not passing muster. Tiffany's got all these ideas about what this day is supposed to be like. I'm already letting her down, and I hate that."

Dax did too. It had to feel like crap. "I'll find the best flowers in town, man. Jeffrey is going with me to pick up some stuff. He'll know where to go."

"Great." He fished out his wallet and handed over a couple hundreds. "Tell him thanks."

When his friend opened the door and hesitated, Dax waited for him to speak, watching his jaw lock.

"Sorry I've been such a dick. Later, man."

Rob was out the door before Dax could answer him, and he knew that was the point. He pulled his wallet out and tucked Rob's ring in there, and then went to find Ariel. She was combing through her wet hair when he opened the door. She screamed.

"Jumpy?"

"As a June bug," she answered. "What is that in your clenched hand? Should I be nervous?"

He unfurled it. "Tiffany wants you to keep her wedding ring. I won't assume it's because she doesn't trust me."

"You shouldn't." Although they both knew he was supposed to keep the two rings according to the wedding checklist. "Who brought these? Rob?"

"Yeah." He leaned against the door and watched her put on some moisturizer, her complexion peaches and cream after her shower. "He's already in the shitter. Forgot some 'day of' gift."

"Oh no! I told Tiffany to tell him things like that. Guys can't read your mind."

"We can't?" Dax imagined Tiffany liked people reading her mind that way. "I'm picking up makeup flowers. Jeffrey will know where to go, I imagine, but do you have a place in mind?"

"Bloom and Swoon. Jeffrey knows it well. All right, plant a good one on me. I've gotta dash."

He swept her into his arms and laid her back, kissing her sweetly but thoroughly. She twined her arms around his neck and sighed. "How's that?"

"Pretty good, honey." She patted his butt as he stood her up. "Pretty good."

She was out of the bathroom and heading to the kitchen a minute later. He followed her. "I made coffee. Let me get you a to-go cup. Banana?"

"Already had a delicious one, thanks," she quipped saucily.

He was laughing as he poured her coffee. "Okay, here you are. Go get 'em, tiger."

She gave him a terrible salute that was somehow more adorable because of it. "You too, Captain. See you later."

"Count on it."

She put Sherlock's leash on and was out the door. He

took his time sipping his coffee, laughing as he ate a banana for breakfast. She was a funny one, his girl. When another more polite knock sounded near eight, he headed for the door.

Jeffrey had a basket of muffins in his hand. He was elegantly dressed in a purple spring suit, white dress shirt with cuffs, and an orange cravat. "Good morning. I'm the resident muffin fairy, hoping to spread good wedding cheer today."

Dax selected a chocolate one. "Thanks. How's that going for you?"

"Tiffany about bit my head off. She couldn't believe I thought she'd be eating something fatty after not fitting into her dress. Terry's and Tricia's reactions weren't much better. By the way, we are not to make one wrinkle on Tiff's dress or she's going to go into a tiff, and we're going to get it. I didn't ask for a detailed description of the torment we'd undergo, but I can guarantee you, it *would* hurt. For days. Oh, and I got us this for extra support."

He set the basket down on the side table and fished into his jacket pocket. "Here. I thought we could all use these. A woman at a local spiritual store told me this is what's called bringing out the big guns."

Holding up the packet he'd been given, Dax eyed the large single blue eye. "Is that the evil eye?"

"Yes, and it's a press-on tattoo." He pointed to his butt. "I put mine somewhere no one but Antonio is likely to see. God, I miss my honey, but thoughts of our reunion are keeping me going. You should...put it wherever you'd like, Captain Hotpants. Ariel will be only too grateful to go on a hunt for its location."

Dax tucked his tongue against his cheek. "Might be good to put it on the best buns this side of Biloxi."

"Ariel would like that." Jeffrey flashed him a wicked wink. "She's in a state already. I caught her as she was tearing down the path earlier and insisted she put on her tattoo. Wait until you see where. Then she stuffed a blueberry muffin in her mouth and said something about picking up flowers for Rob."

"Yes, I'll explain on the way there." He twirled his finger. "Now turn around. Because I'm putting this tattoo on right now. I am not taking any chances."

Jeffrey spun around and put his hands over his eyes. "Never say I'm not a gentleman."

Mouth twitching, Dax affixed the tattoo with some water from his glass and walked to the door and opened it. "Never. Ready?"

Jeffrey made like he was throwing a scarf over his shoulder and strode out. "Honey, I'm always ready."

Their errands went fine. The wedding dress was waiting for them. Dax couldn't believe how much it had cost to press the thing, but maybe it was so expensive because it had been a rush job. Jeffrey said he had the company card, so to speak, but when they picked up the dress whites from the cleaner in another part of town, Dax insisted on paying the bill.

The flower shop was even more overwhelming. Dax had never seen so many choices. Jeffrey went from one floral display cooler after another, selecting flowers like a pro. Even the owner was impressed by his efficiency.

When they left the shop, Dax pulled out his phone since Jeffrey was carrying the giant bouquet.

> We're just wrapping up errands. Mission accomplished. 🥂 You need anything else? Also, how's the tent raising? 🎪

> **ARIEL**
>
> Glad the mission was successful. 👍 We're still putting the tent up. The ground is still really wet in places. 😕 And thanks for asking, but I don't need anything right now. Thank God!

> I'm here for you, babe. 😘 See you soon.

Jeffrey glanced over as a woman passed them, sighing, likely over the flowers.

"Hey! I'll be right back," he told Jeffrey. Following his gut, he jogged back to the flower shop. He didn't know if Ariel would sigh or swoon, but he wanted to do something nice. Hell, romantic. After a few questions from the flower shop owner about the woman he was buying for—he recalled her complaining about pastel colors—he jogged back to the car with a bouquet.

"Ah, good choices all." Jeffrey smiled as he pushed up his green glasses and fingered the edges of the double bloom tulips in red, orange, and purple. "She'll love them. One thing about Ariel is that she professes not to be a girl in such things, but deep down, most of us love to feel appreciated. Few things say it better than flowers."

Setting the bouquet in the back next to Tiffany's, he figured this was a good moment to get more information. "What else does?"

"You asking me?" Jeffrey gave a saucy wink. "A really big dick."

Dax choked. "I'll take your word for it. Jesus, Jeffrey! I'm really glad you're you because I was worried I wasn't going to like anyone in Ariel's family."

"Wait until you meet our dad." Jeffrey turned the car on. "He's a pretty serious guy with his own rules, but he's a good man. He'll like you."

Thank God. Dax knew his family would love Ariel. "Good to hear. Now, let's get back to wedding hell."

Jeffrey wiggled in his seat. "Activating my tattoo and ready for takeoff, Captain."

Dax chuckled the whole way back.

When they arrived, they put Tiffany's wedding dress in Ariel's former cottage, leaving the other items in the car to grab on another trip. Jeffrey arranged it nicely and then pulled out a flask of holy water and made the sign of the cross, making Dax sputter with laughter. The *Lord of the Flies* boys were chasing each other around, screaming wildly when they let themselves out of the cottage.

Jeffrey was wiping tears, wheezing with laughter.

"What's so funny?" Marshall yelled.

Ripp raced over, and the rest of the boys followed. Jeffrey exchanged a conspiratorial glance with Dax before drawing out his flask of holy water and shaking it at the boys. "Here! I bless you—"

The boys started yelling, drowning out the rest of what he said.

Dax was doubling over with laughter when Rob found them.

"Hey! What's the matter with you two? Did you get the fucking flowers?"

Dax pulled himself together. "Your bouquet is in the Mercedes SL parked in front of the lodge. It's unlocked. Your dress whites are in the back with the tulips I bought for Ariel, and we put Tiffany's dress in the bridal cottage."

"Great!" Rob jogged off toward the parking lot. "Thanks!"

"You're welcome," Jeffrey called back. "I hope the flowers do the job, but Tiffany is a notoriously tough customer. Now, let's deliver the rest of the items, with Ariel's flowers being top of the list."

He couldn't wait to see her. "Sounds good."

When he found her, she was standing a few yards from the tent setup, rubbing the base of her neck with Sherlock beside her. A large burly guy was talking to her, pointing to the array of poles sticking out of the ground. Men were setting up white folding chairs off to the right, and Dax spotted Scooter filling a large clear pool of water with a green hose. He called out a greeting to the old guy and then went over to Ariel.

He waited until the guy left before stepping forward and lavishly presenting her the bouquet. "For you, Elizabeth."

She worried her lower lip, hastily looking down, but not before he caught the shocked pleasure in her blue eyes. "This is very unexpected, Stephan, but very sweet. So sweet I'm a little speechless."

Speechless was good. More romantic gestures were in her future. "I aim to please." He gestured to the setup. "How's it going?"

Walking closer, she put her free hand on his chest, holding the bouquet in the crook of her arms. "I'll tell you in a minute. Come here."

He knew what she had in mind, so he lowered his head. She rose on tiptoes and pressed her mouth to his in a slow, languorous kiss. "Thank you."

"You're welcome." He kissed her again because he could and looked over when he heard cheering. "Scooter apparently wants some flowers too."

She laughed, the tension falling from her face. "Yeah. We all do. As for how it's going, it's going. The wet ground is still presenting problems, but we're working it out. The crew has been great. And Scooter mentioned Bumper missing us. I told him we'd have to come by for a visit sometime."

Lips twitching, he turned her around and put his hands on her shoulders, rubbing the knotted muscles there. "That's nice. I like being wanted. Especially by a gator named Bumper. I plan to kiss you senseless in front of him to show him he can't stop the inevitable. Also, I hear we'll have to do a show-and-tell later. With our evil eye tattoos."

She put her hand over her mouth to contain her laugh. "God, Jeffrey is so funny. I was like, do you have more? Like for every wedding guest? But yes, we will do a little show-and-tell when this is all over. Because come hell or high water, this wedding is happening today and I will be getting the deed to my grandma's house. And then I'm going to put my feet up and...I don't know, sleep for two days. Go to a silent retreat for a week. Get a permanent evil eye tattoo. You game?"

"For all of the above except the tattoo." He waggled his brows. "As you know, I'm tattoo-free. If I were to get a tattoo, it wouldn't be an evil eye."

"What would you get?"

He didn't hesitate. "I've met pilots who have their girl's name tattooed on their arm. But Elizabeth might be confusing to some."

She fanned herself. "I like us having a little secret between us."

He leaned in and kissed the side of her neck. "Me too."

His sexy whisper made her shiver. "Well... We can talk more about nickname tattoos after the wedding is over." She turned to Dax and pressed her head to his chest, squashing her flowers. "Assuming I make it."

He rubbed her arms. "You will. Hold on to a vision of you with your feet up in your home in Folly Beach."

She all but melted against his tall frame. "With you and Sherlock sitting next to me as we watch the sun set."

Their eyes met when she lifted her head, and they both smiled. He could already see it, and his heart started thumping in excitement like it did before he took off on the airstrip. "I'm already there."

She touched his chest tenderly. "Me too. Now...all we have to do is make sure everything goes great."

"You tell them about the wig thing yet?"

"No, but I'm about to." She rubbed the spot between her brows. "What's the worst thing that can happen?"

With her family?

The sky was the limit.

TWENTY-THREE

Her mother had a backup wig.

Of course it was the hideous wig she'd originally picked out, the one Dax had gotten her out of buying. Ariel stared at her mother's hard face and the Kardashian-like hairpiece in her hand while Tiffany chewed into Marshall about wearing a tie, an argument Tricia and Terry had already gone through with the other boys. Marshall had held out the longest. She was tempted to channel his rebellion.

Firming her shoulders, she faced her mother. "Mother—"

"I'm not listening to another word, Ariel." She stepped closer, her eyes hard, her hair spray so strong Ariel's nose twitched. "I knew this would happen, which is why I went to the store and got the wig I'd originally wanted you to buy. As for the wig going missing, Jeffrey was involved in this, wasn't he?"

She wasn't going to throw her brother under the bus. "Mother, I really don't want—"

"Ariel!" Her mother's voice put a pause on Tiffany's

mini battle with Marshall in the corner. "You will not be in this wedding if you don't wear this wig!"

Someone grabbed her arm and squeezed gently. Turning, she watched as Tiffany confronted their mother, lifting her chin with sheer Deverell determination. "Mother, I changed my mind. Bride's prerogative. I think Ariel's hair looks perfect as it is."

Terry and Tricia gasped in their matching pale pink robes, clutching their *more champagne than orange juice* mimosas, their towering bouffant blond hair sprayed into perfectly shaped birds' nests, if you asked Ariel. Mother must have gotten Botox sometime before the wedding, because Ariel could tell she was trying to lift her eyebrow in derision. Only her perfectly dyed and waxed eyebrows wouldn't budge.

Tiffany touched the ends of Ariel's short hair. "I think it's pretty. Besides, it suits her. Let's keep that wig for another time. Like always, you have impeccable taste. I might wear it for the next Deverell event."

As she said it, Tiffany grabbed the wig from their mother's hand. A brief tug-of-war ensued before Mother reluctantly let it go, long burgundy nails curving into clawlike shapes before resting beside her peach silk pajamas. "Well, it's your wedding, darling."

That voice was code for: *I'll remember this and you will pay at a future date.*

Ariel was too relieved and deeply moved by Tiffany's gesture to care. "Great!" she pronounced. "So let's let the makeup artist do her thing now that everyone's hair is done, and I'll go and check on the setup. The sparkler contractor is arriving shortly, and I want to make sure the koi fountain has been installed."

At this point she would invent an errand to get out of there.

Tiffany half hugged her, jangly but excited. "It's all coming together, isn't it? There were moments when I thought the wedding was going to be canceled. Especially when my dress didn't fit. But Jeffrey took a picture of it and sent it to me, hanging in the bridal cottage. I can't wait to get into it. Even with the back looking like a bodice. I'm getting married today. Oh, Marshall! Come and hug your mama."

His shoulder lifted, his entire body tensing in defiance, and he didn't move until Terry gave him a gentle cuff to the back of his head. He glared at her before trudging forward, so slow a turtle could have beaten him.

Tiffany rolled her eyes toward everyone after pulling her son toward her, careful not to wrinkle her white silk robe. "Honey, today is going to change everything. We've got a whole new life awaiting us."

"I don't want to move," he ground out.

She kissed the top of his forehead and firmly took his shoulders. "I know it's going to be hard to leave Pensacola. I'm leaving my friends too, but San Diego is going to be great. You'll see."

His mouth remained mutinous as she kissed him again. Finally pulling away, he stormed out of the resort's bridal suite and slammed the door.

Tiffany leaned closer to Ariel and whispered, "What I wouldn't give for a drink."

She caught herself before she looked at her sister's flat stomach. She realized she didn't even know how far along her sister was. Well, there'd be time for all of that after Tiffany made her announcement.

"You're doing great." She patted her sister on the shoulder, hoping to start inching toward the exit. "Thanks for backing me on not wearing the wig."

They both glanced over to where Mother was pouring herself a large vodka on the rocks at the Art Deco bar cart.

"She's going to be wasted by the time the ceremony rolls around," Tiffany whispered.

"Maybe it will make things easier." Ariel did her best not to run to the door. "I'll see you later."

"Be sure and come back so Carly can do your makeup," Tiffany called.

Ariel let herself out. Right. So she didn't have to wear the horrible wig, but she needed to have Tiffany-approved makeup. She could deal with that, so long as she didn't look like a clown version of herself the way she had at Terry's first wedding. Betty Boop mascara eyes had made her look slightly cross-eyed in the wedding photos.

Glad she was wearing her flip-flops and not the cream satin pumps with feathers Tiffany had bought everyone in the bridal party, she crossed quickly back to the wedding site. What she saw had her shoulders finally lowering from her ears. The tent was up. The tables and chairs in the interior were all in place. So were the chandeliers and the oodles of stringy white lights.

Off to the right of the tent, the place where Tiffany and Rob were going to say their vows was also set up. The arbor with the pale roses and other greenery stood romantically at the apex of the groupings of white chairs. The white sweeping mesh curtains blew softly in the breeze. The florist was starting to tie the small bouquets at the ends of the aisles of chairs now that she had something to work with.

"Everything is coming together," Jeffrey called behind her.

She spun around and rushed him, banding her arms around him tightly. "You're a prince for stepping in and helping."

"I know, honey," he drawled and they both laughed. "How did the Deverell women take the wig going missing?"

"Mother had a spare wig—the one she'd picked out—"

"Of course she did! The devil probably visited her in a dream and told her our plan."

When he removed more holy water and made the sign of the cross, she dissolved into near giggles. "All your good juju must have worked because Tiffany stepped in and backed me up. She said my hair was pretty and I didn't have to wear the wig."

"You're kidding me!" He made the sign of the cross again. "What is the world coming to? Has a better day dawned in the Deverell line? Is it possible our spiritual attunements broke the wedding curse at last?"

"I'm sure it was the evil eye tattoos." She gave him a kiss as she heard her name shouted. "That's my cue."

Bubba was waiting beside the sparkler display inside the tent. "You ready for the sparkler show of your life tonight?"

She was so giddy at their progress she did a little knee-slapping dance. "Can't happen soon enough, let me tell you."

"Your fella caught me as I was coming in." He wiped perspiration from his brow. "Told me about the mud pits and all. Bad luck that."

"Yes, but we turned it around." She dug out her phone. "Let me call in the Navy boys who'll be in charge of lighting the displays."

"Do you want to see the final result? I added a little whimsy. Since you're a Gamecocks fan and all."

"Sure." She started typing as she walked.

> I'm ready for you. 🔥 You can't know how much. LOL. Sparkler display training is ready.

CAPTAIN HOTPANTS

> Ready for me, huh? 🥒 Promises, promises. Coming your way. How'd the wig thing go? 😊

> 😎 Tiff backed me over my mother, who'd bought the wig she picked out. She smelled deception in the air apparently. 🥴

CAPTAIN HOTPANTS

> Deception, huh? LMAO. I only smell bourbon. 🥃 Rob is hitting the lucky bourbon hard. Might need to take him on a walk. 🚶 He's a wreck. Nervous as hell. Worse than before our winging ceremony. 😱 See you soon.

She smiled as she pocketed her phone. Bubba was waiting for her beside two large crates. "Let's see it!"

Grinning, he smartly snagged off the tops of both. *Go Navy* was on the right. *Just Married* on the left. Hundreds of sparklers stood at attention. "Awesome! You're the best."

"Glad you're pleased. I added the biggest sparklers we can legally get away with in the corners. They'll last longer and give you a little more fire so y'all should light them first. Hey! Looks like the Navy is here."

Turning toward the wide entrance of the tent, she felt her mouth water. Dax was decked out in dress whites and looking as good to eat as a slice of red velvet cake, which she couldn't wait to have later when they cut the groom's cake. The other men wore their uniforms well, but Dax had an extra swagger. When he flashed her one of his *make her knees weak* smiles, she felt her heart flutter in her chest. Goodness, he was gorgeous. Not that Carson, Perry, Gunner, Frank, and Rob didn't look just as good.

But she had eyes for only one pilot...

When Dax reached her, she gave in to the urge to touch his wings and ribbons before tracing the gold and black epaulets on his wide shoulders. "Goodness," she purposely drew out in a Southern accent. "I'm having trouble concentrating."

He leaned in and kissed her, adept even with his military style cap with the black visor. "You always do that to me."

"Look at these!" Rob fairly shouted. "Better than I could have expected. Man, did you personally make them?"

Bubba patted his massive chest and nodded. "Yes, sir."

"Awesome." Rob fingered a few of the sparklers as the other guys circled the crates.

"That's a buttload of sparklers," Carson remarked with a whistle. "Run us through the lighting process."

Ariel was glad to hear his can-do attitude. She knew he and the other guys harbored reservations, but clearly they'd gotten the memo. Rob wanted to get married. End of story.

"I brought four blowtorches." Bubba gestured to the large canvas bag on the ground and unzipped it, showing off the goods. "You'll have to work in tandem—"

Rob swung his arm around Carson's neck, leaning heavily. "We're used to that. Aren't we, boys?"

Dax put his arm around her and squeezed reassuringly. "Your job today, Rob, is to sit back with your bride and enjoy yourself. We've got this."

She was glad Dax had said this because she wasn't sure having Rob near a blowtorch—not now and certainly not later given how much more drinking he might do—seemed a good idea.

"Ariel!"

The cry of her name was almost a scream. She dashed off in the direction of the sound, Dax running beside her. She heard the other men's footsteps behind them. Spotting Tricia and Terry running in their cream satin pumps, pale pink robes gaping, she increased her pace to intercept them.

"What is it?" she asked when she reached them, heart hammering.

Tricia's eyes were wild. "Tiffany's wedding dress—"

"It's not in the cottage!" Terry was panting, suddenly gripping her arm. "We've looked everywhere."

"What?" She felt like someone had socked her in the face. "Are you sure?"

"We put it in the cottage." Dax's voice was full of conviction.

Jeffrey was running toward them. On the grass. In his shoes. Something had to be really wrong for him to do that. She took off toward her brother.

"Ariel!" He was gasping as he reached her. "The wedding dress is not in the cottage anymore."

Dax reached them. "What happened?"

Jeffrey pushed his green glasses up his nose. "I don't know. Tricia texted me and asked where we'd put it. I told her. She said it wasn't there. I went to show her in case she'd had too many mimosas. But it's not there."

Her stomach felt like it had tumbled from the penthouse to the ground floor. "You're sure?"

His nod was so convincing he had to right his glasses after they slid down his nose. "I looked everywhere. It's like that dress up and left and followed your wig into the ocean."

"But we hung it where we were supposed to," Dax ground out. "How could it—"

Suddenly, Rob was whipping Dax around. "You son of a bitch!"

His fist nailed Dax in the jaw, making his head swivel. Carson and Perry had their arms around Rob before he could take another swing, Gunner and Frank in the wings. Ariel told herself not to step in, but she stayed where she was. Although she was glad Terry and Tricia were screeching, running off until they stood out of range.

Dax touched his face and glared at his friend. "What the hell, man?"

"You took the dress!" Rob's shout had the blood rushing out of Ariel's face. "You didn't want me to get married. You've tried at every turn to talk me out of it."

"Rob!" Carson's grip tightened as he tried to take another lunge at Dax. "Get a hold of yourself. Accusing Dax of something like that would be like accusing me or any of us guys."

"You're talking crazy!" Perry cried, muscling Rob in place as the other men nodded.

Ariel turned to Dax. He was pale, but his green eyes were hot with anger. He'd even fisted his hands at his sides. She didn't know what to do. But one thing was for certain: Rob was totally out of line. This betrayal had to be cutting Dax deep.

"You know I wouldn't do something that low," Dax ground out, his voice clipped.

"Do I?" Rob practically spat, shoving at Carson and Perry. "Well, here's the punch line, buddy. You've been trying to stop something you can't. Tiff and I got hitched in Vegas two months ago."

Ariel's mouth dropped open. *They were married?* How could her sister not have mentioned this?

Jeffrey cried out like a dog who'd been stepped on. "OMG! That's why her dress didn't fit! She's pregnant!"

She whipped her head around to frown at him as she heard Terry's and Tricia's outraged cries. He'd slapped both hands over his mouth, his brown eyes wide with shock. She was sure she didn't look much better.

"Jesus, Rob!" Dax exclaimed, taking her attention back to him. "You're married—and having a baby—and you didn't say a word! To any of us. What the fuck?"

"Yeah, dude!" Carson echoed harshly. "We're your buddies."

"Your friends," Perry added hollowly, looking as hurt as the other two men who were glaring at Rob.

He tried to wrestle free, but they continued to hold him. "Tiff didn't want anyone to know because of something I don't want to go into. It's our private business, isn't it? But maybe I should have told Dax here so he wouldn't steal my *wife's* fucking wedding dress!"

"I didn't steal it!" Dax shouted back, taking his cap off and slapping it against his thigh.

"Who else would have?" Rob tried to wrestle free of Carson and Perry's hold, but they held him back by the arms. "You're the only one who's made a big deal of wanting this wedding to be canceled since you imagined she hit on you."

God, how many proverbial cats could get out of the bag?

"When the hell did that happen?" Perry shouted out.

"It doesn't matter." Rob started struggling again. "Dammit! Let go of me!"

"Not until you get a hold of yourself, man," Carson bit off, his cap tilting to the right. "You're totally over the edge right now. I'm tempted to tell you I took the dress to save you from yourself."

"Give her dress back, Dax!" Rob's voice was cold, his eyes flat and mean. "All she's wanted is a perfect wedding. Don't fuck this up for her. Because if you do, you're fucking it up for me too."

The two men faced off in a silence thick with bad feelings. Dax's ears were bright red from repressed anger. Rob's face was flushed with rage.

Dax held up a hand like a white flag, his jaw locked. "I give you my word that I did not take her wedding dress."

"Bullshit!" Rob started wrestling to get free, fighting for all he was worth. Gunner and Frank joined in to hold him. Dax only stood there silently, his face rigid.

Jeffrey stepped up behind her. "Did you know?" he whispered.

She leaned closer, desperately wanting to put her head on his shoulder, close her eyes, and pretend this wasn't happening. "Only about the baby," she said for his ears only. "When she disappeared that day she told me. She never mentioned being married already."

God, she still couldn't believe it. But right now wasn't the time for shock. Rob was continuing to fight his friends, his hard eyes locked on Dax like he wanted to take another punch at him and not stop.

If they let him go, she knew he would knock Dax on the ground and hit him until he confessed. Someone had to defuse the situation. "Rob, I know you and Dax have had your differences, but he'd never do this."

"Shut up, Ariel!" Rob spat back, surging forward.

Dax was in Rob's face in a hot second. "You don't talk to her like that."

Rob kicked at him, making Dax jump back to avoid

being kneed in the balls. "That's rich, coming from you. Dammit, give Tiff back her dress."

"I don't know where the dress is, man." Dax's jaw cracked audibly. "Listen to me. I didn't take it."

Ariel walked over to her visibly shaken sisters. "You checked to make sure it's not in the bridal suite?"

They both nodded, their faces pale with shock. "We texted Tiffany," Terry said, choking back tears.

Oh God!

"Ariel!"

The air fairly crackled after her sister's anguished cry, and Ariel wouldn't have been surprised if lightning had struck something. A tree. A happily swimming koi in the wedding pond. The four-tiered wedding cake.

Disaster was joining danger in the air, and this time, it had the Deverell name written all over it.

Mother was striding toward them in her silk pajamas, Tiffany right beside her. Hands pumping at her sides, she didn't notice her robe was gaping open. No, there was murder in her sister's wild eyes.

"Where's my dress?" Tiffany practically screamed.

Ariel stood rooted in her spot. Her brain wouldn't process anything but the one problem she didn't have an answer to. She had an entire bag filled with disaster-solving items, everything from wet wipes to extra extension cords, but nothing that would solve this. Checking the time, she noted they had ninety minutes until the wedding started.

Ninety minutes!

The *Lord of the Flies* boys were suddenly running toward them and skidding to a halt, staring up at the adults. When she glanced around, everyone was staring at her. Right. Because she always knew what to do. A surge of nausea shot up her throat like she'd downed a vinegar shot.

She had no answers. Only the urgent pounding of her heart in her ears, making her pant rapidly.

Dax's hand on her shoulder brought her back into focus. God knew how much that had cost him at such a fraught moment. Oh, she couldn't have loved him more.

She walked toward her sister and leaned close to make direct eye contact. "Somehow your dress got misplaced, Tiffany."

"Misplaced?" Her sister's voice was full of venom. "Well...then you'd better find it—or you won't be getting what we agreed to."

She could feel everything inside her drop. Yeah, this was the other shoe she'd feared was coming. Swallowing the ball in her throat, she reached for her famous calm, the kind she gathered when she faced impossible odds. "I know what's at stake. Don't worry. We're going to find it."

Her voice sounded more assuring than she felt. Surely they would find it. A wedding dress didn't just up and walk off on its own. If her family was the kind who could joke, she'd say maybe a bunch of crabs, relatives of the one who'd worn her wig, had taken the dress off into the ocean. Perhaps a mermaid had needed it for her perfect wedding under the sea.

But they weren't that kind of family and never would be.

Her sister's wedding dress was missing. They had less than ninety minutes to find it. And if they didn't, after all this, the one thing she'd wanted all along would never be hers.

TWENTY-FOUR

The wedding dress was nowhere to be found.

Dax stood beside Ariel as the last reports came in from the search party they'd formed. Even the *Lord of the Flies* boys had been eager to help despite their shocked faces, muttering about Dax being blamed for it. Which had only made him want to snarl. Being accused of something he hadn't done—would never do—was new to him, and he hated it. And he had no idea how to clear his name or find the damn dress!

They'd searched cottages.

They'd searched the common areas of the resort.

No dress.

Anywhere.

Focusing on his objective kept him from wanting to shake Rob senseless. Hell, he wanted to clock him for accusing him of such a low, vile thing. How could his best friend think he'd ever hide a wedding dress?

A friend didn't.

They were done.

"I don't know what else to do here." Ariel was tapping a

pen against her temple, standing on their front porch with Sherlock pressed against her leg, looking at the map of the resort. "Where else can we look? Dax, we've got an hour until the wedding starts. Guests are starting to arrive."

"Keep calm." He took the pen away and held her hand while Sherlock nuzzled it. "Let's brainstorm. We haven't found the dress. We need a plan if we don't."

She lost even more color. *"A plan?"* A wild laugh escaped her. "It's a wedding dress! You don't exactly go out and buy one of those."

"Why not? I'm not saying it's going to be the ideal dress—"

"This is Tiffany we're talking about!" Ariel's voice quavered with stress. "Besides, there's the fitting and pressing and the— Someone is going to have to convince her to wear a different dress. One of her sundresses. Oh God! This is awful. In every wedding nightmare I had, this one never came up."

She cradled her face in her hands. Dax could understand. Tiffany's threat had pissed him off. She could lose her grandma's house here. He'd lost his best friend. He looked off in the direction where his buddies had stashed Rob so he wouldn't go after him again. They'd had to practically drag him back to his cottage while the bridal party, minus Ariel, had taken Tiffany back to the bridal suite after Terry and Tricia had started asking their sister nonstop questions about her marriage and pregnancy. Ariel's mother hadn't said a word but her entire face had tightened as if by screws. Dax didn't want to be in either cottage.

Jeffrey appeared, running toward them, his loafers slapping on the path. When he reached them, he put a hand on Dax's arm, breathing heavily. "Tiffany is insistent. There won't be a wedding if she doesn't have her dress. It doesn't matter to her that she's already married. She will not go through with her perfect day—"

Ariel slumped against him. Dax usually had a good head on his shoulders in stressful moments, but even he felt knots forming in his stomach. Her worst fear was here, and he felt helpless in the face of her desolation.

"Then it's all over," she whispered hoarsely. "I won't get my grandma's house. Everything was for nothing. Oh God! How could this happen?"

Dax still didn't know. A wedding dress did not just disappear. "Do you think Sherlock could find it?"

She rubbed the dog under the ears as she shook her head. "I already thought of that, but Tiffany's scent is all over the resort. Yours and Jeffrey's too. It would be like going after a needle in a haystack."

He'd been afraid of that. "Do we start calling bridal boutiques with her size and asking if we could pick up dresses for the bride to try on, this being an emergency?"

Jeffrey took off his glasses and pinched the bridge of his nose. "I already called the most famous wedding dress boutique downtown. They said they couldn't just send us all the dresses in Tiffany's size. Too much liability if something happened to them. I called two other boutiques and got the same answer. No surprise, I guess. We have trouble with a capital T written all over us. The shopkeepers couldn't believe we'd lost the wedding dress. One said she's been in the business for over forty years and never heard of such a thing."

"Great, we're a first." Ariel tipped her head back up toward the sky. "I usually have an answer. In every disaster, there's often something that can be done. Even if it's small. But not today. We simply have to convince Tiffany to wear something else."

Jeffrey clutched his now-rumpled cravat. "Ariel, she swore on Grandma Deverell's grave that she won't do it."

"She has to. She just has to." Ariel uttered a pained moan and started walking down the steps and then onto the path leading in the direction of the bridal cabin. Dax caught up with her after putting Sherlock back in the house—better he be out of the way right now. Jeffrey was on his heels.

"Ariel, you don't have to go in there," Jeffrey called out. "You know how it's going to be."

"I know! But I can't give up without trying."

She sounded so dejected his heart squeezed. "We'll be a unified front."

"I'm not sure you should go in there, Dax." Ariel's pained face glanced his way. "Let me talk to her."

He stopped short. "Wait, you don't think I stole it, do you?"

Her mouth parted. "No, of course not! But Tiffany does, and she will rain hellfire on you."

Jesus, Ariel was right. What would it be like for him and Ariel going forward after this? Her mother and the Three Tornadoes would probably bar him from every family function. What would that do to her? God, he didn't want to put her in that position, but he also wasn't a man to hide from anything. "I told you from the beginning that I'm your wingman. That doesn't stop now."

"I agree, Ariel," Jeffrey declared, locking arms with her. "I'm not going to let Tiffany or anyone else unload on you. This is not your fault. Or Dax's for that matter, so you don't need to protect him. This is the Deverell wedding curse. I was with Dax. We left the cottage together. The dress was there, and I have the photo to prove it."

"When has common sense ever mattered?" She

groaned. "I should have put guards on the door. I should have—"

"Hey there." Dax couldn't stand to see her blaming herself. "Let's not go there. We're both getting knocked around for something we didn't do. We need to remember that. So you go in there and hope she can see that marrying Rob *again* is the most important thing—not the dress."

Jeffrey let out an anguished shriek. "Not the dress! Dax, please don't say that out loud."

Ariel gave a tormented nod of agreement.

Dax patted them both on the back as they reached the bridal cottage. He just didn't get it. Maybe it was a guy thing. But how could you let something like a dress stop you from doing something really important? Like getting married to the person you loved? It was even crazier given they were already legally married.

Jeffrey opened the door for her after adjusting his rumpled cravat. Lifting her chin, Ariel walked inside in determined strides. Tiffany was surrounded by her sisters, crying in front of a mirror. Stormy was holding a large highball filled to the brim, sitting in a nearby chair.

Seeing her, Tiffany hurled herself up out of the chair. "Did you find it?"

Ariel shook her head. Tiffany's face crumpled, and she sank down to the floor, hands in her lap, crying her heart out.

Dax felt Jeffrey's hand on his arm. They halted just inside the door, which was probably a good decision because the bridal party rushed over and settled around Tiffany, their loud cries joining hers.

He'd never seen anything like it.

The wailing made him want to turn tail and walk out, but he stayed for Ariel. He heard her muttering to Tiffany.

"I can't get married if I don't have a wedding dress!" she howled back, glaring at her sister.

More murmuring from Ariel.

"But I can't!" came another protestation from the bride.

"It's too bad I can't pop back to my house in Savannah and let you choose from my old wedding dresses, Tiffany." Stormy took a long pull of her drink. "You're a little chubby, but my empire dress would probably fit you."

"That's it!" Ariel practically shouted.

Dax felt the energy in the room change as she pushed off the floor and stood up, pulling Tiffany to her feet.

"What?" Tiffany muttered, wiping tears and smearing more makeup.

"Grandma has three wedding dresses in the attic to choose from, and you're her size." She grabbed Tiffany's shoulders. "Don't you remember how gorgeous they are? I'll bet one will fit you."

"But they're not mine," Tiffany wailed. "And they're old and not clean."

"Grandma was a neat freak, and you know it." Ariel checked her watch. "They'll be in perfect condition. Okay... If we delay the wedding a little, I can run out to Folly Beach, grab the dresses, and then be back in a jiffy for you to try them on, to see which one you like best. Then we'll steam it real quick and get you married."

"But Ariel—" she moaned, crying jaggedly now.

"Tiff, I love you," she interrupted, hugging her. "But you're going to have to open your mind to a new plan. Think about how romantic it will be to tell your and Rob's children about wearing your grandma's wedding dress."

They shared a look. There was a long pause. Tension thickened in the air.

"Maybe your girls might even wear one, should you and

Rob have them," she followed up, wiping the tears from Tiffany's cheeks. "It could become a beautiful family tradition."

Tiffany sniffed and finally nodded. "All right...but it's not how I wanted it."

"I know, but maybe it's even better this way." Ariel kissed her on the cheek. "I'll be back as soon as I can. Be ready to try some dresses on. Jeffrey! Will you find a couple of steamers? We'll work like an assembly line if need be once she chooses the dress she wants to wear."

"You've got it," Jeffrey called brightly as she passed them in a blur to the door. "And I'll make sure everyone knows it's delayed and keep the rest going like clockwork until you get back."

"You're the best!" Ariel called. "Dax!"

"Coming," he answered, rushing after her as they headed down the path in the direction of the parking lot. "You want me to drive?"

She shot him a killer smile. "I'd love for you to drive. It's been one hell of a day so far, and we're not done."

He did his best not to speed, feeling every minute of the twenty-five-minute journey ahead of them. But he couldn't help that his foot wanted to put the pedal to the metal. When they reached Folly Beach, he wanted to curse. The police were everywhere, and the twenty-five miles per hour speed limit on the island was enough to drive anyone bananas.

Ariel was clearly losing her mind over the snail's pace. She tapped her foot on the floor as well as her fingers on the dashboard, leaning forward in her seat like the mere act would propel them to their destination faster. When they pulled into the driveway, she was opening the door before he'd stopped.

"Hey! Be careful."

Hitting the brakes, he watched her run to the house and take the steps two at a time. He kept the car running but went around to the side to make sure the rear seats were lying flat so the dresses could be laid out. That's what he'd done with his dress whites. Made sense to him.

When he hit the button for the first seat, he spotted the plastic. His mind reeled as his gaze took in the rest.

The wedding dress was here!

In the back of his Bronco...

Holy—

He took a couple deep breaths before walking to the back and popping it open. While he wasn't a superstitious man, he reached out to touch the dress to make sure it was actually there.

Yup.

The plastic made a rustling sound as he carefully unfolded the balled-up dress. He couldn't believe it! Someone had balled up Tiffany's dress and thrown it in the back of his Bronco. Rare panic made his heart race. Surely she'd believe he had no idea how it had ended up in his car. Except shit. Look at Rob—they'd been friends for half their lives and his friend had turned on him without any evidence.

The sound of Ariel's footsteps pounding down the stairs had his head craning to look at her. She held three vacuum-sealed bags in her arms. He looked back toward the wrinkled wonder in his trunk.

Fuck! What the hell was he supposed to say?

Hey, Elizabeth. You aren't going to believe this. Someone threw Tiffany's dress in the back of my car.

But then she was off the stairs and running toward the Bronco and him. The situation hit him.

He'd been framed.

And he had no idea by whom or why.

He stepped a couple feet from the trunk, blocking her view. She was panting and her gaze shot up to look at him. He put his hands on her shoulders and leaned down until they were eye level. "So...I don't think I'm going crazy, but it seems like Tiffany's dress is in my trunk."

Her brows slammed together. *"What?"*

She zoomed around him and let out a closed-mouth shriek before swinging around and staring at him.

"You see it too, right?"

"But...how?" she sputtered. "I thought you and Jeffrey put it in the wedding cottage."

An unholy tension rolled through his gut. "We did. Ariel, I have no idea how or why this dress is in my trunk."

Her mouth parted before she glanced toward it again, her face pale as fresh snow. She stood there, breathing hard, the other wedding dresses lying limply in her arms.

When she didn't say anything, he stepped forward and put his hand on her shoulder. "You believe me, right?"

Her pupils were dilated, and she looked as wild as he felt. She glanced back toward her sister's wedding dress... and then at him. She finally nodded. Slowly.

"But..." She made an inarticulate sound. "I don't understand. Who else—"

"I don't know." He checked his watch, his sense of mission timing never failing him. "Look, we both have questions. But we need to get back. We have less than thirty minutes—"

"You're right. I should just be grateful it showed up."

He loved that perspective. "Right."

She spun into action, laying her grandma's dresses carefully in the back after straightening Tiffany's dress. "I don't have time to take them back inside. Let's go."

He backed out of the driveway and then hit the road. As a pilot on a mission, he hated that sinking feeling of knowing the clock was against you. He felt it today. Even though he knew they could delay the wedding a little, he could still hear the second hand clicking in his mind. Ariel clenched her hands in her lap, staring straight out the window.

"We need a cover story," he finally said in the tense silence of the car.

She turned her stricken gaze his way. "Dax, this looks really bad."

He nodded, his jaw clenching. "I know."

She exhaled loudly, pressing her hands to her knees. "I think we just say that we found it as we were coming back to the resort. In a closet or something."

In a closet? She must be jittery because that didn't make any sense. "Ariel, everyone knows someone moved it. I know it won't be easy for anyone to believe someone put the dress in the back of my car—"

"Dax!" Her cry was totally out of character as she turned in her seat and looked at him, her blue eyes round as quarters. "No one is going to believe you."

He'd lived his whole life doing what was right. Knowing people were going to think the worst of him—Rob and her family and everyone else—was like being told he'd never fly again. "Ariel, I know this looks bad, but we're going to find out who did this."

She started laughing, the stress making the sound tense and ear-grating. "Find out? Like a whodunnit? Oh, Dax! I don't even know where to start because I can't think of *anyone* but you wanting this wedding stopped."

He bristled. "Are you saying you don't believe me?"

Rubbing her throat, she turned away and looked out the window. "I do, but then a horrible little voice starts talking."

His heart felt like it had been ripped in half. "And what does that horrible voice say?"

"Oh, Dax," was all she said in a hoarse voice.

He watched the road ahead and stared at the cars in front of him, going numb. "You think I felt guilty or something and decided to unhide the dress."

She rubbed her forehead. "Dax, I know you... When you tell me you didn't do it, I believe you. But I don't know how this could have happened. Okay?"

Okay? No, it wasn't okay. She was crushing him here.

"I'm tired and I thought I'd lost my grandma's house again." She reached out a shaky hand and touched his arm, her blue eyes glistening now. "It's been a roller coaster. Let's deal with all this after. Please."

If he didn't have her trust, at least he could stand by the truth. "Ariel, I will not say we found this dress in a closet. I'm going to tell Rob it was in my Bronco and that I did not put it there."

"He'll never believe you," she whispered, gripping his hand. "Neither will Tiffany or anyone else. You saw how they are."

He set his jaw and kept driving. "I have a code. I won't break it. Not to make things easier or smooth things over."

Her sharp inhale hurt to hear, and he clenched his teeth, knowing he'd hurt her too.

"Like I do, you mean."

He said nothing.

"That's right. That's my job. To smooth things over. To help everyone get along. To clean up after disasters like this as kindly and politely as I can."

"Lying isn't kind or polite," he felt compelled to say. "I can't control what anyone thinks of me, but I would hope the people who know me would understand I'd never do something like this. If you love me like you said you did, then you would know that too, and you would tell the truth. About me. About this."

Her silence had something dying inside him.

"I do love you, and I do know you." She heaved out a breath. "But I just don't know what to think right now, and I certainly don't want you to tell them where the dress was, because it will only cause more problems."

He kept driving, biting his tongue to hold back his harsh retort, the kind you can't take back. He was aware of her staring at him as he drove, but she said nothing. And when she let her hand fall from his arm, he thought he'd lost one more person he loved.

Her.

TWENTY-FIVE

She was going to lie.

Despite what Dax said, she didn't see a choice. If Rob knew where the dress had been, not even Carson and Perry could hold him back from beating Dax to a bloody pulp. She couldn't let that start up again. Right before the wedding. Right in front of the wedding guests. God only knew what her mother, sisters, and Tiffany would do if they were told where it had been found.

Certainly they'd order him from the wedding.

Maybe have him thrown off the resort property.

She wouldn't put it past her mother to have him arrested for stolen property.

None of that could happen. She knew her family. He didn't. She didn't care that he didn't like it. She couldn't tell them the truth. Even if that put her at odds with Dax. It was in her blood to mitigate disasters. She didn't start them.

She pulled out her phone to text Jeffrey on the sly as Dax drove, his entire demeanor stiff and unapproachable. That she had hurt him she had no doubt, and she hated that.

Except the question remained like a dark whisper in her head. Who else would have hidden Tiffany's wedding dress? And how could it have ended up in Dax's trunk?

She had no answers there, and right now, she couldn't waste her last working brain cells considering the possibilities.

There was a wedding to get done.

> Meet me in the parking lot. Stat. We found Tiffany's wedding dress. I need you to take it to her. 👰

BEST BROTHER EVER

> You what? 😳 Okay. Whew! I'll be there with bells on. God, I need a Manhattan. 🥃

> 💚 Then I need you to come back to our cottage and escort Dax to the wedding. Keep on him like a June bug. 🪲

BEST BROTHER EVER

👍

She pocketed her phone again and stared out the window until they arrived at the resort. Jeffrey was waiting for them, looking rumpled, although his cravat was freshly tied. The minute Dax parked, she was out the door.

"You really found it?" Jeffrey asked, hugging her quickly before pushing back.

"It was in the back of my Bronco," Dax confessed as he came around the front.

She wanted to knock her head against the side of the car.

"Someone put it there," he just had to add.

Jeffrey's eyes widened. "But who? That's—"

When he stopped mid-sentence, she knew he understood the implications. "Jeffrey, I need to change. Will you take Tiffany her dress—"

"I'll handle it." Dax opened the back door, which prompted Ariel to slide under his arm and stand in the way, shaking her head. "Ariel, I am taking that dress to your sister and telling her what we found."

"No, you're not." She put a hand to Dax's white jacket and gave it a gentle but firm push. "Jeffrey is. You are coming with me to the cottage and helping me get dressed. I need you to zip me up."

He glared at her. "You are not keeping me from telling the truth and defending my character."

"Oh, dear sweet baby Jesus in heaven, Captain Hotpants!" Jeffrey cried as he walked to the other side of the car and opened the door, pulling out Tiffany's dress. "This is not the time to be a good Boy Scout. We need to get bridezilla into her dress and get her married off to your asshole friend lickety-split. We've delayed the wedding basically until the bride is ready. The natives are restless, and you're already sporting a shiner. We'll deal with this frame-up later."

He started walking off, but Dax called his name sharply.

Jeffrey only turned and looked down his nose at him. "Honey, I say this with love, but get that stick out of your ass. This is your *make lemonade out of lemons* moment. Listen to Ariel. It's her specialty."

With a flick of his head and a touch of flourish, Jeffrey strode off. Dax glared at Ariel. She glared back.

"So...are you going to zip me up or not?"

His mouth twisted.

She gripped his arm and started walking, aware she was dragging him a little. "I'll take that as a yes."

"Ariel, I don't like this."

His voice was flinty, but he was still coming with her, so she wasn't going to tempt her luck. "Neither do I, but let's take things one step at a time. We can do crime solving later."

He turned and gave her a frigid glare. "You're pissing me off."

"Good!" The cottage was in sight, and he was still following. "Me too! Personally, I hate fighting with people I love. And I'm a newbie over fighting over something like a frame-up. Although Tiffany did blame me for breaking Mother's favorite Waterford vase one time, which I couldn't un-prove. Is that a word?"

"Sorry, but I hate your sister," he spat. "And your whole family except Jeffrey."

"We have that in common, then," she answered, her limbs as heavy as concrete now. "I sometimes do too."

Sherlock greeted them at the door. She leaned down and put her head against his fur, hugging him. He nuzzled her softly, and she felt rare tears fill her eyes.

"Sherlock, you take care of Dax." She took Dax's stiff hand and led him to the couch, pushing him not so gently down. "Sit."

Her precious dog leaped into Dax's lap—all one hundred pounds of him. "I thought you needed me to zip you up."

"Settle down first." She headed to her bedroom, knowing she should be rushing around, but all the life was drained out of her.

Another Deverell family event.

How could she have imagined it would be any different from the rest?

She pulled on her dress after stripping, glad she'd left it

in her closet and not taken it over to the bridal suite. She'd known she couldn't handle being in there with the others. She'd also been hoping to avoid the makeup. Which she had. She almost laughed at that, but she was worried the laugh would turn into a sob.

God, she hoped everything was in place. Maybe Tiffany would be too elated her dress was back to ask many questions.

Oh, who was she kidding?

The crisis had leached all the color from her face, she noted in the mirror, so she went and added powder and a touch of blush along with the nude pink lip gloss Jeffrey had chosen for her.

Staring at herself in the mirror, she brushed her hair. She looked like bridezilla's sister with her glazed-over eyes and pale features. Blush couldn't get rid of that look on her face. And then there was her hair. The curls were sticking out in all directions. She smoothed them with some water and clenched her eyes shut.

Please let this wedding come off without a hitch.

Taking one last look, she tried to smile before heading back to her room and stepping into her heels. Maybe she should go barefoot. Be faster. Then she shook her head. With her luck, she'd step on a nail and end up with lockjaw or something.

Her being hospitalized wouldn't make Tiffany more compassionate.

Then she remembered how her sister had stood up for her about the wig. Later she'd threatened her with Grandma's house again. She just couldn't predict what her sister was going to do. She made a point of strapping on her garter flask. Because she was not going to leave home without it. Not today.

Striding back to the main room, she found Dax where she'd left him, Sherlock in his lap. He stopped rubbing him under his ears and looked up at her, his green eyes missing the warmth and light she was used to. "Your dog has gotten hair all over my dress whites."

She laughed in a high-pitched tone she didn't recognize, then pressed her hand to her mouth. "Sorry."

His mouth gave a twitch before he flattened it. "Can I get up now?"

"Sherlock. Off."

Her dog jumped from Dax's lap and came to her side. She rubbed him gently and smiled into his expressive eyes. He gave a whine. *Yeah, that's how I'm feeling, buddy.*

"Will you zip me up?" She turned and presented her back to Dax.

There was a pause, and then he kissed the nape of her neck. Slowly. Tenderly. Long enough to make her throat ache. The hiss of the zipper finally rent the silence. A knock sounded on the door. She went over to answer it. Jeffrey stood on the other side, his face red.

"Went that good, did it?" she asked rhetorically, lifting her skirt and taking out her flask and offering it to him.

He gave a sputter of laughter before taking a drink and handing it to her. She took one pull herself before handing it to Dax. He waved his hand, refusing.

"Okay, boys. Let's go. Sherlock, I'll see you later."

With another pat, she was outside, her heels clicking on the path. The rub of the cold metal flask against her thigh was a comfort. When she arrived at the wedding site, she scanned the area. The guests were all seated and talking to each other, happy wedding music playing over the loudspeakers. The sweetgrass baskets filled with flowers, a Charleston wedding tradition, graced the Welcome Table.

Everything looked to be in place except for the bridal party, who were likely waiting for their cue.

Then she caught sight of motion in the sky and lifted her head. Pelicans were circling overhead behind the tent.

"Ariel!"

She turned at her name and watched as the event coordinator ran from the tent, skirt flying up as she pumped her arms to reach her.

"What is it?" she asked, rushing toward the woman.

"It's the koi!" She was panting when they met. "The pelicans are diving into the fountain and picking them out one at a time. I tried to stop them—"

"Oh my God!"

She didn't care about lockjaw. Taking off her shoes, she ran for the pond behind the tent where the open bar was situated. Dax was right beside her, she noted, but then she was stopping short at the sight before her.

Eight pelicans were taking turns diving into the clean water tank. Three koi were all that were left, and they were swimming in rapid circles, trying to evade the pelicans' giant beaks. One dove in, caught a bright orange koi, and then hopped out of the water onto the pool's edge, lifted its beak, and tossed it into the air, catching it in its mouth and working its throat to gulp the whole fish down. It disappeared before her eyes.

She stood frozen in shock.

Dax flew forward, crying out and waving his arms wildly. The pelicans flew off a short distance, but there were more of them than there were of him, and they seemed to know it. Worse, he was in the way of the best meal they'd had in weeks—to the tune of a few thousand dollars of sashimi—and they weren't going to let some lone idiot in a white suit shove them off their turf.

"Ariel!" Dax shouted. "Stay back."

Three of them dove at him, their individual wingspans easily reaching twelve feet. He thrust up at first, but they were coming for him, kamikaze moves in their nature apparently, something Dax clearly wasn't ready for despite being a naval pilot.

She started running. She wasn't leaving him. Suddenly the truth in her heart was absolute. He was her wingman, and she was his. She was not leaving him behind, no matter what.

Ariel looked around for something to throw and ran over to the short ice sculpture of a romantic couple sitting on a park bench on the side of the bar Tiffany had insisted on despite the incident at her first wedding. She picked it up, then ran back and hurled it at the closest pelican.

She missed, but the sound of it crashing to the ground sent more of them flying off. She could see their beady black eyes taking her measure.

Running back into the tent, she found the closest place settings and, picking them up, ran back out and started hurling forks, spoons, and then knives into the air at them. Her projectiles struck one pelican, who gave a loud squawk. Dax was still thrusting his arms into the air and yelling like a madman. The pelicans swirled over them before finally lifting up higher in the air. She watched them, gripping rumpled napkins and a single sterling silver fork, glaring at them, hoping they understood she was not backing down.

Not here.

Not now.

They had pushed her too far.

When they'd finally headed off, she looked in the pond, where a lone koi remained, swimming speedily in circles, clearly not certain the danger was over. She walked over to the water, staring at the poor thing. How did one soothe a koi? She knew how to soothe a dog.

"Everything's okay, folks," she heard Dax call out to a few people who'd come running. "Get back to your places."

Right. Because the wedding was going to happen. With only one koi. She stared at it, still in shock.

"Are you all right?"

Dax suddenly stood beside her. His hands gripped her shoulders, and then he was pulling her hard against his chest. She clung to him. And then she started to laugh. Wild laughter. Deranged laughter. The kind that prompted jokes about someone needing to take Valium or be fitted for a straitjacket.

That thought cut off her laughter. Mother might just do it. "God, that was awful!"

He wasn't laughing. No, he was holding her protectively against his chest. "You shouldn't have done that! I told you to stay back. They could have killed you."

"What? Pecked me to death? I'd like to see them try."

When she pushed back and held up her fist, he cupped her face. "You didn't leave me."

She put her hand on top of his, holding his gaze, her heart somersaulting in her chest because the warmth was back in his beautiful green eyes. "No, I didn't, and I don't plan to."

His mouth curved, accentuating the swelling in his jaw. "I'm glad. I was afraid for a minute that Elizabeth and Stephan—"

She silenced him with a gentle hand to his mouth. The very idea made her ache. "Never! Elizabeth and Stephan are meant to last forever."

He pulled her to him again, his hands gripping her like

he was never letting go. Which she was fine with. "I thought so. Glad the pelicans reminded you."

"I didn't need reminding." She needed to see his face as she said this. "You and I got pissy with each other. It happens. Doesn't mean I don't love you."

"Ditto," was all he said amidst the tenderness in his eyes. "I want to go on the record and say that I'd do anything to get your grandmother's house for you, but if it doesn't happen because nothing has gone according to plan —the pelicans drove that home and then some—I promise we'll find our own home and make new happy memories there for our family."

She melted just like the broken ice sculpture lying on the ground beside the lone koi in the pond. "I'd like that." With that beautiful promise, they were back on firm ground. "And I have no idea how Tiffany's wedding dress got in the back of your car. Or how the irrigation system at this resort could have backed up. I also don't know how a... what is a flock of pelicans?"

He brushed his thumb along her cheekbone. "I actually know this one. A squadron."

"How military of them. Which explains their tactical precision today. Anyway, I don't know why a squadron of pelicans decided to pick out the koi from our symbolic little wedding pond. Or how any number of things happen at Deverell family functions. What I do know is that you did not do it, and I'm sorry that for a minute there, we were at odds about it. All right?"

Nodding, he cupped her face in his hands. "All right. Since we're offering confessions, I might have had a stick up my butt a little like Jeffrey said. Sorry about that."

She patted his very famous ass, the one that had been

named the best buns this side of Biloxi. "Everything all right back here now?"

"*Elizabeth...*" The word was positively electric. "Keep your hand there and find out."

Then he was lowering his head, and she was rising on her bare feet to meet him and kissing him with an urgency that reminded her love was everything, and life was precious, even in the midst of disasters.

Just like Grandma always said.

TWENTY-SIX

Dax was back in sync with his girl, thank God.

A gator might have interrupted their first kiss, but it was the pelicans who'd brought them back to the truth of how they felt about each other. Still, he'd rather avoid all animal or fowl interference in the future. At this point, he and Ariel were never going on a date to the zoo. Or a circus for that matter. Because lions were no joke.

Now all he needed to figure out was whether he was still best man. Jeffrey had spread the news to the groom's party that Tiffany had her wedding dress back. But he wasn't budging from Dax's side—not only for Ariel's sake, he'd told him. Jeffrey knew how the Deverells could get under your skin.

Only Jeffrey didn't realize it wasn't the Deverells that had his guts in knots. It was Rob. What the hell was he going to say about the dress? Ariel had pleaded with him, but it was hard to break his code.

"If it helps any," Jeffrey broke in, "you might consider that you're not lying. Only delaying the truth. Also, I might point out that we don't know the full truth yet."

Dax slid him a glance as they walked to the groomsmen's suite. "No, we don't. You sure you don't have any dark thoughts about me taking the dress and then feeling guilty about it?"

Jeffrey snickered. "It crossed my mind for a half sec, but you're too smart to have put it in your car. That dress would have disappeared for good. Ariel was too tired and stressed to think it through. That happens after prolonged exposure to the Deverell women."

He appreciated hearing that. After Ariel had come to his defense during their very own Hitchcock's *The Birds* moment, he'd let go of his hurt. He'd never seen a point in holding a grudge. But Rob did. Even when it made no sense.

"Thanks for the vote of confidence." At the door, he straightened his shoulders—like he was appearing before a commanding officer. "You don't need to go in here with me."

"Yes, I do." Jeffrey nudged him aside with a wink. "If you'll trust an ally, let me do the talking. After the wedding ceremony, you and I are going to head to the lodge and look at the security feed for the parking lot."

He gripped Jeffrey's shoulder, liking the addition of another ally to his party, one Ariel loved with all her might. "I was thinking the very same thing."

"Consider me your Watson." Jeffrey touched up his cravat and straightened his emerald green glasses. "We'll clear your good name, Captain Hotpants, don't worry. Now, let's face the crazy groom."

With another dashing flick of his head, Jeffrey opened the door and sauntered inside. Rob was sitting sprawled in a tall throne-like chair with the lucky bottle of bourbon in his hand. Carson and Perry were sitting on the cream leather couch. At their intrusion, they pocketed their phones and put their hands on their thighs, poised for action. Dax only nodded in their direction.

Jeffrey smiled brightly. "You heard Tiffany's wedding dress was found, right? We're just coming to check and make sure you're ready. Ariel is with Tiffany and the others. I'm waiting for the text telling us when you can go out to the wedding arbor."

Rob grunted and took another pull of bourbon. "Where in the hell was the dress?"

"In a place you'd never expect," Jeffrey bandied back. "We're still looking into how it got there. Now…is everyone ready? Because when we get the text to go, we need to *go*. You flyboys are used to that, I imagine."

Carson and Perry slid to the edge of the couch, poised to grab Rob. "We certainly are," Carson replied. "Rob—"

"Hang on," Dax interrupted, taking off his white cap and slapping it against his leg. "Rob, there were some harsh words before. I'm here to see if you still want me to be your best man. I agreed to the job, and you know I finish what I start."

Rob set the bottle down with a thunk and stood, his wide stance filled with tension. "Don't I know it."

"What the fuck, Rob?" Carson shot up and flicked his hand accusingly at him. "Are you really going to blow a friendship over *a wedding dress*? A dress Dax absolutely didn't and wouldn't take? Man, you need to apologize, shake hands, and move on. Jesus! Maybe I should tell you I took the fucking wedding dress."

"I agree." Perry put his hands on his hips, staring at Rob mulishly. "Because this is stupid, and if you don't have Dax as your best man, maybe you shouldn't have me or Carson stand up with you either."

Dax's heart was beating hard, and while he was deeply

moved by Carson and Perry's loyalty, he didn't take his eyes off Rob.

Dax lifted his chin. "Up to you, Rob. I'll turn around and walk out of here on your say-so, and we don't need to speak again."

The wedding had changed things, and they both knew it. But it didn't have to end like this.

"Do you know why you've been my best buddy since college, Dax?" Rob asked, shifting his weight heavily to his right. "Because you're such a square. That's what makes you a good officer too. You never break a rule. I never needed to worry you were going to fuck with me."

He left the reason unsaid. Growing up in a small town where he'd been treated as an outcast from the wrong side of the tracks, no one had ever had his back. Not until the Academy and the Navy. Where you had to put your life in someone else's hands and work together for a common goal.

"I'm sorry I forgot that." Rob walked over, his bloodshot eyes direct, and extended his hand. "Some things can't be unsaid, so I don't blame you if you won't shake my hand."

Dax gripped it hard, staring into his friend's face. "I'd be a dick not to."

"God knows we've had plenty of dick behavior around here to fill a cargo ship," Carson interjected, coming over and slapping both of them on the backs.

Perry joined them on the other side, and for a moment, it was like they were back in better days, standing together in their dress whites, filled with the possibility of the job and the brotherhood.

Only Dax knew all that was coming to an end. Soon he would be decommissioned. He'd hang up his dress whites and put on a new uniform. Start a new life. It hit him that he and Rob had that in common. In addition, should things go with Ariel like he hoped, they would be brothers-in-law. Crazy to think about, but then again, maybe that was also why Rob had backed down from his earlier stance. Well, they'd cross that bridge when they got there. Brick by brick, as Ariel said.

"Let's get you married." Dax gave his friend a not-so-subtle shove, which he responded to by shoving him back.

Carson and Perry joined in and soon they were all shoving each other and putting each other in headlocks, white caps flying off and thudding to the floor.

"Ah, male camaraderie." Jeffrey sighed, holding up his phone. "I just got buzzed. You're up."

"Let's go." Rob shook with all the guys again and then headed to the mirror, straightening his uniform. "Jesus, I look like shit. Anyone got Visine?"

Jeffrey strode forward. "I do. Let me help. I'll have you looking dashing in no time."

And dammit if he didn't pull it off. Three minutes later, Rob didn't look like a man who'd been drinking bourbon all day and had clocked his best friend over a missing wedding dress.

"There." Jeffrey adjusted Rob's wings and smoothed his epaulets. "Good as new. Come on, boys. The Deverell women do not like to be kept waiting."

"You're telling me," Rob said with a laugh, the first to head out.

Carson and Perry slapped Dax on the back as they followed Rob.

Dax took a moment to run his hand over his jaw, where the swelling was palpable. "Is there bruising?"

Jeffrey nodded. "Yes, but it makes you look even more manly. I wouldn't put any makeup on it."

Dax took him by the shoulders and marched him to the

door. "Jeffrey, I love you, man, but in no universe were you ever putting makeup on me."

His amused chortling had Dax finally smiling as they walked to the wedding arbor where all the guests were seated. The older minister's narrow face was tense with nerves. He'd probably wondered if he was actually going to marry anyone today. Dax checked his watch. They were only thirty-five minutes late.

A new piece of music started, some wedding frippery that sounded like it included a harp and happy little birds tweeting. Not Rob's choice, he imagined. He checked his wallet discreetly to make sure he still had Rob's ring. Check. Then he straightened his shoulders and stood behind his friend as the flower girl appeared—a girl Dax hadn't seen before who looked to be about five. She looked like an angel in a frothy pale pink dress with a flower ring on her head while she threw white rose petals from a sweet-grass basket.

Her companion was Ripp, who just couldn't ditch the *Lord of the Flies* persona. His clipped red bow tie was listing to the right. He had dirt on his right cheek, which only enhanced his sulky expression. The lacy cream pillow in his hands, which bore seashells rather than rings, was crumpled and slightly dirty. Because the kid hadn't washed his hands. Dax fought a laugh right there. He imagined the boy would be hearing about that from the Three Tornadoes.

"Good thing we didn't have that kid usher up the rings, huh?" Rob said under his breath so only Dax could hear.

It was the first normal interaction they'd had, and Dax was glad for it.

Terry appeared first, doing her best to match the steps of the music, but missing it by a half beat. Carson walked down to meet her halfway and escort her to the front. Perry followed with Tricia. And then Ariel appeared, and Dax couldn't do anything but stare.

Her beauty grabbed him by the throat, from the way her hair curled in the sunlight to the softness of the pale pink frothy dress she wore. He'd never seen her so dressed up, so outwardly feminine, and he could feel his temperature rising at the sight. Back in the cottage, he hadn't taken note, but the sun was out and their worries seemed far away when she met his eyes. She held a bunch of pale pink flowers against her chest, and she was smiling, her blue eyes dancing.

Rob had to nudge him in the side to spin him into action. He heard his friend's muted laughter as he rushed to meet her before he realized he shouldn't be rushing. He slowed down, hearing more chuckles from the audience. When he reached her, a radiant grin crested across her face. He offered her his arm, which she took and squeezed.

"We made it, Stephan," she whispered, the breeze ruffling her short, curly hair.

He tucked her arm snugly against his side. "We sure did, Elizabeth."

With that, they walked to the front before parting again to take their respective places. The wedding march sounded, and the guests stood. Dax knew Tiffany was walking up the aisle, but he didn't have eyes for anyone but Ariel. She was watching him too until the last minute as the bride appeared at the front with her father. Then Ariel winked and gave her sister her full attention.

After that, the ceremony began. He held his breath when the minister asked, "If anyone objects, speak now or forever hold your peace," because surely, they were in the clear, and there was no one who'd snuck into the audience to cause trouble.

With the Deverell women, one could never be sure. He watched Ariel's chest fall as she released a huge breath when the moment passed without issue.

Tiffany cried through most of the ceremony with Ariel feeding her copious amounts of tissues. Rob even got choked up while saying his vows, which kinda shocked Dax. His friend was not known for getting sentimental. Shortly thereafter, the minister pronounced them man and wife. Dax watched them kiss before starting down the aisle together holding hands. When it was his cue, he met Ariel at the front and tucked her arm against him.

He smiled down at her beaming face. "You did it!"

"We did it!" She laid her cheek against his side for a moment, and then they were out front with the others.

After that, there were pictures and the screams and cries of children and the hum of conversation. By the time they reached the wedding tent and found their seats at the head table, Dax was feeling fidgety. He almost laughed at himself. One mission down. Now he was raring to launch into the next one. Figuring out who'd hidden the wedding dress.

Ariel was off checking on something for the reception. He couldn't see her in the big white tent, but he spotted Jeffrey at a table in the corner talking to other guests.

He rose, wondering how long he had before he really needed to take his seat. Enough for him to jog over to the lodge and ask them to pull the security feed? He wanted to get this done.

Jeffrey caught him as he was leaving the tent. "The bar is that way," he joked, jauntily pointing in the opposite direction. "Eager to unmask our criminal, Sherlock? Wait! How did I not realize how funny that was until this very second."

Dax hadn't registered the irony either. "Because today has been a complete shitshow. Humor took a vacation for a while."

"Let's hope she's back." Jeffrey waved at someone and gave a tight smile. "Walk faster. That's Stormy's sister, Gail, and she's always been a bitch to me."

They nearly ran to the lodge, but the sound of Ariel calling their names had them spinning around. She put her hand on her hip when she reached them, looking flushed from the chase.

"Really? You're investigating now? Without me?"

He winced. "I didn't realize— Sorry. Can you take a moment?"

She glanced at the thin watch on her wrist. "What's another few minutes. We're already so off-schedule. You don't want to hear what the caterer said about her dinner. She claims it's ruined. Besides, I already called the front and asked them to pull the footage."

He grabbed her by the shoulders, picked her up off the ground, and kissed her on the mouth. Hard. "Elizabeth, this is why I love you."

"That's not the only reason, Stephan," Jeffrey drawled, clearly in the know about their nicknames from Ariel. "Come on, lovebirds, let's go. This mystery needs an ending."

The front clerk did indeed have the security tape ready, and because he'd had the time, he'd already discovered what they were looking for.

They huddled around the desk while he turned his computer toward them and hit play. They watched the culprits run across the parking lot to his car.

Ariel's hum was drawn out and not amused. "How did I not guess?"

Jeffrey blew out a breath. "Because it's beyond deviant."

Dax shook his head. "Those little punks."

The *Lord of the Flies* boys were laughing as Marshall dragged the dress in the dry cleaner bag to the car. Then Ripp opened the back of Dax's Bronco, and Marshall shoved the dress inside and slammed it shut. The boys were laughing as they ran off.

Of course they were. Marshall had just found a way to stop the wedding.

"No wedding dress," Ariel said dryly. "No wedding. How many times did they hear Tiffany say that? But I never would have believed them to be this bad."

"Ariel, honey, those boys have been lost causes since they were toddlers, which is why everyone leaves them alone to their own devices. Also, Captain Hotpants, you should definitely lock your car after this."

Dax rubbed his swollen jaw, considering. "So those little bastards set me up. Smart though. Rob is going to have to really step up if Marshall is going to keep out of reformatory school."

Ariel blew the curls on her forehead up with a giant exhale. "Yeah. Crap. I was hoping it was a ghost."

The guy at the desk cleared his voice. "If you don't mind, I have another part of our security feed to show you. I tracked the boys all the way back to where they picked up the wedding dress."

He took command of the computer again and pulled up another video, turning it toward them and hitting play.

They watched the boys leave their cottage with the dress and run off toward the parking lot.

"There's a good bit of time between them taking the dress from the bridal cottage and then putting it in your car, sir," the man informed him, earning himself a big tip to Dax's mind.

"They were around when Rob accused me of stealing the dress." Dax swore softly after it hit him. "God, they're even more devious than I thought."

"They had the perfect fall guy." Jeffrey clapped him on the back.

Dax touched the part of his face that was achy and winced. "Like I said, smart. Rob's not going to have an easy time with him."

Ariel sighed heavily. "No, he's not. But we have to show Rob and Tiffany what happened. And my other sisters. And my mother even. I want them to know beyond a shadow of a doubt that Dax wasn't responsible for this."

He could get behind that.

"Maybe after the honeymoon?" She threaded her hand through his arm. "I know you'd rather not delay it. What do you think?"

"I can live with that."

"Deverell blood in boys is fairly terrifying." Jeffrey grimaced. "They did the crime, they pay the fine, and let's hope it sticks. Tiffany is going to lose her mind. So will the other Tornadoes. Maybe they'll punish those little shits for once so they learn their lesson."

Dax tapped the top of the welcome desk. "I'll talk to Rob when they get back. Marshall is going to need a strong male figure. Because you don't just hide your mom's wedding dress and blame it on an adult. That's a gateway to bigger problems, if you ask me. Rob was from that kind of family. It's why he went into the Navy."

"Does anyone feel even more depressed?" Ariel asked, putting her elbow on the desk and looking at him and Jeffrey.

"What we need to do is dance like there's no tomorrow." Jeffrey took his sister's hands and led her into a turn, humming a Britney Spears tune Dax recognized. "And we need a drink."

Ariel pulled her flask from her garter, giving Dax a welcome view of her gorgeous legs. She passed the flask around and then pocketed it. "Good, we're fortified. We need to get back. Dax and I have to give our speeches at some point. Let's hope the rest of the night goes well and the food isn't as spoiled as the caterer fears."

In the end, everything came off pretty well, all things considered. Dax got through his speech without too many glares from the bride. Apparently, she didn't completely believe he'd been the culprit behind the dress theft. Ariel delivered her humorous speech with a sweet smile, making Tiffany cry again.

A few people commented on the lone fish in the nearly empty koi pond, which made Dax shudder. Jeffrey was a good sport, telling everyone it was a new concept. The water symbolized the purity of the bride and groom's love for each other while the single fish showed how they were now one in mind and body. One woman pressed her hand to her chest and got tears in her eyes, saying, "Isn't that the sweetest thing I've ever heard."

Dax wanted to gag.

Although honestly, he felt really bad for the koi, losing all his buddies like that.

Dinner came and went. He barely tasted the food but was assured it wasn't half-bad. When the dancing started—after Tiffany and Rob's first dance as a couple—Jeffrey pulled him and Ariel onto the dance floor. He watched brother and sister let loose, imitating John Travolta in *Saturday Night Fever* before strutting like two chickens in a farmyard. He was laughing so hard he was wiping tears before joining in.

Carson, Perry, Gunner, and Frank finally took to the floor with them, saying it was time to show this crowd some real moves. The DJ was good, but the guests were stuffy, mostly sitting and watching with drinks in their hands. Clearly, some didn't approve of their antics. At one point, Dax was sure Stormy would have turned them into a pillar of salt if they'd looked at her.

The cake cutting went off without incident, but the same couldn't be said for the sparklers display. Lighting hundreds of the darn things with a blowtorch couldn't have been considered safe, and Carson yelped when one of the special sparklers flashed extra high and his dress whites almost caught fire. Perry was laughing, as he lit up the Just Married display. The Go Navy display had them spontaneously singing "Anchors Aweigh," with Rob coming over to join in.

People clapped. They handed out the sparklers to the wedding guests, posh watering cans at the ready. No one got burned in the guest sparkler portion of the evening, thank God. Ariel's distant cousin even commented on how charming the cute watering pots were, making Dax want to roll his eyes.

When the time came for Tiffany and Rob to leave, the guests came out to bid them a raucous farewell. Dax had his arm around Ariel as she watched Tiffany hug Tricia and Terry, all three women crying. When they finished, Tiffany turned and found Ariel at the front of the crowd and opened her arms.

Ariel walked over to her sister, and Dax watched as they embraced each other. Then Tiffany removed something from her clutch and pressed it into Ariel's hands. More weeping from the bride before she gave Ariel one last hug and took Rob's hand. They got into the classic white convertible Ford they'd rented and drove off into the sunset. Literally.

Ariel was clutching something to her chest as she walked back to Dax. Jeffrey rushed over and put his arm around her, clearly concerned.

But Dax thought he knew what she held. When she glanced up, her eyes were misty. Her face broke into a radiant smile.

His heart turned over. "You've got it," he called.

"I've got it." She thrust the paper into the air and wiggled her hips. "It's mine!"

"Damn well better be," Jeffrey muttered, hugging her hard before nudging her toward Dax. "You two go to the dance floor. I'll request a slow dance. Something special."

After blowing his sister a kiss, he rushed back to the tent. When Ariel reached him, he tipped her chin up. "Well, Elizabeth. Is this where we say, 'All's well that ends well'?"

She gave an indelicate snort. "Nah...this is where we say, this party just got started. Come on. I have a strong urge to dance with Captain Hotpants."

"Not poor Stephan?"

"Yes, him too. How lucky am I to have three wonderful men to dance with?"

He was laughing as she took his hand. They ran back to the tent, avoiding drunken wedding stragglers on the way and the *Lord of the Flies* boys, whom Dax was only too happy to bypass. When they arrived, they stopped in the center of the dance floor, the white twinkly lights soft on her beautiful face.

She looked up at him, love shining in her beautiful baby

blues. He knew this was another memory he'd hold on to always. Her hair wild and extra curly from the dancing and pelican attack. Her smile filled with joy as she tucked the piece of paper in her bodice, winking at him. Then she sidled up to him and wrapped her arms around his back, setting her cheek to his chest, already swaying.

When the music changed, Dax lifted his head, recognizing the song immediately. "Endless Love" by Diana Ross and Lionel Richie started to play over the loudspeakers. Ariel was already laughing. Dax found Jeffrey standing beside the DJ's table, a hand pressed to his heart.

"Seriously, Jeffrey?" Dax called out, shaking his head as Ariel squeezed him tightly. "My mom used to listen to this song."

"It's a classic," he shouted back, drawing a heart in the air. "Besides, it suits you two."

Dax glanced down as Ariel looked up, her face filled with the kind of love he imagined must have inspired the song. "Yeah, I suppose it does."

Lowering his head to kiss her, he felt her lips soften under his and heard the music swell all around them. He tightened his hold on her, never wanting to let go. They'd gotten through a few disasters together already.

After this? It really would be endless love if he had anything to say about it.

EPILOGUE
ELEVEN MONTHS LATER...

THE SUN WAS SHINING. THERE WASN'T A CLOUD IN THE sky. The salty smell of the sea hung in the air, and the oaks seemed like towering presences as their leaves ruffled in the gentle breeze. Her wedding dress had been exactly where she'd put it after having it pressed—in her closet in her grandma's house in Folly Beach, which she'd shared with Dax from nearly the beginning.

But best of all, Captain Hotpants—because even after leaving the Navy and starting his new job, he still had the best buns this side of Biloxi—stood beside her in a very smart blue suit and tie under the gazebo in Charleston's famous White Point Garden, known to locals as Battery Park. When she'd first suggested the venue to him, not only because they loved to walk Sherlock there but also for its military history, he'd jumped on her plan.

They were like that, her and Stephan.

Sherlock trotted over, decked out in the "perfect" outfit Jeffrey had suggested for their doggie witness: a canine tuxedo with a bow tie and bib, onto which he'd pinned a red rose boutonniere. Ariel rubbed Sherlock under the ears, thinking he was a sport for allowing her brother to dress him up. She couldn't wait to see the wedding photos they were going to take after the ceremony. She and Dax had already picked out a cheesy frame to display one in their family room. Because she already knew the photos were always going to make her smile.

"Looks like the minister is here." Jeffrey straightened the simple veil he'd helped her choose along with her white A-line wedding dress. He wore a dashing cream suit with an indigo blue cravat like he'd been born to it, and the joy she felt inside was reflected in his easygoing smile.

Ariel checked her watch. "The photographer should be here in a second too."

"I see him." Jeffrey blew out a relieved breath, play-acting. "You crazy kids ready to tie the knot?"

She glanced at her very sexy groom and adjusted the red rose boutonniere Jeffrey had brought for Dax today along with her beautiful bouquet of red roses with baby's breath so fresh they still held their light scent.

"Beyond ready," she answered with a little wiggle of her hips.

Dax caught her to him and caressed the line of her cheek, his green eyes filled with a love so strong it made her want to fly. "Me too."

Was he thinking it was the best idea ever to simply get hitched with Jeffrey as their only two-legged witness?

The park was quiet as everyone took their places and photos were taken, Sherlock brightening up when the photographer called out, "Cheese."

This was the other best thing—not a hint of the Deverell wedding curse hung in the air as the minister started the ceremony.

Then again, neither she nor Dax would have allowed

that. Okay, Jeffrey too, since he'd volunteered to plan the wedding.

The Charleston hurricane center she was working at had even confirmed the weather was going to be terrific, a favor they'd granted without her asking just because they loved her and Sherlock so much. She understood. She was totally crazy about her co-workers too.

The great weather was supposed to continue for the rest of the day, which was terrific since she and Dax were hosting their first fish fry at their home in Folly Beach. She, Dax, and Davey had fished for hours to pull in enough fish for their shindig, wanting to make it special. Besides select co-workers, family would be coming—his and hers—but no one knew they were going to show up as husband and wife.

That was perfectly fine with them, although she knew her mother would probably have an opinion like usual, and the Three Tornadoes would undoubtedly make a fuss. Although Tiffany might not, since she and Ariel had found a new appreciation for each other. Last year's wedding might have been a near disaster in some ways, but Tiffany was taking her second chance at both being a wife and mother seriously, along with her relationship with Ariel.

She'd even gone so far as to apologize to Dax, and when she had visited with Rob and the new baby girl they'd named Audrey, she'd made an extra effort to talk to him about his new job. Marshall, of course, had glared at them for nearly the whole visit since they'd busted him, although Rob had stepped in once or twice about it, but you couldn't have everything.

Well, Ariel thought she could. With Dax.

Which was why they had both wanted to take this next step together.

When she'd visited her grandma's grave before the ceremony a few days ago to finalize her vows and lay her favorite camellia blooms on the gravestone, she'd smiled and said softly in the sacred reverence owed to a graveyard, "You know, Grandma, love with Dax is actually all about love. No disasters so far. Knock on wood."

But truthfully, she didn't see any circling in the sky. Or pelicans looking for koi, thank God. Life was easy with him. They laughed a lot. They didn't really fight. Dax said it was what he was used to.

Ariel thought it was a downright miracle.

She couldn't help but enjoy the simplicity of the ceremony as she took Dax's hands, her heart beating solidly in her chest. She got a little choked up hearing he was going to love, honor, and cherish her. Her whole being seemed to rise up off the ground as his green gaze found hers. When he took a fortifying breath, she smiled.

"Ariel," he began in a deep, strong voice, "you know how much I love you. The minute I saw you, I wanted you. I loved being with you. Some people might think it happened too fast, but like I told you, you can get a pilot's license and fly an airplane in forty hours. Why would love need to be more complicated than that?"

Emotion clogged her throat, and she tightened her grip on his hands, always wanting to remember how he looked right now. The light in his beautiful green eyes. The tenderness in his broad smile.

"Ariel, you make me happier than I've ever been. Sherlock too. And I was pretty happy before I met you. Yes, my family is great, and I know ours is going to be too. Because we love and respect each other. Because we treat each other as equals. And because we're a team. You're my eternal wing woman, and I'm yours. For the rest of our lives. Thank you for being in my life. Thank you for being you. I love you, and I'm so happy you're going to be my wife, and we get to do this thing called life together."

She smiled through tears and felt Sherlock nudge her side. They both put a hand on the dog, and she felt that click, knowing they were a family.

Then it was time for her to say her vows, the ones she'd agonized over before finally realizing it was all so simple.

She felt his strong, warm hands tighten around hers. "Dax, I love you so much. From the first day we met, we've never been apart really. We thought it might be smart to do the normal thing and live apart, but it just didn't work. We missed each other too much. And I know why. I found home with you."

His green eyes got a little misty then, and she couldn't speak for a second. But she took a breath and found her voice. Because she could always tell him how she felt.

"I want you to know how happy you make me. How much I love laughing with you. And making important life decisions together. Because those are really easy too. I wake up every day with a smile on my face, and I know it's always going to be like that. Oh, and thank God I love your family."

He started laughing then, and so did Jeffrey. Only the minister seemed puzzled by that comment, which had her laughing for a second too.

"But most of all..." God, she was feeling the burn of tears start. "I want you to know how grateful I am to learn that love can be great and happy. Fun even. No disasters or tornadoes necessary."

His mouth pursed then, and he tightened his grip on her. She sniffed, feeling her heart swell so big she was sure her chest couldn't contain it.

"I promise to love you and make you laugh and listen to you. To support you. Every day of my life." Wiping a stray tear from her eye, she lowered her voice. "I love you, Stephan."

"Oh, Elizabeth, you slay me," he whispered.

The minister leaned forward, his brow slamming together. "Who's Elizabeth?"

They both tried not to laugh.

"No one." Dax cleared his throat. "Please go on, Reverend."

The minister looked puzzled but thankfully took his cue when Jeffrey extended the wedding rings on the hand-painted china tray that had been Grandma's favorite. Then Dax was putting her wedding ring on and caressing it with benediction. As she slid his wedding band on his finger, she squeezed his hand, hoping he could see what was in her heart, a happiness and peace she'd never imagined feeling. With anyone.

Shortly thereafter, the minister was declaring them husband and wife, and Dax was kissing her, his lips filled with all the love and promise she knew was in his heart.

Jeffrey leaned in and said, "Hey, you two. Good job! Now just follow Sherlock."

She glanced over at her brother and kissed him on the cheek noisily for good measure before turning to follow Sherlock, her arm tucked into Dax's side.

When she spotted the sign hanging from Sherlock's backside, she couldn't hold back her laughter anymore. *This Way To Happily Ever After* was emblazoned in a romantic font.

Dax's deep laughter joined hers, and together they headed the way they were meant to all along.

If you liked Love and Other Trials, make Ava's day and leave a review.

Want another laugh-out-loud romance to dive into? Get The Hockey Experiment!
Read on for a sneak peek.

THE HOCKEY EXPERIMENT

CHAPTER ONE

What is it about men?
What. Is. It. About. Men?
WHAT IS IT ABOUT MEN????

"Darla... Why are you shouting in your field diary?" Dr. Valentina Hargrove pointed to her friend's carefully printed diatribe, sensing latent dating anger.

Dr. Darla James screwed up her oval face. "One word: asshole Peter."

Since her longtime research colleague was also her best friend, she didn't point out the use of two words, not one. "Right. He ghosted you. But shouldn't you be writing something more germane? Like the question we're here to study? Look, I've already written it at the top of my page."

Are hockey players modern cavemen?

After a quick glance at Val's field journal, Darla discreetly flicked her hand toward the hockey rink. "Well, *Val*... My question seemed more pertinent than, *What is it about cavemen?* Since I've never met one."

Val gave in to the unacademic urge to snort. The errant swearing and grunts from the Alexandria Eagles muffled any minor sounds in the massive outdoor arena where they were sitting on cold, *freeze-her-bottom* bleachers, fitting for late February in Minneapolis. Difficult to adjust to after returning from the hot and humid Congo.

Although she was also having another unacademic compulsion: to deeply inhale the smell of fresh, cold ice after being away from it for so long. Four years, as a matter of fact.

The happy little two-year-old she'd been when she'd first started ice skating would never have believed she'd be able to keep away from "the magic glass" so long. The young woman who'd won three junior Olympic golds and retired from skating with a peptic ulcer at fifteen easily could.

"I beg to disagree, Darla." Academic discourse had been her salvation after leaving ice skating, and she welcomed the feeling as she leveled her friend a knowing look. "Your last three dates were total cavemen in the slang sense of the word, asshole Peter leading the pack."

"Har-de-har-har." Darla nudged her playfully before leaning forward, her gaze glued to the male specimens slapping furiously to take the puck away from each other during afternoon practice. "You know, Val, some would say we're the two luckiest women in the world to be spending part of a hockey season with a full access pass to these men."

"I don't see how luck factors into it." To her, the hockey players held the same academic interest as the Pygmies in the Congo she and Darla had studied this past year for their newest article in *Cultural Anthropology Today*.

While these professional athletes might not be sitting around an evening fire in the jungle, preparing to eat the dinner they'd hunted themselves, their monosyllabic discourse and guttural intonations held exciting academic similarities. Her insides were completely titillated.

Granted, hockey players didn't wear loincloths with their bodies painted white like Pygmies, but still...

"You just don't get it, Val," Darla said with a sigh as she smoothed her severely straight black ponytail, courtesy of extensions, over her shoulder. She gave Val one of her frustrated looks, the kind that portended personal trouble.

"You're right, I don't, if we're talking about what I think we're talking about," she replied and folded her hands. Even so, her friend's discourse on men and mating rituals never failed to both educate and amuse her. Today, the distraction was also welcome since it was difficult to tune out the beautiful crisp noise of skates on ice. She would have to become accustomed to blocking it out while she was on this study.

Darla tapped her mouth with her fingertip like she was trying to work out a problem. "Val, hockey players make me question my understanding of modern male and female relations."

Yes, please give me something else to focus on. "Outline it for me."

"I like to think I'm an independent woman."

"You are." Maybe it was their over-the-top nerdy assistant disguises that had Darla doubting herself. "With a PhD in cultural anthropology from Oxford. Like me."

Darla's fake tortoiseshell-framed glasses remained on the large males weaving and attacking each other on the ice in white, blue, and red practice jerseys. "All that male...ness has my girl juices swimming. They're all so big. And rough. And *umm*."

"*Umm?*" Darla was already muttering worrisome guttural intonations herself, as if the hockey-caveman similarities were catching. "And that signifies—"

Her best friend since boarding school looked as if she were imploring the heavens, the way they'd witnessed people doing in the last fertility dance they'd attended during the full moon. "You know how I am, Val. Those men make me just want to—"

"Let's take a pause and refocus, shall we? I can tell you're flooding your system with stress hormones."

"Cortisol hates me." She cupped the gentle curve of her belly, hidden under her baggy black T-shirt, identical to the one Val was wearing. "This pudge never goes away, and while I've come to accept my curves—"

"Again, we're refocusing."

Darla went through this same inner turmoil with every study involving the male sex, something they were becoming academically known for in the small, exciting world of cultural anthropology. Some days she had to pinch herself. Hargrove and James were making a name for themselves, almost like Masters and Johnson, and Marie and Pierre Curie—only she and Darla weren't romantically involved, of course.

"Then refocus me hard!" Darla gripped her arm, her golden eyes pleading. "Give it to me, Dr. Hargrove. I admire your ever-present stoicism as always. Especially with men. You're an academic goddess. Perched in Oxford's black robes, presiding at the front of the class, completely in command of herself."

"I wouldn't go that far. A goddess, I am not, while you have had *scores* of marriage offers. Don't you remember how that one chief told me my hips were too small for childbearing? While he thought you were the perfect goddess of a woman come to life. Clearly fertile because of your curves, and powerful because you could also throw a spear."

"Yeah, but the last guy I dated in Johannesburg told me my hips and the rest of me were too big. You can't please men."

There should be a special place in Dante's hell for men like Asshole Pete and the others who'd hurt Darla. "Why try? I think you're perfect as you are."

"That's because you're a girl and you get me." Her friend looked ready to hug her. "We return to my question: *what is it about men?*"

"I have no idea, and honestly, I don't want to." Val choked on a laugh. "These hockey players don't present such quandaries for me. I admire their hard work and commitment, but I can't imagine ever seeing one of them as a male like you're suggesting."

"God, I envy you in times like this." Darla uttered a heartfelt sigh and let go of the death grip on her arm. "Even though I worry about your lack of interest in the male species in your personal life. You study them but you don't want to get down with them much. Outside of carefully orchestrated interactions."

Val was not going to let Darla jump onto *that* topic. Nor was she going to point out she preferred a scientific approach when engaging with life, including interactions with the opposite sex. She preferred it that way after the chaos of her youth. "We knew going into this study that you were going to be affected."

Darla bit her unpainted bottom lip, her black ponytail swaying as she shook her head in distress. "It's horrible! I hate this primal reaction I have to them. It's like I take a giant whiff of their *leave your reason behind and throw off your panties* pheromones, and I turn into someone else. I can't seem to stop falling for really big, gorgeous, tough guys."

"With terribly dangerous jobs, most of the time." Val folded her hands over her field journal, sensing Darla's need to express her frustration before they could move forward. "Diamond smuggling. Mercenary work. Darla, I know you're somehow wired for the kind of man who—"

"Has gorgeous muscles and oozes aggression and charm?" She put her hand to her forehead and tapped it like she was trying to reprogram her neurons. "I swear, Val, it's all my mother's fault..."

Val gave voice to the words she knew would come next. "If you weren't the love child of an R&B singer and her then-married record producer..."

"I'd have better judgment in men," Darla finished mournfully.

Val patted her on the back and consoled her like she had since their first discussion about Darla's taste in men in Swiss boarding school. She certainly wouldn't bring up how she'd figured out a way to turn off her own prurient interest in men, given her own mother being on her fifth marriage and her father having three. To Val, eight marriages by two people was statistically significant. But Darla needed encouragement, and as her best friend, that was her job.

"You'll manage like always." She removed Darla's hand from her forehead and looked her straight in the eye. "Focus on the bright side. At least hockey players won't land you in jail or get you killed."

Darla spurted out a laugh. "You *would* say that."

"Consider this then... Even if you are attracted to one of them, you can't date him. It's completely against our academic guidelines for any study, and you are a serious professional, Dr. James. Despite your intense biological reaction to the male sex."

Val thanked the fertility gods—if they existed—that she had not received such hormonal wiring.

"You're damn right I am." Darla sat up straighter, like she might in a lecture hall on early human migration. "What else have you written down, Val? You're always light years ahead of me in the first couple of weeks of a study, no matter how much research and prep work we do before we hit the ground."

That's why their academic collaborations worked so well. Val had a quick, clinical mind able to define concepts, identify patterns, and draw immediate hypotheses while Darla had a more holistic approach to amassing information and making nuanced conclusions later on. Val observed. Darla empathized. Even better, as best friends they enjoyed each other's company on long field trips around the world, often to places where there were no phones or internet, running water notwithstanding. Another reason they'd taken this job.

Val turned the page of her field diary so Darla could see her initial thoughts, a smile tugging at her lips. She was pretty proud of the conclusions she'd already drawn. Simple and straightforward was always best.

Cavemen: early humans with physically dense, highly muscular bodies; known for aggression and territorialism; capable of using tools like a club; with simple linguistic capability

Hockey players: modern humans with physically

dense, highly muscular bodies; known for aggression and territorialism; capable of using tools like a hockey stick; with simple linguistic capability

"The similarities are striking, don't you think?" The kick of scientific excitement was coursing through her already, as the punch in her usually one-note lecture voice proved. "This is going to be fun."

Her inner war about skating notwithstanding.

Darla looked back to the rink and let out a little breathy sigh. "Physically dense, highly muscular bodies is an understatement. Not to be sexist, but Val, those men are grade A in every way."

Val looked back at the men on the ice. With their protective gear on, they looked even larger than they did off the ice. She knew the player stats for every single Alexandria Eagles player as well as their physical stats. Most of them topped out at around six feet, with the defense and goalie positions running a little taller. The ideal weight requirements were around two hundred pounds. All solid muscle.

Women around the world—Darla included—thought they were gods of masculinity. Val understood why clinically. Their physical stature embodied the ultimate potential of the male body. Their testosterone levels alone would attract female interest, pheromones notwithstanding. These men professionally trained their bodies to be dominant and powerful, and that translated both on and off the ice. Constant competition gave them an edge many other humans didn't possess but could certainly admire.

As a former competitor in figure skating, Val knew all about refining her body to meet an ultimate standard.

Small. Sleek. Toned. Beautiful in a doll-like way except for the beauty mark by her lip. Her skill as much as her form had attracted people's attention and admiration. As a young girl, she'd been uncomfortable with such adulation.

Then again, women experienced attention from the opposite sex differently. She'd felt vulnerable.

Most men, however, puffed out like roosters for being told they were the gold standard of masculinity. As Val had seen in their off-the-ice behavior, most hockey players loved such attention, craved it even. Unfortunately, that behavior was bleeding into the Eagles' performance on the ice.

She and Darla were here to help change that. Hockey alone couldn't have tempted her, but this was her father's team, and he'd asked for help. Coupled with their travel fatigue—and her and Darla's desire for modern plumbing and other luxuries they'd been without in the field—it had seemed like a win-win, the perfect study.

Then Darla had experienced one of her light bulb marketing moments a few days ago, which had excited them enough to order another round of margaritas to celebrate. Helping this team win the Stanley Cup would position them to provide other sports teams, and perhaps even corporations, with their brand of analysis to help management achieve their goals. Human nature was at the root of many conflicts, and they were experts in analyzing such issues and offering solutions.

"Physically, these hockey players might meet the ultimate male standard, but they are championship deficient," she added, tapping her field diary for emphasis. "Which is why we're here to help my father with his team."

Part of her still couldn't believe he'd asked her and Darla to conduct this assignment after finishing their most recent grant. Then again, while he'd never say so, her father would prefer for her to be in Minnesota than a country like Congo. Less parental worry for him. Because Ebola was nothing to laugh at, and that wasn't even mentioning the armed guerrillas and hairy gorillas, as Darla liked to joke. And don't get her started on the large venomous snakes slithering into her tent or the way baboons' enormous teeth shone in the moonlight when they made a surprise appearance.

"This topic of study," Darla said gamely, wagging her finger at the ice, "might be a bit crazy to some, but your father doesn't do anything that doesn't make sense. Or money. I admire him for that."

She glanced at the Eagles' coach, who was barking at someone on the ice about a missed assignment. "This is his out-of-the-box effort to make his new team win the Stanley Cup with Chuck. To date, this team can't win 'the big one.'"

"And your father's identity does not include being a loser." Darla gave Val's chin a playful tap. "He's an overachiever like his daughter."

She wished she were the type of person who could roll her eyes, but it wasn't in her nature. Facts were indisputable, after all, and she *did* meet the classical definition of an overachiever: a person who does more than they are expected to do or who is more successful than others.

Her father was one certainly, and her mother had been the same way, but after winning her last Olympic Gold in her late twenties, she'd retired and pretty much stopped achieving anything. Well, except for husbands. Now she collected husbands like Olympic medals. To Val, her father was the only one who'd been gold.

"Dad and Chuck think our study might light a fire under these players to focus them to win, especially as we get closer to the playoffs."

"While we get to turn in our suitcases and bask in running water and electricity." Darla put her arm around her companionably, and Val didn't have the heart to remind her to be professional. "Val, I do a little dance every time I go into my bathroom. A toilet! Hot water in a shower! A heated floor! It's a miracle every time."

She felt an indulgent smile play across her lips. "I cannot disagree, Dr. James. For me, it's sleeping in my Egyptian cotton sheets with a light comforter. Every time I got tangled up in mosquito netting, I'd wake up thinking I was covered in a giant spiderweb."

"It's almost like a vacation, isn't it?" Darla started a sultry happy dance, a little reminiscent of her mother's last music video for her song "I Need You Like the Air I Breathe," which had gone platinum. "Even though it's Minneapolis."

"I'm pleased with what I've seen so far. No, it's not Bora Bora, but we knew that going in."

Darla gave one of her crowd-attracting husky laughs, courtesy of her voice having the kind of musical quality that screamed Grammys were in her bloodlines. "I tell myself, if it was good enough for Prince... But back to our study. Val, this baby is going to make headlines. Just you watch. And not all the good kind, I think. Because cavemen are one misunderstood bunch."

"That's not our concern," Val reminded her as Chuck blew his whistle in three consecutive bursts, his anger evident. "We observe. We study. We find patterns. We make conclusions. We meet the conditions of our contract. That's our job."

Even though it was her father who was paying them, she'd insisted they follow their normal protocols to the letter. He had wisely suggested that they work in disguise, wearing team badges devoid of their names to keep their identities secret. No hockey player was going to recognize the famous cultural anthropologists, Hargrove and James, of course, but they might not like it if they knew Ted Bass had signed his daughter up to study his new team.

They certainly wouldn't recognize her as his daughter in this outfit, however, notwithstanding the fact that she favored her mother. And since she was in the field so much, few people had captured recent photos of her and her father together. Even so, she had purposefully chosen the most revolting pair of glasses in history to hide her features and make her repellant to the male sex.

"In your world, it's that simple, yes." Darla closed her field diary and nibbled on the end of her pen. "I don't need or want some very angry six-foot, two-hundred-pound hockey player mad at me for comparing him to a caveman without the proper understanding should they hear we're involved."

Val found that highly unlikely. "I still don't understand why they would be mad." She closed her diary as well, studying the rink as one of the hockey players flipped another teammate off—using silent communication to convey dislike or humor, something she would note in her diary later. "While the modern slang for caveman implies an ignoramus, we both know they were quite brilliant. They took down woolly mammoths. They survived the Ice Age."

"Your geekiness is showing, Dr. Hargrove, which I love, but I'm not sure that's how those guys would see it." She threw her field diary and pen in her leather satchel. "Male egos are a tricky business."

"I don't deal with those." Val paused as Darla chortled. "Laugh all you like, but I stopped catering to anyone's ego a long time ago." Her attempts to please her mother had been a PhD study in all the reasons she should stop; it only led to ulcers, literally. "I understand human posturing, but I respect only those whose excellence and talent are real. I don't respect people who lord their talents, real or imagined, over others."

"Which is why I adore you." Darla patted her hand sweetly. "God, these glasses are going to drive me nuts. Not only do they look dreadful, but they keep sliding off my nose." She straightened them before shooting out of her chair with her usual enthusiasm. "Come on, Val. Practice should be over soon. Let's go see your dad."

As Val followed her and walked down the concrete stairs to leave the rink, two men crashed into the plexiglass wall. Val turned toward the commotion. She caught a flash of two large male bodies fighting for supremacy in a flurry of strength, muscles straining, jaws locking, sweat trickling down the sides of their faces. An arresting visual, to be sure. Val appreciated the primal outlet.

But then the man pinned against the wall trained his eyes her way…

His entire focus seemed to latch on to her. It was rather unnerving, the intensity of his gaze.

But she held it, sensing something important.

Some moments happened that way. Everything slowed down, and a connection was forged.

She was aware of her heart rate increasing. Her skin didn't feel as cold as it had previously. Interesting, she noted, and unexpected.

The icy blue eyes holding hers belonged to Brock "The Rock," the Eagles' captain. She'd read articles on him as part of her early research, and his eyes seemed to command as much media copy as his skating, passing, shooting, and stick-handling skills. He was considered one of the most dangerous offensive players in the NHL while also being a guy's guy and a nice one at that. The Alpha in a pack of strong men. Quite the feat, she knew.

He was still staring at her, all his muscles rippling in response to his opponent pinning him to the glass...

Only he seemed in no hurry to end the fight. In fact, despite his position relative to the aggressor, he seemed in charge of the situation.

One more second passed.

And another.

Val reasoned she was a new arrival to his territory, so with his blood up from the sport, it made sense that he'd home in on her to see if she was a threat. Even pinned as he was.

Then his nostrils flared, like she'd seen animals do in the Serengeti when they caught a whiff of their mate.

No, that couldn't be the reason.

But her heart immediately began to pound to a primal drumbeat in her ears.

Totally unnerving.

She watched a trail of sweat trickle out of the curly black hair escaping his helmet. Noted his rock-hard jaw and broad forehead. From this distance, she couldn't make out the scar along his jawline, but she'd seen photos of him and knew it was there. It only added to his hardened masculinity. He *was* handsome. There was no denying it.

Yet it wasn't something she should notice. She fell back on her training. Remained still. Continued to observe. Took shallow breaths to offset her emotional and physical response to him. But her brain started tugging at a question.

Was he responding on some primal level to her as a woman?

She hadn't imagined that possibility. Her outfit was intended to disguise her female attributes and repel interest.

Did pheromones travel easier across cold surfaces like the ice? She would have to look that up. The reptilian brain was a masterpiece of scientific interest.

His regard of her continued as the other player struggled to keep him pinned, grunting as he pushed to hold him in place. Only Brock wasn't fighting him anymore. She thought she heard a growl emerge from him. Her mouth immediately went dry, and she had the urge to wet her lips. A shocking reaction.

She was here to observe, not to engage.

A sharp hit from his opponent to his kidneys knocked him into the wall hard and ended his focus on her, returning it to the fight for male supremacy. She watched as he shoved back against his opponent with all his strength.

Val noted the excitement within her—as if she were rooting for him—as he broke free with the puck, slicing quickly across the ice toward the central line.

She made herself turn away from the rink. Darla was waiting for her closer to the bench—and the action—studying players.

Val swallowed thickly, wishing she had a glass of water.

Her reaction was not appreciated, she decided. Her feet felt heavy, and her respiration was choppy, as if she'd been doing sprints. She forced herself to take a few deep breaths, welcoming the frigid air rushing through her airways, the smell of rubber mats and cold ice filling her senses. A sense of longing came over her. For the ice. It had to be for the ice.

Clearing her throat, she forced herself to walk forward. She would be fine. The moment had been strange was all. But it made sense that her own reptilian brain was acclimatizing itself to the new environment and the dominant players. Like Brock Thomson.

Yes, that explanation made sense.

CHAPTER TWO

"What is it about women?"

He asked the question of his good friend and old teammate as they were packing up to leave. His sister's text had prompted the question, but he couldn't deny a similar question had clanged around in his mind as the water hit his still-electric skin in the showers: *What is it about that woman?*

He still couldn't believe she'd captured his attention: the nerdy one in the mannish, baggy clothes wearing the ugliest glasses he'd ever seen. While Mason had him up against the glass, no less.

He'd seen her enter the arena with the woman she'd sat beside. She was clearly a new employee since he didn't recognize her. She certainly fit Chuck's no fuss, no muss attitude. Another analyst or trainer likely. They had millions of those around.

But that didn't explain why he'd been aware of her throughout practice when usually his complete focus was on the ice.

Then Mason had pulled his usual shit with the body check as Brock had noted her coming down the steps. But he hadn't given the kid's harsh breathing or taunts any attention, because everything other than her had faded to the background. He'd been so incapable of looking away from her that he'd practically memorized her appearance, from her auburn ponytail to the beauty mark just outside the corner of her mouth.

What a weird moment that had been.

Maybe he'd taken too many hits to the head and it was finally adding up, but he hadn't been able to look away. There was just something about her. Maybe it was the way she held herself so still, or how she hadn't flinched away from what was happening. Usually, women balked in horror or got into the blood sport of things. Not her...

The moment had been charged with something he couldn't name. The way she'd stopped and stared at him... Like she was cataloging him completely. He'd felt as pinned by her gaze as he had by Mason's body.

Jesus, he probably needed his head examined. Brock tossed his phone in his leather duffel bag and growled darkly after rereading the last text that had come through, ready to set aside his strange reaction to Mystery Girl.

"Since you aren't dating anyone, I'll assume your sister texted you something about the kids. You said she's out of town for work." Finn clapped a meaty hand on his shoulder in solidarity. "So what is it this time?"

Brock reached deep for patience. He really did. His sister was getting divorced from her deadbeat husband. Her whole world was falling apart. She had two kids to take care of as well as a career as a medical sales rep, which she deeply loved. It would be tricky for her to find a new balance, and in the meantime, he'd agreed to step in and help.

Forget that hockey season was in full swing. Susan was his sister. Kinsley and Zeke were his niece and nephew. Family. She'd called him in tears, saying the only thing that had made Zeke feel better about the divorce was the possibility that they could stay with Brock.

Jesus. Of course he'd said yes! He'd told her they could stay forever.

But he was discovering on a whole new level that he *really* didn't understand women, something he'd already learned after getting divorced in his mid-twenties. "Susan is having the babysitter drop the kids here and not at my house, because she thinks it'll be easier for them if *I* go home with them. Do you know what that even means?"

Finn made a comic face before tugging on his lucky fisherman's sweater from his favorite store in Halifax. Brock was glad he hadn't worn one of the many sweaters Finn had given him over the years since they'd first started playing together in college, or they would have matched like Mystery Girl and her colleague.

"I'm not dating anyone either right now, so I've got no answer for you, man." Finn grimaced, highlighting the cut to his lip he'd gotten in practice. "I love women, but they completely mystify me."

"If that's not enough, Chuck told me to head upstairs to see him and Ted."

"Mason's going to love that when it gets around," Finn said in practically a stage whisper, seeing as how they were still in the locker room. Sure, there weren't too many players left. He'd lingered in a cold shower to reduce the swelling from the bruises Mason had given him on the ice with that last hit.

When he'd stopped and watched that nerdy-looking new assistant. Whom Coach had hired...

The thought of Chuck refocused him. "We just need to do what we're here to do, Finn."

"I'm locked," he said, his eyes going flat.

"That's something I can always count on."

Brock nodded to a few of the other guys who were heading out.

They'd been playing together almost six months since

preseason had started. Brock was still getting to know the team, even though he'd reached out to many of them in the off-season. Working out together and socializing had helped them get off to a running start as a team. But it was nearly March now, and they needed to gel. It still hadn't happened. They had a competitive record, but they were barely scraping by when they won because of stupid penalties and lack of team cohesion.

Mason "The Marvel" was the proverbial stick in their spokes. That punk had taken it personally that Brock had been recruited to play for his old coach and be the Eagles' savior, and he'd been extra aggressive in practice and games since the beginning, trying to prove who was better. They traded who was the highest scorer in every game, and the kid was driven to outdo him.

Brock was having none of it. He'd gone up against talented players with giant egos his whole career and won. He planned on doing the same here. The kid needed to get with the program. Now. They had eight weeks to make the conference championship and make the playoffs.

He clipped on his Swiss watch and checked the time. "Kinsley and Zeke are going to be here in five minutes, and I'm going to have to park them in the executive offices to wait for God knows how long."

"I can wait with them." Finn zipped his worn duffel shut—the same one they'd both gotten when they'd played for Harvard. "No idea what I'm going to say to your niece. Kinsley's a little terrifying right now. When I swung by your house last week, she'd written UNWANTED on a plain white T-shirt with a black Sharpie."

He hated how tight his chest felt. It made him feel guilty that he was so out of sorts because his family was staying with him. Before a season started, he put everything in a particular order, from the suits he was going to wear for road trips—bought by his personal shopper—to the latest magazines lambasting him and his team and their chances at victory. Nothing fed his motivation like doubters and people who outright insulted him and his abilities.

But the magazines were out of order now, covered by Zeke's PlayStation controller and Kinsley's schoolwork. Susan tried to keep the house tidy, but Zeke's numerous pairs of shoes littered the floor. So did the occasional candy wrapper.

Brock was living in an emotionally fraught circus, and it was going to require all of his mental focus to keep his mind on winning and the job he'd come to do, back in his hometown, for his old coach and the Eagles' new owner, Ted Bass.

He could feel tension begin to worm its way into his body. "It's the tent Kinsley's pitched in my family room that kills me."

Finn rubbed the back of his massive neck with a grimace. "She still hasn't agreed to sleep in one of your guest rooms?"

"Kinsley hasn't left her tent." He felt his jaw pop as the image of the teetering green canvas atrocity flashed through his mind. "Despite me promising to decorate her room any way she wants. But what kills me is the big posterboard sign she's taped to the tent. *I am not an inconvenience.*"

Finn cursed as he finger-combed his blond hair. "That's not good."

"*Right?* I don't even know what to do about that. I remember being really pissed off at my dad when I was a kid. He was the principal at my elementary school, so sometimes the whole student and son thing got crossed."

"Understandable," Finn concurred, leaning back against his locker. "Your dad likes his rules."

Something Brock appreciated better as an adult. "But this kind of teenage agony? It's worse than having a tooth knocked out. I wish Kinsley was five years old again, and I could get her a teddy bear and an ice cream cone. I was her hero of an uncle back then. Now I'm just another adult who doesn't understand her. Like Susan and her dad. I don't know what to do for her."

"You're stepping up and giving them all a place to land." Finn crossed and zipped up Brock's bag for him with a knowing look. "Taking care of shit. Man, you're doing more than most would."

Still, it didn't feel like enough. Certainly, it wasn't fixing anything. "I wish I could cut off one of Darren's balls and use it for puck practice while he watches, bleeding and crying from the stands."

Finn's laugh boomed out in the locker room, making a few other players stop dressing and send over inquiring looks. The old guys were still trying to figure them out.

"He deserves that and more." Finn made a slashing motion across his neck. "What kind of man tells his wife that she and their kids are an inconvenience?"

"An asshole." Brock picked up his duffel. "Thanks for watching out for them. I'll be as fast as I can with Chuck and Ted."

"Good luck with that," Finn called as Brock hurried out of the locker room.

Mason was loitering outside of the dressing room with some of the team's younger hockey players. Of course he was wearing his famous black fur coat, the one modeled after Tyler Durden in *Fight Club*. Apparently, Mason's dad used to watch the movie with him before hockey games to get him into fight mode, and the tradition had stuck. Brock had his own so-called rituals and superstitions—a peanut butter, honey, and banana sandwich had been his pregame go-to for years, started by his mother—but he thought Mason had taken the movie a little too far.

Sure, the kid abided with the NHL dress code before games, wearing the usual suit, tie, and pants, but the fur coat skirted the line. And then there was his off-the-ice wardrobe...

The kid had drawn big press for his crazy graphic shirts, silk pants, leather jackets, and aviator sunglasses—many items he'd endorsed, bringing in serious bank. He'd been quoted in *Sports Illustrated* saying he loved the color red because of the movie, since it symbolized blood and violence. Just how he liked his hockey.

Not Brock's style. He usually respected other players and how they chose to carry themselves, but Mason put his particular brand of hockey in everyone's face.

The kid had incredible stats, the reason he'd been named Rookie of the Year and earned the nickname "The Marvel." But even though the Eagles had made the playoffs over the past couple of years, partly thanks to him, he'd racked up more penalties than anyone else on the team, sometimes costing them games.

The Eagles had been brushed with the worst refrain any good team could incur: they couldn't finish. They couldn't bring in the big win. They were their own worst enemy, Mason being Enemy Number One.

Which was why the Eagles had been given a hard spring cleaning this year. The old owner had sold the team to Ted Bass, who had brought in his old friend, Chuck Collins, who in turn had traded two underperforming players to bring in him and Finn. Chuck had coached them at Harvard, and together they'd won three hockey national championships.

Instead of welcoming Brock as a resource who'd help them finally win the Stanley Cup, Mason had brought an enemy and payback mentality to their relationship from the first day they'd met. The kid clung to old grievances, like the fact that Brock had been on a team that had beaten Mason twice in the playoffs. Shortsighted to Brock's mind.

The only thing they both agreed on was what Brock considered their common ground: neither of them had won a Stanley Cup and both wanted one. He tried to remember that whenever Mason put him to the wall or gave him a hard time. Which was about to happen right now. Because Brock knew the kid was waiting for him after that stunt on the ice. He gritted his teeth and increased his stride.

"Brock, my man." Mason held out his arms, his large black fur coat making him seem like a giant grizzly waiting for prey. "Are you feeling a little bruised from where I put you up against the wall? Do you need Mommy to kiss it?"

He leveled him a flat stare. "First, my mother has passed, and second, you're going to have to work harder to get me to cry uncle. Focus on winning instead. I'm not your enemy, Mason. I'm your teammate. You boys have a good evening. I'm off to see Chuck and Ted."

Mason's mouth flattened. According to locker room gossip, he still hadn't met with Ted Bass privately. Mostly because Ted was smart and knew the lack of distinction ate at Mason's ego. When he heard a crash behind him, Brock smiled all the way to the front office.

If only they could channel that kid's energy toward championship success...

But that's why Ted had hired Chuck, who was known for some pretty off-the-wall motivational strategies when their butts were in a sling, as he liked to say. Brock was part of that strategy, but he'd only agreed to stay for a year so they could make their run at the Cup. A one-year contract for ten million, and after the year was through, Cup or no Cup, his professional career would be over. One of the best high school hockey coaches was retiring and wanted him to take over. The job happened to be fifty minutes from Minneapolis, and he would be able to coach his nephew—a dream for both of them.

But first, they had to win so he could meet his final hockey goals. Every day Brock visualized lifting the beautiful Stanley Cup trophy over his head.

He would accept no other outcome.

Dive into The Hockey Experiment!

"...ROMANTIC GOLD – YOU'LL DEFINITELY ENJOY THIS READ!"

~ HOLLY'S LIBRARY LANE

Date a hockey player?? Why the heck would she want to do that?

But study him? Sign her up for that experiment!

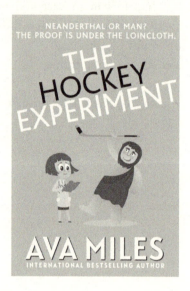

Get The Hockey Experiment!

ABOUT THE AUTHOR

Millions of readers have discovered International Bestselling Author Ava Miles and her powerful fiction and non-fiction books about love, happiness, and transformation. Her novels have received praise and accolades from *USA Today*, *Publisher's Weekly*, and *People Magazine* in addition to being chosen as Best Books of the Year and Top Editor's picks. Translated into multiple languages, Ava's strongest praise comes directly from her readers, who call her books and characters unforgettable.

Ava is a former chef, worked as a long-time conflict expert rebuilding warzones to foster peaceful and prosperous communities, and has helped people live their best life as a life coach, energy healer, and self-help expert. She is never happier than when she's formulating skin care and wellness products, gardening, or creating a new work of art. Hanging with her friends and loved ones is pretty great too.

After years of residing in the States, she decided to follow her dream of living in Europe. She recently finished a magical stint in Ireland where she was inspired to write her acclaimed Unexpected Prince Charming series. Now, she's splitting her time between Paris and Provence, learning to speak French, immersing herself in cooking *à la provençal*, and planning more page-turning novels for readers to binge.

Visit Ava on social media:

- facebook.com/AuthorAvaMiles
- x.com/authoravamiles
- instagram.com/avamiles
- bookbub.com/authors/ava-miles
- pinterest.com/authoravamiles

DON'T FORGET...
SIGN UP FOR AVA'S NEWSLETTER.

More great books? Check.
Fun facts? Check.
Recipes? Check.
General frivolity? DOUBLE CHECK.

https://avamiles.com/newsletter/

Made in the USA
Middletown, DE
29 April 2025

74888360R00252